child of my right hand

A Novel by Eric Goodman

Sourcebooks Landmark™
An Imprint of Sourcebooks, Inc.®
Naperville, Illinois

Published by Sourcebooks, Inc.
P.O. Box 4410, Naperville, Illinois 60567-4410
(630) 961-3900
FAX: (630) 961-2168
www.sourcebooks.com

Library of Congress Cataloging-in-Publication Data

Goodman, Eric K.
Child of my right hand : a novel / by Eric Goodman.
p. cm.
ISBN 1-4022-0306-3 (alk. paper)
1. Coming out (Sexual orientation)--Fiction. 2. Parent and child--Fiction. 3. College teachers--Fiction. 4. Teenage boys--Fiction. 5. Hate crimes--Fiction. 6. Gay youth--Fiction. 7. Ohio--Fiction. I. Title.
PS3557.O583C47 2004
813'.54--dc22

2004013215

Printed and bound in the United States of America
BG 10 9 8 7 6 5 4 3 2 1

For my brave son Ethan

Farewell, thou child of my right hand, and joy;
My sin was too much hope of thee, loved boy.
Seven years thou wert lent to me, and I thee pay,
Exacted by thy fate, on the just day.
O, could I lose all father now.

From “On My First Son” (1603)

By Ben Jonson

PART ONE:

Tipton Levy and the Fry Guy

prologue

Simon could sing before he could talk, a little boy soprano, louder and more resonant than children twice his age. It sounds odd, but even at twelve and fourteen months he was barrel-chested and big-muscled, especially his calves and thighs. Middle linebacker, I'd think, or a tight end like my brother, as I watched Simon toddle after his rubber ball with the joy he had for the enterprise then, the blond Little Lord What's-His-Name curls we didn't cut until he was two, the way he'd put the ball to his mouth and suck on it as if to taste its secrets or perhaps to tell it his, before he chucked it back at me, left-handed.

He was prone to ear infections and slow to speak. Until he was five, my boy lived on amoxycillin like a honeybee on nectar. Ten day runs of the bubble-gum-flavored antibiotic, three teaspoons a day. Then he'd finish, and the ear infection would return, his little hand to his ear, Simon standing in his crib, screaming, and let me tell you, you could hear him down the hall. What lungs! Our first-born, and we were trying to be perfect parents, not pick him up for every little thing. He'd shake the bars, screaming, and you could hear every word, though from twelve to eighteen months, when his first set of ear tubes was inserted, his vocabulary diminished. Imagine trying to hear under water, an ear-eye-and-throat doc later explained. Or listening through gauze. Mommy, Daddy! Mommy! Man, you could hear him down the hall.

Not perfect pitch, he'd say, years later, but almost. I remember him at two and a half, after we'd returned from Genna's sabbatical in Strasbourg, belting out, "Fre-re Jac-ques, fre-re Jac-ques, dormez-vous, dormez-vous!" the sustained note in the second *vous*, pure and distant as the light of a new moon, Simon smiling his cherubic grin when he finished, glad to be the center of attention, even then. I remember him at three in the college preschool, singing, "Row, row, row your boat," so loudly the other kids stopped singing. And I remember the looks on their parents' faces, not the last such looks we'd see, explaining, with a sniff, that some little boys were louder than others.

Genna and I used to wonder where this prodigious sound came from because neither of us were musical. Physically, Simon resembled us both: my chest and seventeen-inch neck, Genna's coloring and dusky blond hair, which in Simon darkened through adolescence until he began dying it. But the voice? We speculated it was the legacy of Genna's biological father, and not just because my field is the history of science and I'm predisposed to think that way. We assumed a genetic link, a biological explanation, if you will, for complex instinctive and performative behavior because Simon's gift was always present, hard-wired, the little boy who could sing before he could pronounce the words.

"Mommy," he said one night when he was four, sitting up in bed while Genna sang a lullaby. Simon with this amazing voice, and our second child, Lizzie, not quite one, but already beginning to talk.

"Mommy," he said and pressed his hands to his ears. "Don't sing!"

We laughed about that for years, even Genna, who was family-famous for being unable to carry a tune. Mommy, don't sing, as if her voice hurt his ears, which it probably did. Mommy, don't sing!

That's how I remember Simon, a sweet little boy of three and four, with this astonishing sound coming out of him—his instrument as we later learned to call it—before all the rest, although there were signs even then. That's my training, to order the unknown, to create a coherent narrative from available fact. Is that science? Of a personal sort. Is there speculation? You bet. As soon as a child is old enough to leave your sight, there are things a parent can't know, influences beyond parental control. What we might have done differently, could have or should have, if only we'd been paying close enough attention.

What I want to remember—and I do, can you hear him, listen—is Simon singing at two and a half, Are you sleeping, Are you sleeping? *Dormez-vous*, his French and English jumbled together, but there's no mistaking that high, perfect note. Like the sun, my son, like first light.

For he is sleeping. *Il dort.*

And this is Simon's song, in three voices: Simon, Genna and Jack's. Jack Barish, impartial researcher. This arrangement is intended to reveal the harmonies and discordances inherent in family life. More importantly, it's the only way I can bear to tell our story. Listen.

chapter 1

On the first morning of his junior year in high school, Simon Barish stood at the bus stop, which was nothing more than a turnaround in one of his new neighbors' driveways. Lizzie waited with him. Two or three other kids, none of whom he knew, hung around looking stupid. At six-forty the sky, through its border of trees, remained dark except for an embarrassed eastern blush. Simon was seventeen, old enough to drive, but there had been trouble last year with his grades. When wasn't there trouble with his grades? And his parents—both of whom, to hear them, had never gotten anything except A's their entire lives and missed no chance to point it out, especially Dad—wouldn't sign for his permit until he achieved a 2.5, which had taken until the end of fourth quarter. Then it was six months to a road test, so here he stood, with younger kids at the bus stop, in the dark, which he was still secretly afraid of. His parents had no idea what it was like to be him, no idea at all.

Lizzie, or Liz, which she now wanted to be called (by next year, he was pretty sure she'd call herself Elizabeth, she was that kind of girl), was in eighth grade, but her body—by which he meant her breasts—had started developing when she was in fifth, so that everyone, especially guys, believed she was older than her age. For two years, while she pretended that what was happening to her body was happening in another state, Mississippi, or even

Montana, Lizzie hid inside his double-X sweatshirts. Then, last year, boom, she emerged from under all that fleece like a swan from under pin feathers, swimming graceful circles through the middle school in tight cotton tops from Old Navy over 34B bras. (He dug through her top drawer when he was alone in the house, Mom and Dad at work, Lizzie at soccer practice. Once, he tried one on. He looked ridiculous, but damn, what a boner.)

So now she stood in her tight top and jeans, looking like the prep he always knew she'd turn out to be, fielding glances from the boys waiting with them as the sky brightened behind the trees of Forest Glen, the development they'd just moved into. Ever since they'd moved to Ohio eight years earlier, they'd lived in Cincinnati, forty miles away. Last spring, his parents, who were always fighting about one thing or another, agreed to move to Tipton, the college town where they taught. They said it was to cut down on commuting and to get out of the city where his mom had never been happy, but he knew the move was mostly about getting him out of the performing arts high school where things hadn't gone well from the start, where they'd never appreciated how great his voice really was.

The school bus ground into view. Red lights above the windshield burned like the eyes of a small frightened animal. Simon hefted his waist pack and stood behind Lizzie, waiting to board.

✦ ✦ ✦

The first days sailed by. Get up at quarter to six, shower, make sure Lizzie was with him to walk up the dark driveway. Boxes everywhere, unhung paintings stacked in the dining room, and his parents' attention, especially his mom's, which was usually on him, focused elsewhere, which was A-OK with Simon. School was a breeze. Simon was signed up for only four academic classes, and considering dropping down to three. American history was the same bell as art, where the teacher, Mrs. Campbell, was really awesome. Floppy hats, hippie dresses, like Mom used to wear. The only problem, since Simon didn't give two craps about his classes, was that instead of being assigned to chamber singers, as he'd been told last spring, he was stuck in concert choir. Only four guys had auditioned for chamber singers, so they'd made it all girls.

Just showed, Simon thought, as he walked down the hall towards second bell, the first Friday of the year, what an ignorant, country-ass school Tipton really was. Concert choir was the worst on planet Earth. The entire bass section, except for Simon, sang flat. Not sometimes, every frigging note. Most of the guys were jerks and didn't pay attention to anything Mister Dolan said. Mister Dolan was short, young, and fat; he had a really bad haircut. The kids called him Donut. Simon felt bad for him, but he felt worse for himself, because there was no set-design class like there was in Cincinnati, which he'd known, okay? But he was certain there would be singing and there wasn't, not really. Just yesterday, Peter, he was pretty sure the kid's name was Peter—tall, thin, kind of cute, with straight brown hair streaked henna—came up to him.

"Hey, Simon. Know what they call this class?"

"No, what?"

"Animal Chorus."

Then he'd grinned and yipped like a coyote, like a wild loon, and Simon grinned too, thinking, This guy likes me.

✦ ✦ ✦

They'd moved into the new house two weeks before school opened, full of hope. The previous four years, Jack didn't know. First he turned forty, then Genna did. His research leaves were denied, not once, but two years in a row. And maybe Genna had an affair and maybe she didn't after he did. But by the time they moved to Tipton where Jack had never thought they'd live because everyone said the schools were no damn good, he felt half-defeated. On his knees looking up, and no, he wasn't talking sexual matters, more like peering up a long garbage chute and marveling at how far away the light seemed.

All summer they packed. The neighbors threw a goodbye party; Jack and Genna explained how sorry they were to go and blamed the commute. The neighbors, mostly good-natured and Midwestern, said they understood. They wouldn't drive fifty minutes each morning, by golly, and they wished the Barishes well. The Cohens, probably their best friends on the street, and the only other Jews, said they'd be sure to stay in touch, and Jack hoped they would.

But it wasn't about the commute. It wasn't about the affair Genna may or may not have had. It was partly about the affair Jack had been having until he broke it off last winter and thought he'd die of it, both the affair and the giving up. It was mostly about Simon, their big troubled boy, as so much of their life was. Simon's weight, Simon's worries, Simon's troubles in school. Simon's gift and what he should do about it. Simon's sexuality and when he'd admit to himself, if not to his parents, what had been apparent or at least intimated since he was five or six and wouldn't give up his Barbies no matter how hard they tried to coax him or what they promised in return.

When he was eleven and down to one Barbie, when even Simon—who'd always been remarkably immune to what other kids thought or wanted—understood he couldn't ask boys to play Barbies anymore, when even the girls he played with had given them up, Genna persuaded Simon to give his last doll to a friend's six-year-old daughter.

Imagine Simon's expression as he handed over his Barbie. Embarrassed, resentful, a proud half smile (Genna had convinced him giving away Barbie meant he was finally a big boy), but oh, the pain as he demonstrated how Barbie liked her hair brushed, and which of her outfits went with which pair of shoes.

So what were Jack and Genna doing moving Simon from the performing arts school in Cincinnati, where everyone agreed the student body was creative, to Tipton High, where only ten years or so ago the Klan had marched? Where the biggest event each week was Friday night football? Where the townie, farm, and trailer kids butted heads for social dominance, but there wasn't much difference except for how much money they had to spend at the mall?

They needed a new beginning, and Simon did, too. Needed out of that house where Jack had confessed the affair and where for most of last winter Genna was gone in the evenings and sometimes most of the night, but always back in the morning before the kids woke up. And Simon? Last fall, he'd nearly flunked out of the performing arts school. He'd alienated teachers. Gotten himself bounced from acting class. And late last winter, right about the time Genna was whirring out of control, Simon was suspended for eight days. The girl who'd loved him the previous six months and whom he'd loved (but not in the same way; he'd refused to have sex with her) lost what little sense she'd ever had and scrawled, Kike faggot! on his locker. He'd written, Nazi bitch! on hers. Although she'd started, they were to be punished equally.

Jack sat in the assistant principal's office, Ms. Moore, a black woman maybe thirty-five, having been summoned from his office in Tipton.

"He shouldn't have retaliated," she said. "He should have come to me."

"Of course, but he's sixteen."

"Janet is fifteen."

Jack didn't like Ms. Moore. The hard angles of her jaw. "I understand Simon has to be punished. But surely you see the difference…"

"Not really. He used profanity. He defaced school property."

"Ms. Moore." Jack was an old hand at massaging school officials. Willing to prevaricate, cajole, bare his large throat, if necessary, for his son. "Simon's been working really hard to bring his grades up."

"He should have considered that."

He hated this bitch's close-cropped hair. The way she looked at him, the kike faggot's father. He'd had to stop work and drive down from Tipton because Simon had to be hauled away immediately, like something dead and rotten. Remember, too, he hadn't slept much the night before waiting up for Genna. "Ms. Moore, you understand how seriously we take the word kike. Kikes ended up in Nazi ovens. Their theory of eugenics…"

"I understand, Mister Barish."

"Kike, it's our N-word."

"Mister Barish." Her eyes gleamed. "I understand."

"But you're going to punish them equally."

"I am."

"Is there anyone I can appeal to?"

"Appeal to anyone you want." She showed her very large teeth, the better to eat him with. "One, he used profanity. Two, he defaced school property. District rules say eight days minimum. If I wanted, I could expel him."

Why don't you, he wanted to say, but Jack exited Ms. Asshole's office without another word. Simon waited, staring numbly ahead, two seats from Janet and her fat mother. To make it even worse, for a time, Simon really did love her.

"Perhaps I could arrange a meeting next week for all of us," offered assistant principal Ms. Asshole Moore. "To clear the air."

Jack glanced at Simon, who shook his head. For once they agreed.

They left, and that was that. It was also the end of Simon being able to do much about his grades. After missing eight days he had to struggle to get up to a C plus for the fourth quarter. And so, the dirty secret. Simon's grades had motivated the move. Tipton High might not be much. It might be filled with ignorami. But the university's primary, and some would say only, concession to town/gown relations was the following: Any Tipton High graduate was automatically admitted. Tipton might not be Harvard, but it was pretty damn good, and because they were faculty, Simon could attend tuition-free. Simon's grades worked out to less than a C for his first two years; Jack and Genna had concluded it was move to Tipton or tell Simon to set his sights on community college.

They put their house on the market. Genna stopped staying out. And two weeks before the new semester, bitching and sweating in the August heat, Simon, Genna, Lizzie and Jack loaded everything onto a U-Haul and moved themselves to Forest Glen, full of crazy hope.

✦ ✦ ✦

Genna loved the new house. Five minutes from her office, it was hidden in the woods. If she had to live in Ohio, and after eight years it appeared she did, at least she could live in a house she adored. Simon and Lizzie had liked the Cincinnati house. Friends invited to dinner parties marveled at its high ceilings. But she'd felt trapped and miserable, turning around and around and around again, like their dog Sam searching for the perfect spot to lie down, without ever finding it.

Now she woke each morning and didn't know what to do, she felt so good. She was jogging three days a week in the nature preserve half a mile from their front door. She was puffing there now, new Nikes biting into a trail that wound between a mix of new and old growth trees and a corn field. Of course there was corn in Nowheresburg, Ohio. But through the trees—and Genna loved the ancient giants, some eight feet around, oaks and sycamores—Six Mile meandered, not much faster than she jogged, twenty-five yards or so behind their golden retriever. Sam loved to lead, another Barish alpha male; she was a bit tired of all that. But the sun winked through the leaves, a summer Romeo. Genna oozed the sweat of honest exertion. She'd only been running two weeks, but God, she felt great, and believed this time she'd be able to stick to the routine. And with running would come a diet, beginning Monday. Protein and grapefruit, a meal of hope. Boiled eggs breakfast. Sliced meat and cottage cheese lunch. Meat and more meat for dinner. Shrimp, raw tuna, roast chicken. Difficult to maintain, and not just because it was so radical, forcing her body to metabolize the fat stored for years around the pillowed contours of her ass. Lord, she thought, jogging to the rhythm of her invocation. Help me with my bottom. Let me not lie down with the pillow-butts, the lard-asses, the double-wides of the Buckeye State. The last time she'd dieted successfully, five years ago, before things began to go wrong with Jack, it was the protein diet that had worked. Trying protein again required hope; for with the diet, Jack might return from whatever marital border he'd fled or been banished to. Big Jack Barish, her own true love.

Genna looked up. Fifty feet further along, Sam gazed back with the insistent good nature that was a retriever's paramount virtue. Since puppydom, Sam had been more Jack's dog than hers, but with the move and her jogging, Sam's allegiance had begun to shift and he waited each morning near the door.

"Go ahead, Sam," she called. "Get going."

He bowed over his paws, a big happy oaf, then raced off, tail bouncing, angling for Six Mile, where he'd lie down in the stirring water as if it were the Ganges to feel his spirit lift. Or was that the Nile? Summer kisses blew through the treetops. The bright leaves sparkled. Another fine day in Tipton, Ohio.

chapter 2

Simon rose each morning before six because it took him forever to get ready. First there was the long shower and for the past six months, no, almost a year, he'd been shaving his calves and forearms. Simon hated body hair. God, how he hated it. It was all Dad's fault. Simon's dad had so much chest hair—brown, black and white twined together—when he lay down, he looked like the Berber rug in the family room. Even his back grew hair. Damn, that was gross. Simon dragged one of Lizzie's purple razors across his calf as warm spray gusted down. His right leg glistened, perfectly smooth, and he moved onto his left. Did Dad care how gross he looked? No, he was conceited about his body and worked out at the university gym. He walked around the house with his shirt off and sometimes just in his boxers. When he saw Dad's body Simon would think in the high-pitched voice that wasn't really his but could be, Oh God, kill me now! for if there were two things he didn't want to be it was hairy and muscular, and it looked like he was going to be both.

He shaved every other day, legs and forearms, underarms, too, and avoided exercise. He already had these humongous legs and shoulders like Uncle Russ who'd played football in college. It was so unfair, Simon thought, moving the razor to his forearm. Why couldn't he be slender like Lizzie or Justin in *NSYNC and hairless like Peter in school. Thinking about those slender, hairless boys with sweet eyes and tipped hair, he began to get hard. Simon set down the razor. He was always getting hard, and wondered if he had time. He'd read somewhere, or maybe someone had told him, that teenage boys thought about sex eight times a minute. He wondered if that was straight or gay, and began to stroke himself. Sitting on the ledge in this shower with warm water gushing down was his favorite way to jerk off. Blood thumped in his ears. Uh-huh. Then he realized the thumping wasn't only in his head.

"Simon!" Dad beat the bathroom door. "Simon!"

He released his throbbing penis. "In the shower."

Thump, thump, thump.

"Time to get out!"

Simon glanced at his waterproof watch. 6:22. He still had to pick his outfit, do his hair, maybe apply a little of the eyeliner he'd been experimenting with. "One minute!"

"Lizzie needs the bathroom!"

"All right!"

Feeling totally jerked around, ha-ha, Simon shampooed his hair, turned off the shower, wrapped himself in a towel and stepped into the hall where Lizzie waited, wearing the blue Winnie the Pooh sleeping shirt he'd given her for her last birthday.

"Jerk. You know how long you've been in there?"

"Use the upstairs bathroom."

"Why don't you?"

"Someone's got PMS."

Her eyes beamed death rays. "Asshole."

Lizzie slammed the door. The toilet seat banged. A moment later, as he was stepping into his room carrying the clean clothes Mom had folded, the crapper door yawed and Lizzie shouted, "And don't use my razor!"

By the time he'd gotten his hair just right (gelled with short spikes), applied the black eyeliner lots of guys in his old school used, selected and rejected several outfits before settling on extra-wide jeans with green velvet patches on the cuffs and back pockets set off by a black Marilyn Manson T-shirt to which he'd added black fish-net sleeves, the bus had long since departed. That was cool. He dreaded the walk up the dark driveway, but now he had to sit in the car with Lizzie while Dad ragged on.

"I'm not a chauffeur. Or a cabby."

"Yes, you are."

She could say anything to Dad and get away with it.

"Cabbies and chauffeurs get paid."

"If you'd let me get my license," Simon said, "I could be driving us."

"Don't start." Dad glanced at Simon in the passenger seat, and a tendon, or whatever it was, popped on his bull neck. "Mom and I didn't keep you from driving, you did."

"That is such crap."

They were passing the campus. Out Dad's side, the sky behind the old trees and red brick buildings streaked pink and gold. Most students weren't awake, but runners in white shorts and t-shirts, tall and lean, short and lean, all of them, lean and buff, ran on the sidewalk.

"I like my idea about the taxi." Dad glanced over his shoulder to smile at Lizzie. "Next time you miss the bus, it's fifty cents apiece for the ride."

"I didn't miss it," Lizzie shot back. "I waited because Simon missed it."

Dad was always scheming to screw them out of what little allowance he gave them. Simon had discovered that if he ignored Dad's threats they usually went away. Talk about lack of follow through. He said, "Here's good."

Dad pulled over across from the high school. Simon climbed out carrying his back pack and waist pack, then waited for the silver Camry to drive off. He edged past the Smokers, a group of eight or ten tough-looking kids, both sexes, who gathered each morning just off school property to burn a last butt. His wide pants swished against the sidewalk, the coolest rags anyone had ever worn to this country-ass school. He started up the driveway knowing he was being watched and enjoying the feeling. Five bells, he thought, till lunch.

✦ ✦ ✦

After fourth bell, which was French—a subject he'd barely passed last year (D was for diploma, he'd tried to tell Dad, who didn't believe it; D was also for Dickhead Dad), and a subject about which he seemed to remember almost *rien* after the summer even though his mom frigging taught it—Simon was approaching the corner in the first floor corridor, walking by himself. This was the fourth week of school but he still didn't know many kids, and no one at all in French where his ignorance prevented him from speaking in class; instead he filled his notebook with elaborate pen and ink drawings. He was singing the Britney Spears hit to himself, "Whoops, I did it again," thinking about lunch and whom he might sit with, when he turned the corner and nearly banged into three guys coming hard the other way. They were all athletic-looking, two of them over six feet (Simon was five ten), the third only five five or six but broad-shouldered with monkey forearms and a neck thick as Simon's. All three sported the bowl-cut hair Simon associated with jocks in general and football players in particular. He didn't know them, just three more faces in the country-ass sea in which he was forced to swim each day. He gave way and they looked at each other and then at him, their mouths blood red in the instant before they banged into him. Then they swept on without apologizing, calling over their shoulders, one of them did. "Die, you faggot."

Tears leapt to his eyes from the blows to his shoulder and to his heart. Then they were gone, and he couldn't have picked them out of a line-up, just three more moonfaced jocks. Simon trembled. He'd always cried easily, but not now, please, not now. Students swirled past, talking, talking. He was the only flower in a world of boulders, the only human in a galaxy of moonfaces. Simon continued on to the lunchroom, ordered chocolate milk, a bag of chips, two slices of pizza, a large salad and sat down beside some animals he knew from chorus.

✦ ✦ ✦

The fall Jack and Genna arrived, Tipton was attempting to pass a school levy. The district had tried and failed to pass levies for a decade, maybe more; during that time funding had dropped to the lowest in the region. German, Psychology, Computer Programming, Art History, all lopped like beggars' hands. Class size had inflated, even in the lowest grades. Varsity teams were pay-to-play, one hundred a sport. Tipton teachers hadn't received raises in half a decade. They were the lowest paid in the county and experienced staff who hung on were surly and resentful. Half the high school teachers were in their first or second year out of college, gaining experience before job-hunting elsewhere. There were persistent rumors that if this levy didn't pass, school buses and all sports except football would be eliminated.

During the years they'd commuted from Cincinnati, Jack and Genna hadn't paid much attention other than to advise new faculty members, as they'd been advised, that Tipton schools weren't worth spitting at. Now that they were local, Genna had persuaded Jack to join a group of faculty and staff working for the levy. It was at an orientation for TUTS, Tipton University for Tipton Schools, that he learned the background of the troubles. He was sitting in the living room of Stan Murray, who taught English. His wife, Lynn, a lecturer in the same department, had baked brownies, chewy and dense. Everyone else had left with packets of flyers and voter registration cards, except for a small, pretty blond Jack hadn't met before.

"Excuse my ignorance," Jack began.

"Ignorance can never be excused," said Lynn Murray, who was large, big-busted and dark-haired, with a hint of moustache.

The little blond winked, her eyes unusually blue and bright. "Except by the ignorant, who tend to embrace it."

"Will you let Jack talk?"

Stan Murray had a sensual face. He liked to eat, he liked to drink, and his small eyes peered out over cheeks flushed with wine and his wife's baked goods.

"I understand Tipton is the largest town in the district."

"It's the only town," said Lynn.

"And the farmers are hard-pressed for cash."

"And don't think their kids are going to college, so what do they care about AP classes?" Stan popped another half brownie in his mouth.

"But no levies passed in twelve years?"

"I can explain." Short hair, stylishly cut, fringed her cheeks and prominent forehead. "By the way, I'm Marla Lindstrom."

She extended her hand and he shook it.

"Jack Barish."

"Until about fifteen years ago," Marla said, smiling, "when I took this job at the age of fourteen..."

"No, twelve," said Lynn.

"...there were two districts, one for Tipton, one for the outlying townships, but only one high school, which the districts shared."

"How did that work?" Jack asked.

"As well as you would have expected," said this Marla, who spoke quickly and somehow lightly, looking directly at him, "given that the Board was dominated by university interests and they've always been so good about respecting the needs of the community. Anyway, the districts merged. And though there weren't supposed to be changes, the unified board voted to close the elementary schools in Roscoe and Milton and start busing into the schools here in Tipton. Since then, Roscoe and Milton residents have voted three to one against new levies. It doesn't matter that they're hurting their own kids." She looked straight at him, and there was an intensity in her eyes, a willingness to make connection he found thrilling, even scary. She added, "It's sad, really."

Five minutes later, Jack was walking out to his car as Marla was walking out to hers, one of the new Beetles, metallic silver, reflecting the cool glow of the halogen street lamp.

"Thanks for the short course in Tipton history. What department are you in?"

"My nightmare ex was in English, which is how I know Stan and Lynn. I'm a guidance counselor at the high school." She smiled, again actively sought his eyes. "That's right. It's my salary the levy will raise. One hundred fifty a month."

Jack glanced at the silver Beetle. As if she'd read his thoughts, Marla said, "My new toy. I inherited some money."

"I hope someone didn't have to die for it."

"They usually do."

"Oh," Jack said, "maybe you've met my son Simon. He's a junior, new this year."

"Oh yes." Something passed across Marla's face, as if she weren't telling everything she knew. "What a sweet kid. Well, goodnight, Jack Barish."

With a flash of slender calves, she climbed in her Beetle and sped off.

✦ ✦ ✦

When Jack arrived home, the kids were downstairs watching *Charmed*. Genna was in her study, where she spent most evenings. She had also volunteered to address students, but Jack had attended orientation for both of them. He knocked and waited. After last spring, which they'd barely survived, they were still tiptoeing, not just around each other, but around the potholes and roadblocks of family life.

"Hey," Genna said, setting down her paperback. "How was the meeting?"

"Slow. They'll set up our talks in a week or two."

"What were the people like?"

"Earnest." He thought of Marla, and since their new policy was to avoid potholes with honesty, he added, "This one woman was kind of interesting."

"Oh?" Genna's face got a wary look.

"Marla Lindstrom, a guidance counselor at the high school. Said she knew Simon."

A worry line appeared between Genna's eyebrows. "I wonder why."

Not, I wonder why, Jack thought, but I wonder what's wrong this time. Simon's official guidance counselor was Tom O'Neill, whom they'd met when they enrolled Simon last spring and again the first week of class.

"Has he mentioned her?" Jack asked.

"I don't think so." The wary look appeared again—a narrowing of her eyes, a slight hunching of her shoulders—and Jack felt annoyed and guilty, because he'd helped put it there.

"Did she seem nice?"

"I guess." He turned to go, guilty again. He hadn't said Marla was pretty. "She's an old friend of the Murrays."

✦ ✦ ✦

Saturday night, Lizzie was out with new friends from her soccer team. Simon, Genna, and Jack stayed home watching the original *Father of the Bride*, starring Spencer Tracy and Elizabeth Taylor. They sat in the family room on the semicircular couch purchased from the previous owners, Simon wedged between them, his dyed hair running into the naturally blond permed curls that fell past Genna's shoulders. Mother and son looked a lot alike, Jack thought, they always had, Genna's oval face grafted onto his big frame. Although Simon weighed two hundred and thirty pounds, when he nestled his cheek on Genna's shoulder and tucked his legs up on Jack's lap, it was as if he were four years old again, just down from riding Jack's shoulders, and they were a young family watching Winnie the Pooh, with baby Lizzie tucked into her crib in the back bedroom of their California house. It felt safe and sweet as it hadn't since Jack couldn't remember when, although earlier in the evening Simon had picked a fight about some damn thing, then groused about what a drag it was to stay home with them.

On the twenty-five-inch screen, all obstacles to wedded bliss had been overcome. Spencer was giving Liz away. It was oh so sweet and schmaltzy. The wedding march played. Jack could feel a lump blocking the back of his throat, for there she was on her screen father's arm, Liz Taylor in a perfect white dress with eyelet lace. Simon said, and though he spoke softly, Jack could hear the grief in his voice, "There's only going to be one real wedding in our family."

Genna and Jack eyed each other. "What do you mean?" she asked.

"Lizzie will get married someday." Simon hesitated, while on the screen Spencer passed his daughter to the man who loved her. "But I can't."

In his wife's eyes Jack read fear and sadness, and he hoped, as he knew Genna was hoping, that Simon would find the courage to go on.

"Why not?"

"Because I'm gay."

He'd finally said it and Jack didn't know whether to cheer or cry or what. It wasn't much of a surprise, no surprise at all, except that Simon had found the courage to tell them. But what to say? Hooray? Oh, shit? We already knew?

"Gay is good," Genna said. "We love you the same as ever."

"Of course," Jack chimed in to be able to say something.

Liz kissed her bridegroom. The soundtrack swelled. Jack's eyes fluttered wet, and he wanted to say something more. "Maybe someday there could be a ceremony where you"—he searched for the right word—"and your partner could each step on a glass."

He tried to imagine Simon under a chupa kissing a guy, but couldn't bring it to mind.

Simon might have said, You guys are great. Or, What if the guy's not Jewish? Instead he responded, "I'm really tired, I'm going to bed." Then he stood and all two hundred and thirty ordinarily surly pounds of him advanced towards the bedroom corridor he shared with Lizzie. Near the door, he turned and smiled his little-boy smile.

Late that night, after Lizzie was home and asleep in her bed, Jack and Genna made love for only the second time in their new house. They'd been tiptoeing around that, too. The moon shone through the picture window onto their bed, lighting Genna's face and the hollow between her breasts. The strange bird they'd been hearing since they moved in gave its odd whooping cry. Who-whoo, Who-weee, Who-whoo, who-weee.

"It's great he could tell us," Genna whispered. "Don't you think?"

Jack nodded.

"It means we've done something right, don't you think?"

She snuggled backwards against him. Jack crossed his arm over her breasts, and they spooned as they had when their path through the world seemed simpler. And in the woods outside their room the bird repeated its eerie cry: Who-whoo, Who-weee. Who-who, who-weee.

chapter 3

✦ Simon was in love or maybe in lust. Hit me from the top, hit me from the bottom, Don't mean nothing, less it's right between the eyes. Rich was a sophomore, fifteen years old. He had curly black hair and lived with his father in the trailer park outside town. Simon had met Rich through his new best friend Rachel. He totally loved Rachel, who lived with her mother and a little wiener dog. She was fine with the gay thing because her mother was gay, which was a secret Simon had promised not to tell anyone.

Rachel had light brown hair, with blonde highlights, that flipped up at the ends, which was what Simon had looked like when he was two and three. Medium height, the tiniest bit plump, smart and popular. She could sit at anyone's table, but she sat with him. Just last Friday he sat down, and Rachel said, "Simon, meet my friend, Rich."

Now, less than a week later, they were walking away from the auditeria, Simon and Rich, Rachel, her friend Ellyn and Ellyn's boyfriend, Rob. Whenever he felt bored during French (the whole freaking time), Simon worked on the note. He'd planned to pass it at lunch, but someone was always watching.

Rich,

I think your cool. I think your hot. Isn't that weird, your cool and hot?

I'd really like us to get together. I think you know what I mean. In case you don't, I bet you have a really nice cock.

Call me. 773-2920.

Simon

He'd outlined Rich in three shades of red and folded the note in a tight, hot square. Now Rachel was saying something to Ellyn, who was thin and pretty but laughed like a donkey. Just as Rich glanced over his shoulder at Hee-Haw Ellyn, Simon pressed the note in his hand and held on. Rich's head swiveled and his eyes locked on Simon. For that magic moment—can't you just hear it?—they walked down the hall holding hands gazing into each other's eyes. Simon didn't care if anyone noticed; he only cared that Rich took the note. Then Rich felt it and moved his hand away.

"Read it later," Simon whispered.

Rich put the note in his front pocket near you know what. With his heart singing a love song, an aria like his vocal coach Yevgeny was teaching him, Simon headed for English, where he'd be bored witless, but he wouldn't notice, he wouldn't even care.

✦ ✦ ✦

Rich called that night. Simon locked his door and they talked for an hour. Tomorrow was only Wednesday but they made weekend plans. Simon wanted to invite Rich over so they could be alone. But if his parents weren't home, how could Rich arrive? If Simon's parents were home, would they allow Rich in his bedroom? They had this rule, no girls in his room, but guys could sleep over, which is how he learned the little he knew about sex. (Someday he'd tell Mom a thing or two about Mark, the son of her old friend, Robin, that would make her hair stand on end! But Mark was just a cock-tease.) They had a similar rule for Lizzie: no boys, not even mixed groups, in her bedroom.

Now that he'd come out to his parents, which he still couldn't believe, he wondered if they'd make a rule he couldn't have guys in his bedroom even with the door open? That would totally suck, but Simon consoled himself that he knew how to get around his parents' rules. Rich said he could maybe come over to his dad's trailer, but Simon worried the other trailer-park people would find out and beat them up.

Simon told Rich he'd work on getting his parents to drive him. Then it was time for *Buffy* and *Angel*, his two favorite shows except for *Charmed*. When Mom heard the television, she called down, "Simon, have you finished your homework?"

Finished? He couldn't remember if he had homework. But these were his favorite shows, and even if he had work, he could do it before bed, or in study hall tomorrow. He answered, "Yes, Mom," and tried to sound really annoyed, like How could she be insulting enough to ask that!

Lizzie watched with him, which he liked, as long as he controlled the remote. Afterwards, he was too tired to check his assignment book. In the morning, during first bell study hall, he wrote Rich a long note in which he described, in some detail, what he'd like to do to that very nice cock he was sure Rich had, and how skilled and experienced he was. (So he exaggerated.) He was, therefore, completely surprised by and unprepared for the pre-calculus test third bell and the French quiz during fourth. He could guess what his grades would be. Between F and F minus, if that were possible, but he couldn't think about that, not even when he sat in French staring at the unfathomable quiz. No, he thought about Rich's curly hair and his cat-like eyes and the note he had to give him; how soon the bell would ring and who would be at lunch, what jokes they'd tell; if Rich would sit next to him and would he like the new long sleeve button down purple shirt Simon was wearing, and would he smile when Simon put the note in his hand and whispered, "Read it later, when you're alone."

✦ ✦ ✦

Sunday night Jack was scheduled to give his first talk, in Sturtevant, a university dorm. Because he'd always enjoyed research, and because at that time he was having to admit that his longstanding project on Nazi eugenics was going nowhere, that he'd been scooped, and he was either going to have to rethink or give it up entirely, he was avoiding his own work and spent the week researching the history of the Tipton school district. Geographically, Tipton was the largest district in Ohio, most of it rolling farmland. In the old days, before the rural and Tipton-city schools were unified, test scores in Tipton were ten percentage points higher than in the rural schools, where each spring and fall farm kids were excused to help with planting and harvest. In the city, there was a significant percentage of staff and faculty families, with the staff, confronted daily by the relatively luxurious faculty jobs, resolving to use education to help their brood advance. Then there were the faculty, who not only prodded their kids to become more successful versions of themselves, there was the politically uncomfortable matter of genetics. Some kids inherited the good genes; others were shit out of luck. Smart kids and dummies, cradle to grave, despite good intentions, where good intentions even existed. What a horrible, retro notion, throwing Nurture out with the developmental bath water.

Did Jack believe it? No. But he had devoted several years to the study of Nazi eugenics, and its relation to American racism in the 1920s and '30s, discovering, but just as another scholar in the field was beginning to publish, that beginning with neighboring Indiana in 1907, thirty states had passed forced sterilization laws, and that these laws were cited by Nazi race scientists as justification for their own theories. The constitutionality of the American laws, which led to fifty thousand sterilizations, had been upheld in 1927 in *Buck v. Bell.* In a majority opinion written by Justice Oliver

Wendell Holmes, the court declared, "It is better for the world, if instead of waiting to execute offspring for crime, or to let them starve for their imbecility, society can prevent those who are manifestly unfit from continuing their kind."

In other words, the court argued that hypothetical persons were presumed guilty of criminal intent even before being conceived, and may not, therefore, be brought into existence. All of this had proceeded, as a sort of nightmare spawn, out of the general Galtian principle that society ought to encourage the genetically superior to increase their numbers and thereby improve the race and culture. There was no doubt certain traits could be genetically selected. Height, for example, probably speed. But intelligence? A heightened moral sense? Jack sometimes thought, but it wasn't the sort of opinion you committed to paper if you wanted to publish, that what most outraged Jewish critics of Nazi racial profiling, was just how wrong they'd gotten it. How could Yahweh's chosen people, linked by blood, with a tradition of intellectual achievement, be lumped with the lower races? What sort of wrong-headed science was that? Answer: science at the service of a political agenda.

Here in Tipton, one population pole was faculty brats, eighteen years and out, with a genetic predisposition to abstract thought. Across the genetic divide dwelled the farm kids, the product of several generations of natural selection which valued manual labor. Then there was Simon, genetically programmed to sing like an angel.

Jack had discovered that the first year after the districts merged, test scores rose for everyone. Maybe it was the synergy of the joined enterprise, the sharing of staff and curricular materials between the elementary schools. During the fall of the second year, however, the central board voted to close the rural schools and to bus kids to the newer and soon-to-be enlarged elementary buildings in Tipton. Test scores rose the second and third years, but once the kids had been moved, fell sharply in the fourth and fifth years, before settling during the sixth at new and unacceptably low levels, where they remained. Working from enrollment figures and test scores he found at the old Tipton Board of Ed. building, Jack determined that by the end of the sixth year, first and fourth grade reading and math scores were 15 percent lower than what the weighted averages had previously been. Not only had the "better" district failed, as promised, to elevate scores in the lesser district, test scores across both groups actually declined.

Was there something poisonous in the shared air, which had yielded a sum less than its parts? Jack shifted his research from the Board of Ed. to the morgue of Tipton's lone weekly, the *Tipton Gazette*. Paging through the oversize, black leather ledgers for 1988 (the year the last levy passed and the school districts merged) to 1991 (when the board voted to close the rural schools) to 1993 (the second year of the steep decline and the year before they'd arrived in Ohio), he found it. Maybe it wasn't the only it, but IT leapt out at him. Nestled between ads for spiral-sliced hams and Easter lilies in the first week of April, 1991, there was a small article: Klan to March in Tipton. The following week, there was a slightly larger article, lamenting permits the Klan had legally obtained and unsuccessful attempts by local groups to have those permits rescinded. The third week there was a front page story with two inch heads and pictures of the marchers: KLAN MARCHES IN TIPTON!

For the rest of the spring the story was front page news. The march, the recriminations, the arrests, the fall-out. What struck Jack as he sat in the *Gazette* morgue paging through old issues was not the fact of the Klan march, which they'd heard about although it occurred three years before they arrived at the university. No, what got him where he lived, that is, where his kids lived, as he stared at the front page photos and the ones that ran inside, were block-printed signs several of the hooded marchers carried. Give Us Back Our Schools.

That was the narrative? School board closes country schools. Country kids are bussed into more affluent, more academic Tipton where they feel second-class and second-rate, and something ugly that is always with us, something that breeds hoods and Final Solutions, wakes and shakes its rodent head. There was a march, beatings, two arrests. School performance plummeted. Then time passed, and hatred returned to its cave. The only long-term effect was that in a university town, test scores continued to be abysmal because of a school board decision in 1991.

Jack closed the black leather ledgers in the *Tipton Gazette* morgue. It was going to take more than speeches to students to undo this, even if student votes would help pass the levy. Jack stood, fearful, worried about his kids.

✦ ✦ ✦

That night, after Lizzie and Simon stopped battling the inevitable and switched off their lights at ten-thirty, Genna entered their bedroom and sat beside Jack on the bed. She looked tired or perhaps just worried. When she was either, her cheeks sagged. The wrinkles at the corners of her mouth showed more prominently and her eyes, which were blue-gray and could present anywhere along that gradient, looked dark as storm clouds.

"We've got to talk," she said.

When a couple's been tiptoeing and feeling as if maybe their hearts could slowly open, it is some scary shit, Jack thought, to hear that particular phrase. Did she want to talk about the affair, to which he'd confessed only in the most general terms? Or was she finally going to confess where she'd been all those nights last winter, a mystery he wasn't sure he wanted solved? "What do we have to talk about?"

"Simon's getting harassed at school. He comes around the corner and kids bang into him. They say, 'Die, faggot,' or 'Die, homo,' and keep going."

"What kids?"

"Apparently, there's quite a few." Her eyes were the gray of grief. "He doesn't know any of them."

"But they know him."

She nodded.

"Maybe," Jack began, and before he uttered another word he knew he shouldn't. But all last year when they'd been having such trouble and the years before, too, when the troubles were building, baby troubles, then toddlers, then troubles learning to gallop on their own, Genna had urged him to get in touch with what he was feeling. Here it was. "Maybe if he didn't wear fishnet sleeves and backed off on the eyeliner, kids wouldn't be calling him faggot."

"That's hardly the point."

He looked at her and she looked at him, and all they hadn't talked about was right there with them.

"For once in his life it wouldn't hurt to fit in."

"That's Simon." She laughed. "So adept at fitting in."

A thousand incidents leapt to mind. At eight and nine, Simon still insisted boys play Barbie. They'd explain over and over he had to choose between getting his own way and making friends. Because he was lonely, he'd always answer, with that cherubic grin, I pick friends, Daddy, but he didn't or couldn't.

Jack asked, "How'd you find out?"

"I came home after driving Lizzie to soccer practice, and he'd made himself this giant pot of spaghetti."

She paused, and just then—his room was directly below theirs, and they'd discovered that although the house was otherwise well-built, there wasn't much sound-proofing—Simon juiced his sound system, and "A Whole New World" from *Aladdin*, which had long been one of his favorites, a comfort song, like spaghetti was a comfort food, blasted through the floor.

"He'd eaten two full plates," Genna said. "I could tell he hated himself for eating so much."

Jack watched her recognize the song; tears swelled her rain-cloud eyes. Simon was a soprano when he first learned "A Whole

New World" to audition for a kid's play in Cincinnati. By opening night, he'd sounded more like Aladdin than the princess. Two more years, and their boy soprano had become a baritone.

"I asked about his day, and it poured out of him. Apparently," Genna pursed her lips, listening for Simon to start singing, "it's been going on for some time."

"Why didn't he tell us?" Before the words left his mouth, Jack knew. And though she didn't say, Because he was afraid you'd tell him not to wear so much eye make-up, she didn't have to.

"It started maybe two weeks ago, then died down. But today was bad again."

Simon started to sing, and inside the operatic baritone booming up through the floor, there was still a little boy in love with magic carpet rides. "A whole new world. A new fantastic point of view."

"Besides," Genna said, "he's been talking to that guidance counselor."

"Mister O'Neill?"

"No one to tell us no, or where to go."

"That woman. The one you found so interesting."

We really do need to talk, Jack thought. Then Simon was singing at the top of his lungs, "A whole new world with you."

Through the floor he heard Lizzie pound on Simon's door, demanding he shut up, she was trying to sleep.

"We're supposed to call her first thing in the morning for an appointment," Genna said.

"I'll take care of it."

"I was hoping you would." She smiled. "I've got a few more pages in my book."

"Why don't you read in here?"

"It's more comfortable in my study." She touched his shoulder. "Don't worry. Everything's all right."

✦ ✦ ✦

In the morning, from his university office, Jack telephoned the high school and asked for Marla Lindstrom. The secretary transferred him to the guidance office, where a student worker—Jack wondered how much the student knew—transferred him to Mrs. Lindstrom's voicemail. Marla's recorded voice was low and melodic, understated. Five minutes later his phone rang.

"Jack, this is Marla Lindstrom."

She could have said Professor Barish or Jack Barish, but no, just Jack.

"Thanks for getting back." Jack's palm dampened the receiver, and he took a deep, steadying breath. "My wife and I would like to come in as soon as possible." What was the proper way to phrase this? "To discuss the problems Simon's been having."

"I'm glad, I was about to call you when I got your message."

"Why?"

"Excuse me a moment."

He could hear background noise at Marla's end. Then she returned.

"I'd like us to meet with Dr. Burroughs, the principal."

"Has something happened?"

"Oh no," she said. "Not really."

He waited for Marla to disclose what hadn't happened.

"The mother of a football player called to say there was a rumor the football team was going to beat Simon up today."

"The entire team?"

"She didn't say. And before you ask, I don't know who the mother was, she wouldn't give a name." Jack heard voices at her end again. "Dr. Burroughs can see us at eleven-thirty. Can you, or your wife come in?"

"We'll both be there."

He hung up and called Genna. When they'd finished speaking, Jack sat in his office, fuming. Why not basketball? Cross-country? Why did football have to be where all the assholes were? He played in high school. He was pretty good, too. Not like his older brother Russ who was second-team All-Ivy at Yale his junior and senior years. But Jack was good enough to start at tight end two years in high school and to be chosen first or second in pick-up games his entire childhood. At Vassar, too, in the dorm games, the intramurals against the other houses, he was always The Man. Good enough that he thought football was something he'd pass onto his son, not only the skill but a love of the game.

When he met Genna in grad school and learned she had played tennis in school and that her younger brother was a star quarterback, he'd cheered silently, knowing it was silly, but thinking, If we have kids we'll breed football players, they'll get it from both sides. It wasn't until later, when they'd fallen in love and it no longer mattered and they were telling secrets, that Genna disclosed she and her brother had different fathers, that the man she called Daddy wasn't her biological dad. Jack, she'd whispered, I think I'm a love child.

She'd laughed and widened those blue-gray eyes which sometimes filled with light. He ripped off her clothes and they'd made love right there on his grad school couch.

"Love child." He hummed a few bars, humming and humping for all he was worth.

When Simon arrived he clearly had Jack's body shape, sturdy legs, barrel chest, a miniature football player, the way some very young children don't look like kids at all, but tiny adults. Such hopes, had Jack. His first-born son! He coached T-ball, soccer, and pee-wee football, but could never capture Simon's interest. At six and seven, he was one of those kids (there were some on every team) who'd stand on the field gazing up at cloud faces or squawking birds while the other kids charged past pursuing the ball or each other. That was the first wedge between them, how much Jack cared that he play sports—In our blood, goddamnit!—pressed up against the reality of how little Simon cared.

Now football was back: the damn football team. And however much Jack hated the fucking Barbies (he used to fantasize about destroying them, as if they were the problem and not Simon), the fishnet sleeves and makeup, he adored his son and would defend him against the football team and whomever else. He called the university information number, got through to Dean McWilliams who was in charge of Diversity and Minority Affairs. When he picked Genna up to drive to the high school, he was armed and ready.

They found Marla in the guidance office. She wore a black two-piece pants suit, very tailored, of the sort Genna would never wear because it would be too tight across, well, everywhere. Much as he didn't want to, he found the woman thrilling.

"Marla Lindstrom," Jack began, "Genna Barish."

"Pleased to meet you." Marla offered her small hand, which Genna took in her much larger one. They seemed to take each other's measure, Jack thought, like wrestlers.

"Simon tells me you've been very kind to him. Thank you."

"He's a wonderful person. A breath of fresh air our school needs."

"Excuse me," Jack said. "It seems to me the school's choking on that fresh air."

"Only certain elements in it." Marla's eyes were the blue Jack remembered the sky being in California. "And these poor kids need to learn how to breathe." She checked her watch, which lay small and golden against her slim wrist. "I've felt uncomfortable these past few weeks not being in touch with you. But Simon asked me not to, and I've tried to respect his wishes."

"We understand."

Genna often slipped into the first person plural when it came to the kids. Jack wondered what Marla thought about that as they followed her to the main office. One-story Tipton High had been built on the cheap sometime in the seventies. The building was beginning to show its age, but there was nothing grossly deficient.

Extra-wide halls permitted students to pass without banging into each other unless they wanted to. The Media Center, formerly the library, was small, the computer lab inadequate. Unlike the Five Towns school Jack attended, there was no formal auditorium. In its place, there was an auditeria: half-lunchroom, half-central meeting space with folding gymnasium seating stored against the walls.

Marla left them front of Dr. Burroughs's office and apologized for missing the beginning of the meeting. They watched her hurry away, heels clicking against the high-gloss hard-tiled hallway. "I can see why Simon likes her," Genna said, and looked up at him.

They entered Burroughs's office together. The Tipton principal was only five-eight or so, broad-shouldered with a hanging gut, and a neatly-barbered brown beard gone gray on his cheeks. Bushy eyebrows and round, magnifying lenses made him look like a badger, or was it a beaver: round, squat, and furry.

"Mister and Mrs. Barish." He stood up from his computer. "Thanks for coming in."

We don't need to be thanked, Jack thought, any parent would. Already distrusting him, Jack shook Burroughs's hand, then sat with Genna across the principal's dark wood desk, the one decent piece of furniture in the office.

"So." Burroughs cleared his throat. "Mrs. Lindstrom will join us shortly. We've asked Simon to come in at the end."

Genna and Jack exchanged glances. Academic life and seventeen years of parenting Simon had trained them to enter meetings knowing what they wanted.

"Dr. Burroughs," Jack began, "I want you to understand where we're coming from. Although we're new in town, we actively support Tipton schools."

Genna interjected, "We've lived the past seven years in Cincinnati."

"My wife and I, we're both professors at the university and we'll be talking to student groups, trying to help pass the levy."

"Glad to hear it."

"In principle, we have nothing against the football team. I played football in high school. Genna's father played. Both our brothers played Division I football in college."

Burroughs looked at Jack through his round magnified lenses as if he suspected Jack were slightly mad.

"My point is, we're not biased against athletes. Quite the contrary. But I also need to tell you, we take these threats from the football team very seriously."

"Now just a minute," Burroughs said, "I'm not sure the football team, or anyone else for that matter— "

"The phone call from the mother this morning," Genna said softly.

Burroughs looked caught out. Perhaps Marla wasn't supposed to tell them?

"And kids coming up to Simon in the hall and saying 'Die, faggot.' We consider those overt threats, and we take them very seriously."

Burroughs's right cheek expanded outward under pressure from his tongue. "We all think it's serious, Mister Barish. That's why we're here."

Jack could feel blood beating in his ears, rage building up inside him, and he struggled to keep the pressure he felt out of his voice. "We think it's so serious that I've spoken to the Title IX administrator at the University, who's informed me that since Ohio and federal laws, and I quote, 'Guarantee students the right to a school environment free from violence or the threat of physical violence,' and since this threatened violence is about sexual orientation and the school has been warned," Jack paused, trying to regain control of his voice, "although I've never been party to a lawsuit, I will sue the district for every dollar I can if anything happens to my son."

"Mister Barish," Burroughs said, looking out through his round lenses as if from inside a cave, "are you threatening me?"

Absolutely, he longed to say, feeling the telltale tendon bulging on his neck. Not threatening—this was schoolyard when he was growing up—Promising, cocksucker! Then he felt Genna's hand on his knee.

"Of course not, Dr. Burroughs. I'm sorry if I gave that impression."

Primordial throat and teeth-baring silence followed, during which Burroughs surely believed he had backed Jack down. Then, with her eyes the balmy side of blue, Genna said, "What we'd like, Dr. Burroughs, is for you, or the guidance counselors, someone, to meet as soon as possible with the football team, and tell them how inappropriate this behavior is."

Jack concentrated on Genna's hand squeezing his knee..

"And how swiftly and harshly Tipton High will deal both with violence or the threat of violence. Something like that."

Genna smiled at Burroughs—how did she manage it?—then at Jack, as if they were twelve, or maybe eight-year-old chuckleheads. There was a knock, and Marla entered. "Sorry to be late." She sat in the last remaining chair and crossed her slim legs. "Simon will be here shortly."

"Before he arrives," the principal began, "I wanted to tell Mister and Mrs. Barish…"

That's Doctor and Doctor Barish, Jack thought, but did not say.

"…that there have been complaints about Simon's behavior."

"From whom?" Jack asked.

"Other students report he's been holding hands in the hall. Kissing his friend on the cheek. That's against school policy, regardless of gender."

Genna and Jack glanced at each other. He said, "What about kids banging into him saying, 'Die, faggot'?"

"I'm not excusing their behavior. Don't think for a moment anyone is." Burroughs glanced at the open file folder on his desk.

"But I see that Simon went to a performing arts high school last year. He needs to understand that this is a very different place."

Genna said, "I'm sure he does."

"We know about the Klan march," Jack said. "That's why we settled in Cincinnati in the first place."

"That was before my time," Burroughs said.

Jack's eyes swung to Marla.

"It was terrible," she said. "There are a lot of ignorant people here."

"Those attitudes remain in the community," Burroughs added. "They just go underground."

Like badgers.

"Walk around the school sometime," Burroughs continued. "Look at all the Confederate belt buckles. You'll see what we're up against." His cheek bulged again, as if full of acorns for winter. "The football team practices this afternoon. If you like, I'll talk to them."

"That would be wonderful," Genna said. "Thank you."

Marla, who'd been seated, legs crossed, at the corner of Burroughs's desk, said, "I have a note from Simon. He's hoping Dr. Burroughs will read it to the team."

Marla passed Jack a sheet torn from a spiral notebook. He recognized the ornate, upright script. The swirls and decoration, Simon's usual misspellings. Your for you're. Fealings for feelings. Genna read it aloud.

Hi,

My name is Simon Barish. I'm new this year. Some of you may have herd things about me. Or seen my clothes and decided your different from me and you hate me. So you've been calling me names.

Well, I have fealings like everyone else. If you see me in the hall, don't think you know what I'm like, because as the saying goes, You can't tell a book by its cover. Come up to say hello, and who knows, maybe we'll be friends.

Thank you very much for listening.

Your friend,

Simon Barish

Genna put the letter down and looked at Jack, eyes glistening.

"That's really something," Marla said. "Isn't it?"

There was a knock, and Simon entered with his gelled and spiked blond hair, his extra-wide jeans with green velvet patches, his too-big belly pressing against a black T-shirt Jack especially disliked: If I throw a stick will you fetch it?

Simon smiled, expectant, simultaneously embarrassed and pleased because he must have known they were talking about him. How remarkable he is, Jack thought. How brave. What a royal pain in the ass. My son, he thought, glancing at Genna, and I love him.

chapter 4

On Friday afternoon, when Simon and Lizzie bopped in from the bus stop, their laughing, querulous voices raised Genna from her study. Although they were deep in the so-called difficult years, they were all her pride and much of her joy, and she hurried out to greet them. In the slate entranceway, Simon and Lizzie had just abandoned their backpacks precisely where every afternoon she asked them not to; Sam pogoed on his hind legs celebrating the arrival of a New Person! thrusting his large, moist nose into the startled face of a slender boy Genna hadn't met before.

"Down, Sam, down!" Simon shouted. "Damnit, Lizzie! Why'd you let him in?"

"I didn't," Lizzie shouted, but grabbed Sam's collar and dragged the offended, hundred-pound oaf out the door.

"Mom," Simon said, "this is Rich." Rich was cute and curly-haired. Fine-featured, almost delicate, he energetically wiped Sam schmutz off his cheek. "Rich," Simon grinned, "this is Mom."

"Nice to meet you," Genna said. "I see you've met Sam."

Rich smiled, said nothing.

In the kitchen, Simon hung with simian grace from the fridge door, allowing cold air to escape. How different, she thought, than in my parents' house, where I wouldn't have dared. Then, looking exceptionally well-fed, Simon declared, bitterly, as he did most afternoons, that there was nothing to eat.

"Mom," he continued, with a glance at Rich. "Can we order pizza?"

Simon was obviously smitten. So she didn't respond, as she normally would have, Do you have any money? Nor did she suggest carrots, an apple, or any of the healthy snacks she stocked the fridge with, not because she minded being mocked (as the mother of teenagers she was inured to all forms of verbal abuse), but because she didn't want Simon to appear loutish in front of Rich.

"There's DiGiorno's in the downstairs freezer."

"All right," Simon said.

Lizzie's head snapped up; she was at the kitchen table reading the morning's funnies as she did most days after school. A long-established house rule (posted on the fridge as part of the Barish House Accords) was that those frozen DiGiorno's, five-ninety-nine a box, were quickie dinners, not snacks.

"Come on," Simon said. "I'll show you my room."

Rich followed Simon downstairs. When the boys were out of earshot, Lizzie asked, "After school pizza?"

"It's Friday." Genna watched Lizzie mentally revise the BHAs.

"Is Simon allowed to have boys in his room?"

Lizzie had inherited Genna's ironic sensibility, but otherwise resembled her not at all: tall and slender, where Genna was neither. Her mother's genes had skipped a generation, re-forming in Lizzie, Genna sometimes thought, like an image in a Star Trek transporter. The original Star Trek.

"It depends on the boy, don't you think?"

Lizzie grinned. What a charmer her daughter was. "What about Rich?"

"He's awfully cute."

Lizzie grinned wider. Genna knew she was about to say something hilarious. One of Genna's unadulterated joys was that Lizzie trusted her sufficiently to say what she really thought. How rare in a teenage daughter. But just then Rich and Simon started up the stairs.

"Puh-lease," Simon sang in his too excited, too loud, too high voice. "That is so disgusting."

Grinning, the boys re-entered the kitchen. She hadn't heard Rich speak yet and tried to find something to ask him. He noticed she was watching him, and his pretty, long-lashed eyes—were they really green?—lost their unguarded glow. Rich, she thought, is a hidden person.

Simon bustled about, much like Sam, who didn't realize he'd grown too large to get up on the bed and was always banging into furniture and sniffing crotches. Rattling pots and lids, Simon excavated the Teflon pizza pan from under the stove, removed the spicy chicken pizza from its box, its bag, its cardboard insert and slid it onto the pan. What a load of garbage.

"Mom." Simon slid the pizza in the oven and set the white egg timer. He liked to cook, and not just microwave popcorn and frozen pizzas. "Can Rich sleep over?"

Lizzie's head snapped up again, her dark brows arched like parentheses.

"Not tonight."

Simon stopped smiling. "Why not?"

"The first time Rich visits"—she tried to make Simon meet her eyes so he would realize she meant it—"he can't spend the night."

"His dad won't care," Simon said. "He lives with his dad."

"And my grandmother," Rich added softly.

So he does speak. "Simon." She was trying not to appear angry; she'd discarded anger in the old house like a dress that no longer fit. "May I talk to you in private?"

She glanced towards Rich, who looked as if light might pass through him. This boy, she thought, has seen his share of discord. She walked to the living room where sunshine poured through the wall of glass. How could anyone not be happy in this much light? Simon entered and stood beside her, half a head taller and half again as wide.

"Dad and I have asked you not to put us on the spot by asking if someone can sleep over when they're standing right there."

"But why not? You can call his grandmother or his dad when he gets home from work."

"The first time someone visits, he can't sleep over. But he can stay for dinner if you want."

Simon's jaw unclenched. "Are you and Dad going out afterwards?"

"We haven't decided." In fact, Jack had suggested a movie, and she'd more or less agreed. But she couldn't decide about leaving the boys alone. "Rich is awfully cute, isn't he?"

"Mom." Simon tried to look angry but failed. Grinning, he bounced out of the room.

At five, Jack called and spoke to Lizzie, who found Genna reading on the deck, and reported that Dad would be home in twenty minutes. Genna had a horror of kids returning to an empty house; most days she arranged to be home by three. Jack got the kids off to school, sometimes waited for her to have breakfast, then left. Genna, who didn't function well before nine—as soon as the kids were weaned, she'd delegated breakfast duties to Jack—left later, returned earlier, but accomplished more. Her last two books had been well-received, while Jack hadn't published in quite some time and was having trouble with his grants. All this, she knew, weighed on him, so she accepted that he'd be home an hour or two later than she and tried to believe he was hard at work all those hours he was gone.

Last winter, after he confessed the affair with some woman he'd met at the conference he attended each spring, she thought she'd lose her mind. Looking back, for more than a month, it appeared she had. He told her in the solarium of their old house one January afternoon. The kids were at school, but for some reason she could no longer recall, neither she nor Jack had driven to Tipton. Maybe the roads were bad. It was gray mid-winter blah in the Ohio

River Valley. The sky was two feet above the ground and no light entered through the uncurtained windows. Genna hadn't seen the sun in days, and it was all she could do not to crawl into bed and pull the covers over her head.

Jack announced it had been his New Year's resolution to make a clean breast of things. Where did that expression come from, a clean breast? Some woman-hating, anti-breast-feeding bias? After nine months the affair was over, but he didn't feel he could go on living with her without confessing.

"Do you love her, Jack?"

She watched his face: blue eyes, broad cheeks, square chin, the athlete's neck which descended almost without tapering from his head to his shoulders. An honest face, almost too open, she'd thought when she met him. Not particularly Jewish-looking, except for his nose, which looked as if it had been broken, though it hadn't.

She watched his face, and there was the truth, sharp as her pain.

"Oh," she said. "I see."

"I don't anymore."

Could she believe him? How could she believe anything in that penumbral room, with gray light sifting like ash to the frozen ground that had been her heart. The one thing she had felt most sure of was that Jack Barish, with his broad, honest face would never be able to lie to her, but she understood now that he must have lied frequently and well.

She rose unsteadily and said, "I have to go now."

She drove to the Bonbonnerie, the best bakery in town, ordered two brownies, two scones, a blueberry cheese Danish and ate them all. She drove to the river and thought about throwing herself in, but that would hurt the kids more than Jack, and why should she kill herself, he was the louse. She drove to Lebanon, the antique town and found all the things she would buy for the house she lived in without Jack. She drove to Tri-County Mall and sat in her car with the heater blasting. She continued to Kenwood Town

Centre and walked the bright halls like a released mental patient.

As February wore on, she found a rhythm. She'd eat dinner with the family then leave. Jack didn't ask where. She prowled the malls. She saw every movie in town, most of them twice. When the malls closed, she moved to the bars in Clifton but soon understood they were college or sports bars; she saw students all day and detested televised sports. She tried the downtown hotels and let hopeful businessmen buy her drinks. One night she went upstairs with a guy named Pete from Portland, Maine, who was thirty-two, handsome and very drunk. She permitted Pete remove her bra, but couldn't go through with it.

Pushing his mouth away from her erect nipple—there had been that, at least—she grabbed her things and dressed in the corridor, then drove around and around and around before parking with her lights off on a dead-end street overlooking the Ohio River. It was on that overlook, two-thirds drunk but remarkably sober, another man's lips and breath still imprinting her breast, that Genna admitted what she'd known all along. She didn't want someone else. She didn't want revenge. She wanted life with Jack to be the way it had been, not only before January 26, but before these past few years when everything seemed slowly to dissolve.

Now, she thought, supine on a padded lounger in the late afternoon on her deck, with the white oaks and sycamores transmuting light to a violent green gold, they had another chance. There were Simon's problems, but Simon always had problems. Parenting Simon was helping him clear a swath through his problems, not eliminating them. But this house felt right, and Genna, who hadn't been able to breathe in Cincinnati, felt in her lungs and in her very bones, that this house was right for all of them. All these photosynthesizing leaves. Even the air was better.

That was why she needed to believe Jack was working all the hours he was gone. If he'd been more successful, he wouldn't have had that affair. (Was she an idiot to think that?) If the new project he'd alluded to, but wouldn't tell her about, would somehow get published, then this new house with its super-oxygenated air would work its magic, and Jack would feel strong enough to resist the attraction she knew he felt for Marla Lindstrom.

She'd sensed it in Marla's office, and again in the emotionally-charged atmosphere in Burroughs's office; several times she'd thought Jack and the squat principal were going to leap up and pound each other. Jack Barish wasn't Pierce Brosnan, but he was handsome enough. Over the years her girlfriends had told her what a hunk he was, and a nice guy, too (she'd always agreed). If she ever tired of him, more than one girlfriend had said, only half-joking, just let her know.

As for Marla, she was one of those bird-like women Genna had always envied. Narrow-hipped, small-breasted, looked great in stylish clothes. She had large, bright blue eyes in which Genna could read the state of play. The smile she'd given Jack when they arrived. The palpable sexual tension in Burroughs's office. How they'd glance at each other then look away.

She didn't exactly blame Jack. In the past he'd been attracted to several of her friends and they'd been attracted to him. What did it matter, she'd thought. Everyone was grown-up; everyone was attractive. Nothing ever came of it, as far as she knew, except some sexy dancing at parties, and she'd felt pleased, honored, even, because the nothing that had happened was one more brick in the storehouse of Jack's love for her.

His confession changed all that. But although half of her wanted to rip those big baby blues out of her little face, Genna didn't exactly blame Marla. Genna gathered she'd been divorced for some time in a college town without many single men. Jack was attractive, and as that weasel Woody Allen said about his affair with Mia's daughter, the heart wants what it wants.

No, she didn't blame Jack or Marla for being attracted to each other; she would blame them if they acted on it. Before January 26, she would have had no doubt. And now? A flash of color. A red-crested woodpecker lit on the large oak near the railing and began drumming its beak into the bark.

What she did know—even the birds were more vivid, and there were deer; she'd seen two yesterday morning on the stone path just below the house—was that she didn't have the luxury of ordering Marla to keep her skinny ass far away from Jack. After yesterday's meeting, it was clear Marla would have to be Simon's advocate. In every school, they'd needed one. The six through nine teacher in the Montessori, the principal in performing arts. It certainly wouldn't be Dr. Burroughs, who really did look like a badger.

So Genna would hold her tongue and hope Marla and Jack would hold their tongues and every other part. Genna reclined on the lounger and glanced up at the late sunlight slicing through the leaves. She watched the red-headed bird attack the tree and hoped saving Simon wouldn't cost her Jack.

✦ ✦ ✦

Jack abandoned his project on the connections between American racism in the 1920s and the rise of eugenics in Germany the morning after meeting with Burroughs. After three years of being able neither to complete the whole nor publish the parts, and then being totally mortified when a writer named Kuhl published a book on the subject, it was time. Perhaps admitting this failure would lighten his spirit. Maybe he wasn't meant to take on such a great historical theme, one in which blame was laid and guilt assessed, responsibility objectively measured and assigned. American eugenicists such as Clarence Campbell praised Nazi eugenics policy and millions of "genetically inferior" individuals were sterilized and murdered. You did that, and that's why this happened. Jack was sick of it.

The first step was to clean out the top drawer of his file cabinet; since grad school he'd reserved the top drawer for current work.

Abstracts, off-prints of articles cited. Hard copies of the six completed chapters. Rejection letters, grant applications. Correspondence with prospective contributors to an essay collection he could never place. All of it out of the drawer and into a file box. All those weeks, months and late nights when he could have been learning to flop a wedge or spin approach shots backwards towards the cup. Jack dropped papers in the box file and felt as if he were filing for divorce.

Sorting, he was reminded of Schrödinger's Cat, a paradox said to have arisen out of a discussion between Einstein and Schrödinger about scientific inquiry and the nature of the universe. Was objective observation possible, as Einstein claimed—"God does not play dice with the universe"—or was the observer, however objective he might attempt to be, inevitably implicated in his observations. Here was Schrödinger's proof: construct a hypothetical Rube Goldberg device around a single atom of radioactive material with the half life of an hour; at the other end of the line was a box containing Schrödinger's cat, which Jack had always imagined to be an orange tabby named Rex. Within the first hour, there existed a 50 percent likelihood that the isotope would emit its electron, prompting a Geiger counter to click, causing a ball to drop, then a hammer to fall smashing a vial of cyanide gas inside the box containing a tabby named Rex.

Thus, if the observer left and returned after an hour, much like God the Absent Creator (the only sort of God Jack's four-year immersion in German eugenics permitted him), it was equally likely but impossible to know if the box contained a living cat or a dead one. Only by opening the box and thereby implicating himself in the experiment could an observer reduce all the possible outcomes of Schrödinger's cat to a single fixed one: Rex on his back, paws in the air, or Rex at the door, mewing to be set free.

Jack's eugenics project was his Schrödinger's Cat: dead when he looked at it. Or maybe, he thought, sealing the box file with packing tape before lugging it to his office closet, all his professional training was in that box: the myth of the objective eye, which had prevented him from seeing himself or his career, and quite possibly from having anything interesting to say about the influence of American racism on the rise of German race science in the 1930s. As a Jew, he was so anxious to leave himself completely out—What me, a Jew? You think that's why I'm interested in this? I'll prove it. I'll provide no point of view at all—that what he produced was virtually unreadable. In fact, for months, even he'd been unable to read more than a sentence or two without needing a nap. (Late-onset narcolepsy was another explanation, he supposed.) But late that night, unable to sleep, he decided to develop a lengthy review of the current biological and genetic research on the causes and development of homosexuality. Was this a subject matter he was implicated in? You bet.

In 1991, Northwestern University's Michael Bailey and others had published the best known study of homosexual concordance rates in twins, and reported, among other findings, that if one identical twin was homosexual, there was a 50 percent likelihood that the second twin would be as well, clearly indicating a genetic component. A 1993 study by Whitam and others found a 65.8 percent concordance in identical twins, as opposed to only 30.4 percent for fraternal twins. (This was against an accepted base rate of 5-10 percent of homosexuality in the general population.) That same year, a team of N.I.H. researchers led by Dean Hamer published an article in *Science* reporting that in their study of forty gay brothers, thirty-three had the same set of DNA sequences in a region of the chromosome called Xq28. This study, which was seized upon by gay activists as if it were manna in the conservative desert of Homosexuality is A Life-Style Choice Not Deserving of Anti-Discrimination Protection, made a star of Dean Hamer (himself homosexual). The study and its follow-up were bitterly attacked by family value organizations eager to refute it as not only a gay rights polemic, but bad science.

In April, 1999, researchers at the University of Western Ontario, led by neurologist George Rice reported in *Science* that their study of fifty-two pairs of gay brothers directly refuted Hamer's study, finding that their Xq28 sequences were no more similar than what might be expected from sheer chance. Hamer stood by his findings, especially since two subsequent studies (one unpublished) supported his findings. He did concede, however, that not every case of homosexuality was because of Xq28. "I expect," he said, "we'll find that many genes are involved. One of them will be on Xq28."

Conservative therapist groups seized on the twin studies. Okay, they argued. Let's assume that the concordance figure for identical twins is roughly two-thirds. That leaves one-third of all genetically identical twins with different sexual orientations. What can that mean, but that there's no absolute gay gene, but only a tendency that therapy can treat. Homosexuals, they argued, were not born but molded from lumps of clay that might look queer but didn't have to end up that way. Depending on the potter, you could end up with a homosexual vase, or a heterosexual flowerpot. In their view, the as-yet sexually undetermined lump of clay, the stem cell, if you will, of sexual orientation, was pushed towards faggotdom by an absent or distant father. In later life, that unmolded son, seeking the approval he never received from his dad, sexualizes the need for same-sex affection. In short: in the Barish household, because Simon preferred Barbie to football, Jack had rejected him and that made him gay.

And on the genetic side? There were no known homosexuals in the Barish family, certainly not his brother Russ, nor his father Henry, a lusty tax attorney, who, if anything, was too heterosexual. (Jack suspected that his father had had his own affairs.) There were no known homosexuals in Genna's family, either. Then again, neither of them were musical, yet Simon's voice was so weighty and mysterious that when he sang at the middle school talent show an auditorium full of adults leapt to their feet with tears in their eyes, stamping and clapping and crying out for more.

Of course, there was the unknown: Genna's biological father. Maybe Mystery Grandad was where it came from, the instrument and the swish, and Jack was off the hook. On the other hand, Simon looked and sounded so remarkably like him (except when they sang), the only difference being Jack exercised and Simon didn't, that perhaps there was an unexpressed gay gene coming from Jack on some as yet-unmapped chromosome. Who could say?

Jack finished setting up the new top drawer, arranged his desk, walked out to the parking lot and started home. Turning into Forest Glen, then onto his long driveway, he thought, Maybe this will work. Maybe we won't have to move back to Cincinnati so Simon can return to the arts high school. Maybe we won't even have to pay tuition and find a family for him to commute with. Maybe Tipton will be all right.

He opened the two-car garage with a garage door opener—the first they'd ever owned—and entered through the kitchen door. He could smell rosemary chicken roasting in the oven. Monk played in the living room. A yellow bell pepper and an English cuke rested on the cutting board like lovers. The kitchen table was set for five.

Lizzie entered wearing one of her tight tops, listening to her Diskman, headphones tangled in her dark hair. She kissed his cheek, and smiling, reached up and rubbed the crown of his head where the hair was thinnest. "Hi, Boppa. How was your day?"

"Fine, thanks for asking." Music escaped her earphones. Blink 182, or Three Doors Down, something loud. "How was yours?"

"School."

"Why are there five plates?"

"What?"

"Turn down your music. You're gonna be deaf by twenty."

She bestowed one of her new teenaged smiles which never failed to knock him out. Translated, he believed it meant, Dad, I love you, but you are so 1990s.

"Who's the extra plate for?"

"Ask Mom."

Lizzie exited, hooked up and bopping. Jack found Genna on the deck, Sam at her feet.

"Hey, darling." He leaned down and kissed her. "Do we have company?"

"Simon's friend, Rich."

Something in the way she said friend. "Rich?"

There was that wariness in her eyes he found so upsetting. "You'll see when you meet him."

"Are they more than friends?"

She patted the padded lounger and Jack sat down. "Simon would like to be."

"What about Rich?"

"He's hard to read." Genna's eyes twinkled. "Just like you."

Jack set his hand on her thigh and kissed his pretty wife. "Am I hard to read now?"

She shook her head, leaned back against the lounger and he kissed her again. Then Sam climbed up, wagging his tail and smiling his big dopey grin.

"Down, Sam. Find your own damn girl."

Jack got down on the deck and pushed the dog over. He growled, then bit the fur at Sam's throat, establishing dominance as he had since Sam's puppy days. Sam flailed and growled happily. His fur tasted of dried mud. His tongue lolled. His open mouth stank of rot, the creek bottom, and who knew what else.

Genna said, "I'm not sure we can go out to the movies and leave the boys alone."

When the kids were young they'd had terrible luck with sitters. They'd cancel. The kids would get sick, or the sitters would. The first weekend they'd arranged to leave the kids, they were called home the first night. Chicken pox.

Jack released Sam and looked up. "Can't Lizzie chaperone?"

"She's going out."

Sam grabbed his right forearm and bit hard enough for Jack to feel his teeth. "Goddamn it, Sam!"

Genna laughed. "You started."

Jack climbed back on the lounger. "You really think we can't leave them alone?"

"Would you leave Lizzie alone with her boyfriend?"

"Does she have a boyfriend?"

"If she did."

Sam bowed over his front paws. Hey, Boss, pay attention to me.

"Absolutely not. Where are the boys?"

"In Simon's room."

Jack thought of his high school girlfriend, now Doctor Shapiro, somewhere in Boston, the games they'd played in her room even when her parents were home.

"I don't think that's a good idea," he said. "Do you?"

"They're probably better off here than anywhere else."

"If they want to make out, fine." He thought about Simon kissing this Rich whom he hadn't met yet. "But anything else? Let him sneak around like I had to."

"I think," Genna said sadly, "Simon's in for a lot of sneaking around."

Jack stood. Sam went for his forearm, and Jack kneed him in the chest. The dog barely noticed. "Down, Sam." Jack kneed him again. "Why don't I pick up videos? Maybe Simon and his friend can cuddle with us on the couch."

"Oh, right. Why don't you see if Simon wants you to get them a video?"

Sam followed him downstairs. Jack knocked on Simon's locked door. He knocked again. Movement within. Then, from nowhere near the door, Simon called, "Who is it?"

Jack hated talking through a closed door. "Dad. Open up."

He could hear Simon thinking, Would you just go away? But a moment later, the door opened part way. Simon did not appear flushed, nor were his clothes disarrayed. A dark curly-haired boy sat in Simon's desk chair. The computer was on. Simon said, grudgingly, "Dad, this is Rich."

He nodded to Rich over Simon's shoulder.

"You guys want a video? I'm going to the store."

"I thought you and Mom were going out."

"Mom changed her mind."

"*Practical Magic*." It was one of his favorites. "Rich, that okay with you?"

Rich nodded.

✦ ✦ ✦

One of the uncomfortable facts of Tipton life was how often you encountered people you didn't want to see. Whoops, the department chair in the dry cleaner. Whoa, a problem student two seats away in the movie theater. There was one of everything. One place to buy the *Sunday Times*, one decent bakery, and one video store, located in the one strip mall next to the only supermarket.

Jack parked in the Valley Video end of the lot, cracked the windows and glanced at Sam, who sat upright in the right front passenger seat. The dog looked mournful, almost, but not quite, resigned to being left. Sam waggled his reddish gold eyebrows; Jack scratched behind his ears. Sam needed to be groomed. He always needed to be groomed. Jack closed the door and his last image, walking away, was of Sam dropping his chin on the top of his seat to stare backwards into the dark minivan, awaiting his return.

Jack was checking titles in the new release aisle, trying not to take too long, thinking about how enticing that rosemary chicken had smelled. When he glanced up, Marla was a few feet away stretching for *American Beauty*, her skirt riding above her slim white knee. Later, he'd wonder how long she'd been there before he noticed her.

"That's a really good movie."

"Hi, Jack." She seemed pleased to see him. "I absolutely adore Kevin Spacey."

"You haven't seen it?"

"Three times." She cut her eyes. "It's a slow night in Tipton."

Was a woman who looked like this really going home on Friday night to watch a movie alone?

"Pretty sad, isn't it?" she asked, as if reading his thoughts.

"What's that?"

"The movie." She grinned, and he felt caught out. "But I like the cinematography, the retrospective narration, and I loved watching Kevin Spacey work out. So what was your favorite part, the rose petals?"

Jack nodded, and she laughed, a clear, happy sound.

"Every man I've asked, his favorite part's the rose petals."

"How many have you asked?"

She didn't respond, and as easy as that, they fell in step and moved to the next rack. "My daughter, Lizzie, has the same relation to Russell Crowe. After three viewings, I refused to pay for her to see *Gladiator* and she began using her own money. This fall she's been listening to the soundtrack on her computer and absolutely mooning over him."

"You think I'm mooning over Kevin Spacey?"

Jack nodded and she beamed at him.

"What about you, Jack?"

"I'm not mooning over Kevin Spacey."

"No, what movie are you renting?"

There was something about her. Maybe just that she was so small and direct, where Genna was neither. He said, "Simon has a friend over, and they want *Practical Magic*." Jack longed to say more. Marla was charming, and he felt charmed, no doubt about it, but that was all he was going to let himself feel. He believed Marla would understand how strange it was for Simon to have a boy over who might be his boyfriend. She might even know Rich.

"I also need a movie for the grown-ups."

At his first oblique mention of Genna, the guidance counselor checked her watch. She started towards the front counter, then asked over her shoulder, "Have you seen *Fight Club*?"

"Not for Genna. Blood's okay, but no psychological pain."

"I think you'd like it." Marla raised her small hand and waved. "Night, Jack. Say hi to Simon for me."

He rented *Practical Magic*, *That Old Feeling* (a Bette Midler romantic comedy they'd seen before and liked), *Three Kings*, and because the fourth was free, Jack checked out *Fight Club*. Driving home, he felt guilty and decided it would be better all around if he didn't tell anyone he'd run into Marla.

chapter 5

For a little guy, Rich had a big penis. At least Simon was pretty sure he did. He'd felt it Friday night through Rich's jeans, till Rich pushed his hand away.

"Your parents are home."

"The door's locked."

Rich gave him the Look: almost a smile, but not. Not happy, not sad. Just Rich. His eyes closed and slowly opened, but the whole time he felt as if Rich were looking right at him.

"I don't care."

Simon almost answered, They don't care. They know and they don't care, but he didn't think Rich would believe him. He wasn't sure he did. Maybe Mom but not Dad, who still invited him to the gym to work out on weekends. What was that about except being a different kind of guy, an athlete like Uncle Russ? Unless it was about losing weight, another forbidden subject, his weight or what Dad called his atrocious diet.

Even if his parents were totally okay with the gay thing, which he didn't see how they could be, since he wasn't—he loved kids and how could he have any?—it was unappealing to have their permission to cop a feel of Rich's cock. So he didn't really mind Rich pushing his hand away, so long as Rich kept kissing him. Rich's tongue snaked around his, then beat against his lips like a moth's wings, like a clever little finger, while Simon's big body lay on top of Rich's smaller one, pressing down, pressing down, pressing down.

Rich had said he'd call Sunday morning when he returned from visiting his mom. Sunday afternoon Simon called Rich's dad's trailer every hour but didn't leave a message because Rich had asked him not to. Sunday night Simon phoned Rachel to ask if she'd heard from Rich, but no, all quiet on the Rich front.

Monday, Simon faced the bathroom mirror. He was considering letting the blond grow out then cropping back to his natural color, but he'd been dying it for two years and wasn't sure what that natural color was. He rubbed gel between his palms and laced his fingers through his wet-from-the-shower hair getting the one-inch spikes just right. Last winter, when he started styling, he'd gobbed on the mega-hold. His spikes were so stiff kids' palms bounced off. One freezing-cold day he was fiddling with his hair, and a big clump snapped off! Now, running his hands through his hair and watching them as if they belonged to someone else, his dad's ham hands, he remembered being two years old, the year they lived in France, or maybe he only remembered France from the picture on Mom's desk. Little Simon with blond curls, a big smile bright as day. He was so cute, I was so cute, what happened?

Lizzie pounded the bathroom door.

"Upstairs, you brat."

"Goddamn you, Simon. It's not your bathroom."

"Eat me, Dizzy!"

She kicked the door. "Asshole! I hate you!"

Her footsteps slashed away, and he looked again in the mirror for little Simon. The upstairs shower snorted; water gurgled upwards through the pipes. How she'd loved to spin, Dizzy Lizzie. In California—he could see it when he closed his eyes—they'd hold hands and spin until she fell down, laughing. Now she acted as if she were more mature than he was, but no way, of course, she wasn't.

Simon opened his eyes and returned to his terribly important hair.

✦ ✦ ✦

He walked down the hall after fourth bell, headed for the auditeria. Bad news and more bad news. Failing pre-calc, which he learned yesterday, and now, failing French. Just wait till Dad found out. You're grounded for the rest of your life. Dad's big ha-ha from middle school. Why did he ever think that was funny?

Simon approached the end of the corridor. Asshole Corner. His palms bled. His heart beat like it did last spring after they made him run the mile, and he nearly passed out. He turned the corner and there they were, three round faces, moon boys with bowl hair and piggy eyes, Big, Bigger, and Little Asshole, and he didn't know where to run or hide.

"Hey, faggot. Faggot, yeah, you."

Simon flattened himself against the wall to let them pass. What a joke, he was too big to flatten against anything smaller than a Winnebago.

"Faggot, you're dead!"

But they swept past without hurting him.

In the lunchroom, Simon looked for Rich. Not finding him, he heaped his tray and sat at Rachel's table. BHA number three: Something green with every meal. With his heart still roaring, Fag-got, fag-got, fag-got! Simon started on his salad. His left leg twitched as it did when his mind was elsewhere: up-down, up-down, up-down.

Rachel gazed at him through sweet doe eyes. "You're shaking the table."

"My leg," he said. "Always does."

"Not always." He sometimes thought she liked him in a boy-girl way. "Would you try? You're annoying people."

He ordered his leg to stop. But like everything, his leg was out of control, and Simon felt a gooey wave of despair crash over him.

He punched his left leg above the knee, punched and punched until it stopped.

"You're such a nut."

He didn't feel like such a nut. "Those guys were calling me names again."

"What guys?"

"Assholes all look the same."

Rachel sipped her Arizona iced tea. "You've really got to do something." She tucked fly-aways behind her ears, then whispered, "Rich isn't coming back."

"What?"

"His dad doesn't want him, so he has to live with his mom up in Earlham."

Oh God. "Where's Earlham?"

"Like two hours north." Rachel touched his arm. "I'm sorry."

Simon demolished his first slice of pizza, then started on the second. Under the table, his leg twitched as if it were running away.

✦ ✦ ✦

Jack spoke to his first student group Sunday night: the hall council in Sturtevant, one of the university's two remaining women's dorms. They met in the ground floor common room where the scent, or was it the aura, of well-bred Midwestern girls had worked its way into the upholstery, the cream-colored walls and drapes, even the slightly frayed Oriental rug around which they arranged their wingback chairs. They were waiting on the final member, a senior named Mandy, whom everyone assured Jack would arrive soon; she was doing laundry.

Jack sat at the head of the oval, sipping Diet Coke while sucking a mouthful of sweet and sour Smarties. His speaker's kit contained: information sheets detailing how grossly underpaid Tipton teachers were and how moderate the tax increase would be; voter registration cards; a map of polling places; and a bagful of miniature Smarties rolls, each of which had a yellow label which proclaimed, Be Smart for Tipton Schools.

The girls were dorm officers and RA's, who'd agreed to live on a freshman hall dispensing hot chocolate and sisterly advice in exchange for room and board. Yvonne, a first-year African American grad student from Jack's department, introduced him, then Jack passed around Voter Registration cards, the information sheets, the bag of Smarties. These were nice girls, concerned about social issues and their own weight; the bag of Smarties came back undiminished. Then Mandy entered, blond hair tugged back in a tight ponytail, wearing a gray Tipton T-shirt and running shorts. Clearly, laundry night.

"Sorry." She took the last available chair.

TUTS strategy was straightforward: get the students to vote. Last spring, after the college kids left town, a levy lost by fifteen hundred votes. No More Taxes (the opposition) spread the word that last spring's levy was trying to revive plans for a new high school, which wasn't true. TUTS was now proclaiming, the statement being at least partially true, that it was in the students' self-interest to bring better schools to Tipton.

"Without good public schools, " Jack began, "the university has difficulty hiring and retaining the best young faculty. As some of you may know, the Director of the Art Museum has just taken a job in Tennessee. In his resignation letter, he wrote, and I quote, 'The poor quality of the public schools was the deciding factor. I had to do what was best for my family.'"

He looked around. Such well-scrubbed, well-meaning faces. Only one or maybe two appeared bored. "For eight years, my wife and I commuted because we didn't want our kids in Tipton schools. Our colleagues, when they recruited us, warned us. Now I don't have to tell you, if someone's commuting an hour each way, they have less time for students."

The girls murmured. No doubt some professor had turned down their request for a late-afternoon meeting.

"You can help by registering to vote in Tipton. If you're already registered back home, you can re-register and save yourself the bother of getting an absentee ballot. It's perfectly legal. You live here." Jack looked at them one by one. Several girls nodded. "Even if you're apathetic about the national election—after all, it's an off year—in Tipton, your vote matters. You know how important a good high school education is. Without it, you wouldn't be here."

Mandy raised her hand. "But we don't pay taxes. Is it really fair for us to vote for a tax increase?"

Jack glanced from girl to girl ending on Yvonne, the only black face.

"You spend money in Tipton. And if you live off-campus next year and the levy passes, your rent will probably be five dollars a month higher to pay your landlord's higher taxes. But that's less than a movie, or a pitcher at Joe Mac's."

The girls grinned. Joe Mac's was a popular student bar. "So even though it may cost you or your parents a little extra, it's the right thing to do. The tax rate is so low, the school district can't retain staff. In the past three years, Tipton schools have had to replace 40 percent of their teachers. It's not right." Jack looked at them one by one. Such fine young women. "And you can help."

✦ ✦ ✦

Monday afternoon, when Jack returned from work, music boomed up the stairs so loudly it nearly blew him out the door. Oh no, he thought, recognizing the melody before the nuns began: How do you solve a problem like Maria? Jack hurried to the deck, where he found Genna and Sam, saving their hearing.

"What's wrong?"

"No hello?"

"Hello." Jack kissed her quickly, the kind of kiss couples share after twenty years. "What's wrong?"

"Why must something be wrong?"

"*The Sound of Music*, max volume, and you haven't made him turn it down."

"He's failing math and French."

"Is that all?"

Genna laughed, Jack thought, a bit hysterically. Damn, but parenting was humbling. Simon was often failing after the first six weeks. He didn't want help, he didn't need help; he wanted his parents out of his goddamn business, that was the only help he needed. So each year they backed off until the first report card.

"No," Genna admitted, "that's not all. Rich moved to his mother's house and changed schools. Simon's heartbroken."

"In the middle of the school year?"

Genna shrugged. Rich's people, Jack thought, were just the shabby sort to do it. He'd driven the boy home Friday night and felt his humiliation as they turned into the trailer park.

"I told Simon we'd talk about his grades after you got home."

"Oh great," Jack said. "Lizzie still at soccer?"

Genna nodded. "She got all A's, one B."

They shared a guilty smile. No time to focus on the child doing well. They reentered the house, descending through a silo of sound. Mother Superior howled, "..ford every stream, fol-low every rain-bow…"

Outside Simon's room, the music was so loud Jack's diaphragm quaked.

"Until…You…Find…Your…DREAM!"

When the song ended, Simon heard the pounding and opened up. His eyes were red. At least three days of dirty clothes littered the floor, or maybe they were just rejected outfit options from that morning.

"We have to talk," Jack began.

"I don't want to."

"I'm turning the music off." Genna stepped lightly between them and fumbled for the power as Julie Andrews broke into that cheerful fantasy of Austrian childcare. In piping voices pumped to six-million decibels, the Von Trapp children answered, "Do, re, mi."

Then the sound went off, and Simon threw himself on his bed.

A year, even six months earlier, Jack would have pushed the clothes into an angry pile and announced the room looked like a goddamn pigsty. Instead, he began, "Mom told me about your grades."

Simon looked at Jack as if he were a giant bug.

"First thing, you're grounded until you pull your grades up. No phone or television during the week."

"That's not fair."

Jack hated that particular expression, which no doubt magnified its appeal for Simon. "What's fair got to do with two F's?"

"I don't care what you say."

"What?" Jack could already feel the tendon bulging on his neck.

"Maybe one or the other," Genna offered. "No television and no phone school nights until we check and see your homework's finished."

He looked so sad, Jack thought. "You always have this problem in the beginning of the year. We know you can do the work."

"No, I can't. I don't understand anything in French or math. Who the hell wants to take pre-calculus anyway?"

"We can work together on the math," Jack said. "Like we used to."

Simon looked at Genna and then at his father. "I'd rather be dead. You're always right. You're always right. It makes me feel stupid."

Genna said, "Maybe we can get a tutor like last year."

"I hate that school, I hate it."

Back and forth, back and forth, and every second Jack was thinking, I'm a terrible father, a terrible father, I make him feel stupid. But he also knew Simon was jerking him around. Simon failed two classes because he did no work. Then the phone rang, and Simon leapt for it.

Genna said, "You better get Lizzie at soccer practice."

Disappointed, his eyes still red-rimmed, Simon said, "It's for you," and handed Jack the portable phone.

"Mister Barish," began an older woman. "Simon's father, that right?"

"Speaking. Who is this?"

"Gladys O'Brien, Rich's grandmother."

Without hearing another word, Jack knew this would be a grievous conversation. That must have showed, because Genna turned, mouthing her words, "I'll get Lizzie."

"Mrs. O'Brien," Jack said. "I'm going to change rooms, would you hold a moment?"

He left Simon's room carrying the portable; he didn't want to chance Simon listening in. Genna walked beside him. "Who is it?"

"Rich's grandmother."

Genna looked as if she'd been gut-punched. "Oh," she said, and hurried up the stairs.

"Mrs. O'Brien." Jack looked out the family room picture window into the trees and down the stone path to the meadow. "Is something wrong?"

"I won't mince words." She wheezed slightly, as if out of breath or asthmatic. "Don't believe in it."

She spoke in the distinctive manner of the country folk of southwestern Ohio, not a drawl, but not a northern rhythm, either.

"Rich's been living with me and my son. Until yesterday, when we decided it would be better for him to live with his mother, up Earlham way."

You're telling me this why? But he knew she'd get to it, and that when she did he wasn't going to like it.

"We got these letters, notes, really, from your son. You know what kind he is, dontcha?"

Through the picture window Jack watched leaves tremble.

"Why don't you tell me, Mrs. O'Brien?"

"These notes is hardcore, is what they are. They describe what your son would like to do to my grandson. Got the picture?"

It occurred to Jack this might be blackmail. "It would be better," he said, "for everyone, if you threw those notes away."

"My son's gointer decide. It was me, I'd burn 'em. My grandson's fifteen."

Jack listened to her labored breathing. He didn't know what to say. Months later, he realized she probably had her own worries about what kind Rich was, too.

"Well," she said. "Just thought you'd want to know."

"I don't see why anyone needs to see those notes."

"That's for my son to say."

After another silence in which he thought he would just fucking kill Simon, Jack said, "Thanks for calling, I appreciate it."

She hung up, and Jack wondered if he should have offered to buy the notes, unseen, unread, no haggling. He hung up and wondered how soon Genna would return. There was no way he'd have this conversation alone with Simon, no way at all.

✦ ✦ ✦

When Genna reached the middle school, a half dozen minivans ringed the soccer field. Years ago, when Jack coached Lizzie's U-11 and U-12 teams, she'd hated being the coach's wife, the star player's mother. She didn't mix easily with stay-at-home moms. She never knew what to say or how to say it, and thought she'd go mad when the women revealed what they really thought about the world. Still, it was an unalloyed joy to watch Lizzie dribble through the opposing team, take a booming shot on goal, and think smugly, Yes, that one's mine.

In Tipton, Genna didn't feel she could leave all the soccer socializing to Jack. She parked her minivan beside the others and joined the gaggle of waiting women.

"Hi," she said. "I'm Genna, Lizzie's mom."

"Lucille," said a short brunette. "Katie's mom. I've seen you at the games."

Two other women introduced themselves, both blondes, but she forgot their names as soon as she heard them.

"Your Lizzie can really play," said Lucille. "We're so glad to have her."

The others murmured, and Genna thought, How awful. One child scorned, the other welcomed because she can kick a soccer ball. Genna checked her watch. Six-ten.

"Excuse me," she said. "Doesn't practice end at six?"

The stouter blonde grinned. "I see you ain't been picking up. Steve never lets them go till six-fifteen, six-thirty."

Feeling properly rebuked, Genna turned and watched the rough and tumble scrimmage: three male coaches and the girls. This was what she hated. The women were catty as hell, and she never knew what to say.

On the field, Lizzie dribbled towards the goal behind which the moms waited. A coach ran at her, forcing a pass, which she delivered left-footed, Genna noted, wondering if the other women had noticed. The left wing, whoever she was, received the pass and flubbed the shot.

"If the levy fails," the small brunette was saying, Lucille, "I hear they're canceling all varsity sports except football."

They can't do that, Genna thought, Title IX. But she kept quiet. Didn't want to seem like a smart mouth.

"I don't believe it," said the larger of the blondes, whose ten-years-out-of-date shag grew from dark roots. "That school board's been threatening us for years with flood and famine if we don't keep letting them stick their hands in our pockets. Nothing ever happens."

"Excuse me," Genna said. "I'm new in town, so maybe I'm wrong. But I thought a levy hadn't passed in twelve years."

"Well, yeah," said the blonde. "But you understand what I'm saying."

Not really.

"If the levy fails," Lucille said, "we're sending Katie to Bishop."

"What's that?" Genna asked, feeling sick to her stomach.

"A Catholic school in Hamilton."

Genna asked, "You think the levy has a chance?"

Lucille, who was thin and fine-featured, another bird-woman like Marla, started to answer, but thought better of it. The big blonde said, "Lost by fifteen hundred votes just last spring."

"Excuse me," Genna said, "what's your name again?"

"Marge."

"That's right," Genna said. "I'm so bad with names."

"Don't sweat it, hon." Something in the way she said it, Hon, which was common usage here and meant to be friendly, Hon this, Hon that, rankled Genna. "There's lots of us, only one of you."

"My husband and I"–Genna knew she should probably zipper her lip, as her mother used to say, Zipper your lip, Genna–"are part of a group at the university trying to register students to help pass the levy."

"Ya know," Marge said, "I'm not against the levy, I'm really not."

But you're not for it, either.

"I've got three kids in school, I know they need money." Marge sucked both lips into her mouth, and for a moment looked toothless, or as if she were trying to be careful of what she said. "But people in Roscoe township, where I live?" She hesitated again. "They're tired of Tipton folk trying to raise their taxes."

"Excuse me," Genna began, noticing that little Lucille and the other blond were slowly edging away, "a levy hasn't passed in twelve years."

"But every year they try, and never once has anyone from Tipton knocked on the doors of me and my neighbors, telling us why we should support a levy. Don't you think that's stupid?"

"Yes," Genna said. "I certainly do."

Marge's mouth opened, but nothing came out. Then she continued, but with considerably less heat, "Now here you come saying you're going to register students, when everyone knows they're not gonna pay the taxes, we are."

There was a shout on the field. A little dark-haired girl had scored a goal.

"That's my Katie," Lucille said. "You watch, they'll call practice now."

A moment later, a whistle blew and the girls trotted off.

"I'm glad we had this conversation," Genna said to Marge, who eyed her suspiciously. Then Lizzie ran up, sweaty, lovely.

"Hey, Mom. Where's Dad?"

"Starting dinner."

Genna grinned at Marge and Lucille. Yes, my man's starting dinner.

✦ ✦ ✦

Jack told her as soon as she walked in, but they agreed to wait until after dinner to tell Simon. Lizzie chattered happily about what a jerk one of the other players was, how she mouthed off and refused to run laps, and Coach Steve let her get away with it.

"That would never happen on the Titans," Lizzie added, biting into a hamburger that bled ketchup and mayo. "Jeff would have made her run six hills the first time, and kicked her off the second."

"Wipe your chin," Jack said. "Do you wish you still played for the Titans?"

Jack rarely asked such direct questions. The conversation with Rich's grandmother, Genna thought, must have really upset him.

"Hell, no." Lizzie grinned, flaunting her newfound right to swear. "I'm always telling the girls they have no idea what a hard coach is like. They are so protected."

"And ignorant," Simon said. "Country-ass ignorant. Half the kids have never been out of Ohio. Soon as I can, I'm moving to New York."

"Then you better pull your grades up," Jack said. "New York's expensive, you'll need a good job."

At the mention of grades, Simon shut down. They didn't mention Lizzie's grades, either, and how unfair was that, Genna thought, not being able to praise one child for fear of wounding the other. After dinner, Simon headed for his room.

"Let's get it over with."

Jack nodded. He looked as miserable as she felt. They trooped downstairs for the second time that day to stand in front of their son's locked door. She glanced at Jack's rugged face, and he knocked, then knocked again. For a horrified moment she thought maybe Simon had hurt himself. Teenagers did that, and Simon had so many struggles. Just as Jack was about to rap a third time, Simon opened up.

"We need to talk to you."

What now? Simon might have asked but didn't.

"That phone call," Jack continued, "was Rich's grandmother. Apparently you've been writing certain notes?"

Simon looked so aghast, at once terrified and prepared to deny the whole thing, that Genna's heart floated out to him.

"What notes?"

She wished he hadn't said that. Jack turned towards her, his neck bulging.

Genna said, "I think we should talk about this with the door closed."

They stepped into the messy room, which accurately reflected the disorder, Genna sometimes thought, inside Simon's head.

Jack said, "The notes in which you talk about what you want to do to or with Rich. And there's no point trying to lie your way out of this. Rich's grandmother and father have the notes, so drop the bullshit."

She hated the way he spoke to Simon without respect, leaving him no role except buffoon, which was how she knew Jack thought of him at moments like this. It was how Simon thought of himself; he didn't need to hear it from his father. Simon leaned back on his bed, shrinking into himself. His upper lip trembled.

"And no crying," Jack added, bitterly, "okay?"

"Jack."

He must have grasped she was this close to beating the crap out of him as big as he was, because he took a deep breath and seemed to come back to himself.

"Simon," she said, "whatever you feel for Rich, you know you shouldn't write such explicit notes. Did you pass them at school?"

Simon nodded. His upper lip still trembled. She hoped for all their sakes, especially Jack's, that he didn't begin to cry. "I feel so stupid," Simon said.

Jack didn't bark, You should. Instead, in a kinder voice than she might have expected, he said, "Never put anything like that in writing."

Genna said, "We don't think anything will happen. Rich's grandmother said his father will decide what to do with the notes."

"I'm not sure what the law is," Jack began, "but Rich is only fifteen, Simon's seventeen."

"They're both still minors," Genna said.

Glancing first at Simon, Jack answered, "Sixteen's statutory rape."

After a moment, still not looking at them, Simon whispered, "We didn't do anything."

She was relieved, but how awful for Simon to admit it. Assuming he was telling the truth.

"Good," Jack said. "Then I don't think anything's going to happen." He smiled at her, and then at Simon. "Just don't put anything in writing, okay?"

She wondered if Jack had followed his own advice when having that affair.

"Can I watch television?" Simon asked. "I don't have any homework."

She glanced at Jack. Simon had had a hard day. Jack shook his head. She said, "Why don't you study French, dear? I can help if you want. Or go over math with Dad?"

Simon looked as if she had suggested he drink urine. "I can do it myself."

Walking out of his room, she heard Simon close and lock the door.

chapter 6

When Rich's father didn't call that night or the next, Jack assumed disaster had missed them like the fourteen-wheeler that had once roared past them on I-80 in the eastern slope of the Sierras, horn blaring, brake linings already smelling of the crash that would occur half a mile down the road.

"Not this time," he'd said to Genna when they passed the overturned truck. "At least not for us."

Thursday morning, buoyed by a similar sense of survival, he phoned a friend in the math department, who called his favorite undergraduate; by noon, without having met him, he'd arranged for someone named Tom Martin, or possibly Martin Tom, to tutor Simon twice a week. Later that afternoon, Marla called his office.

"Jack," she said, "this is Marla Lindstrom."

He was uncomfortably excited to hear her voice. "How are you?"

"Fine, thanks."

Did he note a note of tension?

"I'm calling about Simon."

As if he might think she was calling about him. "Everything all right?"

"Oh, yes."

The screen saver started up on his desktop: Hiya Dad! in three-dimensional red and green script forming and unforming a double helix, with H-I-Y-A, D-A-D! replacing the standard base pairs: his gift, last Father's Day, from Simon and Lizzie.

"Simon tells me you're finding him a math tutor. I've found him one for French." She hesitated. "If you're interested."

"Absolutely. But I feel we're taking too much of your time."

"Don't be silly." She laughed, and the sound surprised him, a giggle from a woman otherwise so very grown-up. "I'm very fond of Simon."

"So am I. Thanks for calling."

"Don't you want the tutor's name?"

Jack wondered if she could tell, through the phone line, how red his face was. He jotted down the name, a high school senior taking French IV at the university. "Thanks again."

"If there's anything else," Marla said, "just let me know. Simon really touches my heart."

Jack hung up, full of questions.

✦ ✦ ✦

Jack had met Dr. Charles—"Call Me Chuck"—Claybourne a few weeks before, walking Sam. Sam had bounded ahead, off leash, but within whistle-shot. Max, a standard black poodle, heeled on a thin leather lead. Sam spied or more likely scented him and charged off ignoring Jack's high-pitch, two note whistle. He shouted, "Sam, Sam. Goddamn it, Sam!"

The next time they met, Genna accompanied him, and Mary Claybourne walked beside Chuck. Mary's pale skin was set off by very dark hair, a contrast she obviously worked to maintain: long sleeves and sunhats. Sam lumbered towards them, nose and feathery tail high and wagging (his tail, not the nose). Max broke out of his heel and bounded towards Sam who'd begun snuffling Mary Claybourne's crotch.

"No, no!" Mary cried, her hat tumbling. "Bad dog!"

"Do something," Genna said. "That woman's having a fit."

Elegant Chuck (dark hair, silver sideburns), one hand around Sam's collar, the other around Max's, struggled to separate the frolicking canines.

"Good boy," Chuck was saying. "Good boy."

Jack grabbed Sam's collar and wrestled him away. "Sit," he said. "Sit."

Sam looked up as if he'd never heard that before. Sit?

Jack pushed his dog's substantial butt towards the ground. "He's friendly."

"But not very well-trained," Genna added.

"I can see," Mary said, untangling herself from the poodle's twisted lead and bending to pick up her hat.

When the invitation arrived a few weeks later, Genna asked, "Aren't those the poodle people?"

Jack nodded.

"They probably want to introduce us to dog trainers."

As it turned out, the Claybournes wanted to introduce them to the other residents of Forest Glen. The invitation, which Jack posted on the fridge, was to the Third Annual Forest Glen Octoberfest Pot Luck.

"Don't tell me you want to go."

"Why not, Gen? Meet some new people?"

"The Octoberfest Pot Luck?" That wary look came over her face. And not just wary. "You know how uncomfortable I'll be."

"We'll go for a little while."

"You never go for a little while."

For two weeks, the invitation had hung on the fridge, like a splinter in their collective psyche. Jack didn't RSVP to say they were coming; Genna didn't call to decline. Friday after work, as he stood in the kitchen sipping wine and waiting for the pasta water to boil, Genna said, "Mary Claybourne called." When he looked vague, she added, "She wanted to know if we were coming to the dog-training party. I told her we'd be delighted. You owe me one, dear."

Saturday night, carrying a covered dish of shrimp fried rice, Jack and Genna strolled up the driveway to the Claybournes's stylish contemporary. Though it was mid-October, the air remained warm and Genna wore one of her favorite summer dresses: blue Indonesian rayon with cutout work at the neck and on the shoulders. She wore also an air of satisfaction, for she had done what he wanted, which for the time being made her the better person.

"Thanks for coming," Jack said.

"It might be fun."

He looked at her, disbelieving.

"I feel different about a lot of things. Look." She pointed to a small white sign at the corner of the lawn. This yard enclosed by Happy Dog. "What's that?"

"Some kind of invisible dog fence."

"I bet you a week of cooking dinner they suggest we get one."

Though he knew she was right, he answered, "You're on."

✦ ✦ ✦

Inside, Genna sipped white wine. In the past twenty years, she'd attended hundreds of dinner parties like this one, at which the principal libation was better-than-jug-but-not-really-very-good white wine. God, what she wouldn't give for a glass of the beyond-their-means Montrachet her mother served. Mother's other staple was celery sticks arranged like smelt around pools of ranch dressing. When Simon and Lizzie were small and accompanied them everywhere, Genna was always saying, "No double-dipping, kids." She missed those days.

In California, a person could count on guacamole. In Ohio, someone always brought spinach dip in a hollow loaf of bread. Why would anyone do that to bread or spinach? For the past two years, since the local Kroger opened an olive bar, kalamatas and oil-cured Moroccans had been staples. Genna glanced around the family room with its tiled floor and French doors opening onto a brick patio and estimated that of the thirty or so adults hors d'oeuvring and chatting, twenty concealed olive pits in their palms not knowing what to do with them.

Unlike most parties they attended, at which everyone was from her department or Jack's, this room was filled with strangers, many of whom did not appear to be academics. There were several white-haired couples, long since retired from whatever work they had once done. Two women with big hair, one blonde, one brunette, wore powder blue pedal pushers. (No academic woman would be caught dead in pedal pushers; it was almost as if universities taught courses on what was and was not permissible. Pedal pushers were definitely not.) There were two black couples, one old, one young, both named Porter, who had brought barbecued chicken wings, which also marked them as non-academics. (Too down-home for African American academics to bring to a racially mixed group.) There was also a twenty-something couple in neo-hippie attire. The woman, who was full-bodied without being heavy was clearly sans brassiere, while the man sported earrings in both ears and barbed wire tattoos on his biceps.

Genna moved to the Octoberfest table. Pitchers of pilsner, plates of spaetzle and schnitzel, sauerbraten and brats, metts, and several varieties of sausage she didn't recognize, which people around greater Cincinnati seemed genuinely to enjoy but which Genna never let pass her lips. It wasn't so much that she was a food snob or anti-pork, but that twenty years ago she had watched a CBS documentary on meat processing.

Jack was working the room, weaving his big body in and out of cliques of party guests. Years ago, she'd been offended by how he left her alone, fearing he found other women more interesting. She no longer believed that, not because he'd proved faithful—he hadn't—but because she'd accepted that gregariousness as part of Jack's nature. He arrived at every party, no matter how meager its prospects, like a child rushing downstairs on Christmas—or was it Chanukah?—morning.

"Have you tried the schnitzel?"

Genna found herself face to face with Mary Claybourne, who wore a pale yellow summer shawl around her bare shoulders.

"Not yet."

Genna immediately regretted her answer. Mary's elegant nose twitched.

"It's my grandmother's recipe," she said. "My maiden name was Krauss."

"Ja," Genna said. "Octoberfest."

"Ja," Mary repeated. "And be sure to try a bratwurst. We buy them in a special butcher in Zinzinnati. Zie gutt."

Not on your life, Genna thought, smiling, as Mary slid away, circulating between her guests, many of whom were heaping their plates. When she looked around and spotted Jack, he was standing beside Marla Lindstrom. Genna's hand went to her hair, fluffing the curls it had taken two hours with rollers to produce. She walked to the hors d'oeuvre table, dipped two carrot sticks in ranch and bit into them. She allowed herself two olives, one Moroccan, one kalamata, swirled the pits between her tongue and teeth sucking off every salty morsel before discretely pushing the pits between her lips into a purple cocktail napkin. She washed the olive taste away with a slug of white wine. Jack was still talking to Marla, and Genna considered going through the food line and heaping a plate with every Oktoberfest specialty, two or three of each, a plate to end all plates, and eating it all, her fat ass be damned, or better still, taking the laden plate, a sinkhole of German gastronomic achievement, to Jack. Here, she'd say, I made it for you, dear.

No, she'd take the plate and stand beside Jack, beside bird-like Marla's tiny breasts and teeny waist, and she'd stuff herself, the grease from sausages that Marla would never in a million years eat glistening on her cheeks. Even after gorging, there would be so much food, her plate would make a really satisfying thump when she hurled it into Jack's rugged face and the non-existent bosom of that skanky bitch.

Instead, Genna pitched her napkin-wrapped pits, refilled her plastic glass with the Claybournes's excuse for Chardonnay, then joined Jack and Marla on the other side of the room.

"We were just coming to find you," Jack said. "Ready for dinner?"

"I *was* thinking about food."

"You go ahead," Marla said, moving away. "I've already eaten."

When the paper plates were in the trash and coffee water was boiling but dessert had not yet been served, Chuck moved to the center of the room. "Now is the time," he began, "for official business. I'd like you to meet the newest Forest Glenners. Jack and Genna Barish are both Tipton professors. Jack's in History of Science, Genna's in French and Women's Studies. They bought the Lessinger house and have two teenagers, although I suspect more of you, especially you joggers, have met their friendly golden retriever, Sam."

There were murmurs. What a sweet dog Sam was, and Oh, they bought the Lessinger house, then a voice called from the back of the room, "Have you told them I sell Happy Dog at cost to Forest Glenners?"

"That's Bill Morris," Chuck said, raising one of his bushy silver eyebrows. "Always trying to do a little business."

Polite laughter rippled through the room, as Jack leaned close and whispered, "What do you want for dinner tomorrow?"

"Humble pie all week."

They stood and introduced themselves, and although she couldn't remember names, it felt warm and friendly, certainly very welcoming, all these suburban strangers inviting her into the group. What next, she'd believe in God or the Republican Party?

Committee heads talked about their budgets and plans for Block Watch, Forest Glen beautification, fall clean up and spring planting. Finally, Bill Morris, he of the Happy Dog franchise (he was also, she learned, a realtor, who over the years had sold many of the Forest Glen houses, several of them more then once) stepped forward. He had coifed white hair like what's his name, the booby-headed anchor on Mary Tyler Moore's old show.

"As all of you know," he began, "there's another Tipton school tax levy on the ballot next month. As a real estate professional— "

How pompous.

"—I believe passing this levy is crucial to homeowners. I have, therefore, gotten permission from our Commander in Chief," Bill Morris directed a smarmy smile at Chuck, "for a representative from TUTS, Tipton University for Tipton Schools, to say a few words. Most of you know Marla Lindstrom, who used to be our neighbor. But before she gives you all the facts and figures she's so good at," Bill Morris turned towards Marla and actually winked, "I want to say my piece, which is this. As homeowners concerned about property values, it's absolutely crucial to the continued growth of Tipton to pass this levy to help fund our schools. Whether or not you have young children, and right now I'm talking to you retired folks, "

"Bill," someone called, "let Marla speak."

There was general laughter, and one of the women in pedal pushers, whom Genna assumed must be Mrs. Bill Morris, stood up and corralled the noted local windbag. Marla stepped to the center of the room.

"Bill," Marla said, "I want to thank you for saying so many of the things I wanted to say, and for inviting me to speak to this amazing Octoberfest pot luck."

As the crowd settled into paying attention, Genna glanced at Jack, who took her hand then returned his gaze to the speaker. Despite Marla's presence, the room felt safe and warm, as if they had joined a group of friends around a fire. How strange and surprising was that.

chapter 7

Just before Halloween, Simon applied for a job at Burger King. Six dollars an hour, was that great, or what? When the manager, a short woman named Helen, who had light, almost colorless, bangs and raccoon circles around her eyes, disappeared with his application, he sweated and fretted and his leg twitched like a crazy man's; he just knew it was going to be no. But when she reappeared a few minutes later, a smile improved her plain round face.

"Simon, could you come in Sunday to be trained?"

He wanted to shout, You mean I'm hired? He would've hugged her, but didn't want to act like a freak. Instead he nodded and filled out forms, then headed home with a visor and a blue BK shirt feeling so full of himself he did all his homework without being told to. When Mom asked if he'd like to jog before dinner, he nearly said Yes, but remembered, just in time, that he hated to exercise.

Sunday morning Mom fixed blueberry pancakes, but Simon felt too giddy to eat more than three or four because he had to get ready. He showered and shaved, dressed in his BK shirt and visor. Okay, he looked lame, but he couldn't stop grinning. If he worked fifteen hours, he'd earn ninety dollars. Ninety dollars a week! Music burst out of him, as if he were starring in a movie musical. He sang, "Super-califragilistic-expi-alidocious."

Where did that come from?

"Even though the sound of it is something quite atrocious."

Simon's feet tapped. His legs moved.

"If you sing it loud enough— "

He sang so loudly the walls cheered. No, Dizzy Lizzie beat on his door.

"Shut up, Simon! Will you just shut up?"

Simon sang and danced for everyone in Movie Land.

✦ ✦ ✦

Simon asked Mom to drive him, but she said Dad would.

"Don't worry," she said, loading the dishwasher. "I'll make sure he leaves on time."

"He's always late," Simon said. "I'm sick of it."

At twelve-thirty—he was due at one and the Burger King was ten minutes away—Simon headed to the driveway, climbed into the Camry he hoped would someday be his, and leaned on the horn.

After eighteen vicious honks, Dad emerged through the front door and walked towards the car. He looked pissed off, probably about the honking. He had the biggest nose Simon or any of his friends had ever seen; he also had one of the biggest heads. What a freak. With his best friend Martin, who visited every summer and sometimes Thanksgiving, Dad was always going, "Big nose, big humph." Then he'd grin like he'd won the lottery.

Could that be true? Simon's nose wasn't large; he'd gotten Mom's nose. The last time he glimpsed Dad's penis he was five or six. They used to pee together, what Dad called crossing swords. Back then, Dad's penis was the biggest thing he'd ever seen. More like a sea snake, or a garden hose, than his own hairless little wiener.

Thinking about his dad's penis was disgusting. Then Dad—he tried to think of him as Jack, but couldn't—climbed into the car with this smirking grin on his big face, as if he knew what Simon had been thinking about

"You're pretty anxious to get to work." Dad backed up, then cut forward to pull out of the long driveway.

"I don't want to be late."

"You're never this anxious to do anything I want. Even when I offer to pay you."

It's not the same.

"Maybe I should have thrown in one of those cool hats."

He glanced at his dad, who was still grinning. Simon grinned, too.

"Shut up, Dad."

"It's enormously cool," Dad said. "Your first real job."

✦ ✦ ✦

They made him Fry Guy.

"Don't worry," Helen said. "It's what everyone does first."

Simon thought, An adult who apologized to kids, what was up with that?

He learned to drop frozen balls of potatoes into one of four baskets, raise the basket to drain when the timer dinged, then dump a glistening lawn of fries below heat bulbs red as Superman's sun. Salt, salt, salt, then he boxed fries, small, large and extra-large. And not just fries! Fry Guy kicked chicken nugget butt: drop, sizzle, fry and dump. Instead of bulbs, a heat lamp warmed them, its space heater coils glowing orange-juice bright. Below them, Fry Guy wore a halo of grease. Grease cologne. Grease deodorant. In his head, the hours chimed like a cash register. Six, twelve, eighteen, twenty-four; within the first hour he'd decided how to spend his money. Buy the Camry from Dad so when he got his license he could drive his friends to school and everyone would say, There goes Fry Guy. Ain't he cool!

Mom picked him up. He emerged wearing his visor, carrying a sack of food. Fountain drinks were free; sandwiches and shakes discounted 25 percent, but Helen gave him a free number five meal because he'd done such a good job his first day. He climbed into the minivan which stank of the cigarettes Mom smoked on the sneak.

"How was it?"

"Fine."

"That's all you're going to say?"

They started down High Street. Fry Guy and Fry Guy's mom.

"I liked it." He saw her eyeing his food. "Don't worry, the food was free."

"I'm not worrying about you paying for it. I'm worrying about you eating it."

"Mom," he said, "don't start."

✦ ✦ ✦

With Rich gone (and unheard from), Simon's fantasies turned to Peter, whom he saw every day in Animal Chorus. They stood beside each other, and Peter's hip grazed his when they sang. Peter often forgot his sheet music, and sometimes Simon hid his when he saw that Peter had remembered, so most days they shared. After Simon had heard a song more than once he didn't need music, anyway. His mind recorded and played back the melodies. If only it worked that way in French he'd tell Peter, who stood beside him in Animal Chorus on Monday morning, how beautiful his eyes looked, *les yeux*, or how handsome Simon found him. *Vous etes tres beau, cheri.*

But Simon's gift lay not in words but in music, which Mom had told him was the food of love. He feasted on Peter, who smiled back without opening his mouth. Peter had a crooked front tooth. Oh hon, Simon longed to say, you don't need to be ashamed. The rest of you is so beautiful!

But he couldn't say that. Not in Tipton, Ohio. So who knew if Peter felt even a little for him what he felt for Peter. But he must, look at him smiling, his left hand coming up to cover his mouth, his right hand holding the sheet music for "Mariah (They Call the Wind)". Even if Peter did feel some of those gay and faggoty feelings (Sticks and stones can break my boner, thought Simon), would he be willing to admit them? Look how much crap I've taken. So even if he wanted to say something—and he did, Peter's peter—he'd promised Mom not to put anything in writing. But saying anything to Peter's face—and what a cute face it was, a dusting of freckles, a button nose and that hennaed hair—was impossible, at least in school. That left the phone. He'd been thinking about calling Peter for a week or two, since Rich disappeared, but he didn't know Peter's number. Every day for at least a week he'd thought about asking, but he didn't have the balls. Simon Barish didn't have the balls, but the Fry Guy might. He grinned. Peter returned the grin, then his left hand covered his mouth.

Fry Guy imagined lowering a basket of fries into bubbling oil. He imagined a visor on his spiked blond tips, a blue BK shirt on his chest.

"Peter," he whispered. "What's your phone number?"

Peter looked alarmed. "Why?"

Simon was almost too nervous to answer. Then he saw the music teacher, whom they called Donut, stand up from behind his desk and shuffle his papers, which meant rehearsal was finally going to start.

"Maybe we could hang out sometime."

A gaggle of emotions flew across Peter's face. Donut approached the music stand in front of the room. He'd had another haircut over the weekend, his worst ever. His ears looked like wings on a bowling ball.

"Let's start with 'Mariah,'" Donut said. "Section leaders pay extra attention. We'll do break-out later."

Donut had designated Simon section leader for the basses. Not that he had much choice. No one else could sing one frigging note. But it made Simon proud to be one of the leaders. Not the bell cow, Donut had joked. The bell bull. Carry the other basses on your big strong back.

Donut said, "Basses and baritones come in on four. And-one, and-two, and-three, and..."

Simon glanced at Peter, who smiled shyly. They sang, "Away out west, they got a name..."

Simon forgot about Donut, he nearly forgot about Peter, and listened to his section. That wimpy fucker on the end, what's his name, wasn't even singing! Simon sang louder, the bell bull of all bell bulls, and the others lowed behind, "...and they call the wind Mariah. Ma—ri—aaah."

Donut waved his soft hands, and music flew through the air like kettling birds.

✦ ✦ ✦

The weekend before the election, Jack agreed to canvass apartment complexes in the student ghetto south of campus. These were cheaply constructed two and three story brick walk-ups: eight or ten contiguous entrance ways, arranged in U's around a parking lot. There was a shortage of student housing in Tipton and even the shabbiest, butt-ugly ones stayed full. Genna had also signed up, but at the last minute decided to canvas in Roscoe Township, which many of their university colleagues and TUTS co-workers referred to as the Redneck Quadrants, although technically, Tipton was too far north to have rednecks.

Saturday morning, Jack kissed Genna goodbye in their driveway. Ten minutes later, he climbed out of his Camry in front of Fairview Commons on South Elm, carrying a small backpack and a plastic shopping bag emblazoned with the pro-levy logo: Be Smart for Tipton Schools! Eyeing the first of twenty identical complexes, he felt the loneliness of the political grunt. The last time he'd gone door to door, he was an undergrad working in Carter's first campaign. What a part of history he'd felt, leafleting a working class Poughkeepsie neighborhood, Greeks and Italians in row houses, Jack with his curly hair long then and all the world and future before him. As he stood in front of Fairview Commons, it was hard not to feel that the world and his place in it had diminished. Then, a presidential race, now, a school levy fight in Tipton. That's life, he thought, stepping inside entryway one. Those teachers deserved raises, the students needed languages and sports. And if it were more virtuous, as the argument had been made to Galileo, to believe the Church's geo-centered explanation of the solar system in light of contradictory scientific evidence, was it not more virtuous to work in a school levy than in a national election?

He knocked on the battered door of apartment A. He knocked again, then wedged a folded flyer into the crack between the door and its jamb just above the knob, crossed the hall and tried apartment B. An old black man answered, leaning on a cane. A yellowed undershirt showed beneath his white short sleeve dress shirt; the whites of his eyes were slightly yellow, too. He was not the white Tipton undergraduate Jack had expected.

"I'm Jack Barish, here to ask you to be smart for Tipton schools." He paused to gauge reaction; the old man didn't seem to have one. "Are you registered to vote in Tuesday's election?"

"Yes, sir, I am."

"Then I want to urge you to vote for the school levy. Tipton hasn't passed one in twelve years and the schools..."

"Let me stop you, young fella. My kids are grown and gone."

"The schools still need more money." Which I have not got, Jack imagined the old man replying, though he didn't speak. "A community is judged by its schools."

"Then Tipton is in trouble, isn't it?"

Jack grinned. "Not if we pass this levy. Can we count on your vote?"

"You always could."

Jack handed him a flyer and a roll of Smarties. Be Smart for Tipton Schools.

"My niece is gonna take me to vote. She's got two kids."

"Well then." Jack passed him a handful of Smarties rolls. "Thanks again."

It was unrewarding work. Most apartments were empty. In more than half of the apartments with someone home, the inhabitants, mostly students, weren't registered to vote or were registered at their parents' address. The apartments, which he glimpsed through half-opened doors, were uniformly small and dingy. In one of them, four students trading bong hits didn't bother to hide it as a marijuana cloud rose to the ceiling. Another entranceway smelled strongly of Indian spices. Graduate students, he assumed, but when the door opened, a small boy with enormous eyes stood beside an Indian woman Jack's age, quite a lovely woman, too, with jet-black hair.

"We are not being citizens," she said, when he finished.

Jack gave her Smarties for the boy and a flyer to pass to a friend. He descended the stairs and exited entryway six of Fairview Manor. The November sun shone weakly. The storm front, he thought, looking up, would be here sooner than later. He set out for entryway seven. After just forty-five minutes, Jack wanted to pitch the Smarties and flyers into one of the green dumpsters dotting the apartment complex landscape. Instead, he stepped into entryway seven, and knocked on apartment A. Be strong, he thought, and waited.

✦ ✦ ✦

Genna parked her minivan in front of a gray double wide set back from the main road. She'd been working her way south from Tipton for two hours and had just entered Roscoe. A hundred yards ahead, the Roscoe Roadhouse hunkered beside a one-lane bridge. The old Roscoe School, if she remembered correctly, was half a mile further, on the road to Milton.

God, she thought, but Roscoe was the end of the line. If she lived here, she would rot from the inside out, like an apple too long in the crisper. As a teenager she'd felt the same way every time she crossed her parents' wide front lawn pimpled with dandelions. *Help! Someone, help me!* Daddy, not her real father as they said back then, but the only father she'd known, sipped Chivas—Cocktail hour, Genna—most afternoons on the screened porch and in the evenings in his study. Judge William O. Gordon had retired young. No fault of his own, he always said, but the Democrats. As a teenager, Genna felt everyone was watching them, the old-money Gordons *sans d'argent*.

Staring at the chain-link protecting a trailer in Roscoe, Ohio, she had a sudden whiff, as if she could again smell Daddy's study, of what it was like to grow up on Kingsbury Court. Her tall, elegant mother (from whom Lizzie got her height) patrolled the kitchen, scorching meat. As a child, Genna had thought all steaks and chops were cooked so dry it hurt to chew. I wasn't born to cook, Doris always said. Later, Genna came to understand that brutalizing food was how her mother stayed so thin and that if she wanted anything palatable, she'd have to look outside the house or cook herself. What a childhood. In the greater world, she stalked around proud yet ashamed because her name was Genna Gordon, while at home, within the crumbling walls, she studied hard and swore she'd get as far as she could from Kingsbury Court. And she had. Dr. Genna Barish, who married a Jew.

Most of the people she'd spoken to this morning, and she'd spoken maybe to twenty in two hours of canvassing, had listened politely, though she understood most intended to vote against the levy. Perhaps she'd changed two or three votes, maybe four or five, by pointing out that the difference in their taxes would be twelve or fifteen dollars a month, but that those twelve or fifteen dollars added together across the district would save buses and sports for the high school, reduce class size in kindergarten and first grade, maybe even bring back Latin and computer programming.

Genna climbed two cement steps to a porch covered in translucent green plastic siding. She knocked, and a small blond boy answered.

"Is your mother or father home?"

"No." He closed the door. A moment later, it reopened, and a slightly older girl with a pinched face, maybe seven or eight years old, stood beside her brother.

"My brother said my parents ain't home." She blinked once and then a second time. "But they're industposed."

"Thank you." Genna passed the girl a flyer and three rolls of Smarties. "Would you give this to your parents for me?"

The little girl eyed the Smarties. "Ain't supposed to take candy."

"Save it until your mom and dad are dustposed," Genna smiled. "They must be very proud of you, dear."

Genna started up the street. Strangely, she'd never felt her own parents were proud of her, and she'd worked hard to ensure Simon and Lizzie knew she treasured them. Which was it? Were her parents proud, which she somehow didn't feel? Or weren't they? She'd gotten A's. She played varsity tennis. She was pretty enough, and from eighth grade on, when her breasts developed, had never lacked for boys' attention. She wasn't tall and regal like Doris, and she hadn't stayed home and made a great stinking pile of money like her brother Billy, but no one expected that of a girl back then. She hadn't married anyone with money, that must be her crime. Or maybe she never stopped being a reminder of her mother's sole indiscretion.

Genna stopped in front of an enormous sugar maple that had shed half its leaves. Those that remained were crimson. In the words of the Motown song she'd listened to obsessively growing up, Genna used to believe she was a Love Child, never meant to be! Her biological dad? Some random her mother couldn't admit to. A one-night stand, a sperm provider, a knife-point rapist!

"No, Genna," Doris had assured her, over and over. Finally, during Genna's senior year in high school, Doris produced a marriage certificate with the groom's name x'ed out. "He was just some boy. Then I met Daddy, and we all got on with the lives we should have had."

Genna thought of all the times her mother had implied she did not have the life she ought, the one in which someone else cooked and she didn't have to worry about money for a new roof.

"Then how come you won't tell me his name?" Genna asked, realizing how petulant and childish she sounded, how come? She stared, furious, at her tall, raven-haired mother, more aware than ever that in her shorter, rounder blondness she resembled someone who wasn't there.

"Because of the foolish notion I see in your eyes right now." Doris tucked an errant strand of hair, bad hair, into her neck bun, then lit a cigarette from the one already burning in the ashtray. She'd brought it home from her one and only trip to France, when Genna was twelve and Daddy was still a judge. Painted yellow and green in country bistro style, the ashtray's sentiment was black-lettered on its rim: *Les enfants sont les fleurs en le jardin de la vie.*

"But Mom."

"Because of how it would hurt Daddy. Who has raised and loved you as his own."

"But Mom."

"When you're older."

Then Doris rose from the couch and strode to the kitchen to burn dinner.

Five years later, in May of Genna's first year at grad school, her mother died of cancer, still thin, still elegant, forty-five years old. And if Genna had expected a deathbed confession, some baring of her mother's cloistered soul, she would have been disappointed. But Genna had expected no such thing. She'd met Jack and had decided he would be her future. He visited with her in March, between winter and spring quarters. He fixed little things around the house, ingratiating himself with Daddy, and though her fix broken windows." She inserted the key, but it wouldn't turn. "Damn."

"Let me." Genna pulled the heavy door towards her, turned the key and felt it ease. The lock sprang; the door opened in; a puff of musty air escaped.

"You're handy," Marge said. "I like that."

The flooring was hard, brown linoleum tiles; the walls, once green, were dark with age. Cobwebs shrouded old-fashioned globe lights. Marge ran her fingers along the wall. "My dad and his pals ain't much on cleaning." She grinned. "Then again, I ain't, either."

Genna followed her down the windowless hall to the second classroom on the left.

"I had good times in here, all right. Second grade. My mother was the teacher. Boy, did that make me feel special."

Genna smelled mold, moisture. There was a black blackboard, and two rows of wooden flip top desks, with small cut-outs in the top right corner.

"In Dad's day, these were ink wells, and boys would dip girls' pigtails, he said, just to be boys."

Genna ran her fingers across a oak desk top. Refinished, in New York or L.A., it would probably fetch a small fortune.

"You might wonder why I'm taking your time." Marge pushed a hand through her short bangs. "Unless you see how the geezers keep the place up, all these years later? You couldn't understand how much the school meant to this town. How it made us a town."

"I think I do. Your mom was really your teacher?"

"I'll tell you something. My mom was the only teacher who lived in Roscoe." Marge walked to the blackboard then turned to face the classroom as her mother must have. Genna tried to imagine Doris a second-grade teacher. Impossible. "Mom was extra strict on me, but I felt like a queen. The spring they closed the building, I was pregnant with Megan. Mom moved up to Reynolds

Elementary in Tipton. When she got sick her second year there, breast cancer, Daddy blamed that on the move, too."

"How old was she?"

"Fifty-eight when she died."

"My mother died at forty-five."

"I'm sorry," Marge said. "How old were you?"

"Twenty-three. We were never that close." Genna wondered why she was telling this stranger. "I still miss her."

"Of course you do." Marge reached into her giant black purse and produced a piece of chalk. "When I get to missing my mom, I come to her classroom and write a note on the board." Marge turned her back to the room and printed, Hi, Mrs. Williams.

"That's what I had to call her in school, Mrs. Williams. Why don't you write something to your mother? Erase it afterwards, I always do." Marge set the chalk on Genna's palm. "I'll wait outside."

Genna rolled the white chalk between her fingers and faced the board. Hi Mom, she wrote. I miss you. She stared a moment, erased Mom and replaced it with Doris. Maybe I should go see Daddy. Genna smudged the board with her palm and walked out of the classroom then out of the old school. Marge waited in the parking lot, blond and blowsy, smoking.

chapter 8

Election Day dawned dry, bright and pretty as any campaign manager could hope for. Returning from the top of the driveway toting the *Cincinnati Enquirer*, which most mornings only enraged them, the air felt so clear and energizing, Jack believed, perhaps for the first time, that the levy would pass. Such a beautiful morning, how could anyone vote against small shining faces, public education, apple pie?

Jack and Genna punched ballots at the middle school after breakfast. The balance of the morning he labored to educate the young minds of Ohio, which, frankly, did not seem much engaged or enlightened by the glories of Renaissance science. From three to five he distributed leaflets outside the Taft Student Center, where most undergraduates were assigned to vote. Distributed, Jack thought, what an old-time, mouth-filling word. Maude distributed freely her favors. Karl sought in vain to redistribute the wealth of the ruling class.

Through Stan Murray, they'd been invited to an Election Night bash at Grandma's Barn. Neither Genna nor Jack had ever been to the Barn, a Tipton fixture, but at eight o'clock, they left Simon and Lizzie in front of the television and drove into Tipton then west out of town towards Indiana. It was full dark and a light rain had begun to fall as they turned onto Miller Road and angled past a field of standing corn. Why, by early November, it hadn't been harvested, or combined, whatever farmers did to corn, he didn't understand. But there was a lot Jack didn't understand about life in the corn belt.

"If the levy doesn't pass," Genna said suddenly, "we'll have to move back to Cincinnati."

She turned towards him, and in the dazzle of approaching headlights her eyes shone, he thought, with unshed tears.

"Even if it does," she continued, "I'm not sure we should leave Simon in that school. It's so awful for him."

Jack thought, disloyally, Simon's had problems in every school he's attended, maybe it's not the school, it's our son. But he said, "Has something happened you haven't told me about?"

"No."

Just ahead, an illuminated sign appeared through the murk like a message from beyond: Grandma's Barn—Functions and Parties.

"What about our house?"

"You think I want to move?" Genna smiled a sideways smile. "But kids before houses, I've got that much straight."

They started up the graveled drive. A large pond, an acre or more, dimpled with rain. Parked cars covered the available lawn on their right. The barn, maybe two hundred feet from where Jack pulled over, loomed through the mist, square and red with white trim, very charmingly barn-like. Genna and Jack crunched up the driveway in the light rain holding hands.

"The levy's going to pass, I just know it."

"Why, Jack." She smiled. "That's the most optimistic thing you've said in months. Maybe years."

Just then, the barn door opened, and the party spilled out into the rain. The interior of Grandma's Barn had been completely redone, down to a high gloss oak floor. At one end of the long room there was an elevated stage. At the other, two half-kegs floated in tubs of ice. Beyond the kegs there was a long bar on which someone had laid out twelve-foot subs parsed into four-inch squares, hot wings, bowls of chips, dip, and enough miniature pigs in blankets to depopulate several miniature hog farms. A crowd of strangers filled four rectangular tables. Who were all these people? Tiptonites. Other party guests surrounded the kegs, watching a projection screen illuminated with the ABC News home page.

It was an off-year, no national campaigns, and not much of local interest except the levy. Jack looked around, feeling out of place, which, he knew, was how Genna felt, only more so. When they were dating, she'd beg him not to leave her alone at parties. For years he didn't, although it wasn't in his nature. At parties, he liked to float, Jack the Giant Barishfly, and he soon left Genna, beer in hand, with some women she seemed to know from Lizzie's soccer team. Jack plunged into the crowd circling the keg to refill his mug, which was where Stan Murray found him.

"Jack," Stan said, "glad you made it. You remember Marla Lindstrom, don't you?"

Marla wore a short dress the same blue as her eyes. The neck scooped almost to the tops of her small breasts. She looked wonderful. Overdressed, but wonderful.

"Who could forget Marla?"

He'd intended nothing, but it didn't sound like nothing, and Stan, munching his way through a mound of finger food, started to inflate. His eyes bulged; his cheeks swelled. Jack tried to remember the Heimlich. Then Stan coughed a miniature wiener into his palm.

"Stan," Marla exclaimed, "that's remarkably gross."

Stan wiped his lips on a napkin.

"Genna and I have been seeing Marla at the high school. Our son's been having some difficulties." Jack glanced from Marla to Stan, who was still working on his lips and perhaps his dignity. "If the levy passes, perhaps the district can use some of the money for a diversity sensitivity class."

"Why's that?" Stan felt sufficiently improved to begin gnawing a chicken wing.

"Simon's come out, and he's being harassed."

Stan set the half-chewed wing on his plate and glanced at Marla.

"It's been bad," she admitted.

"Sometimes," Stan said softly, looking around under his dark brows, "I wonder why we work so hard for this school district, it's such a fucking embarrassment."

"By the way," Jack asked. "The levy is going to pass?"

"The first results should be up any time."

They walked towards the front of the barn, where a media station had been set up on a card table: phone line to a laptop patched to a projection screen. A short sandy-haired stranger in a Reds cap sat at the table, typing.

"Jack," Stan said, "this is…"

But he didn't hear the rest, because just then the projection switched from the ABC home page to a text-only screen from the county board of elections. The computer operator, whoever he was, scrolled down to the Tipton School levy, proposition eight. With three of twelve wards reporting, the vote was 586 Yes, 470 No. The room erupted in hoots and clapping.

"Great!" Jack shouted to Stan, who ignored him and leaned over the computer operator.

"Small," Stan said. Could the name really be Small? "Can you tell which wards have reported?"

Small moved the cursor, changed screens twice and declared, "One in Tipton city, one in the township, one in Roscoe."

"What was the vote in Roscoe?" Stan asked.

"This is only one of three wards," the computer guy said. "But it was 206 No, 152 Yes."

Jack calculated. "That's like four to three against. That's really good news."

The room buzzed happily. Stan said, "There are six Tipton city wards, that one in the township, then three in Roscoe, two in Milton. Small, what was the vote in the city ward?"

Small clicked at his keyboard. "Two hundred forty-seven Yes, fifty-two No."

Jack could feel himself grinning and grinning. Then his eyes found Marla, who was standing close enough for him to smell her light scent, violets or lavender, and for Jack to imagine the weight of her small frame against his.

"Gotta love it," she said.

The twelve-foot sandwiches shrank to six then four then two, and completely disappeared. The hot wings took flight. Shortly before ten, three more wards reported; two from the city, which voted four to one for the levy, and one from Milton, which voted three to two against. With half the votes counted, the levy was leading 1601 to 1230, and the campaign coordinator, a small dark-haired woman named Eleanor, got up on stage.

"It's too early to know for sure," she began, "but I want to thank all you volunteers. Not only are we winning big in the city in the student wards—"

Jack smiled at Genna who was standing beside him.

"—but we're running at 40 percent in Milton and Roscoe, twice what we got there last time."

A cheer went up from the sixty or so volunteers still in the room.

"I know how much work it's been for all of you…"

Small, the computer operator, who was standing just to the side of the stage shouted: "I haven't seen Ellie in weeks!"

Oh, Jack thought, they're a couple.

"…because I know how hard I've been working. But if this trend keeps up, it will be a great victory, not just for those of us who worked for the levy, but for all of Tipton."

More speeches followed, short and jolly, with everyone thanking everyone. Then Genna wanted to leave to ensure the kids got to bed on time. Jack glanced around Grandma's Barn, which was starting to empty. Pretty soon, it would be just the hardcore waiting for final results, which they'd been told should come between eleven and midnight.

"I'll drive you," Jack said, "but I want to come back."

He dropped Genna and started back to the Barn. The rain had stopped, and mist rose from the blacktop as he drove west from Tipton. Though the first trip had felt interminable, it wasn't more than fifteen or twenty minutes from their house. Hell, it wasn't more than fifteen or twenty minutes from anywhere to anywhere in greater Tipton, and Jack turned onto Miller Road with a sense of urgency. He pulled into the driveway for Grandma's Barn, parked near the pond and looked around. Perhaps twenty cars remained, but none that he recognized, especially not a certain silver Beetle. He crunched up the driveway as shadowy clouds crossed the moon. He'd been over and over the numbers, and it was all but a mathematical certainty the levy would pass. They'd be able to stay in town.

Inside, he looked for familiar faces. Eleanor and Small were still there; Small hunched over the laptop, clicking, stringy hair falling out the back of his Reds cap. Eleanor and several of the other levy officials leaned against the bar watching the projection screen. Jack approached Eleanor.

"We haven't met," he said. "I'm Jack Barish. I worked with Stan Murray and TUTS."

"You guys did a great job." She smiled and squeezed his hand.

"Any more updates?" For a small woman Eleanor had a fearsome grip. "When I left to drive my wife, six wards had reported."

"Not yet," said one of the others.

Then Marla reentered from wherever she'd been. "Hey, Jack. I thought you'd left."

"I came back." He found himself grinning. Stepping away from the others, he added softly, against everything that was reasonable and good, "I was hoping you'd still be here."

Marla didn't answer, but he knew she'd heard him; her eyes gave this blip of recognition. Then a cry went up. Not because Jack had said what he shouldn't have and found in Marla's eyes confirmation of what they'd both suspected, which is why he was silently shouting, Huzzah, huzzah! Oh, God no! But because new results had posted. With ten of twelve wards reporting, the Tipton School levy was 63 percent Yes, 37 percent No.

"Quite a night," Marla said. "Isn't it, Jack?"

It was quite a night.

✦ ✦ ✦

Helen, the shift manager, loved Fry Guy so much she'd scheduled him Thursday and Friday four to eight, Saturday one to eight, Sunday noon to seven. Twenty-two times six, one hundred thirty-two dollars (Simon was an early whiz at multiplication; math and musical gifts often appearing in tandem, hinting at some genetic link), more money than he'd had at one time, except for the day after his Bar Mitzvah when his parents let him keep two hundred. They'd claimed the rest for his college fund, but Simon believed they'd spent it; when he suggested using Bar Mitzvah money to buy him a car, Mom and Dad's faces got long and weird, like, What money?

His dad's big face wore that same pissed-off money expression right now. It was Saturday morning, and they were driving to Cincinnati for Simon's weekly session with Yevgeny Keratin, the Ukrainian-born vocal coach he'd been studying with since eighth grade. Yevgeny foretold a fabulous future, "Ef only Simon vould vork harder."

Yevgeny had been a wunderkind, with his own fabulous future foretold, until his mother emigrated to Israel. Three months later, Yevgeny was expelled from the Kiev Conservatory. How Yevgeny, who was short and broad and looked like the men in Dad's family, smooth-cheeked with very white skin and dark hair, made his way from Kiev to Cincinnati, Simon didn't know. But Yevy loved Simon's voice. Vhat an instrument! he'd exclaim. Like a grown man's. Simon, who disliked lessons on adolescent principle, especially with men (which reminded him of studying math with Dad), had been happily making his way to Yevgeny's studio one evening a week for three years, and since they'd moved, on Saturday mornings.

Between Yevy's and the Fry Guy, Simon was scheduled from nine in the morning to eight at night. He was meeting Peter soon afterwards so he needed to be driven home to shower then back to the movie. He also needed an advance of oh, fifty dollars from the paycheck he'd get next Thursday. But would Dad say yes? Did he ever? No! He got this whacked-out look with that throbbing thing in his neck, then started muttering about financial responsibility, how Simon was always borrowing against his allowance, and now that he had a job, he needed to learn to save and wait until payday. And blah, blah, blah. Simon had screamed. You never say yes. You make me feel like crap!

For twenty minutes they'd ridden in radioactive silence, Simon with his seat cranked as close to horizontal as he could manage, eyes sealed, plotting revenge. If Dad didn't start showing him more respect, he'd move out. Dad could be lying half-dead in the street, bleeding from his nose, ears, eyes and everywhere else. Simon would pretend he didn't know him and keep right on walking.

"Simon." Dad touched his shoulder; Simon feigned sleep deep as the ocean. "We're almost there."

Simon slit his eyes as if Dad were a big-nosed vermin.

"I've been thinking, Simon."

I doubt it.

"Maybe I will advance money against your paycheck. But just this once, because you haven't been paid yet."

Simon lifted his bleeding pater off the pavement.

"But why do you need so much? Fifty dollars for the movies?"

Simon dropped his dad like a hot rock. "What does it matter? It's my money."

"No." Dad braked and moved towards the exit ramp. "It's my money, which you want to borrow. Who is this Peter anyway?"

"A kid from school."

Simon looked straight into Dad's eyes, daring him to ask more.

"Are you paying for him?"

"Why would I?"

"Just wondering why you need fifty dollars." But Dad didn't say it very loudly and he didn't say anything else, like Is this a date? So Simon knew he'd get the money.

✦ ✦ ✦

In Yevgeny's small waiting room, Simon sat across from Dad and flipped through an old *People*. Classical guitar runs ran towards them from the nearest lesson room. In another, a beginner played C, G, then A major scales on a piano, over and over again. Down the hall, in Yevgeny's studio, the tall redhead whose lesson preceded Simon's trilled some Italian aria. For reasons Simon didn't understand it seemed to be Little Italy week in Yevgeny's Kiev-by-Kenwood; his new piece was "Se Vuol Ballare," from *The Marriage of Figaro*. Simon disliked opera. Musical theater, he loved. *NSYNC. He'd been telling his parents for years, but did they respect his opinion? No, they listened to Yevgeny who said Simon had a vone in a million instrument for opera, but too much jellybelly to dance.

Simon glanced from the photo of Jennifer and Brad (was he ever hot) down at the watermelon pressing out from inside his green Old Navy tee. He wore a collared over-shirt to obscure his middle, but there was no hiding that he was a fat boy with tree trunk thighs and a massive chest, when all he desired was to be skinny and cute like Brad Pitt or even better, like Jennifer Aniston. He also wanted his parents to get off their collective butt and find him an agent so he could become famous like the guys from his old school in 98 Degrees. But no, he had to sing opera, about which no one under sixty gave a rat's ass.

Down the hall marched Yevgeny and the soprano.

"...next weekend," she was saying, "I have to..."

The soprano was bony-kneed, tall, and skinny. Yevgeny's dark eyes found Simon and his face splintered in a grin.

"Leave message on machine," he said to the redhead without looking at her. "Simon, how heve you been? Everyting good?"

Simon turned to his father, praying he'd keep quiet. Simon followed Yevgeny to his studio, which housed a grand piano, floor to ceiling bookcases, a cassette recorder, and a large desk piled with newspapers and sheet music in half a dozen languages. Yevgeny's thick hair fell almost to his shoulders. He sat at the piano and played scales. Simon sang the ascending notes making the full, resonant sound Yevgeny taught.

"Not here, here," Yevgeny had shown him years ago, sliding his hand from Simon's throat to his diaphragm. "Make sound like growling bear. Natural sound."

They warmed up for ten minutes. Yevy kept after him to relax his jaw. "Why so tense, boy like you? You have girlfriend? Girlfriend make you tense?"

No, Simon wanted to say. But I hope to have boyfriend.

They skipped the recitative—what a relief, Simon didn't know the words yet—and moved to the main section of the aria. He didn't know what it meant, word for word, but Mom had explained this evil Count whom Figaro worked for was putting moves on his girlfriend. Figaro was pissed, but couldn't show it because the Count could have him killed, then really do the nasty with his true love. So Figaro had to figure out how to get the Duke or Count, whatever he was, without letting on how mad he was. Simon could relate. It was like fighting with your parents, who were always saying it was their house, their money, so they made the rules.

"Simon," Yevgeny asked. "You ready?"

He nodded and Yevgeny played an intro, swaying over the keys then looking up through his dark hair.

Simon sang, "Se vuol bal-la-re, si-gnor con-ti-no."

You know what it was really like? Simon thought, and it was so weird. He was singing and thinking at the same time as if he were two different people. The person stood apart from the instrument, which filled the room, the tone rich, round, and large, like the low notes on the organ in the Plum Street temple in Cincinnati. It was like being gay, and someone who doesn't know asks about your girlfriend and you have to smile and pretend whoever she was really was your girlfriend. Or it was like asking Peter to hang out, the movies, whatever, and hoping he understood that what you really wanted wasn't going to the movies. Slow, devious and smart was Simon Barish, just like Figaro.

Now Yevy glanced up at him, the instrument him, peering through a mask of hair, playing with just his left, his cupped right hand signaling near his throat, open up, open up, the fingers unbending like an old man's, because here came the high note, the F which he couldn't hit but Yevgeny said he could, Ef only he vouldn't tighten his throat and jaw.

"Il chi-tar-ri-no le suo-ne-ro, si."

He sang and tried not to strain and imagined putting his hand on Peter's shoulder as if it meant nothing, Peter shyly covering his mouth with his hand,

"Le suo-ne-ro si!"

as the F expanded out of the other Simon's throat like silver underwater bubbles floating up to the light.

When he finished, Yevgeny grinned "Not bad. Vhat you think?"

"I hit the F," Simon said, coming back to himself.

"Yesss." Yevgeny laughed. "Pretty damn good, for American boy. Now this time," he winked, "even better."

✦ ✦ ✦

It happened so fast Simon didn't know what he'd done. One moment he was dumping a basket of nuggets. Several had lodged in the corner, and Fry Guy always got every one. He raised the fryer basket, shook and shook harder. His left forearm brushed the heat lamp; his skin sizzled like meat. Simon screamed, dropped the basket, and stared at his smoking arm as Helen came running.

"It was so hot," he was saying hours later to Peter in the back of Mom's minivan driving to the movies, "it didn't hurt. The skin just bubbled and fell off."

"That is so weird."

"Look." Simon turned on the overhead reading lamp. He moved his arm until the mini spotlight illuminated his hairless forearm (shaved that morning), and let the light play the length of the pink scar. It ran for maybe six inches, the width of the coil, swooping and graceful, before doubling back on itself.

"It looks like an S." Peter touched Simon's wrist with a slender finger. "S for Simon, Super Simon." Peter smiled and covered his mouth with his hand.

"I wasn't feeling very super. I was screaming and running around. My arm was smoking," Simon made a face like Jim Carrey in that movie. "Then Helen, that's the manager, asked where it hurt most, did I want to go to the emergency room, and I realized it didn't hurt much at all. My skin just singed off. Like eyelashes."

"That is so weird," Peter said.

He liked the way Peter said weird. "That's why we could pick you up. I got off early."

"And because your mom is so nice," Mom called from the front, glancing in the rearview.

Simon rolled his eyes and grinned at Peter, who didn't look away or cover his mouth. Simon remembered the shock of the burning coil then Peter's cool finger, and his heart beat faster. He wondered, if he touched Peter's hand in the movies in the dark, would Peter hold his hand or pull away? He was betting, hold his hand?

chapter 9

Genna dropped Simon and Peter in front of the Rialto. As they entered the theater side-by-side, Simon inclined his big face towards Peter and whispered. Peter smiled. Watching, Genna felt so happy and fearful for her son, she had a crazy notion. Buy a ticket and sneak in to watch the boys watch the movie. Simon was seventeen and this was his first date. Oh, how she loved her big strange boy!

She remembered little Simon, so cute and serious, imploring her, "Please, Mommy, don't sing!" Re-imagining him tonight in the back seat with Peter, ten times as large as his former self though still cute, she smiled, then put the Town and Country in gear. Instead of turning towards home, she started out of town towards Indiana. Genna had always enjoyed driving. But since last winter when she drove night after night, the Woman Who Drove, she craved the van's quiet, the plush front seat, the whispering of rubber rolling over empty blacktop. She couldn't think as well if she weren't in the car, or perhaps she thought simultaneously of too many things unless half her mind was occupied with the minutiae of locomotion: steering, signaling, which way to turn, how fast, how slow, her life's problems weeded by the dialectic of pedals, gas and brake.

The Town and Country nosed past housing developments which soon became farmers' fields that would someday yield more developments. This afternoon she'd phoned her brother Billy.

Forty-three years old, and frankly never all that smart, Billy had done extremely well: senior executive vice-president of the largest commercial bank in St. Louis. Billy had employed his charms and the power of Daddy's connections, who were happy to do for the son what they couldn't or wouldn't do for the father. Or maybe Billy was brighter than she gave him credit for. He was certainly personable and athletic. In high school, he'd starred in football, basketball, and golf, and still shot in the seventies. Then there was Billy's smile. Billy smiled, and the heavens applauded. His dark hair was now attractively silver at the temples, and he possessed, oh, she didn't know, a certain social grace, which made even the jocks he'd hung around with in high school content to lose to him. Billy had also inherited their mother's elegant jaw and long limbs.

In high school, it would have been easy to hate him. He was homecoming king his junior and senior years, for God's sake, and although she was a year ahead everyone thought of her as Billy's sister, not the other way around. But despite it all, an all which had included freshmen girls accosting her to gush, "Ooh, you're Billy's sister. What's he really like?" she didn't hate him and never would. Billy was warm-hearted, a good brother and a loving son, who supported Daddy in a manner to which he'd happily become accustomed.

As adults, sometimes even Genna had trouble remembering that Billy was the younger sibling. Credit the Rolls, the bank job, the twin girls in private schools, the stay-at-home wife, the large house in Ladue.

Genna's minivan purred past corn fields stubbled brown. Smoke plumed from a chimney on the next rise. After the rain on Election Night, the weather had turned; for the first time all fall, the wind blew coat-piercingly cold from the north. That's what had prompted her to call Billy. Although the families rarely gathered at Thanksgiving, Genna wanted to. And because she needed Daddy there, and in the eight years she'd lived in Ohio she'd only coaxed one visit out of him, she'd thought it best to ask Billy to invite them to St. Louis.

"Delighted to, Sis."

Sis, what he'd called her since always. In high school, he'd tried out Sissy—he had a crush on the actress—but she wouldn't respond. For a year or two after she finished her degree, he'd called her Doctor Sis, which she had rather liked.

"Carolyn's whole family is coming, I can sure use some back-up."

Then in her study and now in the front seat of her dark van as she passed a welcome sign, Indiana—The Hoosier State, Genna imagined the ironic twist of her brother's lips. He barely tolerated Carolyn's parents, especially his mother-in-law.

"Will Daddy be there?"

"Of course," Billy answered. "With Gwen."

Gwen, whom she'd never met, was Daddy's current friend. Women of a certain age and social class found Daddy excellent company; there had been quite a few friends since Doris died twenty-two years ago next May.

"If you want," Billy added, "I'll invite the aunts. It'll be a proper family reunion."

"What will Carolyn think?"

"She won't much like it. Damn, I put up with her family year-round, she can put up with mine on turkey day."

In the awkward silence, she heard Billy sip from an ice-filled glass.

"I'm kidding, Sis. Do you want to stay with us?" He hesitated. "It might be a bit snug."

What nonsense, a snug six-bedroom house. "We'll stay at the Holiday Inn. The kids like the pool."

"Great, Sis. It'll be fun."

Replacing the receiver, she remembered Billy in high school. Short, nearly-black hair, his slash of a smile. Twenty-five years later he employed the same cheery teenage phrases. Great, Sis. Genna checked the illuminated dashboard clock. She'd been driving for forty minutes. Tipton Professor Disappears in Indiana. She sometimes imagined she could drive for days and no one would notice except Simon, who'd wonder why his laundry wasn't done. No, Jack would miss her. So would Lizzie, and Sam would miss his morning runs. Jews, she thought, searching for a place to turn around, at least the Jews in Jack's family, would never suggest a close family member stay in a motel. Cultural difference, she thought, directing the Town and Country into a cutout in a farmer's field. Genna reversed, then started back towards Ohio. A full moon just above the treetops spilled light across the bare fields. Beautiful in an empty way, she thought. Like Marla. Then she put that woman out of her mind and drove towards Tipton where she planned to sip chai in a coffee house until Simon and Peter's movie let out.

✦ ✦ ✦

When Genna and Simon came through the kitchen door Jack was in the family room watching *Saturday Night Live* with Lizzie. He bounced up from the couch as if there were a spring attached to his substantial bottom, and Lizzie's eyes swung towards him, as if to say, Don't get all crazy, Dad. Then she looked back to the screen where the president was being lampooned. Jack and Lizzie had spent the evening together, as they frequently did before boys and teenagerdom had snuck up the Barish driveway. Over the years they'd had such fun; Lizzie was the easy child, which might have been nothing more than Lizzie fitting in around Simon's vast psychic shadow. Competing with Simon must have been like trying to arm-wrestle an earthquake. Lizzie couldn't have known what to grab or which way to push. From time to time they'd worry, lying in bed before sleep, that Lizzie was too out of touch with what she thought or felt, though wasn't it remarkably convenient that she was so undemanding.

But Jack had always thought Lizzie's easiness was more than how difficult Simon was. She was more like him. More like Genna, too. (Though Simon looked more like him than tall, lithe Lizzie ever would.) Better at school. More athletic. More psychically and perhaps, more genetically in tune; if their DNA were unraveled and lined up side-by-side then sequenced, any lab tech could look and see, Yes, yes, I see how we got there from here.

That evening, even if she hadn't been attuned to her dear old dad (or Boppa, as she'd taken to calling him, introducing Jack with a smirk to her new eighth-grade friends as Boppa Barish; "Isn't my Boppa a cuddly old bear?"), she couldn't have missed how upset he was. Every ten or fifteen minutes he'd jumped up to check the driveway to see if Genna were returning.

"Maybe Mom decided to go to the movies," Lizzie suggested after his third or fourth trip upstairs. "Or maybe she's out driving." He looked at her warily. As a family, they hadn't discussed the events of last winter, but the kids must have their suspicions. "You know how Mom likes to drive."

"I guess that's it," he'd said, and pulled her close. "How's your new school? Tell me the truth now."

"The kids tease me about Simon."

"You want me to talk to the principal?"

"Dad." She regarded him with that new, half-pitying teenage smile. "I've been teased my whole life about Simon. I can take it."

What a heartbreaker she was going to be some day. Those dark, dark eyes. He said, "I love you, Lizzie." Then, remembering hearing Lizzie use the word, Jack added, "You're the bomb."

She laughed. "The bomb." She shook her head. "I love you, too, Boppa."

Now, with Genna and Simon's voices falling down the stairs, he suspected Lizzie was right. Genna had been out driving. But why, and with whom, if anyone, he hadn't a clue.

Jack hurried up the basement stairs and nearly banged into Simon who was coming down.

"How was the movie?"

"Awesome."

"Awesome good or bad?" he called after Simon's broad shoulders as they dropped from view. Simon didn't answer, instead headed for the couch where he demanded the remote from his sister.

"NO!" Lizzie shouted. "I'm watching this."

Jack abandoned the kids to their nightly battle for electronic dominance. In the kitchen Genna was pouring a glass of white wine from last night's bottle.

"Where were you?"

"Sipping chai in Java, the new coffee house."

"For two and half hours?"

She glanced at him, gray-eyed, over her glass. "I lost track of time."

On Election Night, Jack had returned long after all returns were in. The next morning, he explained he'd lost track of time while celebrating the levy's victory. He said, "I was worried."

"You have nothing to worry about."

Or was that, *You* have nothing to worry about. Jack was unused to such obliqueness. The old Genna would have blurted what was on her mind. He almost said, You have nothing to worry about, either. Instead, he replied, "I'm glad you're safe," and emptied the Chardonnay into his own glass.

Later, with their television tuned to a *Golden Girls* rerun, Genna and Jack sat up bolstered by large pillows. On the screen, gravel-voiced Bea Arthur was explaining to Rose that Blanche went through men as if they were a box of chocolates, sometimes not even bothering to unwrap them before eating.

"How was Simon's date?"

"I don't think he'd call it a date. But it went extremely well."

"I wonder," Jack moved his right leg closer to Genna's left, "if we can get in trouble if Simon becomes sexually active."

"How?"

Their knees touched. "For pandering." He dropped a hand on Genna's upper thigh. "These boys are all underage."

"I don't see how." Genna turned towards him, and if she'd noticed his hand or felt his knee she gave no sign. "Unless every parent of a sexually-active teen could get in the same trouble."

"Don't be naive."

"It's been a long time since I've been naive." She placed her hand on his knee.

Jack glanced at his wife's hand then back up at her face. "How about horny?"

"Watch the television," she said, smiling, "and give the kids a chance to fall asleep."

Later, much later, since it had become almost impossible to out-wait the children, who tended to stay up later than their parents, nor did it seem plausible to enter their rooms and order them to sleep so their parents could have a noisy sex life, they'd made love quickly and quietly—efficiently came to mind—and were about to fall asleep when Genna said, "I spoke to Billy. We're invited to St. Louis for Thanksgiving."

Jack snapped awake and wondered if this was why she'd come on to him. "You know I don't like going there."

"Of course, I know." Her voice sounded disembodied, blooming out of the dark. "But they're my family, and I'd like the kids to know them."

Jack thought about the first time he'd met her parents, the Judge pickling himself, her mother thin, almost gaunt, wasting away but still elegant, as if trying to disprove the adage about the impossibility of being too thin or too rich, which they clearly weren't although the Gordons liked to pretend otherwise. Lying beside Genna he had a sense, sudden and brutal, of what he had felt arriving for the first time in that funky, falling down manse, feeling so completely the outsider, the Jew, with a capital J, New York New Money, which he had decided was better than no money at all.

In the short time he knew Doris, he'd come to like her, perhaps more than Genna did.

"Jack," Genna whispered, her voice floating towards him so feathery light it would not have moved tracing paper in front of her lips, so gentle, in fact, he would not have sworn he'd heard it until she added, "Are you still awake?"

"Barely."

"I want to learn about my biological father. I'm going to ask Daddy."

"Good," he murmured, but didn't ask, Why now? Not because he thought he knew (he didn't), but because he could feel sleep advancing so rapidly he couldn't form words. "Good," he repeated, and looped an arm over her breasts, gave the right one a friendly squeeze.

"So I want you there, and I don't want you to make a scene."

"Unh," Jack mumbled, and then he was gone, pressed up against her. And if she explained herself it was only to the dark and his slumberous embrace.

✦ ✦ ✦

Mom and Dad bundled them into the car pronto, crack o' dawn, the Wednesday before Thanksgiving. Simon had often observed to Lizzie, when he was condescending to speak to her, how totally gung-ho Mom and Dad were about school. You had to do this, blah-blah. You had to do that, blah-blah-blah or the sky would f-ing fall and you'd be grounded until you were twenty-one—unless it interfered with their travel plans. Then it was fine to ditch for a day or two or three. So it had been up and out at seven, the minivan loaded the night before. Simon had stumbled into the garage carrying blankets and pillows and claimed the back seat (Lizzie always said she couldn't sleep in cars, anyway). Fine, Mom called from up front, but she had it next.

Dad backed out of the garage and the last image flickering on Simon's retinas was Sam sitting up in the driveway, his big head

(Dad said was so noble it belonged on the back of a nickel) following them, brown eyes pleading, How? How can you leave me? Next thing Simon knew Lizzie was shaking him awake somewhere outside Indianapolis. He tried to slap her hand, but she was too quick, a prissy little gnat. Mom called, "Rest stop in two minutes, then I'm in the back!"

"No, Mom, no!" he shouted, warm and comfy under his blankets, safe and adored in the rhythm of this and other road trips.

Mom and Dad had been popping them into minivans (this was the fourth they'd owned) for weekend outings for as long as he could remember. Four, six, eight hours, no problem, especially in California, where they were always driving somewhere. They'd bundle him into the back and Lizzie into her car seat to camp in the sequoias or to stay in some Mexican hotel. He'd play on his Game Boy, and Lizzie would whine to use it, until Mom and Dad bought a second one. He'd listen to his Walkman for hours. God, how he loved those tapes, *Jungle Book*, *Little Mermaid*, *Mary Poppins*. He even loved Raffi, one strange dude. Simon would sing louder and louder, until Dad would shout, Pipe down, Lizzie can't hear her tape. So he'd pipe down, and the miles would unroll, four, six, eight, and later twelve hours to New York to see Dad's family after they moved to Ohio. When they were little, he and Lizzie thought everyone took such trips. Later, when he learned most of his Ohio friends hadn't been anywhere, except maybe Indiana, and certainly hadn't spent their childhoods rolling up and down the interstates, he began to complain. But he didn't complain long and pissy—goddamn, he was a good complainer when he wanted, a good arguer, too; to get what he wanted out of Mom and Dad, he had to be—because riding in the bubble of the family van, Simon had always felt warm, safe, and loved, a small boy even now that he was huge, wrapped in the embrace of his family.

Dad pulled into the rest area. The Barish clan donned shoes and sweatshirts, hurried up to the rest rooms. Unzipping inside a closed stall, Simon could hear Dad at one of the urinals. Simon used a stall whether he was just peeing or not; when he was younger he didn't want anyone to think he was sneaking a peek at their penis because they might think he was gay, now that he was gay, he didn't want anyone peeking at his penis in case it was the wrong size or shape. Dad whistled that off-key whistle of his, something from *Man of La Mancha*. Damn, it was embarrassing. Dad's urinal flushed, and still Simon waited, unzipped but not yet pissing, because he didn't want Dad to hear. He couldn't say why that mattered. Damn, he didn't want to think about it. He glanced at the gray stall wall. Someone had printed in red marker: For a good time, call Bob. 789-4242. Next to that, someone had scrawled, Faggots suck! A third someone had answered, You bet we do! Simon heard Dad move to the sink; water started to flow. He wished Dad would get the hell out; he had to piss like a racehorse. Then Dad started to sing. He was actually singing in a public bathroom.

"To dream the impossible dream..."

Simon thought he would die, he was so freaking embarrassed.

"To fight the unbeatable foe..."

God, he had to pee. Then Dad called, "Simon, you alive in there?"

Not in a million years, Simon thought, am I going to answer.

"To try when your arms are too weary..."

God, but he had to pee.

Dad called, "It's all right. There's no one here except us."

"Will you leave me alone?" Simon hissed. "So I can piss in peace?"

"You're just taking a leak? What's taking so long?"

"Dad!"

"All right." Dad started laughing. What an asshole he was sometimes. "I'll be out in the car."

Dad moved away from the sink. Simon could see his legs and big feet under the stall wall. The men's-room door opened and banged shut. Simon's stream hit the bowl like the blast from a fire hose, strong enough to extinguish a second-story blaze. The toilet bowl frothed. Simon's bladder eased and he remembered some camping trip, he must have been nine or ten. He'd had to pee right now! And Dad pulled over on a country road. He'd stepped outside and started to pee, shielded from the world by the van. Mid-pee the van started to roll. Next thing he was running after the van, holding his shorts up with one hand, holding his penis with the other, still peeing, trying not to laugh but cracking up, while from inside he could hear Mom, Dad and Lizzie laughing and laughing. After maybe ten feet Dad stopped, but they never forgot it, any of them, little Simon running alongside the van taking a leak, holding his dick.

Simon shook himself dry, flushed and unlocked the stall. Good, no one. God, he thought, grinning, but Dad could be an asshole.

✦ ✦ ✦

They rolled west on I-70 across Indiana and into Illinois. Mom snoozed in back under a mountain of blankets. Simon sat in the middle captain chair, hooked up to his Discman, singing along to the new Britney Spears. Lizzie sat up front beside Dad. In between songs, he could hear them chatting, easy and relaxed, and he felt a switchblade of regret, a rose petal of sorrow. Dad loved Lizzie better, just look. If he were a girl, or good at sports, Dad would love him as much.

He remembered elementary school, their first year in Ohio. Dad was always coaching back then; such a big-ass jock and he hoped Simon would be, too. That spring, Dad was the assistant little league coach; he stood near third and waved the kids around. This one game, Simon hit a double and an inside-the-park home run. Man, he really socked it. He could still remember Dad's face when he chugged by, arms pumping, slogging towards home. That's my boy! But Simon couldn't keep the rules straight—When did you slide? How many foul balls?—and he was afraid of the ball. No, not afraid, f-ing terrified.

Later that same spring, some idiot pitcher on an opposing team, one of those moonface jocks who could throw really hard but didn't know where it was going, hurled a pitch at Simon's head. He tried to duck, but his legs wouldn't obey, and the ball rushed towards him big as a planet. He turned just in time, and instead of hitting his face, the ball smacked him in the middle of the back. Simon felt like he'd been harpooned, and the rest of the spring, every time he stood at the plate, he'd feel the ball smack him—Thar she blows!—and lurch away from every pitch like a sounding whale, like a sissy, the other kids said, even if the ball was a mile away. That was the last spring he played baseball.

In middle school, Dad convinced him to try football. Dad the Jock had been throwing to him in their backyard for years. Buttonhook, he'd shout. Post. Down and out, or some other code Simon never got, as if it were the secret handshake of a club he wasn't allowed to join. He knew this much. He had to run out. Dad would whip the ball at him, and if he wanted to be loved and applauded, he was supposed to catch it like Dad's big brother Russ, the family hero, except he never could. It would bounce off his hands, as if the ball and his fingers were repulsing magnetic poles. Or he'd flinch and miss it completely. Then Dad would shout, "It's not going to hurt you, what the hell are you afraid of?"

"Nothing."

Which was a big, fat, whopping lie, because back then he was afraid of everything. Not just the ball, but the pissed-off look that would smirch Dad's face when Simon demonstrated yet again that he didn't share the Barish gift for football. He was so afraid of that look in eighth grade, when he was bigger than almost everyone, over two hundred pounds, and the middle school football coach stopped him in the hall one day and said, Hey, why don't you come out for the team? He decided he would, even though he hated football.

They made him a lineman, and though he didn't know the rules and couldn't follow the plays, he dressed in the locker room with the other guys. He put on shoulder pads. He put on a cup, thigh pads, knee pads, cleats and a helmet, and for part of every game, they'd put him in and let him bang into some other kid. This one time, he was opposite some poor schlub he must have outweighed by sixty pounds. He kept knocking the kid back and falling on top of him. No matter what the play, he'd do the same thing. Man, he was pancaking that kid, he was bulldozing him. In the stands Dad was shouting, "Way to go, Simon. Way to go!" which Simon thought was pretty great.

Then one play the kid didn't get up. He'd sprained an ankle or maybe broke his leg and lay on the ground crying. The other team's coach came out on the field and carried him off. He was just a little kid. And though everyone said Simon hadn't done anything wrong, he never played hard after that, and he was grateful when his first and final season ended, although he did miss the locker room. After that, he pretty much gave up on sports, and Dad, he thought, pretty much gave up on him.

✦ ✦ ✦

When they were two hours east of St. Louis, he moved into the back seat with Mom, who was sitting up reading. "Mom," he said and put his head on her shoulder. "How are you doing?"

"Just fine." She smiled her special Mommy smile, which he believed she reserved for him and only him all these years later, her eyes crinkling a bit. "And how are you?"

"I'm good."

"I'm better."

"I'm the best," Simon said, just as he used to when, oh, he didn't know, he was five or six, and he'd crawl up on her lap. They beamed smiley beams at each other, and he wished, not for the first time, that he could still fit on Mom's lap without crushing her. "Tell me about your Mom," he added, thinking, as he always did, who I never knew.

"I already told you, Simon."

"Tell me again."

"She was tall, thin, and beautiful. Lizzie looks quite a bit like her. She had jet-black hair. She curled her eye-lashes. She was very glamorous." Mom got this faraway look, and he wished he knew where she went. "She hated food, which was how she stayed so thin. She died when I was twenty-three."

"You've told me all that. Tell me something new."

"She died so long ago, I'm not sure there is anything new."

Simon looked out through the van's tinted windows at farm land rolling past like a river. "Tell me your happiest memory," he said. "Then tell me your worst."

"Oh, Simon. Sometimes you're really so wise."

A happy glow spread through him like food coloring diffusing through a glass of water. In the whole world no one else thought he was wise.

"When I was eight years old I was walking with my mother in Vandervoort's, which was the fanciest department store in St. Louis. I don't know where my brother Billy was, it was just the two of us, which was rare."

Mom paused, and her eyes got their crinkly look.

"We were all dressed up—I can't remember why—and we walked through Vandervoort's holding hands. Everyone who saw us smiled. I knew my mom was the most beautiful woman in the world. But that day she was also the nicest. We arrived at the fancy-dress department, where everyone knew her. 'Oh hello, Mrs. Gordon,' they said, 'so good to see you.' As if she were a queen or a movie star, and it wasn't because she spent lots of money, because I know now she didn't. 'Oh hello, Mrs. Gordon, how are you?'"

"All the salesgirls gathered around us, and in those days they weren't girls, they were grown women. Doris said, 'I'm extra-wonderful today, because my beautiful daughter Genna is with me. Isn't she just a doll?' I felt so happy, Simon, I can't tell you."

From the front of the van, Simon could hear that crappy punk music Lizzie listened to, either from the front speakers or escaping her headset. The kid was going to be deaf by eighteen.

"So what was your saddest memory?"

Mom looked out the window. When she turned back, tears like tiny pearls spun on her lashes. "That was both. She never said it again, so I knew she didn't mean it. I don't know why it mattered so much—it shouldn't really—but it did to my mother. No matter what else I did, she never forgave me for being a little bit plump, pretty but not really beautiful. My mother," Mom paused, then continued, speaking as she sometimes did, as both judge and jury, "was a shallow woman."

Simon didn't know what to say. He thought about how Dad made him feel, like he didn't really love him because he didn't play football and all that. But he also knew Dad did love him, and he thought, wonderingly, that Mom was stuck in her childhood. All grown up but still worried her dead mother didn't love her.

"I think you're beautiful, Mom." He kissed her cheek then grinned. "For a mom."

"Thank you, Simon. I think you're beautiful, too."

He laid his cheek on Mom's shoulder and let the joy of the moment overtake him as they rolled west towards St. Louis.

PART TWO:

Journeys of Discovery

chapter 10

They splashed in the pool, bubbled in the Jacuzzi, then consumed slabs of animal protein in the hotel restaurant, although Jack annoyed her by arguing it would have been cheaper and probably healthier to eat anywhere else. Give it a rest, Jack, she'd said, the kids are tired. Later, those same tired kids stayed up half the night in their room watching MTV and *Seinfeld* reruns. It had been years since the Barishes managed a single hotel room, and then only because until she was twelve or so, Lizzie liked sleeping on the floor. Before saying goodnight, Genna had warned the kids that if they charged movies they'd pay for it out of their allowances, and both kids got this expression on their faces—Yeah, right—because neither she nor Jack had ever managed to enforce such a threat.

The next morning, lying in a contented ball in Jack's arms on Thanksgiving morning, Genna concluded a few movies, even at hotel prices, was cheap for a whooping orgasm. In a hotel bed, on clean sheets, with miniature shampoos already stashed in her make-up bag, and a soft-core, soft-focus video on the box, they remained hot for each other. What conference? What woman?

As if once again they were Jack and Genna, starting out, when they were so hot for each other she'd suck his fingers and other digit with such urgency he'd joke afterwards he thought he and it, all of him, were going to disappear inside her like smoke inside a genii's bottle. Mmm, she thought, snuggling, feeling Jack's stubbly cheek abrade her shoulder, she could still hear the joy ripping out of her—OOOOOH, Jack!—as she came last night and he pushed her up on her knees and entered her again, mashing her face into a pillow, his fingers reaching up from beneath her to pinch her nipple, his cock—his COCK, upper case, OH YES! HIS UPPER CASE COCK!—pounding so far up and down inside her it was a pile driver and she was the pile, Jack the wave and Genna the ocean floor he broke against wet and dripping. My God, she thought, and shuddered against him, where did that come from?

Later, after they'd dressed and eaten and dressed again in their holiday best—which for Simon meant the extra-wide Ginkos with red velvet pocket patches, now what would her family think of that?—and she sat around while the kids watched more reruns, and Jack gazed with longing—she might even say the ineffable sadness of lost youth—at the first of several college-football games, the family climbed back into the Town and Country and drove through beautiful downtown Ladue to Mellon Drive on the tree-lined east side of town. Here the houses, substantial as aircraft carriers, were protected from the eyes of pedestrians (maids walking large dogs) by brick walls and battle groups of juniper hedge. Jack eased up to the wrought iron gate, the only opening in Billy's high brick perimeter. Each of the gate's vertical members, elongated like a Giacometti walking-man sculpture, ended in a well-defined, anti-welcome exclamation point, intended to discourage the unwashed and uninvited from popping in unannounced.

Jack rolled down his window and pressed the large tab on the security keypad. A moment later Billy's voice found them in the van, right there, remarkably static-free.

"Welcome, Jack, drive right in."

"In former times," Jack said, *sotto voce*, "the heads of Jewish martyrs were mounted on that gate."

"Don't be ridiculous," she said as Jack eased the van into gear. "The front gate was reserved for Catholics. How did Billy know it was us?"

From her captain's chair, with more than a dollop of teenage scorn topping her vocal sundae, Lizzie answered, "We're always last, Mom."

Jack said, "There was a mini security camera, smart-ass."

They proceeded up the tree-lined drive. Maples, Genna thought, though the leaves were down. It was disorienting to see Billy so mummified in the signifiers of wealth. Each time she visited, which wasn't often, she was like, as the kids would say, Are you kidding, Billy?

They parked in a turn-out near the house, where silver sedans sparkled like sterling teasets in the November sun. For a moment she wished they'd washed the van before coming over, then put it out of her mind. Jack parked beside a low-slung roadster.

"Look at that Beemer!" Simon exclaimed when they were out of the van, collecting themselves and the cut flowers she'd bought, straightening their clothes. "That car is awesome!"

They proceeded up the front steps in family order, Jack beside her, their ducklings trailing behind, and stood between Doric columns supporting a second story portico. In the center of a carved door, the brass jaws of a lion's-head knocker opened wide as a gnu's throat. Below the bell press there was an engraved golden plaque: House of Gordon, Established July 4, 1992; the year Billy and Carolyn had bought and refurbished their pleasure dome. Genna pressed the buzzer and somewhere inside a chime played the opening measure of Beethoven's Fifth. Sometimes—du-du-du-DUM—she believed her brother had lost his way.

A uniformed maid admitted them to the front hall. Billy entered, smiling his smile of smiles, face tanned and handsome as ever, though perhaps a bit fleshier above his yellow cardigan. "Hey, Sis," he cried, and here came the flash of teeth, that light in his eyes, the recapitulated elegance of Doris's jaw. "It's so damn good to see you."

He kissed her cheek and she kissed his, which smelled faintly of Aramis. It was damn good to see him, too. Carolyn entered wearing one of the black sheaths she favored, cut just below the knee to show off her trim calves, a double strand of pearls against the black—what was it, cashmere—the diamond on her left ring finger prominent enough to denude Genna's. Oh, who gave a good goddamn. Genna offered up her cheek. Carolyn offered hers, first one then the other, a European embrace in the heartland. Carolyn's straight hair, bobbed just above her shoulders, remained the same almost-black Billy's used to be. For years, she'd suspected Carolyn dyed hers to match Billy's; it was that similar, and Carolyn was that shallow a girl.

"So good to see you," Carolyn said, then moved onto Jack, who pulled her against him, the Barish hug—which was how he greeted everyone, especially pretty women—Genna thought, watching Carolyn flinch then readjust her smile when Jack released her. Carolyn moved on to Lizzie and Simon, exclaiming over how beautiful and grown-up Lizzie appeared (Damn right) and what a big man (now it was Genna's turn to flinch) Simon had become.

Billy said, "I'll fetch the girls," and returned a moment later with his twins, Nicole and Tara, who were a year older than Lizzie. Nicole had her parents' pale skin and black hair. Tara's hair was honey brown. When they were younger, Carolyn had dressed them identically. Pink dresses. Lavender tights and tutus. White cashmere coats with fox-fur collars. Summer shorts and blouse sets. As the girls grew, however, Carolyn had given that up because they were fraternal twins, after all, and matching clothes only magnified how little they resembled each other. By their tenth birthday, it was hard not to think of Tara as the smaller, prettier one. Her parents' dark good looks and Doris's lean elegance had miscombined in Nicole, as if square base pairs had gotten stuck in round double helix holes. Nicole's long jaw and neck, and her over-large teeth neighed, Horse-face, Equus, freaky-looking.

"Aunt Genna," Tara said and kissed her cheek, then Nicole did, too, finishing her pretty sister's sentence as Genna remembered she often did, "so good to see you."

The twins moved on to be mauled by Jack, then stopped awkwardly in front of their cousins; at least Nicole did. Tara smiled, as she remembered Billy smiling at her age, confident the world would be smitten. Poor Nicole, Genna thought, as she watched the teenagers file out, first the twins then Lizzie and Simon. What she'd suspected before she hugged her nieces was anatomically true: Tara had even gotten the bigger breasts, her figure lush like Lizzie's while Nicole was knobby as a two-by-four.

Then the kids' noise and angst and bustle were gone, and the couples stood uncomfortably alone except for the maid, who'd returned for their coats. Billy said, "Come on, Jack, let's get you a drink," then turned to her. "Daddy's eager to see you."

Then where is he? She trailed Billy and Carolyn into the living room where split logs burned in a hearth large enough to accommodate a spitted stag. The mantle looked as if it might have been transported, tile by hand-painted tile, from a manor house where the masters had ridden to the hounds and cried, "Heigh-ho!" Instead there was Daddy, with the inevitable sweater vest under a gray flannel suit, his gold watch chain running from his belt loop up to his vest pocket. His right hand cradled a scotch, which she knew without knowing was Chivas, one rock, thank you. Daddy stood with his back to the fire conversing with Carolyn's father. Carolyn's younger sisters occupied the couch; their husbands stood across the room, talking to each other. Truth was, she could never remember which husband went with which sister. For years, she'd tried to stay near Jack, who remembered everyone's name. Okay, she thought, I'm a terrible family member, a passive-aggressive snob, but the sisters' husbands really did look quite a bit alike, more so, say, than Nicole and Tara. Wait, one of them was divorced, yes, that was the news. The tall one with the blond moustache was new. She couldn't be expected to know his name. He didn't look anything like the other one, thank goodness, though they wore the same blue banker suit. And the older woman with short-cropped blond hair seated in the armchair beside the couch must be Daddy's friend, Gwen.

She hurried towards the hearth, feeling the room's eyes follow her. Daddy turned and smiled. He drew his watch from his pocket and flicked the golden case. "You're late. Some things don't change."

It was the kids' fault, not mine. "Very little changes, Daddy. How are you?"

"Wonderful. Warming my brains." He smacked his buttocks. "Come give us a hug."

She felt the familiar grit of his cheek. He seemed a little shorter, frailer. She stepped back and examined Daddy's long, lined face, the ironic blue eyes, remembering how he'd looked all those afternoons in his study when she'd come home after school and he'd been drinking. World-weary, cheeks flushed.

"There's someone I'd like you to meet." He led her to the red velvet chair. "Gwen, my dear." He offered his hand—Daddy had such impeccable manners—and helped Gwen rise. "My prodigal daughter, Genna."

✦ ✦ ✦

Jack never knew exactly what the old boy had against him. Oh sure, there were the slow-moving Jungian rivers of resentment and woe. Jack was not only banging his daughter, he'd arrived on the scene when the Judge's wife was dying and the next thing he knew not one but both of his women were gone, and no bride price, either. But Genna had been away for years, and the old boy never really seemed to miss Doris. Within weeks, there was a line of moneyed matrons out the door. Whatever he was giving those rich women he should have bottled and sold through men's stores. All right, the Judge was better-looking than Jack ever was. Saturnine was a word that leapt to mind, though Jack wasn't exactly sure he knew what it meant. The old boy could drink like a fish, an aquarium of fish, clouds of silver bait darting this way and that, always the best scotch and always someone else's, without lowering that arched eyebrow, that almost Southern grace, as if he were a patrician from some other time and latitude, noble, doomed and too proud to ask, whom it was the world and its rich ladies' joy and duty to care for.

The Judge hadn't worked since his early fifties, supported first by the women and then by his son. Now Billy, what a gift for gelt. Money stuck to him like gum to a theater seat, like shit to a straw, and on and on. Okay, maybe Jack was a little jealous. Billy was so damn nice, sweet, and dumb and stinking rich.

They stood sipping scotch in front of the hearth, which must have been twelve feet wide—you could have burned ten foot trees in it—when Gwen, the old boy's girlfriend, suddenly asked, "And what do you do, Mister Barish?"

"Genna and I are professors at Tipton University." That didn't register, and he added, "In Ohio."

Gwen wore one of the most remarkable items of clothing Jack had ever seen: an orange and brown Thanksgiving sweater on which a black-hatted Pilgrim on her right breast fired a musket at the turkey on her left.

"That's right," Gwen said. "Daddy told me."

Jack glanced at Genna who stood a few feet away chatting to Billy. She had also heard Gwen call her father Daddy.

"What's your area of expertise?"

Now that's an interesting question. "I'm writing about homosexuality."

"A memoir?" asked the Judge, bestirring himself and turning, his eyebrow arched an inch or more.

"Not exactly."

The Judge sipped his Chivas. "Handbook?"

"I'm in the history of science." Jack nipped his own drink and felt in the growing silence a whooshing drop in air pressure as everyone in the room turned towards him.

Carolyn's youngest sister, Ellen, said, "That's so interesting. Tell all, Jack."

"I'm reviewing the new emphasis on genetics in homosexuality." Ellen and the others stared blankly. "The so-called gay gene, and what the societal implications would be if the existence of a gay gene could actually be established."

"And what would that be?" the Judge asked.

"Depends how you feel about homosexuals." Jack glanced at Genna, who was silently shaking her head no, which he ignored. "Not long ago, Frances Crick—who won the Nobel Prize with Watson, the double helix guys?—Crick said he thought pregnant women could have their fetuses' DNA tested, and if they discovered it carried the gay gene, they could choose to abort and no one would blame them. Now, most people think that Frances Crick is a quack, but still."

"Do you?" the Judge asked.

"Do I what?"

"Think he's a quack?"

"Yes, I do."

The Judge nodded.

"What if the military decided to test the blood of new recruits before allowing them to enlist as a way of screening out homosexuals? Would that be constitutional, Judge? An invasion of privacy?"

"I don't think homosexuals should be allowed in the military," the Judge answered. "Too much fun in the showers. "

"What," Jack continued, knowing he was being baited but rising to it anyway, "about other employers? If the military can test, why not Anheuser-Busch? You wouldn't want homosexuals getting near those proud Clydesdales. What if HMOs could screen out homosexuality as a pre-existing medical condition, citing higher HIV infection rates? Or women carrying a gene that indicated risk factors for breast cancer, years, even decades before the disease developed. What if insurers could screen them out?"

Although his hands appeared steady at his side, Jack could feel them shaking. What the hell? He glanced at Genna, who said to everyone listening, which by now was the entire room. "Jack gets a little worked up about these things."

"Understandably," Billy said. "Now let's eat; I'm sure the soup is ready."

They entered the dining room, and what a splendid table awaited them, a groaner, twenty-two places. Lalique crystal, sterling flatware engraved with ornate G's, a six-headed candelabra supplemented by so many single tapers blazing around the paneled room it could have been a wake, Jack thought, or a seance to raise the spirit of his departed mother-in-law, Doris. Who had died, he suddenly remembered and wanted to smack himself in the head, of breast cancer.

Assigned seats were indicated on name cards on each antique Havilland setting. Jack pocketed his: Dr. Jack Barish. Couples were seated opposite each other, with Billy's family at the head of the table, with Carolyn at the foot, half a time zone away. The teenagers were grouped near Carolyn, with the entire table arranged by age and the respect it was due; the Judge sat on Billy's right, opposite Gwen. Jack was between Gwen and Carolyn's mother, Betty, opposite Genna, who sat between Daddy and Carolyn's father, Earnest. When everyone had taken a place behind their chairs, Billy said, "Will everyone please join hands?"

Jack glanced across the glittering table at Genna who rolled her eyes. There was whispering then aspirated laughter from the teenage end of the table, one of the twins and Simon, from the sound of things. Jack wondered what they'd said and wished he were sitting with the kids. Then he took Betty's long-fingered left hand in his right, and Gwen's short, bejeweled fingers in his left.

"Lord," Billy began, "bless this house and all its inhabitants on this day of thanks giving. We are especially grateful for the presence of loved ones who have traveled a long way to be with us."

Jack smiled across the table at his wife. Damn nice of Billy.

"We'd also like to give thanks, as we sit down to this feast, for the memory of loved ones no longer with us, who cannot be here today for this meal. May my mother Doris, enjoy her turkey with you in Heaven. Amen."

Many voices murmured, "Amen." Jack released Gwen and Betty's hands, wondering what Gwen must think of dear departed Doris and celestial fowl being mentioned, what the etiquette of that was. He held the chair for Gwen. Watching him from across the table, the Judge said, "You know, if Doris is up in Heaven eating turkey, which I doubt, I bet she asked for the smallest portion of all the heavenly host. My wife, perhaps you remember," the old boy winked at Jack, apparently forgiving the lecture in front of the hearth, "ate less than anyone I ever met. It was unnatural."

Then the Judge sat and the maids circling the table swooped in to collect soup bowls. When the bowls returned, filled with consommé, Genna leaned towards him across the crystal, the silver, the burning tapers. "No matzo balls." She grinned. "*Tant pis*."

✦ ✦ ✦

After Simon ate slices of turkey awash in a river of gravy the color and consistency of his poop the time he was sick in Mexico, but not cranberry sauce, nor the stuffing which was studded with oysters, gag me; oven-baked mashed potatoes decorated with that orange spice, what was it; yams sprinkled with brown sugar and belly button marshmallows, now you're talking; and that weird string bean and cream of mushroom casserole that Mom sometimes made; then apple and pumpkin pies topped with ice cream or whipped cream, both if you wanted it, for at Uncle Billy's Thanksgiving more was not only more, more was better, so that even the most ordinary foods were combined with something extraordinary; he followed his cousins upstairs to their suite of rooms, which was two bedrooms with this amazing bathroom in between, and told them he was gay.

He hadn't planned to. At least the conscious portion of his brain was astonished when the word popped out of his mouth moments after they closed Tara's door.

"I'm gay," he began, as if it were no big deal, as if he were saying he was cold, so please turn up the heat.

"You're kidding," Tara said. "Right?"

She sat beside him on her brass four-poster with its silk spread and matching pink pillows.

"He's not kidding, you stupid cow," Nikki shot at her.

Boy, did she have a mouth.

"Why would he be kidding?" Nikki sprawled near Lizzie on the pale pink carpet. She turned to Simon. "Are you?"

"Who you calling cow, Horseface?" Tara asked.

"Cow, tits like udders."

"Least I have tits." Tara's full lips parted to reveal a mouthful of perfect teeth; everything about Tara was perfect. "You know," Tara continued, "we had to stop riding lessons because other families kept trying to saddle Nikki. It was so embarrassing."

Simon caught Lizzie's eye. One of the delights of visiting was how much the twins fought, their insults an art form he and Lizzie repeated for weeks afterwards.

"So," Nicole asked, "are you kidding or not?"

"I'm not kidding."

"Does that mean," Tara grinned at her twin, then turned back to him, "that if I put my hand on your Willie, nothing will happen?"

"Something will happen." Simon laughed. "I'll knock it away."

"That proves it," Nikki called from the floor. "All the other guys, when Tara puts her hand on their Willies at school dances, their eyes roll back and their Willies get big."

"Not everyone." Tara threw back her head, exposing her ballerina neck. She was such a pretty girl. "Sean Williams' Willie is tiny."

"Oh, Tara, oh Tara!" Nikki moaned, and thrashed around on the floor. "You're sooo beautiful."

"How many Willies have you touched?" Lizzie asked, the question coming out as a single word, HowmanyWillieshaveyoutouched?

"Lots," Tara said.

"Oodles of Willies," Nikki cried. "She's the Willie queen of St. Anne's."

"Bow down, Dude." Tara rose and extended her hand. "Queen Willie the First."

"Bow down, Dude," Nicole shouted, and knee-walked towards her sister, "and the queen will kiss your Willie."

"Ooh," Simon said in his too-high, too-excited voice, "that's so nasty."

"What about you?" Nikki asked, "how many Willies have you touched, not counting your own?"

"His own, he touches like fifty times a day," Lizzie called, getting in the game.

You little bitch, thought Simon. "More than you."

"Not me," Nikki said. "I don't touch Willies. That's my sister."

"Fuck you, Nikki," Tara shouted.

"Don't you wish," Nikki shot back.

"Then lots more than Tara," Simon said and hoped Lizzie, who was looking at him like he was crazy, would keep her mouth shut around Mom and Dad, or he'd get her back, that was for sure.

"That's easy," Tara said, "because I haven't really touched any."

"Liar," Nicole shouted, and Simon didn't know who to believe. "What about J.D. Harris's Willie?"

"Shut up, Nikki," Tara cried. "You are so mean."

She was mean, Simon thought, and had been since they were little.

"What about Aunt Genna and Uncle Jack?" Tara asked. "Do they know?"

Simon nodded.

"And they don't care?" Nikki asked, that mean edge muscling into her voice.

"They say they don't." Simon still didn't quite believe it.

"I bet they do," Nikki said, "and they're being nice."

"Our mom would have a cow," Tara said.

"She already did!" cried Nikki.

"Fuck you, Horsey!" Tara tossed a pillow at her twin's head, then they were pillow-fighting like they used to when they were little. After he'd nailed Lizzie, pow, upside the head, she shouted, "Simon, you always hit too hard. You're such an asshole!"

To aggravate Lizzie (for yelling at him in front of their cousins), and because he really had hit her too hard, even if he wouldn't admit it, Simon said, "I really love my sister." He wrapped her in a bear hug from which Lizzie struggled to escape. "Ain't she purty?"

"Jerk," Lizzie muttered, but her heart wasn't in it, and the cousins sat on Tara's bed in comfortable, nostalgic silence.

Then Simon said, "You can tell your parents, you know."

"Really?" Tara smiled her beautiful smile.

"Really." Simon nodded and felt it, this need to tell his family, to be as large as his appetite before the Thanksgiving meal. "I wish you would."

chapter 11

Friday morning the family splashed madly in the Holidome pool. Still feeling stuffed—that turkey, those candied yams!—Genna opted to skip breakfast and waved goodbye to Jack and the kids from the Jacuzzi. Lolling in the hot water, bubbles beating against her bottom—that pie, that oyster dressing!—Genna watched a bead of condensate wiggle across the steamy skylight above her head. The droplet enlarged and slid, gathering size and speed then plopped into the bubbling spa. Now there's a lesson, Genna thought. The great circle of life. Maturation, brief escape, heady freedom, then back in the soup. Last night, for hours, she'd tried to work up the courage to tell Daddy she wanted to speak to him alone. Finally, as the party was ending, she'd found him in front of the hearth. Forty-four years old and her heart yammered like a girl's.

She blurted out what she wanted, and Daddy's eyebrow arced like a wave. "Dare I mention you're talking to me now?"

She glanced nervously around. Carolyn stood near the couch with her sisters, three life studies for the same sketch: dark hair, long legs, button noses.

"I'd like to talk to you alone, Daddy."

"If it's a loan, you'd do better with Billy."

"It's not a loan." Now she was grinning. "Would I ask you for money?"

"Too clever by half, aren't you?"

Didn't take cleverness.

"What is it then?" His eyebrow arced again nearly into his hair line. "Fatherly advice?"

He made it sound preposterous. Why had he desired this total abnegation of parenting? She didn't believe it was the same for Billy, and she felt the blade of that familiar sword. Daddy continued, more gently, "Are you in some sort of trouble, dear?"

Across her mind's sky, a single, towed banner. Jack had an affair last year, and I'm afraid he's starting another.

What would Daddy say? Been there, done that?

"I'd just like some time with you. Lunch tomorrow, my treat?"

He grinned, relieved to be back on more solid ground. He named Ladue's most venerable restaurant. "Shall we say one, one-fifteen?"

"Whichever."

"One, it is. You remember where?"

She nodded. "Clayton and Price."

"I'll reserve a table. And Genna." He winked. "Do try to be on time."

Genna rose, dripping, and headed for their room to plan her outfit. At precisely one o'clock, she stepped into Busch's Grove, having abandoned Jack and the kids to the pool and MTV.

"Why can't I come?" Simon had demanded. "I'd like a fancy lunch."

That boy, she thought, stepping towards the maitre d', who was on the phone, never willingly skipped a meal.

"Because Mom's having some father-daughter time," Lizzie said, with a wistful look at Jack.

"We could get our own table," Simon said.

"No," said Jack.

"It's not fair," Simon declared and she watched the tendon bulge on Jack's neck.

"Courage," she whispered as she kissed him goodbye.

"You owe me." Jack brushed his lips against hers. "Tell the old boy hi."

"Gordon, table for two," she said as the maitre d' replaced the receiver and looked up quizzically. Wasn't she dressed well enough? "Is Judge Gordon here?"

The maitre d' shook his head fussily. "Your reservation is one-fifteen."

Daddy—she thought, eyeing the maitre d's white shirt, black pants—You old skunk.

At one-fourteen—she was paying close attention, unaccustomed as she was to arriving first—Daddy sauntered in and looked around, dark hair combed impeccably back from his face. She wondered if he still used hair creme, if they still manufactured his brand, or was Daddy bonded to mega-hold gel, like Simon. When she was growing up, Daddy had looked quite a bit like that most atypical of St. Louis celebrities, T. S. Eliot. For years he cultivated the resemblance, down to the rimless glasses. Daddy had long since shifted to contacts, or had he tried that Lasik procedure he'd been talking up last year? He spied her from across the elegant room—white guests, still all black servers as in days of yore—raised two fingers in greeting, then strode towards her with impressive energy. No shuffling baby steps for Daddy. Genna rose and offered her cheek, which he gallantly kissed.

"You're late, Daddy. I've been here since one."

"I'm not late. I always told Doris fifteen minutes early, too, except when I told her twenty. Now you know all my secrets."

I doubt it. They ordered cocktails, Chivas, one rock, for Daddy, white wine spritzer for Genna.

"What a girly-girl," he announced, when the drinks arrived. "Barely enough alcohol to souse a fly."

"I'm just drinking to keep you company."

He clinked his rocks glass against her fluted stem. "What say you really keep me company, eh, Genna?"

She ordered a scotch, which arrived with the first course. (If she were paying for Daddy's appetizer, Genna didn't see why she shouldn't have one, too. Her protein diet would start Monday.) Later, when she was in the ladies' room—it must have been then because she didn't see it happen—Daddy arranged for a third round which arrived with their entrees. By the time Daddy had consumed half his osso bucco, complaining it was a trifle tough today, she'd managed only a few nibbles of risotto. Chivas washed through her arteries as some distant estuary must have washed the prawns dotting her rice, like drowned raisins in the cream of wheat Doris had served all those lifetimes ago. Genna was half-plotzed, two-thirds, no five-sixths, which must have been what she wanted; there was no point matching Daddy unless the Land of Plotz was your destination. Now she'd arrived, and her fingers had no bones.

"Well, Genna." Daddy raised that rakish lash, oh arched inquisitor's brow. "Ready to ask whatever it is?"

"My biological father." She hesitated, not wanting to look too closely, but eager to see the pain Doris had predicted would stain Daddy's face. If there wasn't any, not that she wanted Daddy to suffer, but she wanted to touch him a little, perhaps not as much as Billy... "Doris's first husband."

"Your progenitor." Daddy set down his cutlery. "As I suspected."

"Really?" She reeled through a river of scotch.

He took up his knife and fork. "I've been waiting all these years. Good God, Genna, haven't you wanted to know?"

"Of course." She was spinning, and for a moment Genna feared she was going to be sick in the middle of this memorable lunch. Then the river rushed on, and she added, "But Mom wouldn't tell me. When I asked..."

"You asked?"

Daddy clapped his hand to his forehead like a Victorian thespian enacting surprise.

"And what did she say, your mommy dearest?"

"It would hurt you too much." Genna brought Doris's face to mind, her elegant jaw and neck, and with it, her sense that Doris would have told her all if she'd asked at the end, "and how it wasn't fair, because 'you'd loved me as your own.'"

"Ah, Doris." Daddy threw back his scotch and looked around, Genna thought, for their waiter. "What a piece of work." He caught their gray-haired waiter's eye, halfway across the salon, raised his empty glass and twirled his index finger beside it. Satisfied that re-supply was forthcoming, he began, "She used to tell me when I asked, and I did, I assure you, that you'd told her you didn't want any information about—"

Daddy smiled, drawing it out.

"—Denny Sweetwater, 'because you loved me as your very own,' the only Daddy you ever wanted. Just like her, playing both sides."

"Doris was married to a man named Denny Sweetwater?"

Daddy sliced meat from his veal shank and raised the fork to his lips without changing hands, another example of what he'd always considered his superior manners. "Who said anything?" He chewed, swallowed and raised another shimmering shred of osso bucco. "About marriage?"

The waiter arrived with another Chivas, one rock, for Daddy. He glanced her way—she didn't know what showed on her face, Denny Sweetwater?—but Daddy caught the waiter's hand. "Charlie, another for my daughter."

"I'll be too drunk to drive."

"I'll drive you."

"You're too—"

"Never." Daddy speared a cube of oven-roasted potato, slick with gravy, and brought it to his lips. "Now." He popped the potato through. "Any questions?"

Genna thought of all the questions flapping through her mind like the small birds she'd glimpsed recently driving from Tipton to

Cincinnati. Hundreds and hundreds, thousands, so many they looked like black bees against the sky.

"Tell me how you knew I was going to ask."

"Sweetwater, you know, was one of them. The pink-socks brigade."

"Daddy."

"A homosexual, like Simon."

"What do you mean, like Simon?"

"He hasn't told you yet?" Daddy sipped his Chivas, one rock. "He announced it to his cousins last night and asked them to tell their parents, which of course Nicole did. What a mouth on that little bitch. Takes after Doris. Billy called me this morning. Surely," there went his eyebrow again, "I'm not telling you anything you didn't know?"

"Of course I know. But I didn't realize he told the whole family."

"Why not? Sweetwater was very out front for his day too, according to your mother." Daddy wiped his lips and set his knife and fork, perfectly aligned, on the edge of his plate. Somehow, he'd finished his entire bucco, while she'd barely touched her lunch.

"Have you considered therapy? Billy tells me they're doing wonderful things; he read sexual orientation could be changed."

"I don't think so."

Their water boy approached with her third drink.

"What about shock therapy? Every time Simon has a homosexual thought, you plug his unit in an outlet."

"That's not funny."

"I suppose not."

Their water boy set down her drink and hurried off, mincing a bit, swinging his hips, and she could almost hear Daddy's thoughts—or were those hers—wondering if the water boy was one of them, too. She sipped the undiluted top quarter-inch of her scotch.

"Anyhoo, when Billy called this morning, I was certain you wanted to ask about Sweetwater. Jack must be anxious for an explanation that doesn't involve his side. A big strong jock like Jack, this must be hard on him."

She eyed Daddy's long face. He was really very smart, if also mean. Well-matched with Doris. Jack had always claimed the old boy didn't like him, didn't like Jews, and she'd only half-believed him. With greater assurance than she probably felt, Genna said, "No, Jack's fine with it. It's not what we hoped for; I mean, it makes Simon's life harder, especially at the high school in Tipton. But it is what it is. Simon's Simon, just as Tara and Nicole are Tara and Nicole, and not each other."

Daddy's eyebrow arced, as if to declare, If you believe that my dear, I'll pretend I do, too. He raised his Chivas, one rock, and she knocked her stubby glass against it.

"To what is," he said.

"To what is."

"And now," Daddy added, "if you're not too schnockered, I'll tell you what I know about your pater veritas, Denny Sweetwater."

✦ ✦ ✦

When they set out from the Holiday Inn for the long drive east, Genna sat up front beside him. She'd returned yesterday from lunch drunker than he'd ever seen her except for a memorable camping trip years ago. The first night, beside a blathering stream, they pitched a new Northface dome, purchased for this, their first backpacking adventure. In the heady redwood-scented dark, they put away a bottle of B & B then wobbled beneath the velvet sky hollering whoopee. Genna was so intoxicated she kept falling, swearing she wasn't drunk, oh no, that darn freeze-dried food! In the middle of the night, when she got up to pee, she lost her footing and tumbled into the stream bed. Roused by her cries, Jack hauled Genna off the slick stones then held her hand to keep her from tipping over again while she squatted to relieve herself. The next morning, she moaned and groaned, carrying a heavy pack up and down the switchbacked trail, swearing she'd never touch B & B again, which, he believed, she hadn't.

"Denny Sweetwater," she murmured, as their mud-and-snows sang over the highway, Go-in home, go-in home. She'd told him the name but not much more, when she returned yesterday from lunch. "Would you have married me if my name was Genna Sweetwater?"

"I was so wild for you, I would have married you if you were named Engelbert Humperdinck." He touched her hand, which rested on the arm of her captain chair. For a moment, before looking back to I-70's three lanes roaring with holiday traffic, he wondered, After what's happened, can that possibly be true? Yes, he thought, and added, "I still am."

"Doris and Denny Sweetwater," Genna began, her voice pitched low to escape the kids' radar, "were close friends in college. She went to Webster, you know, in St. Louis."

"I didn't know."

Jack glanced in the rearview. In the captain chair behind Genna, Lizzie was hooked up to her Discman, reading, her head bopping to some punk rhythm. In the way back, Simon hibernated in a blanketed cave.

"According to Daddy, Sweetwater was an actor and a singer." Genna's eyes met his, then danced away. "Outlandish, Daddy said, a bad boy, who scandalized the campus by drinking and taking drugs…"

"That doesn't sound so scandalous," Jack said. "Even I did that."

"Not in 1959. And by being openly homosexual."

Got me there.

"And Doris, who was always something of an ice queen…"

"The old boy said that?"

"I'm saying that. There was this quality about my mother, an icy elegance, as if she never got laid enough…"

"I met your mother."

"I know."

"You keep talking as if I hadn't."

"Jack, will you just listen?"

An SUV, one of those mammoth Expeditions, zoomed up behind them and flashed its fuck-you lights. Asshole, Jack thought, and accelerated.

"Doris, who was a virgin—"

"How do you know?"

"I'm speculating—lusted after Denny Sweetwater down to the marrow of her skinny bones."

Jack would have loved to watch her face, but the SUV was on his tail.

"For years she watched him screwing guys, which, knowing Doris, must have made her tremendously jealous. According to Daddy, everyone said they looked like the perfect couple, but he wouldn't sleep with her, only his boys. The spring of their senior year, just before or after graduation, Doris got Denny drunk, or maybe he got her drunk, and they did it once or twice or who knows how many times, for old times sake, or because they loved each other, or maybe he threw her a charity fuck…"

A charity fuck? Jack glanced over his shoulder at Lizzie, who hadn't heard.

"Then Sweetwater moved away, and she never saw, or even spoke to him again, Daddy thought, and Doris—who had her own notions about many things, and Catholic relatives on her mother's side—decided to have me, come hell or damnation. That's when Daddy rode up wearing a white hat for the one and only time in his life. He was older than Doris, already a lawyer. Their families knew each other and maybe he'd always wanted her, or maybe he watched her grow up and felt responsible. 'But I made,' he said, can't you just see him," Genna made her Judge face, an eyebrow arching into her hair-line, "'a semi-honest woman of your mother, and she never let me forget it.'"

"What do you think he meant by that?"

Genna shrugged and scrunched down in her seat. The driver of the Expedition flashed his brights again. Jack swore and moved to the center lane. As soon as the Expedition passed, he moved behind it and pulled up close, flashing his own brights. He stayed there for a mile or two, doing eighty-five, snatches of his impromptu Thanksgiving speech about the gay gene flashing through his mind.

"It's really immature," Genna said, "driving like that."

"A taste of his own asshole medicine." Jack slowed and changed lanes. "Do you want to find Sweetwater?"

"I can't decide. What do you think?"

Jack glanced across at his wife, who seemed to be disappearing into herself. "Why wouldn't you?"

"So many reasons."

"If you hadn't wanted to know, you wouldn't have asked the old boy in the first place."

"That's what Daddy said, too. So you think I should call him?"

"You have a number for your father, and you're asking if I think you should call him?"

"I don't have a number. I don't even know if he's alive."

"Of course you should call him. Did the Judge know where he moved to?"

"He thought California." Genna lowered her seat, curled into it, and pulled a blanket up around her. "I'm going to try to get some sleep now. I hope you don't mind."

Genna placed one pillow behind her, a second over her eyes to block the light. She sighed, and Jack turned his attention to the road. Ten or fifteen miles further east, he passed the big, bad Expedition, stopped on the shoulder, right directional still blinking, an Illinois state trooper parked behind it, bubble gum lights whirling. Yes, thought Jack, sometimes life is good.

chapter 12

When Simon returned to Tipton after Thanksgiving break, everything had changed. There were two, not one, two, phone messages from Peter. Ms. Cherry, the drama teacher had posted the name of the spring musical, *Once Upon a Mattress*, which Simon had never even heard of, but Dad said was funny. Years ago, he'd seen a TV version with this actress, Carol Someone, whom Simon had never heard of, either, and Dad rolled his eyes, like Simon was some kind of retard. Simon knew more about movies, music, and actors in one tiny corner of his brain than had ever pooped inside Dad's entire fat head. But Dad was so clueless, he didn't know he was clueless. He was always trying to discuss music with Simon's friends when he drove them around until Simon wanted to die or piss his pants, or better yet, Dad's pants.

Early in the fall, he told Dad, and very politely too, how his friends hated it so much when he acted friendly, they wanted to barf. Dad got all wounded, his eyes big and mopey like Sam's, with that vein thing popping on his neck. He said he had great rapport, whatever that meant, with his students, who weren't much older than Simon's friends, so he didn't believe they wanted to barf, thank you very much. All fall, driving them around, he insisted on chatting. It was so embarrassing, with Dad acting hip in front of his friends, that Simon swore he'd rather walk than ride with Dad, which no one believed; everyone knew Simon hated to walk further than he had to.

Luckily, Simon thought, with a glance at Dad, who occupied the passenger seat of the Camry, while he, Simon Blake Barish, luxuriated behind the wheel, that was another of the fabulous changes that had occurred since they'd returned from St. Louis. On Tuesday, he'd started Drivers' Ed. In three weeks, as soon as class was over, he could take his road test. He'd been hounding Mom—Simon had raised Mom-hounding to a high art—and she'd promised to make the appointment. If everything worked, he'd have his license in time to share the drive to Florida, and he would never again ride the bus with all those losers.

"Simon," Dad said. "The light changed."

Damn. Simon jammed the accelerator; the Camry burst forward. It was Wednesday, early dismissal, and they were out in the country. Dad didn't need to make a big deal out of everything. But that was Dad's deal, to make a big, hairy deal. Simon turned south onto SR-127. The left side of the road was crop land, brown and gloomy this time of year. The right side grew houses. Simon grasped the wheel at ten and two and drove thirty-five miles per hour.

"Turn right," Dad said, "the next time you can."

Simon nodded. An eighteen-wheeler raced towards them. Simon's palms poured sweat. God, how he hated trucks, so large and noisy, always calling attention to themselves. His hands were sopped sponges squeezed by the wheel. The semi roared past inches from his side, roaring like twenty trucks, like an army of trucks, so close the slipstream nearly sucked Simon's eyes out of his head. He screamed, "I hate trucks!"

A moment later, Dad said, "You can probably speed up, son."

Heart thumping, Simon glanced down. Twenty miles per hour.

"Look straight ahead and pretend they're not there," Dad added gently. "That's what I do."

A half mile further, Simon turned onto Ogden Road and pulled over.

"No," Dad said, "you drive."

Simon looked at his father's nose, a flesh-colored slope, humped like a mogul. "I have to be at work soon."

Dad grinned. "Then you better drive faster."

Simon had never driven himself to work. Mom, who usually took him out, limited lessons to back roads.

"You can do it, you're good. A little bit chicken-shit," Dad grinned again, "but that's better than reckless."

Simon dried his palms on his jeans. He checked the driver side mirror, no one, flipped on his blinker and pulled onto Ogden Road, headed towards Tipton.

✦ ✦ ✦

At ten-fifteen, Simon still wore his Fry Guy clothes. He'd just gotten home and needed to shower. His feet throbbed as if a giant had stomped them. His hair, his clothes, Simon reeked of grease, but he needed to call Peter, who lived alone with his mom, before it got any later. Peter's dad, who drove trucks, had moved out years ago. Peter saw him once a month. Simon wondered what that would be like, if Dad were gone, being the man of the house. My mom is overprotective, Peter said last night on the phone, 'cause I'm all she has.

Simon considered checking his homework planner, but that would only depress him. He raised his arms. Ugh, a whale's armpits, stinky and ripe. He dug through the crap on his floor, dirty clothes and balled up Kleenex from blowing his nose and who knows what else, until he found the purple cordless. He wasn't supposed to make calls after ten on school nights, but what Dad didn't know. Dad used to rip him for calling kids Friday afternoon or Saturday morning for sleepovers, as if that was why they said no, all those skinny boys in his fifth grade Montessori class, who liked sports and had known each other since they were three or four. If only he'd called Wednesday, they would have wanted to be his best friend and come over to play Barbie.

But Simon could see maybe Dad wasn't totally wrong, but not for the reasons Dad thought. Simon didn't call until Saturday morning because at ten years old he was smart enough to know those boys just didn't like him It was less painful, he realized now, to wait until they had other plans, instead of being rejected simply because they thought he was weird.

Simon touched in Peter's number. They could order pizza, see a movie. Afterwards, they'd hang out in Java, order chai or hot chocolate. Maybe Peter would hold his hand under the table. Or they could sit close on one of the couches and Peter would cover his mouth to hide his crooked tooth, which was really so cute, both the tooth and Peter's shyness. It would feel like a date, wouldn't that be something, not to be the freak all the goddamn time. Just two guys on a date, a guy and a guy, you know what I mean?

Peter's mother answered. "Oh, hi, Simon. I'm afraid Peter's asleep."

Was she lying? "I just got home from work, or I wouldn't have called so late."

"Where do you work?"

"Burger King."

Simon thought he heard another voice. Maybe she was going to let them talk. Then Peter's mother said, "I'll tell Peter you called. I know he'll be sorry to miss you."

Simon hung up. It was nice of Peter's mom to say that, I know he'll be sorry to miss you, as if maybe she approved, as if maybe the path of true love which Simon longed to follow, Aladdin and the Princess, Brad Pitt and Jennifer, wasn't always blocked by forests of thorns.

Simon removed his visor and Fry Guy shirt, and dropped them as a lady in waiting might let slip a lace hankie. He stepped over socks and boxers, the heaped jeans and clean shirts he'd tried on and rejected, opened his bottom desk drawer where he hid the cache of color pictures downloaded off the Web. Young Studs with Giant Cocks dot com. Simon thumbed through his sweethearts until he found the boy he loved best, a Leo DiCaprio look-alike: same smirky smile, blond tips and a boner like a frozen garden hose.

Simon locked his door, reclined on his bed and reached for the pump bottle of dry skin cream he'd filched from Mom. The unzzzzzzzipping of his jeans got him hard. A rocket emerging from its silo, a broom stick he could fly straight to the parted lips of the boy in the picture. When he was younger, Simon measured his erections against a twelve-inch ruler. Was six enough? Was eight good? Ten too much? Stiff dreaming. There was a world of cocks outside Tipton, and someday he'd touch them all. Didn't that cream feel good, didn't his hand! Oh yes, it did, it did.

✦ ✦ ✦

Jack hadn't seen Marla since Election Night, except for one morning early last week. He'd driven to the high school to drop off a notebook Simon had forgotten, and before he knew it, he was walking past the guidance office just to see if Marla was there. A trio of students waited outside her door: one white kid; a light-skinned black guy; and a pimply blonde, who couldn't have been more than fifteen—one year older than Lizzie!—but who looked six months pregnant. Jack stuck his big head in the outer office and waved. Marla smiled and waved back, then Jack was on his way feeling he'd gotten away with something.

So he was more than a little worried—but admit it, Jack, excited, too—to discover a note in his mailbox Thursday morning: Call Marla Lindstrom, then the number of the high school guidance office. The message had been taken yesterday afternoon by the department secretary, when he was out driving with Simon.

Jack swiveled his desk chair ninety degrees to the right, then one hundred and eighty left, stared at the bleak November sky. No, December first. Simon hadn't mentioned trouble at school, but he wouldn't. This could mean anything, or nothing. Maybe he should phone Genna, halfway across the central quad, to tell her Marla had called. Genna might understandably ask why he hadn't called Marla to find out what she wanted? Might not calling his wife first sound like a muted admission of guilt, or at least of desire?

But Jack didn't want to be calling Marla or any other woman without Genna knowing about it. He'd done that last year, and although the sex, what there was of it, had been exhilarating, and for a time he believed he was in love and that was even more exciting, the entire experience, even before he'd confessed and everything went ka-boom, made him feel his brain was a zygote undergoing meiosis along the spindle of his heart. Twin Jacks in one body. Clean Jack, Jack Dirty. Here the smile for his wife and kids after he'd gotten off the phone with his lover; here the smile on the days he hadn't. Before he ended things, he was beginning to confuse which was which, and experienced both smiles as equally inauthentic, as if his one true heart had ceased to exist.

Or so it had seemed at the time.

Jack rotated in his chair, then dialed the guidance office. When Marla's voicemail picked up, he realized how hard he'd been gripping the phone.

"This is Jack Barish," he hurled into electronic space. "Simon's father."

He disconnected and tried to clear his mind. For several weeks, his own work had been going well, having progressed from a hazy notion to an actual plan which linked his earliest work in Galtonian eugenics to current research. He wanted to determine—and was preparing grants to fund the research—what percentage of prospective parents would employ a test for the gay gene if it became available. He speculated the figure would be fairly high: 10

to 20 percent of the population that would consider genetic testing in the first place. Of that population, he wondered what percentage would consider terminating a pregnancy if the gay gene were found. It was a complicated question and a complicated answer. The inclination to perform such testing, which presupposed a desire to know, would indicate that quite a significant percentage might want to terminate the pregnancy. Why else would they want to know? Yet if there were a genetic, and hence a familial link to homosexuality (as every study had shown), might not such couples, who would have known gay family members or recognized same sex sexual impulses in themselves, be more likely to embrace such offspring? Or might the opposite be true?

What would the results be if the gene tested for were a predisposition to alcoholism? That also ran in families, yet some kids inherited a thirst, others didn't. If a religious ban on abortion were factored out, how many prospective parents, themselves alcoholics, or the children or siblings, the grandchildren of alcoholics, would re-roll the genetic dice to create offspring without a desire for John Barleycorn? What if the trait being tested for were a propensity for criminal violence, such as that associated with an extra Y chromosome? What if a genetic link could be established for individuals unlikely to honor their fathers and mothers, or to be 50 percent more likely covet their neighbor's wife, as he suspected his own father had, or their son's guidance counselor?

O, brave new world. Then the phone chirped. Jack stared at the new beige handset and decided to let it brrr-ing or warble, whatever it was phones did these days. On the fourth whatever, his answering machine interceded. His outgoing message, then Marla's voice: "Jack, Marla. I'm at my office until four."

On the top left corner, the message minder mutated from a crimson zero to a crimson one. Jack stroked the hump of his nose with his right index finger. Ridiculous, what if Marla was trying to reach him for something important? And what was he so guilty about?

He dialed the guidance office.

"Why, Jack, or is this Simon's father?"

"One and the same." He touched the bridge of his nose. "Everything all right?"

"Simon's fine. I would have said more in my message." She hesitated, and in the silence he could see her blue eyes, bright as a bird's. "But I didn't know who would hear it."

"Just me."

"Could you come by around four?"

"Let me check." He flipped to today's page, though he knew he was free. "Four's good. Should I bring Genna?"

"I don't think that's necessary." She laughed. "See you at four."

Later, after he'd finished preparing his two o'clock, Jack decided to call Webster College, which he'd determined was now Webster University. It had occurred to him—not because he was feeling guilty about Marla—that the way to find Denny Sweetwater was through Webster's development office. If he'd learned anything in academia, it was that universities made it their business to stay in touch with alumni, just in case there was money to be wheedled out of them.

He made a few notes. Doris had died in 1982, at the age of forty-five. Subtracting twenty-three years, put her in the class of 1959, which sounded about right; Genna was born February 12, 1960. That meant Denny Sweetwater was also the class of 1959. All he had to do was reach the Webster alumni office and convince them to share contact information for Dennis Sweetwater. Then what? Genna would be grateful? The mystery of Simon's homosexuality would be explained, with no genetic input from the Barish clan? (Wouldn't Russ be relieved.) A mini-origin revealed, not of species, but of sexuality? Jack swiveled in his chair, one hundred and eighty degrees right then the same half arc in reverse. For every action, an equal and opposite reaction. What a bitch to mistrust your own motives, or to be fully aware of them.

He asked directory assistance for the main number of Webster University and added it to his research notes for Denny Sweetwater. Did he have time to call before his two o'clock class? If he hurried.

✦ ✦ ✦

When Jack barreled into the house just before dinner, she wondered where he had been. Oh, she knew him. She could read his broad face, with its Roman-by-way-of-the-Ukraine nose, like a second grader's haiku. And what did she read when he entered the kitchen (she was reducing the cream sauce for her boneless chicken with shitake mushrooms), wrapped his arms around her from behind, and kissed her just below her ear? Oh, no, what's wrong? It wasn't the first time he'd grabbed her like this, a two-handed squeeze of her breasts, memories of sleepy Sunday morning intercourse falling over her like a shadow, Jack pressed up against her from behind.

"Glass of wine?" Jack slid towards the fridge. He poured them each a glass from an open bottle, Chardonnay sparkling like sunlight. "I've got something to tell you."

"Oh?"

She sipped her wine. Jack gulped his. "Don't look so worried."

"The last time you had something to tell me, Jack."

His eyes flipped, as if they were diving into a shallow pool. She sometimes forgot how blue they were, Jack's eyes. Why hadn't the kids inherited blue eyes, what about that recessive gene business?

"No, this is good news, I called the Webster alumni office to see if they had an address for Denny Sweetwater."

"What made you do that?"

"Love."

Now her eyes must be the ones twirling. "Did they?"

"I think so, but they wouldn't give it out."

Jack refilled his glass, and she felt a beating in her chest, lub-dub, dub-lub, as if emotions long denied were waking.

"They confirmed Dennis Sweetwater was the class of 1959, and said," his eyes were sparkling now, "if we wanted to send Mister Sweetwater a letter, they'd be happy to forward it. So I figure we write one, maybe enclose a picture or two, and if he's alive, and I get the feeling he is,"

"Why's that?"

Her right hand, which held the wine glass, was shaking. Forty-four years old, it was such a surprise.

"Because when I mentioned his name, there was this pause."

"You're making that up."

"I'm not. And anyway, whoever I was talking to, this sweet young thing, checked their database, and if Mister Sweetwater were deceased, she wouldn't have told me to send a letter, now would she?"

She sipped the wine and peered at Jack through batted lashes. "I guess not." Imagine, flirting with her own husband. "Against the code of behavior for sweet young things."

"That's right."

Genna set down her glass and the slotted spoon with which she'd been stirring the sauce, and hugged him, pressing into Jack, her breasts flattening against his chest. Her hands reached around his broad back, then rooted in the back pockets of his jeans. Saturday night, she thought, with the kids gone, not Sunday morning.

Simon pounded up the stairs from the family room, trailed by the dog. "Awww." He burst into the kitchen. "Mom and Dad are making out. Isn't that sweet?"

Sometimes, she wanted to kill that boy.

When the kids were in bed, and Jack had turned off the family room television—*Sports Center* must be over, she thought and glanced at the clock, Yes, eleven-thirty—she listened to Jack mount the stairs and remembered that ghost story from all those years ago in summer camp. Who stole my golden arm? Who stole my golden aaaarm? You did. She remembered lying in her girlhood bed on

Kingsbury Court listening to the creaky stairs, thinking of herself as the second-best loved child. If they were coming to kiss anyone goodnight, it wouldn't be her. How old must she have been, eight, nine? And even if they did kiss her, it would be after Billy, who was Daddy and Mommy's favorite. Listening for Jack—had he turned towards the kitchen to grind his morning coffee? No, he was hurrying towards their bedroom—she picked up the novel she'd set down some time ago just so she could peer up over it to see if he registered the night gown she was wearing.

"Hey," he said, coming towards the bed. "Haven't seen that in a while."

"What?"

"The nightgown you only wear when you're hoping to have an orgasm."

"Jack Barish, you have the romantic I.Q. of a gnat."

He grinned. "You're not only wearing that come-hither nightgown, in which you look incredibly beautiful and sexy."

"That's better."

He sat beside her. "But your book? Upside down."

She set it on the night stand without checking to see if he were right. "I thought you'd never get here." She leaned forward and kissed him, sucking his lower lip between hers. "I'm really, really grateful you called Webster."

"And now you want to thank me?"

She nodded and felt her heart flutter.

"What if I write the letter to Webster?"

She slid her hand from his shoulder down his arm to his lap. His erection pressed against his jeans like an eager puppy. He pushed her against the pillows and lay down beside her. Through the satin of her negligee, his thumb and forefinger coaxed her nipple. She switched off her reading lamp; the room plunged into darkness. She fumbled at Jack's belt and felt his leg press hers apart.

"Are we back?"

He touched her. “Front and back.”

She found his eyes in the dim light. “You know what I mean, Jack.”

“Yep.” He snaked his finger into her panties. She moved against it and shuddered. “Yeppity-yep,” he said. “We are.”

chapter 13

In January, Simon tried out for the spring musical. He danced, he acted, he sang. His voice quaked during his monologue; his tree trunk legs trembled. But when he sang "Some Enchanted Evening," handing the sheet music to Donut, then coming in on key, on time, full-voiced, he blew the listeners away, he just knew it. He turned towards Ms. Cherry with the final note glowing in the practice room air as if high beams were reflecting off droplets of rain. She had a cute, round face, Ms. Cherry, ringed with curls. On her dark lashes, tears hung. Or maybe he only imagined the tears, but he was certain of what she said next, because he embraced those words for the next three days, through call-backs and all the rest, held on as if he were six and her words were his beloved blue blankie.

"That was so beautiful, Simon."

She clearly meant it, Ms. Cherry, who was only twenty-two, not much older, really, than he was; when the cast list appeared, he'd been picked for Sir Harry, who sang more than any other guy, including the most famous song, "I Love You Less."

That was two weeks ago; they'd rehearsed every day since. What timing! Simon had his license and except when Dad was being a dick, he took the Camry to school so he could drive himself home after rehearsal. Next year, when she started high school, Lizzie would ride with him; for now she was stuck with the moonfaced assholes. Not me, Simon thought, I'll never ride that freaking bus again.

He turned onto Cottage, two blocks from school, and cruised for a spot. Next year, he'd rent one in the school lot. Twenty-five dollars and seniors had dibs. This semester, he was stuck on the street. Although he already drove better than Dad—who talked too much, drifting from lane to lane in terrifying fashion until Simon exchanged looks with Mom, My God, did you see that?—the one thing he hadn't mastered was parallel parking. Instead, he arrived early to find a spot either just before or after a driveway.

He spotted one big enough for a dump truck. He slid towards it, shark-like, set the brake, and snapped off the engine. Dad was always yammering at him to turn off the heater and the radio, so they wouldn't drain the battery when he restarted the engine, and blah, blah, blah, but that, he thought, climbing out of the Camry, throwing his hip-bag strap over his shoulder, and bending to check his look in the side-view, was totally crap. He'd been leaving the heater and radio on since he started driving, and nothing bad had happened.

Simon began the three-block hike to school; the red velvet cuffs he'd added to his pants swished like skirts. It was seven-twenty, cold January, and his breath puffed like the cotton balls Dad's mother, Grandma Babs, removed her eye shadow with last month in Florida. When he was little, he watched her apply make-up whenever he visited. Eye-liner, shadow and mascara, liquid foundation, rouge, some weird metal thing-y to curl her lashes. A better show than any Saturday morning cartoon, except *He-Man*.

Simon approached the Smokers' Club, who were lined up, puffing like blowfish, across the street from school. What jerks, and not just because they smoked, which he would never do because it would ruin his voice, and without his voice, he would die. No, these kids were giant assholes. Even the girls made smoochy noises when he passed. And who else but a jerk would smoke right across from school, then act all surprised when even brain-dead Doctor Badger knew they smoked.

Hel-lo-oo!

Some days, Simon walked out of his way to avoid the Smokers. Some days, he'd had enough of their shit and walked right by. Today, there were four or five guy Smokers, two or three girls. This one guy, Nick Fleming, a senior, was the biggest dick of all. Until he got booted for smoking, he'd played basketball.

Hey, how did Coach find out?

Simon poked his index finger into his cheek.

You think he saw me across the street each morning? Nah, musta been the fat faggot.

"Hey, faggot-boy."

Right on cue.

"Look, here comes the faggot."

The other Smokers and the moonfaces who harassed him in the halls were butt ugly, but Nick Fleming was a hottie. Six-two, a cleft chin and black hair like Superman. He was rich, too. His father and uncles were the biggest builders in town. Simon saw their red, white, and blue sign everywhere: Fleming Construction. Nick went out with skinny Tina Murphy, who played Simon's love interest, Lady Larken. Before the opening curtain, what Ms. Cherry called back-story, Sir Harry had knocked her up. Yeah, right. They wanted to marry, but no one in the kingdom was allowed to until the Prince did. Only the Queen, the all-time possessive mommy, didn't want to lose her son, so she kept creating tests no girl could pass. In the second act, after the Swamp Princess won the Prince, Simon had to kiss Tina Murphy. They hadn't practiced The Kiss yet, but Simon suspected that Tina, who had a thin, sweet soprano, wasn't any more interested in getting started than he was.

"Hey, faggot," Nick Fleming said. "Want to suck my dick?"

Simon looked from Fleming, who was blocking his way, to the other Smokers. Tina stood to one side, embarrassed. Before rehearsals started he hadn't even known who she was. He almost said, If you really, really want me to, Dick. I mean, Nick. Instead, he answered, "No, thank you. And I'd rather be a faggot than an asshole."

Nick Fleming punched his shoulder.

"Leave him alone, Nick," Tina said.

Then the light changed and Simon started across the street to begin another jolly day at Tipton High.

✦ ✦ ✦

When fifth bell rang, Simon hurried to the auditeria to set down his hip bag at Rachel's table. On Mondays, Pizza Day, he tried to arrive early. Imagine his surprise when he discovered that not only wasn't he first at Rachel's table, but that the black hair and cat's eyes that looked so much like Rich's, features he'd been seeing in the hall or uptown in Tipton (sometimes he'd walk up close for a better look then spin away at the last moment), really was Rich, back from the dead, no, Indiana.

"Rich!" Simon exclaimed, an enormous grin splitting his face. "Whatcha doing here?"

Rich's eyes slowly closed and opened. "Waiting for lunch."

Simon's face hurt from grinning.

"My dad decided he couldn't live without me." Rich's eyes closed again then slowly opened, like a kitten's. "Actually, my mom decided she couldn't live with me, and it was Dad's turn."

"Cool." That's so sad, Simon thought. "Well, I'm glad to see you."

"Can you lend me a dollar?"

"No way." Simon grinned again. "But I'll buy you anything you want. I'm working at Burger King."

"Anything?"

Rich's eyes sparkled, but he didn't look happy. He rarely did, even when he was smiling. Then Simon remembered. Rich never had any money.

"Anything," Simon said. "A salad. Two slices."

"Wow." Rich's tone was always slightly mocking. "Welcome back pizza." He stood, shocked Simon's forearm with an electric fingertip. "Thank you, Simon. It's good to see you, too."

Rachel flounced up wearing her favorite knee-high brown boots and the yellow hippie dress she'd bought for two dollars at the thrift. Lips to Simon's ear, she whispered, "You look happy."

The rest of the day all he could think about was Rich. Rich's eyes, Rich's lips, Rich's very splendid penis which he'd felt that one time through his jeans. In his last class of the day, which this semester was French, the last forty-four minutes before freedom rang—Freedom! Mel Gibson shouted in *Braveheart*. Freedom!—Simon sat head down trying to avoid eye contact with Monsieur Robinson, who was teaching not his first, not the second, but maybe the eighth lesson on the imperfect tense. *Classe, dit* Monsieur Robinson. *Classe*. I was traveling for two months *Je voyageais pendant trois mois*. That's imperfect tense, *non?* A repeated, or continuing action in the past. Now, *maintenant. Ecoutez bien*. One day, I ate onion soup. *Un jour, j'ai mange du potage a l'oignon*, that's a completed action, and so we use the *passe compose? Oui? Comprenez-vous, classe?*

Who could possibly *comprenez-vous* such crap, although Simon had just comprehended this. Now that he had a license, seeing Rich wouldn't be hard at all. Never again would he have to convince his parents to get Rich, leave them alone, then drive Rich home. He did have rehearsal every day, the Fry Guy, and he didn't know Rich's number. What if Rich wouldn't give it to him? But he'd said, 'We should get together,' and Rich answered, 'Why not?' in his ironic way, just like Alanis Morissette. No problem, Rachel would have it.

Now here came Monsieur Robinson, who could be a pain in the butt-hole, walking up the aisle, waggling gray eyebrows that were long enough to braid.

"Simon, yesterday, I ate french fries."

He couldn't remember the word for yesterday. "Uh, j'ai mange des pommes frites."

"Tres bien," gushed Monsieur Robinson. "Bon, bon."

Sometimes Simon thought Monsieur Robinson must be gay.

"Maintenant, Simon, try this. Every day last summer I was eating—"

Rich's cock.

"—french fries."

"No wonder he's so fat!" someone shouted from the back of the room.

"Who said that?" Monsieur Robinson shouted

Fuck 'em, Simon thought. "Tous les jours, je mangeais des pommes frites.

"Tres bien, Simon." Monsieur Robinson smiled damply at him. "Tres, tres bien."

Assholes, Simon thought, and returned to his reveries of Rich.

✦ ✦ ✦

Genna started a letter to Denny Sweetwater the week before Christmas.

You have a daughter, you know, and I'm not half bad.

It was so humiliating, this pimping for herself, that she tore it up. When they returned from visiting Jack's mother in Florida, she tried again.

Surprise! You don't know me, but I think you'll remember my mother, Doris Krebs? Everyone else does, or did.

She crumpled that attempt, too, and pitched it in her study paper basket. This was impossible. Striking a tone simultaneously perky and self-pitying, which was an original, but wildly unattractive rhetoric. What did she want to tell this stranger? I never thought I'd be writing such a letter, but if you're the Denny Sweetwater who slept with Doris Krebs on or about May 15, 1959, then I'm your daughter.

That wasn't it, either. Something about Simon. After all, Simon was why she'd first asked Daddy. So she wrote and mailed the third attempt, before she had a chance to self-censure:

Dear Denny Sweetwater,

My name is Genna Barish. My mother was Doris Krebs, who died twenty-two years ago. I've just learned that you are my biological father, and if it wouldn't be too much of a shock or an imposition, are you sitting down? I'd like to begin a correspondence. I am a professor of romance languages at Tipton University in Ohio. I'm married and have a teenage son and daughter I'd like you to meet someday. If this letter finds you, I hope it finds you in good health, and I very much hope you are content to be found.

Sincerely,

Genna Barish

Then she added her phone number and home address, slammed the mess in an envelope addressed to the Webster alumni office, and tried not to think about it. She'd never done such a thing, but then, who had? As days then weeks slipped past, she found herself fantasizing about Denny Sweetwater at the oddest moments. It was the inverse—or was that the converse? one of those words of art she remembered from Simon's geometry course—of the amputee who still experienced pain in a phantom leg. She was beginning to feel pain that was a kind of pleasure in thinking about the phantom father she did have. She stood now in the narrow corridor outside the kids' rooms sorting laundry, the most quotidian of her tasks, and nearly a daily one with teenagers, both of whom wore two or more outfits a day. How did they soil so many clothes? Teenage angst, sweated into several layers of cloth; neither would wear a winter coat even on the coldest morning.

Pulling Simon's gray, ribbed-cotton tee from inside a long-sleeved button-down, she tried to conjure Denny Sweetwater as Daddy had on Thanksgiving. How old would he be, sixty-six or seven? Blond, if he still had hair, and a bit plump, at least a bit, if it were Denny she took after. What would a gay man of his generation look like or be like, and was she even certain he was gay? It was only Daddy who said so, and maybe that was his way of diminishing a long-ago rival.

Genna started on the whites, pulling the socks right-side out, squirting stain remover on the cotton inserts of Lizzie's panties, on hers, too. What was always leaking out them—and not just during their periods, but body fluids at all times—like a drip inside a cave? And why couldn't either male do a better job of wiping his bottom? Why was there always a shit smear? And how had her life devolved to this, the shit and stain queen?

Genna poured bleach into the narrow bleach slot. She added detergent and had pushed in half the whites when the phone rang. She crammed the rest of the clothes then raced for the family room, thinking, What if it's Denny Sweetwater? But it was only Jack, saying he'd be home late: grading papers. She was feeling annoyed, a low-grade burn, by how frequently Jack arrived late and expected her to handle everything domestic, as if she were the back-up team, although she had a deadline from her publisher for revisions on her manuscript. How many papers could Jack possibly have, anyway, and why couldn't he grade them at home? She picked up the green handset to ring him back, then set it down. What if he weren't at his office? Better to do extra housework a bit longer, and hope for the best.

Genna returned to the sorted laundry. Behind her bedroom door, Lizzie click-clicked, IMing her friends. Inside his room, Simon was singing and dancing to a new version of the gay nation's Bar-Mitzvah anthem, "YMCA," by the Village People. It would just kill them, she thought, if anything went wrong between her and Jack. They were still so dependent in their oh-so-mature teenage way. Baby birds, waiting to be fed, and she smiled to think of Simon and Lizzie with their mouths opened wide for a worm.

She hoped Jack understood that, too.

Simon sang, joyously, "It's fun to stay at the Y-M-C-A," as she sifted through the pile of dark clothes for the trash he often left in his pockets, the candy wrappers, tissues and folded squares of paper that would otherwise dissolve coating all the clean clothes.

"It's fun to stay at the Y-M-C-A."

In the jeans Simon had worn yesterday, she found a sheet of lined paper torn from a memo pad on which Simon had scrawled "Simon and Rich 4-ever," enclosing their names in a pink heart. Outside the heart there was a phone number, which appeared to be in a different handwriting.

"They have everything for you men to enjoy, you can hang out with all the boys."

Oh my, she thought and started upstairs, wondering if this were an old note resurfacing in Simon's jeans like a piece of eight rising from the sand on a deserted beach, or something new. Genna turned towards the kitchen to start dinner: turkey burgers, rice, and salad, one of her kid-food standbys, and glimpsed Denny Sweetwater in the hall mirror opening her letter and nearly being struck down with joy.

Genna, he'd say when he called. Genna, this is your dad, Denny Sweetwater.

She shook the vision from her head and began to shape ground turkey into patties.

✦ ✦ ✦

Saturday night, Lizzie had arranged a sleepover at the house of her new friend, Alanna, who lived several miles south of town. Jack missed a turn and got lost in the January dark, a cold night without moon or stars. By the time he corrected his mistake, cursing the miserable Barish sense of direction—not enough iron, he supposed, in his brainpan—Lizzie had stopped speaking to him. He could feel her outrage building like thunder heads, or more appropriately for Lizzie, like a zit begging to be popped, as she sat beside him in the dark compulsively flipping back and forth between the punk rock stations she favored. When he finally circled to the correct road and pulled into Alanna's driveway almost thirty minutes late, Lizzie bounded out of the car without so much as a Goodbye, thanks for the ride, and he sat alone in a familiar parental stew of rage and resignation.

But Jack had promised Genna he'd meet Alanna's parents. He climbed out of the Town and Country (now that Simon had a license, he rarely drove the Camry), and picked his way through a front yard dimpled with frozen turds and car parts. There was a large wood pile at one end of the covered front porch. At the other, Lizzie waited under a yellow bug light. Inside the house, dogs yowled. Then the door swung in, and a girl about Lizzie's size stepped into the circle of yellow light. Dark eyebrows, high, prominent cheekbones. Wide swaths of dark curly hair had been dyed purple, but it was hard to be certain because of the ambiguous light. Maybe her hair was pink? She hugged Lizzie as two black and tan mongrels, hounds with some other breed intermixed, maybe burro, rushed onto the porch and began snuffling Lizzie's ankles.

Lizzie said, "Sorry I'm late. My dad got lost."

The girls turned to escape inside. Jack said, "You must be Alanna. I'm Lizzie's father." He shot Lizzie a look, half-smile, half-reprimand, for failing to introduce him. "Are your parents home?"

One of the dogs began humping Jack's leg.

"I'll get my dad." Alanna disappeared, trailed by Lizzie, but not by the dogs, which appeared to be litter-mates. Short-legged, thick-bodied, forty or fifty ugly pounds. Jack pushed the one dog off his leg, but it climbed back on. Next thing he knew someone had booted the dog's ribs and it slunk off, whimpering, towards the dark end of the porch.

"Sorry, them dogs ain't well-trained. Wally Burns."

Jack shook the proffered hand, small and hard-callused.

"Jack Barish."

"Don't worry." Burns was several inches shorter than Jack, with the same broad face and thick, dark hair of his daughter. "We'll keep an eye on 'em. There's some of her so-called friends we won't let come over no more. Too damn weird-looking."

Oh, really. "What time should I pick her up in the morning?"

"She sleeping over?" Burns put two fingers in his mouth and whistled. "Guess my wife forgot to tell me. How about noon?" He whistled again, a sharp, three-note trill.

"See you then," Jack said.

"Goddamnit, Duck. Commere!"

The dog that had been humping Jack's leg crawled up out of the darkness.

"This here's Duck, other's Daffy. I shoulda named 'em the other way around." Burns scratched behind the dog's ears and grinned. "Don't worry, Jack, we'll keep an eye on them gals."

Jack crossed the yard and started home in the dark, trying not to feel that he'd delivered his daughter up to the Philistines. When he arrived, entering through the kitchen door from the garage, Genna called from the living room. He hung up his coat and rubbed his hands, wishing he'd remembered to wear gloves. In the living room, Genna sat on the couch wearing her winter nightgown and fleece-lined slippers. She stared out into the bare trees, sipping what at first blush looked like white wine but turned out to be champagne.

"What took so long?" she inquired, smiling. "You didn't get lost?"

"Don't you start, too," he said, taking a second sip from the glass she had waiting for him. This is pretty good, he thought, wondering if she'd broken out the Mumm's they'd been saving. "I got so lost and Lizzie was so pissed, she wouldn't speak to me." He spied the bottle of Mumm's on the mantle in front of the family portrait they'd had done four years ago for Simon's Bar Mitzvah.

How young and sweet the kids looked. Lizzie was such a pretty kid, with bright shining eyes. God, he thought, but that Burns house gave him the creeps.

"What's the occasion?"

"Denny Sweetwater called. He lives in San Francisco." Her eyes glowed oh-so-blue, no gray at all. "He wants to meet me." She slid across the couch and wrapped her arms around his neck. "I owe it all to you."

"You asked the Judge."

"I would never have thought of Webster." She moved her lips to his ear. "I'm so excited, Jack."

Genna closed her eyes waiting to be kissed. Before he moved his mouth to hers, he thought, She looks so happy. Despite everything I've done wrong, I guess I've done this right. Then he kissed his wife and felt her full lips press against his.

"What did he sound like, Mister Sweetwater?" wondering in the tiny back corner of his mind if this was going to support his thesis.

"Funny, smart, and you'll never believe what he does."

"What?"

"He owns a candy shop on Castro Street. Sweet's Sweets." Genna smiled. "Hand-crafted chocolates."

"I guess you really are his daughter."

Genna, whose taste for sweets was wide and deep as the ocean, nodded. "He said he had no idea, never heard a word from Doris."

Jack wondered if that could be true. It was certainly what he'd tell a daughter he'd never contacted.

"I thought we could all go out and meet him during spring break. We don't have any other plans, do we?"

Jack thought about some provisional arrangements a certain guidance counselor had been urging on him. "None that we couldn't change. This is so great."

"He's lived with the same man for twenty years," Genna said. "It turns out he and Marty, that's his lover, met the same fall we did."

"When Marty met Denny." Jack grinned. "By the way, is Simon out?"

Genna nodded.

"If I put the champagne on ice and turn the heat way up, would you change your nightgown?"

Genna raised the gray flannel nightgown over her head, shook out her hair and smiled. She was wearing a black lace teddy he'd never seen before.

"Way ahead of you, Jack." She walked to the mantle and hoisted the bottle of Mumm's. "The ice bucket's in the bedroom."

"Then I guess we should be, too."

Jack followed his smiling, surprising wife towards the waiting bucket of ice and his marriage bed.

chapter 14

Valentine's Day was Saturday, three days away, and Simon wanted to buy Rich something special. They'd been to the movies twice since Rich returned to Tipton, trailing a comet's tail of possibility. Simon paid for everything: tickets, popcorn, Mountain Dew, a giant sack of Gummy Bears. Money? No problem for the Fry Guy; he was still working sixteen hours a week. After last Saturday's movie, they hung out at Rachel's, and Rich let him slip his hand inside his pants. Simon felt it, hard and warm, growing like a bean stalk. Simon adored Rich's penis; he longed to sing a ballad to it—On the Cock Where You Live, or Riiiiiich's Penis, where the wind comes sweeping down the plain!—although Rich made him take his hand away after a second. Rachel was walking back down the hall to her room.

What to buy him? Simon didn't have time to shop. Friday, he worked four to eleven. Today and tomorrow, rehearsal until six, and he'd promised Mom to come straight home to study for his stupid French and English tests. Saturday morning was his lesson with Yevgeny, so what he had to do was convince Mom to let him drive alone to Cincinnati for the first time. Afterwards, he could shop at Kenwood Towne Center.

Maybe, Simon thought, as he walked down the deserted hallway with its cheesy Go Braves! red construction paper signs on the wall, he and Rich could park somewhere on Saturday night, and something might happen. Maybe Mom and Dad were going out, and he could sneak Rich into his very own bed. But he'd been noticing that on romantic occasions like their anniversary and V-Day, Mom and Dad often didn't go out. Instead, they tried to arrange it so the kids were gone. Was that disgusting or what? He and Lizzie discussed it. She was almost fun to talk to now, after years of being a brat. At first, she wouldn't believe him; he wasn't sure himself if Mom and Dad still did it.

Then one night last fall, it must have been just after Thanksgiving, long after he was usually asleep on a school night, he heard this noise in the ceiling, thump-thump, thump-THUMP, as if someone were moving the bed. All of a sudden he knew what the thumping was, and he lay awake, horrified, just horrified, afraid he was going to hear voices, moaning, his own mom moaning, and realized he was listening for their voices. He hurried to Lizzie's room and shook her awake. She whispered, "Let's go back and listen."

"That's gross."

But he followed her, and they lay on his bed with just the hall light on. The ceiling thumped softly once or twice, and he glanced at Lizzie's face beside his. She was growing up, little Lizzie. She was so beautiful, and he wished he were, too. The next thing Simon knew it was morning, and Lizzie was asleep beside him, her face buried on his pillow.

Simon turned into the guidance office and asked the secretary, Mrs. Rogers, who was old and plump but had a head full of red curls, just like Annie—Tomorrow, tomorrow!—if he could see Mrs. Lindstrom.

"Is she expecting you, Simon?"

I love you, tomorrow. Everybody knew his name, he loved that. "I have an appointment."

Mrs. Lindstrom had approached him yesterday in the hall. He must have looked worried, because she said, Nothing's wrong, and smiled like she was smiling now as Mrs. Rogers led him into her office.

"How are you, Simon?"

She was so little and cute, seated behind her desk, with soft blond hair touching her cheeks. If Simon were a woman, he'd want to look just like her.

"Fine, and you?"

She smiled again, and he felt warm and happy.

"I'm fine, too." Mrs. Lindstrom glanced at her hands. Such nicely shaped nails. Real ones, not like the black press-ons he sometimes wore. "I asked to see you because I care about you. I really like you, Simon."

"I like you, too."

She smiled again, and Simon felt all gooey inside.

"Ms. Cherry's worried about your grades."

"But I don't have Ms. Cherry."

"Of course not. She's worried about your grades and the show."

"I thought if I passed everything last semester, I was fine."

"That's right." Mrs. Lindstrom looked so concerned Simon began to freak out. "But we don't want you falling so far behind you can't catch up when the show's over. I've checked with your teachers, and though it's early in the semester, you already seem to be having trouble."

Simon thought about his tests on Friday in French and English. About the pre-calc and history tests—he was pretty sure they were next week—he hadn't even told Mom about, and thought he might cry. "Ms. Cherry's kicking me out of the show?"

"Oh, no, Simon. Ms Cherry adores you, and so do I." Mrs. Lindstrom smiled, and he smiled back, not comprehending. "But I was thinking, maybe I could move you into this special study hall I run. Until the levy passed, the superintendent's office was going to cut it, but now they won't. There are only five or six students. Like you, they're smart kids who have trouble getting their work done. I'd have to rearrange your schedule, but you'd have all the same classes, just at different times."

"You'd make sure I'd get my assignments written down, things like that?"

"Like having another parent in school."

Simon wasn't sure he wanted more parents.

"Why don't you think about it, then have your dad call me?" Mrs. Lindstrom smiled again. "Or your mother. I really think it would be good for you."

The bell rang, ending fourth period. He thanked Mrs. Lindstrom and hurried back to art to collect his books, then continued towards the auditeria. The only problem, he thought, as he navigated the sea of strangers, with Rich returning, was that he didn't know how to act with Peter. They still stood next to each other in Animal Chorus, but since Rich returned they'd stopped sharing music. It wasn't like anything had happened. They'd never kissed or even touched, and that night they went to the movies when Fry Guy burned his arm and Peter called him Super Simon, he'd chickened out and didn't try to hold Peter's hand.

But Peter liked him, at least as a friend and maybe more. He liked Peter the same way. But the kid wasn't on to himself; he couldn't admit he was gay, even though it was totally obvious to Simon and everyone else. Just yesterday, standing on the risers in Animal Chorus, Peter dropped his music. Bending to reach it, Peter started to fall forward and squealed like a little girl. Then he covered his mouth and looked around. Who me? I didn't make that sound. No straight teenage boy would. Even Simon wouldn't squeal like that, no freaking way, and he wasn't trying to pass.

The other thing, and this was nothing bad about Peter, but Rich was really, really hot. There was something about his black hair and how sad and ironic he was, like he didn't give a crap about anything, that excited Simon. Simon wanted to have wild sex and take care of him at the same time. And if what he felt for Rich caused him to hurt Peter's feelings, he was really, really sorry. Simon was the king of getting his feelings hurt, he knew what it felt like. And he also knew, as he turned into the auditeria and looked around to see if Rich was at Rachel's table—Not yet—that Rich didn't like him nearly as much as Peter did. Rich often hurt his feelings without meaning to because he didn't care about anyone, not even himself. Simon couldn't help that. He was just a boy in love. Hit me from the top, hit me from below, Just hit me hard, yeah, so I know. Simon set his hip bag on Rachel's table and joined the food line. He was trying to lose a little of his belly, but he was so damn hungry all the time. Salad, he decided. For the rest of the week, he would only eat salad. Maybe a small bag of chips.

✦ ✦ ✦

Thursday morning Genna rolled over to check Jack's alarm clock. The face was angled away, preventing her from seeing the red numerals. Though she depended on Jack to prod the kids into action, he slumbered beside her, a breathing, blanketed mound. Sam held down the floor, her side of the bed, whimpering softly, perhaps dreaming of the spring bunnies he could never catch. Wraiths of light twisted through the drawn curtains. Why weren't the kids awake? She strained to read her watch, but the early light and the damn changes in her eyes (she'd always had such perfect vision) thwarted her, and she nudged Jack, once then harder.

"Why aren't the kids up?"

"It's a snow day."

Suddenly, she remembered. She had been up, Jack too. Shouts and murmurs from downstairs, then she must have fallen back asleep. She didn't recall Jack returning to bed, or anything but this. It was February 12, Lincoln's birthday, also her mother's. Doris would have been sixty-six, or was it sixty-seven, old enough to collect full social security if she'd worked, which she hadn't. It was hard to think of her mother so old. In her mind's eye, Doris remained the same age. Never a gray hair or a day older. Doris would have liked that. On her next birthday, Genna would be as old as her mother had been the year she died. Was Doris's eyesight fading when the breast cancer got her? Lying under the warm covers beside Jack, who was snoring like a faint, whistling teapot, she tried to remember Doris wearing glasses, or straining to read, Daddy joking, "Arms too short, Doris?" but drew a blank. Maybe it happened while she was away at college. Or maybe it never happened at all and Doris had slipped the indignities of middle age by popping off this mortal coil, like Keats or Shelley, without lingering into tendentious old age like Wordsworth.

I've never forgiven her, Genna realized. Doris would have chosen dying young to wrinkles. Doris had been so proud of her skin, which she shielded from the sun like that woman at the far end of Forest Glen, what was her name? Mary, the one with the standard poodle. Doris had also been enormously vain (a pattern here?) that her birthday was a school holiday. She'd been outraged when they'd conflated Lincoln and Washington's birthdays to Presidents' Day.

"The world is going to hell, don't you see? This is yet one more example."

Then she said something, which Genna had forgotten or more likely repressed, which made her wonder if Doris had really said it. Senior year of high school? No, she was home from college, sitting in their kitchen.

"If you ever have kids, Genna, make sure they know my birthday. It used to be so easy." She patted her hair into place. "When it was a national holiday."

Did Doris know she was going to die, Genna wondered, years before she told me? Could the cancer have been in remission? Or maybe she knew nothing, and Doris was just being a drama queen, Genna thought, trying to remember if the conversation had, in fact, occurred. Yes, she decided, slipping out of bed. I'll tell the kids.

Later, when the kids had stopped grumbling because she hadn't let them sleep in and everyone was in the kitchen cutting into Sunday breakfast on a Thursday—the kind she rarely made even on Sunday—Genna doused her blueberry pancakes in maple syrup. "Simon, Lizzie?" She glanced at the amber lake on Simon's plate. "Today was my mother's birthday." She cut into the stacked cakes and took the first bite. "I promised her I'd tell you."

Suddenly, she was sobbing. She was so surprised, stunned, really. The kids looked at each other, Simon at Lizzie, Lizzie at Simon, then both kids at Jack, as tears soaked her cheeks. She'd had a whole speech planned, an appreciation of her strange, hard-to-know mother, but did she get a chance to deliver it? No, first she was blubbering, then choking on the doughy cakes.

"Do something, Dad!" Simon shouted.

Lizzie was shouting, too. Jack stood, pounding her back, though she'd told him, time and again, it didn't help, they'd done new studies. Her larynx cleared. She'd somehow got the pancake down despite the pounding, and her eyes were tearing, not with sorrow, but the ack-ack of nearly choking to death.

"Will you stop hitting me, Jack!"

"Dad was trying to help," Lizzie said.

She's so protective.

Genna sipped orange juice and cleared her throat. "As I was saying. You never knew my mom. I sometimes think I didn't know her very well myself." Genna glanced at Lizzie, the long line of her jaw, the dark brow she'd gotten from Doris. "Sometimes mothers and daughters go through a phase where they don't get along that well."

"From what you've told me," Jack said, "that phase lasted your entire life."

The kids glanced at her apprehensively. Would she commence choking and blubbering again? Lose her temper? "That's true," she admitted. "But I kept hoping it would change." She felt herself tearing up. "Way back then, when I was a girl, February twelfth, Lincoln's birthday, was a school holiday. My mom thought that made her special. Every year she told me and Uncle Billy the holiday was in honor of her birthday but we shouldn't tell, it was our secret. Until third grade, I believed her."

"Aw, Mom," Simon said. "That's so sweet."

"So here's to your Grandma Doris." Genna raised her orange juice.

Jack said, "I doubt she would have wanted to be called Grandma."

"Well, she wouldn't have had any choice," Genna answered, feeling some of the old resentment return.

"Happy birthday, Grandma," Simon said.

"Whoever you are," Lizzie added.

They clinked glasses and settled in to inflict serious damage on the cooling hot-cakes.

✦ ✦ ✦

Snow fell for twenty-four hours. Then the temperature dropped to six above, and Tipton schools were closed for a second day. Even the university canceled classes, the first time that had happened in his eight years in Ohio. It felt to everyone, Jack thought, as if Old Man Winter stood on their chests, howling. It was all anyone could talk about, at home or around the department. How cold. How much snow. Have you heard another storm is coming? The woods behind their house filled up, one foot, two feet, it was hard to tell. Saturday morning, while the family slumbered, Jack decided to take Sam and see if the small stream at the edge of their meadow was still flowing. He laced his Timberlakes over two pairs of wool socks. He found the heavy parka with a wolf fur collar Simon had bullied them into buying for him two years ago then abandoned when he learned how unfashionable real fur was, and how much he resembled an igloo inside the enormous off-white coat, which was too warm for southwestern Ohio except for two or three days a decade. But it was perfect for this Valentine's Day morning. Jack stepped out of the family-room door with the dog behind him and felt the cold smack his cheeks but nowhere else. Sam bounded ahead through the unbroken drifts.

What joy the snow inspired in Sam, a joy that Jack felt, too, as if there were something beyond or before words, produced by kicking through knee-high powder. Something about childhood and innocence, a full bursting heart, his big brother Russ a few strides ahead of him as they attacked Jimmy and Fat George's snow fort in the next yard. Sam launched himself halfway down the hill then intentionally flopped on his back and rolled, his golden legs kicking upward as if he were a beetle tipped on its shell. Look how happy, Jack thought, rubbing Sam's chest, which was clumped with small balls of snow. When's the last time I felt that way, Jack wondered, continuing down the snowy path towards the stream, happy without reason or qualification, but pure animal joy?

"Come on, Sam!" he shouted, and could have added, Show me the way! But there was no need. Sam bounded up and pushed ahead, always eager to be first. In fact, Jack thought, watching the dog's wide-hipped gait and ferocious ears, little puffs of snow and frosted breath rising off him, he had every reason to be happy. When Genna informed him a week ago that they were going to San Francisco to meet Denny Sweetwater, he began casting about to find some way to write the trip off. With all the genetic work being done at Berkeley, Stanford, and UCSF, someone or several someones must be working on genetics and homosexuality or the genetic component of another complicated social behavior. That would be enough for his taxes; the IRS was more often lied to than any institution except the American Association of Deceived Spouses. Not funny, Jack thought, feeling the cold on his cheeks. But not only had he found someone whose work would pass the IRS standard of appearance, on Wednesday he'd come across an abstract in the most recent issue of *Science*, written by Rajiv Menard, a geneticist at UCSF. They'd spoken and arranged to meet when Jack was in town. It was exciting work, and Menard hinted he hadn't included the most exciting aspects of the study in the abstract.

Why then, Jack wondered as they reached the bottom of the path and started across the small clearing towards the stream, did he feel this terrible sense of foreboding? The kids were fine. He was fine. Genna seemed happy. And if there was this unresolved flirtation, this thing with Marla, she was pursuing him, not the other way around. He was intrigued, but guilt-free.

"Sam!"

Sam turned, mouthing a toothy retriever grin. Together, they clambered down to the snowy creek bed where Jack kicked through the dry powder to a layer of ice. He kicked once then again, and his heel broke through. Below, water was running, not much, but water; he could hear the shush over wet stones. "Sam," he called. "Look."

Sam barked then pushed his muzzle through the snow and drank. A moment later, master and dog climbed out of the stream bed and started back up towards the house. The first rays of sunlight broke through the skeletal trees and sparked on the drifted snow. Jack labored up the hill, cheeks flushed, filled with foreboding.

chapter 15

Simon knew it, goddamnit! His parents weren't going out. Dad said it was too icy to drive to Cincinnati. Not with the weatherman predicting another storm.

"You should really take Mom somewhere," Simon replied, sitting across from Dad at the kitchen table. Simon couldn't remember the last time he'd sat next to his father. "She'll think you don't love her."

Dad extracted his face from the sports section, the dumb jock. He'd been out walking Sam, and his cheeks were pink as a baby's ass.

"Mom knows I love her."

"You should take her. It's Valentine's Day, for God sakes."

A mocking glow lit Dad's eyes. He peered down his big nose as if a sign had been switched on—Eat, eat!—because he'd realized Simon was up to something. Among Dad's many hateful expressions, this was the one Simon hated most of all. Of course he was up to something. He was a teenage boy, a gay teenage boy, with secret business. It was hard to say what infuriated Simon more: Dad suspecting him of trying to get them out of the house so he could sneak Rich into his bedroom—whatever happened to trust?—or Dad being right. How he hated Dad being right! How it enraged him, affronting his manhood. In all the world, in the history of all the world, there was nothing more infuriating than the look on Jack

Barish's big-nosed, big-headed, big-assed face when he suspected Simon was up to something. With this crappy little grin tinkling on his face like "Chopsticks," Dad asked, "Other than your concern for Mom, is there a particular reason you want us to go out?"

"No."

"Is Lizzie going out?"

Lizzie was going out, to a party at her purple-haired friend's house, but count on Dad not to know that. "You know, Dad?" Simon curled his lips. "I really don't know what Lizzie's doing."

"Well, I do." Dad grinned even wider. "She's got some party—"

Damn.

"—at the Crapsters house."

"Who?"

"Family with all the dog shit in their yard."

"That's really mean."

"Have you seen their yard?"

No freaking way Dad was going to make him laugh.

"Anyway." Dad snapped the sports section and looked oh-so-pleased. "I was wondering if you wanted us to go out so the house will be empty?"

"No!" Simon shouted. "Because I care about Mom's feelings!"

"You're saying I don't?"

"If you did, " Simon couldn't stop shouting, "you'd take her out for Valentine's Day."

"You don't know anything about it!"

"I know more than you think!"

A shadow crossed Dad's face. Then it passed and that vein thing in his neck was jumping. "What the hell do you mean?"

Simon hadn't meant anything in particular. But from Dad's reaction he knew it had something to do with last year when Mom was out driving all the time.

"Nothing." Simon looked away. "I meant nothing."

Dad said, "When I was your age—"

Blah, blah, blah. Dad took a long pull from his coffee mug, which was covered with stenciled renderings of summer fruit: strawberries, cherries, and plums.

"—starting to date, I sometimes wanted an empty house to come home to."

He sipped again and glanced meaningfully at Simon, who blanked his eyes.

"I thought that might be why you were so eager for us to go out." Dad banged the mug down, empty. Eat, eat! cried his wolf eyes. "I guess I was wrong."

✦ ✦ ✦

With his parents' change of plans, Simon had to think fast. He'd bought Rich a lava lamp for V-Day, which he knew Rich would adore since he'd gone on and on—for Rich, about two sentences—about how much he liked Simon's. Simon had wanted to buy something more personal, a ring or bracelet, but thought that might spook Rich, who was still terrified of his father and grandmother finding out he was seeing Simon.

They'd worked out this geniusy system. When he called Rich's trailer, he let the phone ring once then hung up. Exactly two minutes later he called back, and if Rich were home he answered the first or second ring. Simon hung up before the third. For pick-ups, Rich waited two streets away, at the entrance to Pleasant Acres. But with the terrible weather, Rich shouldn't wait outside. He might freeze, he was so skinny. And on a day like today, if Rich just walked out the door his father might suspect something. Simon had planned to bring Rachel and send her into the trailer to fetch Rich, but now that his parents were going to be home—goddamnit!—what would he do with Rachel? He'd planned for her to hang out in the family room. Or upstairs. Now where would Rachel be? In the back seat, blindfolded?

Late that morning, Simon dialed Rich, hung up, and feeling like a spy—Bond, Simon Bond—called back exactly one hundred and twenty seconds later. After he spoke to Rich, he phoned Rachel, who agreed, if he bought her movie ticket and popcorn. Fry Guy said, Yes, oh yes, no problem. At six, he stood before his bathroom mirror putting the finishing touches on his hair. He'd tried and rejected six different outfits then settled on the one he'd started with: black sweater vest over his long-sleeve purple shirt, his Ginkos with the red velvet pocket patches. He fastened a heavy choker around his neck, little silver balls, ha, ha. Inserted the turquoise stud in the second hole in his left ear: perfect behind silver hoops. Simon hated gold; the Fry Guy was all about silver. Then, down the hall, the telephone shrieked. Soon, Lizzie was pounding the bathroom door.

"Who is it?"

But she'd already left, the little brat. He cast a longing glance in the glass, then rushed to his room. Covering the receiver, Simon shouted, "Hang up, Dizzy Lizzie!"

Rachel breathed in his ear, "Simon."

"Hey, hon, what's up?"

"My mom won't let me out. She says it's gonna snow."

"But, but…you promised."

"Don't blame me."

He wanted to scream at Rachel, but she'd click him, she did all the time. Losing patience, she said, with his drama queen shit. "Let me talk to your mom, she likes me."

"No."

"If I tell her how important…"

"It's not that important. And it is gonna snow."

"What am I going to do?" Tears of vexation leapt to his eyes. "Rich is expecting me."

"You'll think of something."

"Thanks for nothing."

Simon clicked Rachel—now didn't that feel good!—and stood in the center of his room wishing he had something to throw besides the phone. God must hate him, that must be it, or he wouldn't be gay and fat. It wouldn't be snowing and Rachel's mom wouldn't make her cancel. It probably wasn't even her mom, it was Rachel, goddamn the bitch to hell! Sobbing, Simon flopped on his bed and had himself a good cry. When he felt better, he dialed Rich's number to tell him to wait at the entrance to Pleasant Acres. (What a joke. It wasn't pleasant and there weren't any acres, just shitty trailers on concrete slabs.) The phone rang busy and stayed busy for twenty minutes, until it was time to go. Simon raced upstairs, grabbed his good gray coat and hurried towards the door before his parents could stop him.

"Simon," Mom called as his hand touched the knob.

"What?"

"Have fun. And if the snow gets bad, or anything." She smiled the special Mommy smile she reserved just for him. "Just call. Dad will pick you up."

"Don't worry." Now that he could drive he would never let Dad pick him up. "I'm fine."

Then he was out the door. The air tasted metallic. Simon drove through Tipton, Britney blasting from the speakers. Tiny snowflakes spun through the street lamps. Introducing, Simon Barrrrrrish! He didn't know what scared him more, driving in snow or knocking on Rich's door. I'm Simon, he'd say. Rich's friend.

No, no, no! He braked and turned carefully, perfectly, better than Dad could, into Pleasant Acres. He wouldn't give his name, just ask, Is Rich home? The trailer park was badly lit, and he struggled to see street signs. Rich lived on Birch Trail, just after Oak Knoll. When he'd driven through the park before, middle-schoolers would stop beating the crap out of each other and stare. Tonight, Pleasant Acres' empty streets were drifted with snow. The plow don't come here much, Rich had said the last time they spoke, when he still thought Rachel would come, the bitch. Snow fell in profusion. The flakes were larger, too. Simon tapped the brake pedal to turn onto Birch Trail, and the Camry fish-tailed right then left, before the front tires bit in the frozen tracks. Shit, he thought, pulling up in front of Rich's trailer, trying to ease to a stop without braking, his hands pulling back on the wheel as if it were a horse he was trying to whoa, I can't do this.

He set the emergency brake, crossed the street, and walked up three steps to the crappy wooden porch someone had added on, maybe Rich's father, maybe someone else. Simon squared his shoulders and knocked. He had nothing to be afraid of, but oh, his knees knocked and his heart yammered. A bare bulb shone above his head. Wind-blown snow swirled through the light, then the door opened, and Rich filled the doorway, wearing a work shirt and jeans, his black curly hair lit from behind. He almost said, Rich, I'm so glad it's you. Then a voice not Rich's, like his, but deeper, asked, "You lost or something?"

Simon saw, full of fear, that it wasn't Rich, but someone who looked very much like him. "Is Rich home?"

"I'm Rich Senior." It was crazy. They had the same green eyes. "You must mean my son, Rich Junior. Come in out the cold."

Simon waited in the living room, narrow as a tunnel, no bigger than his bedroom. Or maybe it just seemed small because there were matching maroon recliners in front of a giant screen TV. An older woman with gray curls sat in one recliner watching *Roseanne*. Simon tried to make himself invisible. On the wall behind her, a wooden plaque warned, 'This Home Protected by Smith & Wesson.'

Rich Junior followed Rich Senior from the bedroom. They looked so alike it was freaking eerie.

"The apple don't fall far from the tree," Rich Senior said. "Do it?"

Simon caught Rich's eye. Rich was shaking his head. Simon said, "I look a lot like my dad, too."

"He also a big fella?"

"Football star in high school," Simon said, glad of that for the first time in his life. "And my uncle, he played in college."

"What about you?"

"I played in middle school," Simon said, thinking that the kid whose leg he broke must have been about Rich's size. "I wasn't very good."

"At least you tried. Hey, Rich." Rich Senior back-slapped his son. "Aintcha gonna introduce your friend?"

"Dad." Rich's eyes slowly closed then opened, but otherwise didn't change expression. "This is Martin Long. Grandma?"

The old woman on the recliner turned.

"This is my friend Martin."

Rich Senior stuck out his hand. "Pleased to meet you, Martin Long."

Simon squeezed hard like his father had taught him. A firm handshake makes a good first impression. Especially from a faggot, Simon thought, and grinned, as he saw Rich Senior wince.

"Quite a grip." Rich Senior didn't seem like such an asshole, not like Rich had said. "Maybe you can teach my son."

Rich threw on his coat, then they were out the door and into the storm.

"Martin Long?" Simon asked when they were in the car. "Where'd you get that?"

"Where do you think?"

Simon blushed and put the car in gear. The snow was really coming down. He drove slowly, barely moving, out of Pleasant Acres, and turned onto Route 37, which had been plowed, thank God. "Where do you want to go, Spyder Creek?"

Rich peered out the dark passenger window. "It's fucking snowing. Let's rent some vids and go back to your house."

"But my parents…"

"You rather hang with Rich Senior?"

They ate at Domino's, rented *American Pie, I* and *II*, and motored, slowly, towards Forest Glen. It was snowing so heavily Simon could hardly see. When he turned into their cul-de-sac, his tire tracks from before were totally covered up. He'd never been so glad to see the lights at the end of the long driveway.

Mom and Dad were in their bedroom. Simon and Rich tiptoed past the closed door and descended to the family room. A few minutes later, Dad appeared. His collar was up and his shirt was untucked. It wasn't too hard to guess what he and Mom had been up to. Nasty.

Dad said, "I thought you were, ah, out for the evening."

"It started snowing real bad." And then, because he wanted something big from Dad, and that required sucking up, he said, "You were right not to drive to Cincinnati." Simon waited for the appreciative smile to appear. When it did, he said, "I was wondering if Rich could sleep over, so I wouldn't have to drive in a blizzard."

Simon followed Dad's eyes to Rich, who sat a few feet away on the couch.

"Let's see what your mother thinks." Dad started upstairs then stopped. "Lizzie's sleeping over at that party. If Mom says okay, maybe Rich could sleep in her room."

"Why not?" Simon asked.

Outside, wind-blown snow blasted the windows.

✦ ✦ ✦

Genna sat propped up wearing her sexy green nightgown. She'd downed half a bottle of merlot and had been this close when high beams swept the shutters like searchlights.

"Oh, God," she'd yelped. "Simon's home!"

Jack thrust one last time; her breath caught. She teetered on the mountain top, but it was no good, no use, married sex! Jack withdrew and she felt his member, hard and wet, land on her thigh. He kissed her neck, and she pushed him away. "Get dressed."

He stood, muttering.

Now she sat watching some Jimmy Stewart western, feeling tensed up and deprived. She'd been having such a fine Valentine's Day night. Kids gone, lights down, a whooping orgasm moments away. Jack had bought her a silver bracelet, told her he loved her. He still had such clever fingers, and now this. Purgatory!

"Genna," Jack said, knocking. "It's me." He slipped inside the room wearing trouble like a mask. "Simon wants to know if Rich can sleep over."

"That'll end our sex life." She felt her anger rising. "What did you say?"

"I'd ask you."

"Coward."

Jack opened the shutter covering the front window. "It's really coming down."

"I know," Genna said bitterly and felt herself retreating into her asexual, wife-and-mother-of-two self, the self inside which she dwelled most days. A tented camel, a curtained window. Getting shit stains out of Simon's boxers.

"What should I tell him?"

"Are you having an affair with Marla Lindstrom?"

"What?" His eyes swelled into silver dollars. "Where did that come from?"

She wanted to shout, From deep inside me. Where I am still driving around like a crazy woman. "Well?"

"Absolutely not."

"If you do, you'll let me know, won't you?"

"Genna."

"I know, I know. You'd never consider such a thing." She looked into Jack's broad face she used to believe could never hide anything from her. "I want you to promise."

"I promise."

She heard Simon tromping down the hall. One knock, then he

entered, per usual, without waiting for an answer. "Can Rich stay?"

Genna turned from Jack, *too bad*, to her son, who looked love-struck and on a mission.

"Is the driving really terrible?"

"I skidded twice."

She turned to Jack, who nodded.

"All right," Simon said.

"We have to call Rich's father."

Simon shook his head. "I'll have Rich call."

"We should, to make sure it's okay."

"No."

Jack said, perhaps too loudly, "I agree with Mom."

"No!"

"Then he can't stay."

Simon shouted, "You're always making threats, Dad. That's all you know how to do."

"We're not going to argue about this. We speak to his father." Jack started towards the door. "Or I drive him home."

Simon's face registered defeat, then connivance displaced anger. "Wait, it's just." Simon tugged at his ear, the one with two earrings. "Rich introduced me to his dad as someone else. Remember, the letters last fall?"

Jack thundered, "You want us to lie?"

"You're the ones who want to speak to Rich's father."

"What did he call you?" Jack demanded.

"What does that matter?"

"Think about it," Jack said, and turned to her for support.

"If we're going to do this," Genna said, "we need to know."

Simon raised both shoulders nearly to his ears, looking very much like the darling little boy he used to be. His shoulders fell. "Martin Long."

Genna fought back a smile. "Let me talk to Dad in private."

✦ ✦ ✦

Jack knew in his bones that this was a bad idea, but still spinning from Genna's accusation, the wine, and coitus interruptus, definitely the coitus interruptus, he'd consent to whatever she wanted. The door closed behind Simon. Jack sat on the bed beside Genna, who still wore her bosomy, only on love-making-nights nightgown. Had Simon noticed? Of course.

"Who's calling," she asked, "you or me?"

"If you want, I'll call, but I have an idea."

Genna seemed to be fighting a smile. "Martin Long," she said and guffawed, the laughter bursting out, Ha, ha, ha!

"Do you think?" he asked.

"What do you think?"

"I think I love you, and you don't have to worry about Marla."

"You're the only one who knows, Jack."

He kissed her hard on the lips. "I'm so frustrated," he whispered, "I could die."

Her hand fell to his knee. "What are you going to say to Rich's father?"

Months later he would regret this. "Why don't we let Rich call? If anyone's going to lie, let him do it."

"What if he asks to speak to you?"

"Then I will."

"Mister Long?"

"Absolutely."

"How are we going to monitor them?"

"You know, maybe we shouldn't let him stay."

Genna, who could never deny Simon anything, shook her head.

Jack continued, "Then why don't we tell him, Rich can stay if he calls his father, and if he's in Lizzie's room, alone, by midnight. If not, he can't come over again."

"You really don't know how to deal with Simon without threatening him."

They stared at each other for moment, then Jack stood up, offended. "I'll send Simon in to talk to you."

He resisted the temptation to add, You might want to change your nightgown. Instead, he threw open the bedroom door then continued down the hall. From the family room rose the sounds of television and adolescent laughter. Starting down the stairs Jack glanced out the long, vertical windows behind them. In the glow from the house, snow fell thickly, without sound.

chapter 16

Whatever had happened with Rich and Simon had happened, and Jack resolved to put the Valentine's Night disaster out of his mind. But it wouldn't stay put out. Details kept erupting. After all the discussion, neither he nor Genna had called Rich's father. Simon reported Rich had, but really, who knew? Not Jack. Who wanted to know? Not Jack. Sunday morning after a late breakfast, he volunteered to drive, but Simon insisted he'd drop Rich on his way to Burger King. Later, after giving county work crews enough time to clear secondary roads, Jack retrieved Lizzie at the Crapsters and drove home feeling clear-headed and refreshed, which was how time alone with Lizzie had always made him feel, and often still did: as if the sunlight ricocheting off fresh-fallen snow reflected their easy and unambiguous affection.

Now, barely three days after the storm, the thermometer outside his office window topped sixty degrees; roof-melt pattered on the ledge. Jack's thoughts had turned to California; he'd been corresponding regularly with his new best friend, Rajiv, the UCSF researcher. They'd arranged to meet his first workday in San Francisco, and had been discussing ways to co-author an article. Jack was answering Rajiv's latest email when the phone rang.

"Jack Barish."

"Jack, it's Marla."

"I recognize your voice." He could have gotten off, explaining that his wife didn't want them talking, which wasn't what she'd said. Less ambiguous was that since Saturday night, there had existed between Jack and Genna a persistent, unresolved tension, emotional noise, an ambient hum of distress; they'd never gotten back to lovemaking. Instead, they climbed into bed and feigned sleep. "How have you been?"

"Neglected." Marla trilled that girlish giggle. "I mean, neglecting my duties."

Don't, a voice whispered.

"I revised Simon's schedule to move him into a support study hall. I'm supposed to have parental permission."

Jack's hand warmed against the receiver. For no reason at all—it was a blind courtyard—he drew the shade. "You have mine."

"When I spoke to Simon last week, I asked him to have you call me."

Jack felt a palpable thrill of excitement.

"But then I said," Marla's words spilled out, "to have his mother call because I didn't want to cause trouble."

"How so?"

"Fishing for compliments, Jack?" He didn't reply, and she added, "It's pretty obvious I'm very attracted to you."

Flattered, distressed, Jack felt himself falling, falling, falling, and heard himself reply, "I'm very attracted to you, too."

"I know, I don't allow myself to be attracted to someone I don't already know is hot for me." She giggled again, or something very like a giggle. "At our age, it doesn't seem proper."

Proper? "Simon didn't say anything. About calling you."

"If he could remember to tell you, he wouldn't need the special study hall. He's a really sweet boy, Simon. Sometimes makes me wish I'd had kids."

After a nervous silence, Jack asked, "Do you know his friend, Rich? Curly hair?"

"Rich O'Brien. I'll tell you all about him. Cup of coffee?"

Jack stared through the drawn shade. It was exciting to be pursued, never happened before. And no harm, he thought, in coffee. "Love to."

"I make a mean cappuccino."

Alone in his office, Jack flushed. "I was thinking of someplace more public."

"You're not afraid to be seen with me?"

"Why should I be?"

"Are you sure?"

"You want to have coffee or not?"

"Starbucks in thirty minutes, Jack, okay?"

He hung up feeling wicked.

✦ ✦ ✦

Jack was early. Marla was late. Four-thirty, a bright winter's day. Jack sipped a grande cappuccino near the front window, feeling like a prize puppy in a pet store. Steven something, one of the students in his senior seminar, nodded hello walking in, and again walking out. Jack asked himself a dozen times what he imagined he was doing. The whole world could see him here. Wasn't that the point? A friend, a co-worker in the levy campaign, which had restored Latin to the high school and reduced class size in first and second grade, by golly, his son's guidance counselor, who just happened to be beautiful, or what passed for beautiful in middle age. Been around the block, no obvious signs of wear and tear, but he'd have to look under the hood. God! Jack's leg trembled under the table; it must be the caffeine. If she knew, Genna would be so offended just by the car analogy she'd slap him. Then the door opened and Marla entered wearing a gray spring coat, double-breasted. She must have been fixing her hair while she kept him waiting; it couldn't have looked this perfect at Tipton High.

"I hope you haven't been here long."

"Just arrived."

She glanced at his cappuccino, half-gone, froth fallen. "I like that in a man."

"What?"

"Discretion. Or give me another word for it."

"'You who are so good with words.'"

"I can't believe you know that."

"'Your eyes were bluer than robin's eggs.'"

"Why, thank you." Her knee brushed his beneath the table. "'My poetry was lousy…'" She slipped the coat off her shoulders, revealing a blouse of shimmering green. "Diamonds and Rust, one of my favorites."

Jack drained what was left of his cappuccino. "You might be right about sitting here. I've already seen one of my students."

"Can I interest you in another cup?"

Jack recalled the affair he'd had last year, the first and only in nearly twenty years of marriage, how he'd promised himself and Genna it would never happen again, and how during the affair (he'd seen Jan twice, three times if he counted the conference at which they'd met) he'd been grateful she lived hundreds of miles away. He wondered if some rogue gene, long suppressed and only finding expression in middle age, was causing him to act against what he not only believed was moral, but against his own best interests.

"A second cup would hit the spot."

They looked at each other for a moment, no doubt wondering, what spot would that be? Then Marla said, "Give me a ten minute head start." She reached into her coat and passed a yellow square of foolscap. "Directions."

Her lips pursed, too briefly for anyone to notice unless he or she were watching as closely as Jack. Then Marla slipped out the door and Jack slid the directions in his pocket realizing she'd written them out in advance. That was spooky, but also thrilling. He waited ten minutes. When the foolscap in his pocket failed to ignite, Jack exited onto Main Street, where behind the First National Bank building the sun was setting and the Ohio sky glowed pink and mauve.

He followed directions written in a neat, upright hand to a country road he'd never heard of. Marla's house was an A-frame at the end of a long driveway, no neighbors. Jack drove intentionally past before turning around at the first four-way intersection. On the passenger side, the land fell away towards the horizon which was still bright but no longer pink. Jack turned up the long drive and parked behind Marla's new Bug. It was five-fifteen, and he had to pick Simon up at the high school at six. (What a battle to get his own car for the day.) Jack hurried up the steep wooden steps. There was melting snow everywhere. Rock salt crunched underfoot. He opened the storm door. Before his hand touched the bell, the inside door opened.

He followed Marla into a large kitchen. A saxophonist, maybe Coltrane, maybe someone else, played something low and sinuous through hidden speakers. On a center island, a large white cup, piled high with foam, rested on a saucer.

"Let me take your coat."

When he handed it to her, feeling very large and sinful—he was six-one and two twenty, she couldn't have been more than five-two and weighed who knew how little—she exited and he watched her hips swivel under the green blouse and black leggings. Everything in the kitchen looked new and expensive. Blond oak floors. Hand-painted tile counters in Southwestern colors. He wondered where the money came from; surely not her salary at Tipton High. Marla returned, sipping white wine.

"It took you an awfully long time to get here."

"I missed the driveway."

"It's been three months since election night." The boldest blue eyes he'd ever gazed into. She glided to the counter, picked up the cappuccino and passed it to him. "Sugar?"

He could smell her perfume, light and floral. He shook his head, took the cup and saucer from her hands and bent to kiss her as she rose on her toes, open-eyed, to meet him. When he opened his eyes, the taste of her wine on his lips, she said, "You better put that down."

He nodded, tongue-tied.

"How long, do you think, we can keep it up?" Marla asked.

"The double entendres?"

She nodded.

"I have to leave in twenty minutes to pick up Simon."

"Rehearsal?"

He nodded.

"Then you better put that cup down, if you want to see the rest of the house."

Jack set the cup on the counter and followed Marla out of the kitchen. When he left twenty minutes later, he hadn't taken a sip, but the froth on the cappuccino had subsided, leaving a half inch between the dark liquid and the rim. Jack rushed out to his car and threw it into reverse. He arrived at the high school as Simon was spilling down the auditeria steps with the rest of the cast. Jack waved. Simon caught his eye and smiled.

✦ ✦ ✦

Genna called Denny Sweetwater Sunday morning, one week after Rich slept over. She could foresee a time when she would call him every Sunday, as she'd called Doris and Daddy her first year at college. She remembered those long ago Sunday nights, sitting cross-legged on her single bed, shielding her eyes and her personal affairs from Sarah, the perky freshman roommate from Des Moines she'd never much liked. Sorting laundry in the family room (perhaps she should propose a graduate seminar in cleaning products and laundry techniques; she seemed to spend more time at this than any intellectual work), she wondered if they'd have the same family tradition when Simon left for school. Or would he end up at Tipton (she hoped not), with no need for a scheduled call because he'd be home every Sunday so she could wash his clothes?

Denny said, "Call when you get to town, dear." Such a cheerful, reassuring voice. "We'll have you and the family over for dinner."

She'd felt a twinge of disappointment and now, folding boxers, realized she'd wanted Denny to want to see her alone and for herself.

"You don't have to cook," she said. "We'll go out."

"Not a problem."

She tried to imagine what he looked like, but could only conjure her own face, older and masculine.

"Marty handles the cooking, I do dessert. I hope you like chocolate."

"Do I ever."

"That's my girl."

Who knew what he'd meant, no doubt just the figure of speech. But conversation had paused before resuming much like lights flicker then come back on during an electrical storm. Instead of blinking numbers on clocks and appliances, nervous laughter had marked the bolt, and she'd gotten off, promising to call the following Sunday when she knew where they'd be staying.

Genna left the kids' laundry in the family room (they were still asleep), and walked upstairs with hers and Jack's. What a week. All that snow, then the rapid thaw. The weatherman was again predicting highs in the sixties. Then the Marla business. Just Saturday night she was accusing Jack of having an affair. A few days later Marla called at work to tell her about a special study hall she'd arranged and to suggest they get together at school, or if she had time, over lunch to discuss Simon's situation. She'd thanked Marla profusely. That sort of monitoring, what some might call nudging, was exactly what Simon needed. She arranged to see Marla the week before spring break, and to be in touch at least once this week by phone, just to make sure, as the guidance counselor said, that Simon stays on track. As if he were a train, Genna thought, who might derail.

After hanging up with the guidance counselor, Genna had been smitten by guilt. How could she accuse Jack, and on Valentine's Day! When she returned home after speaking to Marla on Wednesday, she guessed it was, or maybe Thursday, she tried to apologize for raving out, but Jack wouldn't listen. He looked annoyed or embarrassed, she couldn't decide which. It was nothing, he tried to say, though they both knew it wasn't. At best, a misunderstanding. More fallout from last winter. Then, last night, Lizzie went out early. An hour later, when Simon drove off, she waited for Jack to make some genial attempt to pick up where they'd left off last weekend when the snow fell and Simon returned home with Rich. Instead, they ended up at the dreary four-plex in town, some predictable shoot-em up starring Tom Cruise, who'd left his wife, the jerk.

She waited again for Jack to make a pass on the ride home, and then in their bedroom, growing annoyed, then angry he hadn't found some way to make it up. She'd catch him peering at her over the book he'd picked up and she over the edge of hers, nine-thirty on a Saturday night, sitting next to each other in bed like the old married couple they were, Ma and Pa Barish. He'd look away as if he were afraid or shy, although he wasn't either, until she almost burst out, Okay, Jack, you've punished me enough. I'm going to sleep.

But Genna was a modern woman, a liberated woman; she didn't have to wait for her prince to come or anyone else. In the bathroom she slipped on the green come-fuck-me nightie she'd been wearing last Saturday, returned to the bed, took Jack's book out of his hand, took his glasses off his nose and sat down beside him. She set her hand on his knee, moved his hand to her breast, that ought to give him the idea, and kissed him on the mouth. When they came up for air, his hand had slipped under her nightgown, and she was finger-dancing across his crotch.

"You don't have to say that again," he whispered

"What did I say?"

He moved her hand to his nipple, inserted his tongue between her lips. When next they paused, her panties dangled from an ankle, and his finger moved inside her.

She'd whispered, "Nothing wrong with your hearing."

Now, carrying their clean laundry, Genna opened the bedroom door. "Come on, Jack." She kissed him below a drowsy ear. "You, me, and Sam are going for a run."

✦ ✦ ✦

Every day at three, Simon sang Sir Harry. That was how he thought of it. He didn't play Sir Harry, he sang and sometimes danced him. During the production, he'd wear a red velvet tunic (Ms. Cherry had said he could design and sew it himself if he wanted) and carry a long wooden sword wrapped in foil to make it look like steel.

When he was little he'd loved swords. He spent years as He-Man slicing up Skeletor, but he was also He-Man's best friend Teela, the woman warrior. What astonishing boots women super-heroes got to wear; he was always jealous. Simon had two poseable Teela figures, Brown and Red Teela, with different colored hard plastic hair. He'd slash and dash, playing Teela when he fought with his sword and shield wearing the bathrobe he pretended was Teela's short dress. How freaky was that! Teela was always beating the whiz out of everyone, the little dyke! Dad was always trying to get him to play football, but he wanted to play Teela and Skeletor. Some of that must have stuck, because here he was in grade eleven, running across the auditeria stage in his wide pants with velvet cuffs (too femme for Teela) to meet Tina Murphy who wore her blond hair up as Lady Larken, to announce his mission had succeeded. He'd found the Swamp Princess, who in her eagerness had swum the moat and climbed the castle wall, a real princess, if a little tacky and uncouth. Soon, You and I, oh my Lady Larken, will be married.

"Stop!" shouted Ms. Cherry, seated at one of the lunch tables in front of the stage.

Simon glanced at Lady Larken, who had a red zit like a Hindu prayer dot in the middle of her forehead. He ought to lend her some foundation. Lady Larken shrugged and looked annoyed, as if to say, What could they have done wrong, they hadn't even said their first lines?

Ms. Cherry, five-foot-one with bouncing curls, popped onto the stage.

"Simon, don't take this wrong." She glanced at Tina then back to him. "I don't like the way you run."

"Not fast enough?"

Ms. Cherry shook her head.

"Too fast?"

"Too..." Ms. Cherry's button eyes seemed to search his for the right word. "Too swishy, I guess."

Simon's cheeks burned.

"Look," Ms. Cherry said. "I'm not trying to embarrass you. But Sir Harry is like this big macho stud. He's running to tell Lady Larken he's done it! But instead of taking macho strides—"

Ms. Cherry retreated to stage left and ran towards them in a caricature of a manly run, swinging her arms, her little feet (no more than a size six, he thought), thudding against the stage, Oh, Lady Larken! she called, and grinned at them.

"—you're taking tiny steps and using entirely too much hip."

She ran at them again, and Simon had to admit, she looked just like him. Little baby steps and lots of hip, like Marilyn Monroe in some old movie. "But that's how I run."

"That's not how Sir Harry runs. Watch me again."

Ms. Cherry ran across the stage, arms swinging, feet thudding, her curls bouncing, a campy version of a masculine trot.

"You try," said Ms. Cherry.

So Simon ran across the stage with his wide pants swishing, his big feet thudding, swinging his arms, trying not to swing his hips, imitating Ms. Cherry imitating a man. When he drew up beside them he could see Ms. Cherry trying not to laugh.

"Pretty bad, huh?"

Ms. Cherry started to say something polite. Simon loved Ms. Cherry; it was almost like he could read her mind. She began to giggle, and it popped out of her. "No lie."

Then he was laughing, and even Tina Murphy—who sometimes looked at him with this expression on her narrow face, like, You expect me to play a love scene with this????—was grinning.

Ms. Cherry said, through giggles, "Don't worry, you'll get it."

"I can work on it with my dad, he's a jock." He glanced at Tina, who was still grinning. "Or maybe you can get your boyfriend, Nick, to teach you, and you can teach me."

At the mention of Nick Fleming, the mirth left Tina's face.

"Take it from the top," Ms. Cherry said, starting down the stage steps.

"You want me to run in?"

"If you think you can."

Simon retreated to stage left. He took a few, exaggerated running strides towards Lady Larken, gathered her in his massive arms and hugged her.

"Lady Larken!" he cried. "I have great news!"

chapter 17

Simon would never forget his first visit to Castro Street. They'd arrived in San Francisco the day before, Saturday afternoon. After they checked into the Bridge View—totally a dump, but San Francisco was expensive, Dad said, be grateful for beds, forget about a pool—they motored across the Golden Gate. They parked the rental—this really hot Mustang convertible (what had gotten into Mom and Dad?) that Simon begged to drive, but Dad kept insisting, No, he wasn't insured—on the shoulder below the tower of the bridge.

They climbed the path in reverse family order, Lizzie, Simon, Mom, and Dad, hiking as they used to in their California dream life, with a cloudless sky soaring above them like a blue cathedral, the rust-red tower rising up and up. Across the bay, a neighborhood of white matchbox houses huddled together, thousands and thousands. Far below—Simon almost couldn't bear to look—roiled the purple-blue waters of San Francisco Bay. Tiny sailboats, their wakes too small or light to be seen from such a height, dotted the Bay, while a massive cargo ship (Container, know-it-all-Dad said), steamed in from the ocean, cutting a path in the smooth tableau.

"It's really something." Dad draped his arm over Simon's shoulder. "Isn't it?"

"Beautiful," Simon admitted, wishing Dad would take his arm away.

"When Mom and I were courting, we used to come here at night and make out."

Gross, Simon thought, then Dad removed his arm. Thank God.

Dad added, "I'm really glad I got to show it to you."

Mom and Lizzie approached. They'd been off for a girls-only moment; Simon felt a pull of jealousy. Then Dad—he was always doing this kind of thing, Simon used to think he did it just to embarrass his kids, but no, it was just Dad in his Dadness being Dad—cornered some tourist, who already had a camera hanging from his neck like an anchor and asked him to snap their photo. The Barish family lined up with the bridge behind them and the cathedral sky overhead.

A few months before, Simon would have refused; he didn't like having his picture taken, and he certainly didn't appreciate Dad, who stood in the middle next to Mom, putting his arm around him again. But that was a few months ago. Today, they were touring San Francisco, gay capitol of the planet, and tomorrow, they were meeting his gay grandfather, how weird was that! Simon grinned; the tourist went snap-snap, then bowed and returned Dad's camera. Simon could tell it would be a great picture; he knew about such things, composition and light, the interplay of sea and sky.

Then they hiked down the hill and drove into Sausalito with all the beautiful hillside houses, the expensive shops, and sparkle of light on the Bay. Simon decided he would live here after he made his first million as a singer. Dad bought burgers (Simon and Lizzie), fish and chips (Mom and Dad), followed by this awesome Hawaiian ice cream, and didn't say a word when Simon ordered three scoops and sprinkles. (What was up with Dad?) They strolled and shopped until the day was swallowed by night.

As excellent as Saturday was, it didn't touch Sunday. Mom had been priming him for weeks. Dad had helped her find her biological father. Simon had never really liked Daddy, who was a stuck-up jerk most of the time, and not very nice, not even to Mom. Simon could tell Mom was incredibly pumped about meeting her real father, though she kept saying she wasn't, and that the most significant reason for the trip was for Simon to experience a gay-friendly world.

Who believed that? This was her dad (and his partner!) they'd be meeting, but Mom couldn't admit something this big was for her. So she'd talked for weeks in that way she had—like a professor, for God sakes, with all her opinions presented as facts, she couldn't help herself, that was Mom!—about the life-affirming gay images he'd see, the positive role models. Why, his grandfather and his partner had been together twenty years! After Mom's pep talks, Simon had concluded that San Francisco would be the opposite of Tipton, sort of like the Bizarro World in an old Superman he'd read. Gay guys would be the moonfaced assholes; as long as there was a world there'd be moonfaced assholes, assholes everlasting. Amen. They'd accost straight kids in high school hallways, growling, 'Die, Straight-ee, die! You eat pussy!'

Because Simon didn't want to be mistaken for straight, and because Mom said he'd have an hour or two to walk around by himself before going to dinner with his gay grandfather and his partner—he still couldn't get his thoughts around that; he grinned, almost giggled when he said it in his head—Simon chose his outfit with utmost care. He was awake long before Lizzie, trying on combinations. Definitely big pants, but red velvet cuffs or green? After thirty mirror minutes, while Lizzie slept like Rip Van Ludes, he selected the green then the red, then the green and finally the red, because it made him look just a little bit thinner. He'd wear his gray ribbed cotton tee, but which over shirt? Fish-net? The long sleeve blue button-down? After he'd modeled everything in his suitcase twice, he asked Lizzie, who pillowed her face and refused to look, the little brat. Simon knocked on the connecting door to Mom and Dad's room.

Dad growled, "Who is it?"

"Simon."

"Go back to bed."

He put his mouth near the door, whispered, urgently, "I need to talk."

Voices, footsteps. The door opened; the curtains were still drawn. Dad's big butt in boxers retreated to the bed, where Mom sat up, rubbing her eyes.

"What is it?"

"I was trying to decide what to wear." He held up the blue button-down, then the red short sleeve tee to which he'd sewn fish-net extensions. "What do you think?"

"It's seven-thirty in the goddamn morning."

Jerk.

"The blue," Mom said. "You're going to find the gay community dresses more conservatively than you think."

She held out her arms. He hugged her, and she smelled like morning Mom, musky, fusty, slumberous.

"You want to crawl in?"

Simon remembered all the times he'd slept between them, warm, protected. He shook his head.

"Let Lizzie sleep, you know she likes to." Mom stroked his cheek. "You'll look fine, dear, you're really very handsome."

He didn't believe her, but smiled and let himself out. Hours later, they went to breakfast. Hours after that, after examining every T-shirt in every T-shirt shop on Fisherman's Wharf, they drove to the Castro. The first thing Simon noticed, still in the car, were rainbow banners arching over the street, then rainbow flags in all the shop windows. And men, men everywhere. Tall men, short ones, white men, brown ones, bald men holding hands. Men with bare muscular arms wrapped around each other. The Barish family rental coasted down Castro. Simon's left leg twitched so badly he thought he'd explode into song. Whoops, I did it again!

Dad found a spot on a side street two blocks from Castro and backed into it; good job, Simon admitted, parallel parking. Soon they stood on the cool, sunny pavement. An old guy, maybe fifty, bald and hulking, strode towards them, black leather pants and vest, tattoos twining up and down his biceps. Simon watched him pass, avoided eye contact, his heart fluttering like a bird's.

Mom said, "Let's walk to Castro."

"Are you crazy?" Simon hissed. "I'm not walking with you."

"Until we find Sweet's Sweets." Mom glanced anxiously at Dad. "Where we're going to meet later."

"I'm not walking with you."

"We could be halfway there," Dad said. "If you'd stop fighting."

Simon crossed his arms. "I'd rather be dead than walk with you."

"Drama queen," Lizzie said.

"What?" Mom exclaimed.

"Mind your damn business, Dizzy Lizzie." He'd get her for that.

"That was out of line, Lizzie." Dad playing peacemaker, imagine that. "And Simon, think about Mom. You're not the only one stressed here. Why don't you walk twenty paces ahead? We'll follow behind like chattel."

Simon had no effing idea what chattel was, some kind of cow? "No, I'll walk behind you. What the hell is Sweet's Sweets anyway?"

"It's a chocolate shop." Mom's lip trembled. Her nostrils quivered as if she might start crying. Then she was crying.

"Mom!"

She wiped a single tear from each cheek. "A chocolate shop my father owns."

Mom looked as if she might start crying again. His mom crying on the street! In the Castro! He stepped forward and hugged her

"I'm sorry." He stepped back. "I'll be right behind you."

Dad mouthed, Thank you, then he, Mom, and Lizzie started. When they were almost to the corner, Simon threw his shoulders back, checked his collar was straight, ha-ha, and Simon Barish, young gay god, grandson of a gay grandfather, set out after his family, to cruise the Castro for the very first time.

✦ ✦ ✦

Simon walked away from Sweet's Sweets. They'd given him twenty dollars (he'd asked for fifty, eyes wide, extravagantly hopeful), then arranged to return in an hour and a half. Genna watched Simon's big jeans with red velvet cuffs until they disappeared in a sea of narrower, less flamboyant inseams, mostly khaki. How she loved that boy, who was always himself no matter the context. Who could have imagined this eighteen years ago, feeling the baby kick? Taking her gay son to the Castro and waving goodbye as he walked off as if for his first day of kindergarten. Or this: Simon at the bima for his Bar Mitzvah, surrounded by all the beaming Barishes, by Billy and his family, too, who'd looked pleased but out of place, which was very much how she felt right now.

"Well," Jack asked, "are you going in?"

Of course. Hadn't she mortified the children with her crying? Jack looped an arm over Lizzie. She was getting up there, taller already than Genna, but still Daddy's girl, even in her new independent phase.

"Lizzie and I will come in, or you can meet him alone. We won't be insulted."

Lizzie nodded, hair and dark eyes shining.

Genna admitted, "I would like to."

Behind the plate glass store-front, on a bed of doilies, rose a three-tiered display of cut-glass candy dishes topped with truffles and creme-filleds, fluted shells of white, dark, and milk chocolate, an array of dried fruit, apricot, pineapple, mangos, and others she didn't recognize, dipped in bittersweet. Small pink signs promised Homemade Fudge and Gaylord's Gelato. At the bottom right corner, black letters painted directly on the glass proclaimed: DENNIS

Sweetwater & Martin White, Proprietors. Genna glanced at Jack, and for the first time in years and years she heard her mother's voice deliver a favorite admonition: Genna, don't slump. Professor Genna Barish, nee Gordon, rolled her shoulders up and back, grasped the heavy brass knob and entered Sweet's Sweets, which was small and perfumed, over-decorated, stuffed with antique display cases. A tall black man eyed her from behind the oak counter. Receding cropped hair, gray temples, lengthened an already long and narrow face.

"My guess, you're Genna."

She nodded.

"Marty." He circled the counter, legs sheathed in gabardine, and presented an elegant hand. "Sweets," he whispered and motioned with his eyes, "is hiding in back."

She clasped Marty's cool palm.

"Mister Sweetwater!" Marty called. "There's someone here to see you."

The bead-covered back doorway parted. A medium-sized portly man looking neither old nor young stepped through. He had a fleshy face, a nose remarkable for how straight and narrow it was, luxuriant gray-white hair combed straight back. He wore a silver ascot tucked into a pale peach shirt and gazed at her with blue-gray eyes.

"Denny?"

"Call me Sweets, everyone does."

She pressed her cheek to his. They were nearly the same height.

"Please," he said, seeing she was weeping. "Please, don't."

His face was worn and warm, endearing when he smiled, attractive, if not classically handsome, much like Simon's. At the thought of Simon, she began to cry again.

"If you keep it up," he said, "I'll be crying too."

"Believe it," said Marty.

"My mascara will run." Again, that smile. "Is that really the first image you want of your father?"

She wiped tears from her cheeks for the second time in an hour. Denny (she couldn't yet think of him as Sweets) and Marty (Dark Chocolate, she would learn, in his performing days, and she saw how it must have been, the double and triple entendres between them, creme-filled), each offered her a hankie. She waved them off, asked for a bathroom; Marty directed her to a small room in back. When she returned, puffy and red-eyed, the shop was hopping. Three young men with short, tipped hair, pointed into the display case behind which Marty crouched. Jack and Lizzie stood near the door with Denny.

"Here she comes." Sweets smiled at her. "My beautiful daughter."

"You've met?"

"They charged in, sabers drawn, when you disappeared in back."

From the counter, boyish laughter burst from the shoppers.

"I assured them," Denny grinned, "you were safe."

Jack touched her hand. "You look a lot alike. Especially the eyes."

"Why, thank you." Sweets half-tossed, half-nodded his head, a gesture she could only think of as coquettish. "And this gorgeous creature, my granddaughter?" He reached for both of Lizzie's hands; to Genna's astonishment, she extended them. "Looks so much like dear Doris, gave me the absolute chills when she walked in."

Sweets gazed at Lizzie until she looked away. The three young men passed, babbling. When the door closed, Denny, who still grasped Lizzie's hands, asked, "Do you know what I do when I get such chills?"

Lizzie shook her head.

"Chocolate, my dear. I eat chocolate."

Later, Jack and Lizzie strolled down Castro. Genna waited for Simon. Sweets was sixty-six, Marty just a few years older than Genna herself. In between customers, they caught her up on their twenty-year romance. Marty declared being with Sweets had saved his life.

"The early Eighties? Before we knew The Killer? Come on! A young," he grinned at Sweets, "beautiful black man like me? I would have been vaunting all over town. If not for Sweets, I'd be dead, and he'd be one tired old man."

"Marty likes to think he keeps me young." Sweets smoothed his ascot. "But I keep him young by being so terribly old every single day. All that gray hair, yet always the young one. But for all his delusions, there's no denying loving Marty has brightened every day of my life for twenty years."

"That's so sweet," Genna said, wondering if Jack would say that about her.

Simon returned sooner than expected. Genna looked up and there he was, eyes shaded, peering in the shop window. She hurried out to fetch him. Before she could speak, he said, "Some guy tried to pick me up."

"Really?" She kissed his cheek and led him inside. "How nice for you."

"Mom!" A Gay Pride button adorned his shirt. "He was like, Dad's age, and he put his hand on my butt."

"Really." She caught Sweets's eye. What was wrong with her? Why didn't she find all this disgusting or at least terrifying? "What did you do?"

"Told him I had to meet my parents." Simon looked around. "Then I ran up here."

Sweets said, "Perfect. Don't talk to strange men, or take candy from them, either." He extended his hand. "Simon, I'm Sweets, your grandfather. And that young man behind the counter—"

Marty, who was re-filling a dish of truffles, waved.

"—has been my companion for twenty years, which makes him your grandpa, too."

Genna couldn't decide who looked more astonished, Marty or

Simon. Sweets shook Simon's hand. Although their eyes were different, they had the same face and round body, although Simon, taking after Jack , was much larger.

"Now that we've been introduced, may I offer you some chocolate?"

"Simon doesn't like candy."

"Mom!"

She caught Sweets's eye and smiled. This whole business of genes and genetics, bowler hats off to Gregor Mendel. If not the gay genetics Jack had told her he was writing about, there was no mistaking the basic phenotypical expression of body type, nose, face, and maybe even soul, passing unbroken from Sweets through her to Simon.

"Actually," Genna said, "Simon loves chocolate."

"Ah," said Sweets. "The nougat doesn't fall far from the wrapper."

They dined at Sush-He, a Japanese restaurant a few blocks away, where the all-male staff wore tiny tight shorts like volleyball players. Sweets refused to let them see the bill. She glanced at Jack, knowing he'd be torn between wanting to be manly and pay their share, and his concern about how much this trip was costing. But she couldn't read Jack's eyes in the aqua restaurant light, or find his thoughts in the New Age surround sound; he seemed alone and adrift in this undersea world in which she and Lizzie were the only females.

Marty and Sweets walked them to their car. Simon and Lizzie led the pack, followed by Marty, who was long-legged as a fawn. Sweets walked to Genna's left, Jack on her right in the fog that had rolled in after dark. Genna rubbed goose flesh from the backs of her arms, wishing she'd remembered a sweater.

"You don't know what a dream this is. Not just you," Sweets touched her hand, "but the children. I'd thought only Marty would outlive me. Now all this extravagant life from one night of drunken fumbling with Doris Krebs." He grinned. "What a beautiful, unhappy girl she was. Half the straight men were in love with her. The gay men wanted to be her."

In the fog-muted glow of streetlights, she glanced at Jack.

"Doris declared she could never love anyone except me."

Genna thought that may have turned out to be true.

Sweets continued, "I was very dashing, you know, leading man in Webster's productions of *Camelot*, *South Pacific*, and *Showboat*. Doris announced, she was so imperious, for graduation and as a celebration of our four years of friendship she wanted to sleep with me just one time. Though once we got rolling," Sweets smiled, remembering, "we kept at it all night. Doris was very determined, and I did have feelings for her. In the morning, the first and only time I woke up beside a woman, she hugged and kissed me tenderly. 'See,' she said. 'You've changed!'

"Part of me wished it were true, but I knew who I was. And part of me was furious. How could my best friend not know? After all I'd put up with, and told her about. And part of me, well, we were twenty-two. So I didn't say the whole time I was fantasizing about this cute freshman Freddy Parker. I said, 'It was a one-time gift, Doris, pure magic.'

"She wouldn't let go. 'You could, you could, you could if you loved me.' Over and over. And this still breaks my heart—"

Sweets looked down his narrow nose, placed his hands on his substantial hips, and her long-dead mother stood beside her.

"'Denny, I can do whatever those boys do for you.'

"I should have kept quiet. But I was young. 'That's just it, I don't love you, Doris, not like that. And what those boys do, I'm sorry, but you can't.'

"She went nuts. I'd ruined her life, I'd humiliated her, and someday I'd feel what she felt. I would learn that love could turn to hate." Sweets stopped walking. "Maybe that's why she didn't tell me about you. To settle the score."

"Could be," Genna said. "She didn't like me very much."

"That's not true," Jack said.

She felt a flash of rage. "Trust me, Sweets. Doris loved me, she wasn't a monster, but she didn't really like me."

Sweets asked, "Did you know her very well, Jack?"

"Less than a year."

"She was formidable. It's so sad she missed all of this."

Sweets spread his arms to encompass the vanguard of Marty, Simon, and Lizzie, who'd stopped in front of the silly convertible Jack had talked her into renting when the Alamo agent offered it for a mere fifty dollars extra for the week. What about our budget, she'd asked.

A mid-life fantasy that's not X-rated, and seven dollars a day? What more could you want? A car that won't blow my hair around?

Sweets said, "Nice ride, children."

Simon said, "They won't let me drive it."

"He's not insured on a rental," Jack said.

"Some rules," Sweets replied, "are made to be broken."

Even in the dark, she could feel Jack's annoyance.

"Yeah, Dad."

"Maybe when it's not so dark and foggy." Genna glanced at Jack, who looked unmoved and immovable.

"Maybe," Marty chimed in, "we shouldn't be telling Jack and Genna what rules to make, Grandpa."

Sweets turned towards her. "When do we get to see you again?"

"We're free all week."

"I'm busy during the day tomorrow," Jack added. "But otherwise…"

"Why don't you come over Tuesday? Marty will prepare a Thai feast."

"Spice okay?" Marty asked.

She glanced at her family. She was certain they were nodding.

"Come by the shop," Sweets said, "at six."

Everyone hugged everyone. They climbed into the ridiculous convertible and drove off. Sweets and Marty waved, a round white man and a tall black one, diminishing then disappearing in the foggy night.

chapter 18

Jack dropped Genna and the kids at the Exploratorium then continued on to meet Dr. Rajiv Menard. In his student days, Jack had loved the drive through Golden Gate Park. But he'd been gone so long, he feared he'd miss the turn. So much for a relaxing ramble. Soon he was winding out of the park headed south on Nineteenth Avenue through a neighborhood of modest homes, immodestly priced. If only he'd bought one or even better, two, back in grad school. His parents would have loaned him a down payment, as they later did in Ohio. If he'd been prescient enough—Jack glanced at the bright sky reflected in the windows of the white row houses lining Nineteenth Avenue—they might have had some way, financially, out of Tipton. The profits on San Francisco real estate would dwarf a lifetime of his professor salary. Now that, Jack thought, as he approached Nordstrom Plaza, was a dark thought on such a brilliant day. To live and die a wage slave in Ohio.

Fifteen minutes later, he was striding past a reflecting pool in the UCSF research quad. Rajiv Menard was thirty-six; other than that, Jack knew little about him, although his name suggested a mixed racial heritage. Just then, spray from a fountain in the pool stung Jack's cheeks. Smelling, almost tasting, the chlorinated needles, he wondered if there were a meteorological lab nearby, and if this damp, wind-blown plaza was designed to recreate the micro-climatological patterns of the Bay. Unlikely,

Jack admitted, as he entered the high rise lobby, glass and gray stone.

He pushed the button for nine, and checked the collar of his sports coat in the burnished doors after they slid shut. Snazzy, distorted Jack. When the doors reopened, his footfalls preceded him along the tiled corridor to 916, inside which Dr. Menard waited. Rajiv was medium height. Straight, nearly black hair and light Indian skin under which a five o'clock shadow already gathered in a dark and spreading blush. His lips were full, cheeks rounded. On his left hand he wore an expensive watch, but no wedding band. The man was quite handsome, Jack thought, in a soft sort of way.

"Welcome, Jack." Menard smiled and extended his arm, a narrow wrist unbending out of his lab coat. "I've been keeping an eye out."

"Rajiv," Jack answered, feeling exceptionally pleased; he couldn't say exactly why. "Delighted to meet you."

The scientist's face was smooth and perfect, as if he were a Bollywood star. "My directions were fine?"

"Perfect." If Rajiv had European—make that Caucasian—blood, Jack couldn't detect it in his features.

"Come on," he said. "I'll show you around."

It was only then Jack realized it was probably time to stop shaking his hand.

After a quick tour, they headed out to a Starbucks where they sat in adjacent armchairs warmed by sunlight through plate glass. Rajiv drank a machiata or some damn thing, teasing apart a poppy seed muffin with long, slim fingers. Jack sipped cappuccino, he could never think of anything else, and recalled the last time he'd been to Starbucks; he and Marla in the front window, puppy lust on display.

"It's funny you should arrive today." Rajiv moved a wedge of muffin to his lips. "I've just finished an interesting book, *Reinventing the Male Homosexual,* perhaps you know it?"

Jack shook his head.

"The author questions the political advisability of gay gene research." Rajiv glanced up from his dissection of the muffin. "As you know, when Hamer first published, everyone cheered because it seemed to trump the conservative argument that homosexuality was a lifestyle choice that didn't deserve equal protection."

"Yes, of course."

"But in ways I hadn't exactly been thinking about, the biological explanation, even if it's only partial, leaving room for environmental factors, which is what I believe— "

"So do I," Jack said, although he believed Simon had been born gay.

"—re-pathologizes homosexuality, but moves the disorder from the mind— "

Jack wondered if he'd told Rajiv about Simon.

"—to the genes, where once again, if Hamer's work is valid, it's maternal over-influence that produces homosexuality. What's interesting, and I must admit troubling—"

Rajiv fed another piece of the poppy seed muffin to his full lips.

"—is that when psychologists officially removed homosexuality from their list of disorders, they lost control of the subject, as if forces on the Right were saying, 'If you can't cure the faggots, just shut up.'"

Rajiv picked some crumbs from the napkin in front of him and moved them fastidiously to his mouth. If Jack hadn't been sure before, that gesture convinced him: Rajiv was gay.

"So here I come, thinking I'm advancing the cause. When in fact, I'm adding ammunition to the homosexuality as feminized pathology argument. It's not as if I hadn't thought about this. You'd have to be an absolute ass not to realize that isolating a marker might lead to prenatal testing and hence, a 'cure.'"

"I've been writing about that myself."

"You told me." Rajiv looked straight into his eyes in a way, Jack realized, that straight men did not. "But my unexamined assumption, that the only site to check was the x chromosome, as if it couldn't possibly be on the y, and therefore the influence of the father— "

"The presumptively straight father."

"—embarrasses me."

Rajiv raised his mug and drank deeply. Jack rarely met a man so passionate about his work; then again, he didn't have colleagues at Tipton with whom he discussed his research. He used to talk to Genna, but she'd hated the eugenics project—Who would want to think about the Nazis day after day, and our connections to them?—and he doubted she'd feel any better about this one. What if he and Genna had been able to test for the gay gene, would they have done so? Jack loved loving women. Perhaps too much, and too variously. But if given the choice, would he have really wanted to produce a son who didn't?

"But what if you're right?" Jack asked. "You're a scientist first, an activist second."

"Ah," said Menard and smiled. "There's no innocence, Jack. Surely, as a historian, you're not going to argue that."

"I suppose not."

Behind his dark lips, Rajiv's teeth looked moist. He tapped Jack's wrist with his index finger. "So what brought you to the subject?"

"My son came out last fall. He's seventeen."

Rajiv covered the back of Jack's hand with his own. "Should I be looking on the x or the y?"

Jack flushed. He felt, admit it, a whisper of excitement. Handsome Rajiv Menard was flirting. How flattering. But he didn't want to give him the wrong idea. "Probably the x. We met my wife's biological father for the first time yesterday. He owns Sweet's Sweets, the candy shop on Castro."

Behind the counter, the cappuccino maker hissed.

"I've been there." Rajiv patted Jack's wrist then removed his hand. "What you're saying is this grandfather's gay?"

As a three dollar bill.

"Have you heard," Rajiv asked, "of the theory of sexual antagonism?"

Jack shook his head.

"It's my current favorite amongst the sexual anthropology theories."

Jack's hand still burned where Rajiv had held it. "I've read the kinship theories."

"Of course. Then there's status. Young men, think Rome, fucking older high status men," Rajiv winked, "to gain status thus making themselves more likely to have lots of children. When you think of it, that supports Kinsey's version of sexuality: sexual acts, not a sexual identity."

Before he knew what he was saying, Jack asked, "Have you ever had sex with a woman?"

"What makes you think I'm gay?"

Jack burst out laughing. "Everything."

"A very long time ago." Rajiv grinned. "I didn't much like it. What about you, Jack?"

"With a man?"

Rajiv nodded, and Jack shook his head.

"A pity," Rajiv murmured, "from a research standpoint. Now, sexual antagonism. What if some gene made men very sexually attractive to you. If you're male and have that gene, you're gay. If you're a woman, men would appear very sexy to you and you'd have more sexual contact, and hence, more children. What about your wife, Jack, she a sexpot?"

He thought about Genna's shy smile, the way they were in bed. "She's a professor of romance languages and women's studies."

"Was she slutty?" Rajiv drained his mug, and wiped a moustache of steamed milk from his lip. "I mean, before you met her?"

"I don't think so."

"Well, it's only a theory. But let's say this gene, wherever it's located, functions by inhibiting the production of testosterone. That would make men less butch, and since testosterone slows down menses in women, a woman with less testosterone would reach menses earlier, hence providing her with the possibility of bearing more children."

"Of course," Jack said, "there's no proof of this, is there?"

"That's why it's a theory. And theories, you know, are like assholes." Rajiv winked and stood up. "Why don't we head back to my lab? There's something I want to show you."

✦ ✦ ✦

They saw Sweets and Marty every day except Monday and Thursday when they drove to Big Sur and stayed overnight, returning in time for Friday dinner at the Grandpas. (They'd settled into that, the Grandpas, Sweets and Marty.) Marty, she thought, turned out to be a remarkably adept chef: Thai Tuesday, French Wednesday. Friday's meal was haute Mexican. Guacamole with homemade chips, prawns in chipotle salsa, chicken mole, and Genna's favorite, chiles rellenos in a batter light as tempura.

"Who cooks at Casa Barish?" Marty asked, finally sitting after serving the rellenos and setting the platter on the sideboard. "Lord knows I'm the kitchen help here."

"Mostly Mom." Simon filled his plate for the third time, "But I'm learning."

"Oh, really?" Marty occupied the foot of the table, Sweets the head. "What do you cook?"

"Stir-fry," Simon said, "and pasta with meat."

"Anything with meat," offered Jack, who teased Simon about how much he ate, although he often ate as much himself. "Lots of meat."

Marty said, "Too much red meat's not good." He glanced at Simon and added, mildly, "But I'm sure you know that."

Sweets beamed from the head of the table, oddly quiet tonight. Jack wasn't his usual verbose self, either, and hadn't been for days. Lizzie never said much around adults, which left the conversational burden on Simon and Marty.

Suddenly, Sweets asked, "I was wondering if Simon, and Lizzie, of course, could spend the night? We'd feed them, maybe take them shopping"—Simon's eyes lit up—"and get to know them better. You kids," he smiled at Jack, "could have a night alone."

She knew Lizzie wouldn't want to. On the drive up from Big Sur, Lizzie had announced she was dirty and needed to sleep. And Genna knew without asking, that Jack would think it too weird to leave only the gay child with the gay couple, although since he'd started his new project, she wasn't sure what he was thinking.

Lizzie asked, "Can we?"

Genna felt a rush of shame.

Thinking, perhaps, of his sex life, Jack replied, "If it's all right with your mother, it's fine with me."

"What about clean clothes?" Genna asked.

"No need," Sweets said. "We'll take them shopping as soon as the stores open, I promise."

"On one condition."

Simon glanced at her. She'd been working on him all week and he'd refused.

"Simon has to sing for us."

She watched him weigh the pluses and minuses. Shopping spree, a night with the Grandpas?

"He doesn't have to," Sweets said. "He's not some organ grinder's monkey."

"And I'm not an organ grinder. But if he wants to stay he has to sing."

Simon said, "I don't have my music."

"'Some Enchanted Evening,' you know the words."

She glanced towards Sweets, who must have performed the song when he knew Doris, but Sweets's face was unreadable. Later, after they'd retired to the living room with its wingback chairs and dusky rose Victorian settee, Simon stood in the center of the room, wrists crossed below his waist. Last spring, she'd watched him perform "Some Enchanted Evening" at a talent show sponsored by a Keep-Our-Kids-Out-of-Trouble church group in Cincinnati. Most of the performers and audience members packed into the grade school auditorium were black. Hip-hop and rap predominated; boys in sweats and Air Jordans, girls in matched skintight coveralls, shaking teenage booty, competed for cash. Halfway through, Simon strolled out in wide pants and a black shirt, smiled into the spotlight, and crooned his selection, which was half a century and several cultures removed from Pleasant Ridge Elementary.

"Damn, that boy can sing," a woman in front of her exclaimed when the applause subsided.

"That's my son," she'd said, kvelling. Jack had taught her the Yiddish: kvell: to brag, or boast publicly.

"Some enchanted evening," Simon began in the Grandpas' living room. Jack caught her eye. Lizzie, poor dear, looked bored: listening yet again to Simon. But it was the Grandpas she couldn't get over, seated together on the settee. Marty covered his mouth with his left hand. With his right hand he grasped Sweets's left, and it was her father's rapt expression she would remember after they'd returned to Ohio, Sweets mouthing the words as Simon sang.

"...and somehow you'll know, you'll know even then..."

Simon seemed in exceptionally fine voice. If she closed her eyes, which she did often when he practiced, she could imagine a Technicolor Enzio Penza stepping off the big screen to stand before her, the only difference being Simon's voice might even be a little better. She preferred it; not quite as heavy, more youthful and romantic. She didn't dare close her eyes now; she couldn't miss a moment. Then Sweets stood. Actually, Marty pushed him out of the settee.

"Sing, Grandpa," Marty said.

Oh, no! Simon hates it when anyone sings with him. But Simon nodded and Sweets joined him in the center of the room. They started from the beginning, or was it the second time through?

"Some enchanted evening, you may see a stranger…"

Sweets's voice was lovely, not nearly as resonant as Simon's (she'd never heard anything that was), but the voice of a man who'd sung proudly his entire life. She could hear, she thought, the voice her mother had heard. On certain notes, their voices blended so perfectly, she couldn't tell them apart. Not Enzio Penza, when she closed her eyes and listened, but one voice, joined through her, the mysteries of heredity on display. She watched them, both faces similarly shaped, as Simon and Sweets built towards the crescendo: "Once you have found her, never let her go. Once you have found her,

…NEV-ER…LET…HER…GO!"

Sweets's voice quavered on the top note, but what of it? He kissed Simon's cheek, hugged him, then took his hand. Like cast members, they bowed from the waist, while Jack, Marty, and even Lizzie applauded.

This, Genna thought, this, she would never forget.

✦ ✦ ✦

They flew home Sunday. Simon had a window seat, 28A, and a new button on his book bag: F.A.G. Fantastically Accessorized Gentleman, a gift from Marty. Lizzie occupied 30A. Mom and Dad sat a few rows behind Lizzie. That's how they traveled now. Everyone at the window except Dad who didn't care.

Simon gazed down through fluffy clouds to mountains topped with snow. The Sierras, Dad declared when they flew out, which felt so long ago Simon was a totally different person. Despite the weirdness of Friday night, he'd never had a better time. How weird? He told Lizzie he'd effing kill her if she told Mom or Dad. So far, she hadn't. But he couldn't trust her, the little sneak. If it were her secret, he wasn't sure he could keep it, either. Friday, after Mom and Dad left, he and Lizzie had been watching TV in the guest room. First Marty knocked and asked if they needed anything. Then, just before eleven, Sweets arrived in a silk dressing gown, a style Simon had seen in old movies. Smiling, Simon felt again how tightly Sweets had gripped his hand when they finished singing.

"May I talk to you a moment?"

He wanted to say no. He was loving *Mrs. Doubtfire*, but that wouldn't be polite. He nodded, and Sweets asked Lizzie, "Will you be okay for awhile?"

He followed Sweets downstairs to the living room where a pot of mint tea and a dish of chocolates filled a silver tray. After he'd eaten two coffee creams and washed them down, Sweets asked, "Tell me, Simon, have your parents ever spoken to you about sex?"

Was this weird, or what? "Not for a while."

Sweets looked straight at him. "What did they say?"

"You know, eggs and sperm." He remembered Dad sitting him down in ninth grade. What a joke. "And always use a condom, Dad's big on condoms."

"What about gay sex?" Sweets's lips formed a little smile. "What have they told you about that?"

Simon thought he should be embarrassed, but he wasn't. "Nothing."

"Of course not." Sweets popped another chocolate and wiped his lips. "How much have you figured out on your own?"

Simon looked away.

"Simon, you're blushing."

He was.

"I'm asking because I've invited a young friend over. Danny is only a few years older than you. He's very good-looking, disease-free, and from what we've been told, extremely skilled." Sweets smiled again. "He's yours if you want him."

Simon's heart clanged. "What do you mean?" he stammered.

"I mean, Danny's perfectly delightful, and I've asked him"—Sweets wiped his thumb and forefinger across his lips, removing a smudge of chocolate—"to initiate you into the joys of homosexual love. If this is too embarrassing for you," Sweets hesitated, "just say so."

Simon shook his head.

"It's a tradition," Sweets said, "in many societies, for elders to arrange for their young men's first sexual experience to make sure it's the right sort. Makes perfect sense, don't you think?"

Simon wasn't sure what he thought.

"My first experiences were with older, ugly men in unfortunate, even degrading circumstances. I don't want that for you, Simon."

Sweets smiled, Simon thought, like a fairy godfather, getting him ready for the ball.

"This will have to be our secret, of course. Not a word to your mother. And if it makes you uncomfortable, now or at any time, just say so, and Danny will stop. I've already told him. What do you say?"

Simon gazed at the sun reflecting on the silver wings. Remembering Danny, tall and slender, a rose tattoo blossoming from the dark of his pubic hair to the knotted skin of his navel, a pierced right nipple, Simon felt an erection tenting his jeans and glanced at the old woman beside him. If she noticed the bulge, he'd just die! Simon lowered the tray from his seat back and smiled at Missus Wart and Wrinkles, who smiled back, unaware. He replaced his headset, turned on his Walkman, and tried to focus on the music, but couldn't stop remembering how Danny's cock had tasted in his mouth, salty and hard. How amazing his had felt in Danny's, the first time anyone had done that for him, warm, close, and moist, how totally exciting when what must have been Danny's tongue licked it up and down. He'd never thought of that! Danny was a god!

Simon glanced down. The effing tray was bouncing! The old lady would know for sure. Good cock! No, bad cock. Not his cock at all, his twitching leg. The granny smiled sweetly—if she only knew—and he smiled, too, kitten innocent, remembering how Danny had made him lie half on his stomach, half on his side and whispered, "This might hurt a bit, Sugar, I'll stop if you don't like it."

But he liked it very much, oh, he really liked it, this was what it was all about! And he kissed Danny, who had a face like Leo DiCaprio's. Then Simon went back upstairs. He was so happy, he couldn't not tell Lizzie. Or maybe she guessed. Anyway, he confessed everything, and now he'd kill her if she breathed a word to Mom or Dad.

The clouds were thicker; Simon couldn't see the mountains. Or maybe they'd passed them. Then, through a break in the puffy white, he spied the ground far below, flat and brown, and felt a rush of fear. They were approaching the land of moonfaced assholes. Who in Tipton could he even tell about Danny? Rachel had been acting strange before he left. Not Rich, who would trust Rich? Maybe Peter, but Peter might be shocked and tell his mother. Sometimes Peter seemed to know he was gay, other times he didn't. Peter's mother must know. No reasonable adult could miss it. The first time you heard Peter squeal or watched him walk, you suspected. The second time, you knew. But Peter's mother, Mrs. Warner, might think she had to protect poor innocent Peter from Simon, or maybe Simon from himself, so she'd feel obligated to tell his parents.

He couldn't tell anyone. He shouldn't tell anyone. The greatest thing that had ever happened in his life—though there were moments when it felt a little weird, his first time with a total stranger—and he couldn't discuss it. Tipton really sucked. Thank God he had the play.

Simon put his cheek against the cool glass. The clouds were too thick to peer through. After a moment, he asked the old lady to let him out. She stood without a word, and Simon walked down the aisle, past his sister and parents who looked asleep, their heads resting on each other's shoulders—Aw!—to lock himself in the tiny airplane and dream his dreams about Danny, far from the world's prying eyes.

PART THREE:

The Kiss

chapter 19

Monday after break, Ms. Cherry assembled the entire cast. Twenty-four days to opening night, Kiddos! Have you memorized your lines like I told you to? (Simon hadn't.) Time To W-O-R-K!

Work they did, every day after school for three hours; Saturday and Sundays were work days, too. Forget your life! Ms. Cherry had proclaimed their first day back, a floppy-curled, pint-sized, non-stop motor, tap-dancing across the stage. Next three weeks, ta-da, arms stretched, this is your L-I-F-E ! ! !

But Simon's life wouldn't stay forgotten. There was schoolwork, going as badly as ever; well, not quite as badly. Mrs. Lindstrom insisted he show her his assignment book–everyone had to, five or six losers, mostly freshmen and sophomores—so he had to stop drawing true-love hearts, Danny and Simon 4-ever—and copy his French and English assignments. Not that he had a *prie* of finishing the French most days, but if he didn't have an assignment written down, Mrs. Lindstrom sent him back. For a small, pretty woman, Mrs. Lindstrom was surprisingly tough and kind of weird. He'd catch her big eyes on him. Sometimes, she'd ask him to say hello to his parents. The first day back she quizzed him about San Francisco, which was also odd. He hadn't told her they were going.

Tonight, Saturday, was Simon's last shift at Burger King until after the show; nineteen days to opening night! As soon as he got the part, he told Mary he would need a few weeks off. But she said he forgot, and now she was all pissy. You're scheduled all next week, what in hell am I supposed to do?

Cram it up your hiney, he'd wanted to shout as she stood before him, round Mary, face like a seat cushion, pinball eyes super-sized behind her glasses. But she'd always been kind: Fry Guy's first night. So he didn't snap back, not because she was his boss, but because he suspected she might be having a bad day. Did this mean he was growing up?

At five to ten, Fry Guy manned the register: visor, greasy shirt, black pants, heavy shoes. His feet ached; they always did at work. Some doctor had said his feet were flat. If there was ever a draft, he wouldn't have to go. That's not the only reason, Simon thought, bored during the nightly lull: too early for the bar crowd and in between movies. They wouldn't have to ask him. Oh, Sergeant, Hon, I've got something to tell you!

A mob of high-schoolers burst in. Simon plastered 'May I help you?' on his puss and looked up to assist the first people on line. Tina Murphy and Nick Fleming.

"Lady Larken. May I help you?"

Tina said, "I didn't know you worked here."

"It's my last night till after the show."

Fleming furrowed his dark brows. What a hottie, that blue-black hair and Superboy chin. J. Crew pocket tee tight across his chest. "They don't let you touch the food?"

"Nick," Tina whispered, "don't be a jerk."

He was starting to like Tina; they hung out at rehearsal. "I touch everything, Nick. I work here."

"Come on." Nick grabbed Tina's arm.

Behind them, Simon recognized a pack of Smokers.

"Let's go to Wendy's." Nick flashed a mouthful of teeth. "Where they don't let faggots make the food."

Nick started towards the door drawing Smokers like leaves in his slipstream. Tina pulled away. "I'm gonna stay."

Nick's eyes glittered.

"I like the food better." Red circles spotted Tina's cheeks. "I'll be there soon."

"You're coming."

"Nick," she said, "just go."

Fleming glanced furiously around. His dark eyes seized Simon. "You're dead, fat-boy."

He stormed to the door and tried to slam it behind him, but the hydraulic closer wouldn't let him. Suddenly, there was sound, light, movement. Plastic forks scraped. An old woman coughed. In the kitchen, fries sizzled in oil. Mary came out and stood beside him. "I heard what he said. Want me to call the cops?"

Simon shook his head. "Lady Larken, what would you like to eat?"

Tina Murphy turned. She stood maybe ten feet away, near the service island stacked with napkins and ketchup. The spots on her cheeks burned brighter.

"I don't want to cut the line."

But there was no line, just two college girls, and the short, dark one said, "You were first."

Looking more and more like Lady Larken, Tina returned to the register, where the Fry Guy, feeling quite a bit like Sir Harry, said, "Whatever you want, it's on me."

Mary smiled. "Don't forget your employee discount." Then she disappeared in the back.

Tina said, softly, "Nick's such a jerk. He thinks, because of his family, he can tell everyone what to do."

Sir Harry replied, "I'm used to it."

Lady Larken, even softer, "You must think I'm a jerk for going out with him."

"Whopper, Lady Larken? Chocolate shake, perchance?"

"Fish sandwich, Sir Harry. King Size fries. And Simon." She touched his arm. "You're really nice, you know?"

✦ ✦ ✦

Sunday, after rehearsal, Simon drove towards Pleasant Acres. He was meeting Rich at the entrance at four-thirty. At four-forty-five, still no Rich. Simon could only hang out until six. He promised Mom he'd work on an English project he'd forgotten about until this morning when she made him check his assignment book: a three-page paper on *Beowolf*, due Tuesday. Beowulf was pretty cool, a superhero for his time—Simon couldn't remember what time that was—who whacked off a monster's head. It turned out the first monster wasn't the bad one. That was Grindel, no Grendel, the mother of all monsters who was totally pissed when she learned her baby monster was dead. Beowulf slew her, too.

Simon wondered what his mother would do if someone slew him.

Outside the Camry, a posse of middle-school boys on banana seats hurled sticks and insults at each other. Your momma's so fat she needs a telescope to see her own ass!

You need a microscope to find your own dick!

Your sister didn't!

Everywhere, it was spring. When they arrived home last week from the airport, purple crocuses and white snowdrops bloomed in their front yard. They didn't even know they had them! This week, daffodils had opened. Even the Pleasant Acres sign was ringed by yellow mouths. Where was Rich? They'd spoken on the phone yesterday morning, today, too, before rehearsal when Simon told him about Danny.

No way, Rich replied, you're such a liar.

I'll show you.

Simon waited, heart thudding. At five, Rich still hadn't showed. This was why he needed a cell phone. But Dad was being a dick as usual. You're working. Pay for it yourself. Simon started the Camry and drove cautiously into Pleasant Acres. Soon, he came up on the middle-schoolers. He honked, trying to pass. The boys turned, their mouths dark slashes in white faces. Instead of yielding, they flipped him off, one by one, like a marching band. Simon leaned on his horn. The kids pedaled even more slowly, fanning out to block the street. Simon imagined flooring it and speeding through them, bicycles flying like pins in the bowling alley Dad used to take him to. Instead, he pulled over. He wanted to murder those brats! When he'd calmed down enough to stop strangling the wheel, he put the Camry in gear and drove slowly to Rich's street and parked across from the trailer. The crappy steps looked even worse than before, as if they were held on by crooked fingers. The dashboard clock read ten after five. Maybe he should just go home. But he really needed to see Rich. Ms. Cherry had mocked him because he flubbed his lines. Simon started towards the trailer. What was that name? Oh yes, Martin Long.

No one answered. Get back in the car. Then heavy footsteps. The door opened in, and Rich's grandmother peered out through the screen, her old face creased by silver mesh.

"Is Rich home?

"And you are?"

"Martin Long."

"Hold on, Mister." She opened the screen door and stepped out. "I know that voice. You're the one talked all that filth this morning! Rich Senior!" she shouted into the trailer. "That one— "

Simon took two steps backwards, turned and leapt. The lowest step snapped in two. Stumbling, he put his hand down like a touch-back, a fullback, whatever, a big stud footballer, and raced towards the Camry, thick legs propelling him. He pulled the driver's door open, stabbed the key in the ignition and roared off as the old monster and her son burst onto the porch sharking their fists. Simon flew off Rich's street bearing down on the middle-schoolers who tumbled from their bikes as he drove past, horn screeching.

Eighteen days to opening night.

✦ ✦ ✦

Jack hadn't spoken to Marla since California. But she'd left two messages on his office machine. Now here he was, a week later, angling across the main quad, crisscrossed by guilt and indecision, like a map that had been folded and refolded a hundred times. He consoled himself: he hadn't pursued her. Her place, her cappuccino, frothed but never sipped, her genuine concern for Simon much of the attraction. Jack filled his lungs with soft, spring air. Blossoms had burst on the sapling red buds Tipton groundskeepers lined the flagstone path with last fall. Song birds chorused. Boys sailed frisbees and coeds sunbathed in shorts and midriff blouses, bare shoulders and knees pushing from the grass like dandelions, as sure a sign as any that winter was over.

Jack stood for a few moments in front of Osborne Hall watching the tableau of campus life. When he spied Bob Henderson, one of his least favorite colleagues, crossing the quad, sunlight rebounding from his glasses like tracers, Jack hurried inside, a serial adulterer, a man attracted not just to other women, determined to make matters right.

The message minder on his office machine flashed a bold three.

Jack, come home as soon as you get this.

Jack, come home.

Jack, where are you?

Genna's tight, *There's a problem and I'm barely keeping it together* voice propelled him out his office without a second thought for Marla or anyone else. When he tried to turn off the cul-de-sac onto their driveway, two Tipton Township police cruisers blocked the way. Jack parked and ran down the driveway past the squad cars and daffodil soldiers guarding their woods. In the front flowerbed, near the preening Japanese maple, a four-foot-high cross smoldered, horizontal arms burnt black.

Sam bounded towards him smiling a toothy retriever grin. Jack rubbed Sam's muzzle then hurried on. In the living room, sunlight streamed through the windows. Genna sat on the couch opposite two uniformed officers, whose hands shot toward their holstered revolvers.

"It's my husband," she said, and the cops, both of them as big as Jack or bigger, one dark-haired, one nearly bald, returned their hands to their laps.

"Where are the kids?"

"Safe," Genna said. "Simon's at rehearsal, Lizzie has practice. You saw it?"

He crossed the room and hugged Genna, then faced the officers. "Jack Barish."

"Sergeant Heinsohn," said the older, nearly bald one, removing his hat from his lap to stand and shake Jack's hand. "My associate, Officer Trent."

Officer Trent was a mountain, six-four or five, two hundred eighty pounds; his neck rose from granite shoulders. Offensive lineman, Jack thought, grasping Trent's hand.

"Professor Barish," Heinsohn said when they were seated. He removed a notepad and a black pen from his coat pocket. "Can you think of a reason why anyone would do such a thing?"

"They're ignorant assholes?"

The officers exchanged glances. Trent fished a notepad and pen from his pocket. Genna squeezed his hand, as if to say, Whoa, Jack.

"Of course you're upset." Heinsohn's bushy eyebrows wagged on the blank screen of his forehead. "I want you to know, we share your outrage."

"When I returned from walking Sam," Genna said, "about two thirty, the cross was burning. I was gone maybe twenty minutes, half an hour at most. I don't know if whoever did it was watching the house and waiting for me to leave?"

She turned towards Jack, eyes leaden.

"Or, as I told the officers, they saw no car in the driveway, and assumed no one was home. Most days, if there's no car, there is no one. But I worked at home today, and because our son drove to school, there was no car."

"It's lucky you weren't home," Trent said. "It could have been terrifying."

Oh crap, thought Jack.

"I'm sure finding the object was frightening enough." Sergeant Heinsohn turned towards him. "So I ask you again. You know, your family's not black."

You noticed.

"So why would someone burn a cross?"

He turned towards Genna, who nodded a go-ahead. Why would he be anything less than honest anyway? "One, we're Jews. Two, our son is the only out gay kid in the high school." The cops exchanged glances. They looked like father and son, Heinsohn and Trent, with Trent a younger, buffer version, jaw-line tight, hair dark, eyes bright. "Anyway, I've always considered the Klan equal opportunity bigots."

"Who said anything about the Klan?" Heinsohn asked.

"Wasn't there a march here," Genna said, "maybe ten years ago?"

Trent said, "I never heard of the Klan burning a cross on no one's lawn but a black man's."

"Maybe they got the wrong house. Maybe," he glanced at Genna, "on top of everything else, we got us a stupid bigot."

The cops scribbled. After a moment, Heinsohn looked up and wiped sweat from his forehead. "I'd like you to think of anyone who might bear you a grudge. Anyone, who for any reason," his lips pursed, "might be angry at you."

Marla, Jack thought.

"No one," said Genna. "Jack?"

He shook his head.

"We're going to canvass the neighbors," said Heinsohn. "See if anybody saw anything. When will your children be home?"

"By six." Jack turned towards Genna, who nodded.

"We'd like to come back," Heinsohn added. "Your son might be the cause of all this."

"The what?" Genna demanded.

"Don't take me wrong," Heinsohn said. "Not that he's to blame."

"Then he's the object of an unprovoked attack," Genna said. "Not the cause."

"That's what I meant, ma'am."

Heinsohn replaced his hat. He looked different with his head covered. College professors, Jack could imagine him thinking. Liberals. Jews. No wonder. Trent replaced his officer's hat and Jack walked them towards the door, very conscious of walking between two men who were larger than he was.

Outside, Heinsohn said, "I hope I didn't upset your wife." His bushy eyebrows moved up and down. "My English ain't never been the most precise."

"Don't worry," Jack said. "By the way, the Klan still active around here?"

"Not that I know of," Heinsohn said. "But I might not know."

Trent asked, "Okay we come back around eight?"

Jack nodded.

Heinsohn said, "Don't worry, Mister Barish, we're gonna catch whatever vermin did this."

Trent yanked at the scorched wood, which came away easily. Not knowing whom to trust or believe, Jack watched them advance up the tree-lined drive, two large cops carrying a cross.

✦ ✦ ✦

After dinner, Simon and Lizzie bracketed Genna on the couch. Funny, Jack thought, lugging the reading chair's hassock towards the coffee table then straddling it. Well, not funny, strange, how much more he felt Simon resembled Genna now that he'd met Sweets and saw the origin of features. Simon lay his head on Genna's shoulder. If he could have climbed onto her lap, Jack suspected he would have. Even Lizzie, who usually maintained a minimum physical distance, the objective correlative to her psychic perimeter, crept close. Like puppies, which was Genna's favorite description when the kids were little. Puppies craving contact, soft, piled bodies, the available teat.

Four mugs of Ibarra Mexican hot chocolate rested on the coffee table. Comfort on a cool night after a warm day.

Jack said, "I know you don't want to talk about this, but we have to. Have you thought of anyone who might be angry enough to do this?"

Lizzie shook her head and glanced across Genna's bosom at Simon.

"Half the fucking school," Simon said. "Why does everyone hate me?"

"It's not your fault." Genna patted his shoulder. "They're just ignorant."

"They're assholes. I wish we'd never moved here."

He sobbed and buried his face on Genna's shoulder. One thing, Jack thought, we've completely abandoned keeping the kids from swearing.

"Say something," Genna mouthed.

For a moment, while guilt washed over him, he couldn't speak. Then, raising his head above the swirling waters, he said, "They're ignorant and they're assholes, which is a deadly combination. Like beans and a long car ride."

Genna groaned. "A Barish joke, kids."

"That stinks, Dad." Lizzie laughed. "Really stinks."

Simon bit his lower lip. He could go from seventeen to seven in a heartbeat.

Genna said, "I know it's hard, but you've got to tell us."

"If I give them names, some won't be right, and they'll get back at me. So what's the point?"

"The point"—Jack felt the vein in his neck wake and stretch—"is some cowardly asshole or assholes, they're usually in groups like cockroaches, burned a cross in our yard, and we have to do something about it."

"They'll get back at me," Simon said. "Not you."

He wanted to say, You're a big guy. Just stand up to them. But he could read Genna's eyes. Stop blaming the victim. Jack hoisted a mug, inhaled the chocolate-cinnamon aroma, and blew across the rim.

"Is it cool enough to drink?" Genna asked.

He nodded. Lizzie leaned forward and cupped a mug between her hands to warm them. "Simon," she began, blowing into her cup. "If you don't tell, I will."

"Shut up, Dizzy!"

"Tell what?" Genna asked.

"What happened yesterday."

"You brat!" Simon lunged across Genna and shoved Lizzie. Hot chocolate spilled over her hands and onto the table.

"Ow!" Lizzie screamed and kept screaming. "OwwwWWWWW!"

Jack raced for the kitchen, returned with a sponge and paper towels; chocolate dribbled off the low table onto the white carpet. In the hall bathroom, he could hear Genna running cold water over Lizzie's hands. Simon sat on the couch, arms folded, staring out the picture window into the trees.

"Help, goddamn it!" Jack tossed Simon the paper towels and swallowed the urge to say more. Together, they cleaned the table, then Jack started on the rug, blotting the spilled chocolate, and flushing the stain with cold water. Genna emerged from the bathroom with Lizzie, realized what he was doing, and screamed, "Is that water cold or hot?"

"Cold."

"Damnit, Jack! Cold sets chocolate."

So he raced down to the family room and returned with their Little Green Machine. When he'd done all he could—the carpet still looked soiled—it was five to eight. The cops would arrive any minute.

"So what did happen yesterday?"

Simon bit his lower lip. "I'll tell Mom."

"What about the cops?" Jack demanded, thinking Sissy boy, and hating himself for it.

"Jack, be quiet. He said he'd tell me."

"Tell them about Grandpa Sweets," Lizzie said, dark eyes glistening. She rarely displayed emotion, but when she did, it was often followed by a total meltdown. "Tell them about Danny!"

"You're dead, you little bitch!"

"Simon!" Genna shouted.

Lizzie ran into the front hall then turned back. "I hate you!" she cried, her face streaming tears. "I hate being your sister!" She wrenched the front door open and slammed it behind her.

"You shouldn't let her talk to me like that." Simon stood, angrily. "She should respect her elders."

Then he fled, too, pounding down the family room stairs.

"That went well." When Genna didn't respond, he added, "What do you think she was talking about?"

"I'm afraid to ask." She stood, grimly. "But I will."

Genna followed Simon downstairs. He considered pursuing Lizzie, but knew it would take her a half hour or more to calm down. Until then, he'd never find her. Jack checked his watch; the cops were late. Then the phone rang. Now what?

What turned out to be Harold Mackey, editor of the *Tipton Gazette*. Mackey, who asked to be called Mac, said he'd heard about the "incident," and wanted to come over and do a story in time for this week's edition.

"How'd you hear?"

"I have my sources, but can't reveal them."

There was some sort of background buzz, as if the editor were in a theater lobby, or more likely a bar. "Unless I know how you found out"—Jack heard a car in the driveway and walked towards the sink window to peer out—"I doubt we'll agree to be interviewed."

"Tipton police," Mackey said. "I'll be over in half an hour, what do you say?"

✦ ✦ ✦

When Jack knocked on Simon's door, Genna called, "We'll be right up."

Jack muttered through the door. When his footsteps receded, she whispered, "Don't mention the business with your grandfather to the police."

"You think I'm stupid?"

Simon looked scared. Inside that big body, he remained such a little boy. He was right to be scared. She was scared. "I think you have to mention Rich's father." Simon looked even more terrified. "By now, they've probably figured out the Martin Long business."

"Or beat it out of Rich."

She couldn't process what Simon had just told her about Sweets. "So they probably know you wrote those notes last fall."

"That's why I shouldn't mention them, either. If the police question them, I'll get in trouble."

She didn't know. She just didn't know.

"And if I mention Nick Fleming and it's not him?" Simon bit his lip. "Tina will be really mad, and it will mess up the play. So I'm not going to mention Nick, either."

How could Sweets do it? That's all she could think, how could Sweets do it?

"You promised, Mom, you wouldn't make me tell if I didn't want to."

She wished the cops would go away and no one would ever mention this again. "Come on," she said. "They're waiting."

Upstairs they marched, towards the living room, where the two giant cops sat on the couch sipping hot chocolate; Jack must have heated up what was left in the saucepan.

"Ma'am," said the younger one, standing.

Lourdes, his name was, no, Trent, some cathedral town. "This is our son, Simon."

The older cop smiled. Why couldn't she remember names? He said, "You look kinda familiar, Simon."

Oh, no, Genna thought, and turned, panicky, towards Jack.

Simon said, "Two whoppers, king size fries, chocolate shake, large coffee, cream and sugar."

The sergeant grinned and patted his substantial gut. Heinsohn, that was his name. "My home away from home. Quite a memory you got there, Simon."

Genna's eyes went to Heinsohn's ring finger. No wedding band. He must eat there often if Simon, who did not have a particularly good memory, remembered his order. Everyone sat. It felt like a blind date. Trent said, "This hot chocolate's really good."

"First-rate." Heinsohn drained his cup to the dregs. "Now, Simon. Do you have any idea who might want to do something like this?"

Simon shrugged his big shoulders.

"Someone who might be angry at you?"

Again, he shrugged. When he wanted to, Simon could look blank as a bar of soap.

Trent asked, "What about kids who've been passing remarks on account of your outwardness?"

The young cop glanced at her, and it was all she could do not to hoot.

"Your parents said you've been getting lots of remarks."

"Not lately."

"What about before?" Heinsohn asked.

"I don't know their names."

Jack glared at her, the vein dancing in his neck.

"None of them?"

"They look the same. I call them the moonfaces."

"So you have no idea," Heinsohn said.

Simon shook his head.

Jack whispered, "Can I talk to you in the kitchen?"

Genna was afraid to look at him. This was wrong, she knew it was wrong, but she couldn't seem to stop it. She followed Jack, a chastised woman. Steam was coming out of his ears, like a cartoon character who was all burned up. He closed the louvered pocket door.

"What the hell is going on?"

"He's terrified."

"The cops know he's lying. How stupid do you think they are?"

"Outwardness?"

He almost smiled, then his anger won out. Oh Jack.

"He's making us look like fools."

As if that's what matters.

"What about all those things Lizzie was talking about, that Simon said he'd tell you?"

But all she could think about was Sweets's betrayal, and Jack's last year, all her men driven by their goddamn hormones.

"For Chrissakes, Genna. Lying isn't helping, it's really not."

Then he slid the door open and stomped back to the living room. When she followed, Jack sat on the couch beside the cops, three large inquisitors facing Simon, whose back was towards her. An air of unease, like a bad smell, hung over the room, and Officer Trent looked somehow altered. After a moment, she saw what it was: a hot chocolate moustache arched over his pink lips.

Heinsohn said, "We'd like to question your daughter. Maybe she, you know, can shed some light."

She looked at Jack. Jack looked at her. Simon's shoulders slumped a little more. Jack said, "She, uh, went for a walk."

"When do you expect her?" asked Trent.

Heinsohn whispered something to Trent, who wiped his mouth with the back of his large hand. "It's still there," Heinsohn said.

Genna handed him a paper napkin; Trent was someone's son, after all, and not that much older than Simon. This time, when Trent wiped, his lip came clean.

"She'll be back soon," Jack said, "but we're not sure exactly when."

"She really likes to walk," Genna added, smiling.

"I guess we'll be going then," said Heinsohn.

The cops stood and replaced their hats. They really were large.

"If you think of anything else…"

Heinsohn let the ellipse lengthen until it lasted long enough to take in their entire house and the budding woods beyond.

"…call day or night." He passed Jack a card and handed her one, too. "I got both numbers, home and the station. I know this isn't pleasant for you. You're not from around here, so I want to say again how sorry I am. This ain't the real Tipton."

Yes, it is, Genna thought.

"It's probably just kids," Trent added.

"Racist, redneck kids." Jack started towards the door.

"There's bad apples in every barrel," said Heinsohn.

The four adults had reached the front door. Simon hung back in the living room.

"One last thing," Heinsohn said. "And this goes double for you, Simon. Don't talk to no one about this, especially not at school. Anyone asks, you say 'I'm not allowed to talk about it,' unnerstand?"

Simon nodded. Jack asked, "What about the newspaper?"

Trent and Heinsohn exchanged glances. Trent said, "Mackey call you?"

"He's coming over."

"No way," said Heinsohn, black eyes narrowing under his hat. "He wants anything, tell him to call me."

She glanced at Jack. When had this happened? Oh yes, the phone.

Jack said, "Of course, ongoing investigation."

The cops nodded. Finally, she believed they were thinking, these professors *unnerstand* something.

Heinsohn said, "We'll be in touch."

"And ma'am," said Officer Trent, "I want to thank you again. That chocolate was really tasty."

The cops moved into the cool evening. Before Jack closed the door, she glimpsed Sam bounce up to be petted, and maybe to sniff a little peace officer crotch.

"We need to talk," Jack said, back inside, eyes aggrieved.

"I don't want to." Simon started down the family room stairs.

"Get back here!"

"Let him go," Genna said. The oaken risers moaned under Simon's weight. "We should talk first."

She heard Simon start down the basement hallway to his bedroom and turned towards Jack, her gray eyes wary.

chapter 20

They met in the principal's office Tuesday afternoon with Doctor Burroughs, Marla Lindstrom, and the drama teacher, Ms. Cherry, whom Genna felt she already knew because Simon had said so much about her. What a cute, cheery young woman, who clearly valued Simon for the right reasons. Ms. Cherry—Please, call me Rona—immediately offered to let him out of the show. Suspecting this might happen, Genna had questioned Simon before school. Oh no, Mom, the show must go on. So Genna shook her head and tried to sound braver than she felt. Whistle a happy tune, Genna. The young teacher's face lit with joy. Broadway! Dimples! I'm so glad, Mrs. Barish. We wouldn't have been nearly as good without him.

Dr. Burroughs, whose appearance was even more badger-like than in the fall, gave his little gray head a shake. He'd warned them, hadn't he, that these attitudes still existed in the community? They nodded, miserably. But if that was the family's decision, he'd support it one hundred and ten percent. Or some such nonsense. Only a few hours had passed, but she couldn't precisely recall the platitude that had dribbled from the principal's bearded lips. Genna was more interested in what Marla had to say. The entire meeting, forty minutes when it could have been five, she focused on Jack and Marla, trying to intuit the state of affairs—affair?—between them. She wasn't sure why—maybe how much time he was supposedly spending in his office, an unwillingness to meet her eyes?—but she'd begun to fear again that her Valentine's Day suspicions had been correct. She and Jack had fought so badly last night she was absolutely raw on the subject of Jack and Marla, Jack and Simon, Jack and anything at all, and found herself wishing as she waited—her spirit drip, drip, dripping, spirit water torture—for the meeting to end, that Jack would slide a proprietary hand onto Marla's slender thigh, or she on his. As they exited Badger's office, it was all she could do not to whisper in the guidance counselor's shell-like ear, If you want him, honey just take him somewhere, and hump him.

Instead, she and Jack thanked everyone oh-so-blandly, then returned to their car in frosty silence. How self-indulgent, with everything that was going on, to be fighting with Jack, to be jealous of Marla, as if that were the issue. All the way home, with Jack an uncommunicative block behind the wheel, they didn't speak. They entered the empty house through the garage. Last night's hot-chocolate pan remained in the sink, unwashed.

"I'm going to my office," Jack said. "If that's all right."

"Why wouldn't it be?"

He looked as if he were about to fire back, then walked out. A moment later, she heard the car reverse out of the garage. In her study, Genna found the junk paperback she'd been reading, *Excess of Hope*, from the Nexus fantasy series, by E.B. Gomez. Now that Lizzie's teenage chill limited how much they spoke, she tried to read the same books to stay in touch that way. She'd linger where she believed Lizzie had: to sniff a black rose or to watch the violet sunset on the third moon of Zeron.

After her mother died, Genna had struggled to keep her alive by recalling places they'd been together. That was emotional life with Doris: remote sharing. With Daddy, she'd shared hardly anything at all, not just because he wasn't her real father, as they said back then, but because he was so tall and male, remote as a mountain.

That's what scared her about Lizzie, the distance she sometimes felt, as if an alien gamete had passed through her, unmarked by thirty years in her ovary. A genetic second coming of Doris. Just add semen and wait. And Simon, in whom she saw so much of herself, and now that she knew, so much of Sweets, she didn't need a book to know how he felt. What was upsetting her—other than a goddamn cross in her yard!—was that she'd returned from San Francisco feeling she'd made that sort of connection to Sweets and now this. Although Simon didn't use the word, and maybe he didn't even understand, Sweets had apparently provided him with a male hooker, a very proficient, and to hear Simon, a gorgeous one at that. What was she supposed to do? Pretend it hadn't happened? Lose her father a second time? Insist Simon get tested for AIDS? She was so distraught she didn't know what to say to Jack, and so she'd said nothing.

Genna desperately wanted her mother, never mind that in life Doris had resisted being the sort of mother on whose bosom she or anyone else could pour out their troubles.

I'm scared, Doris. I'm scared, you frosty old bitch!

Now you're talking, Genna.

Scared for myself, scared for Simon.

Don't slouch.

I opened my heart to Sweets.

Doris—or whatever this was, some rancid trick of a worried mind?—raised a weary eyebrow on the left margin of page 206 of *Excess of Hope*.

Like mother, like daughter.

Can I trust him?

I could, except where it mattered most.

"Sam," she called. "Sam!" The big dummy poked his golden muzzle into her study. "What say we go for a run? What do you say, Sam?"

A toothy grin.

✦ ✦ ✦

After the article appeared Thursday in the *Tipton Gazette*, their phone rang off the hook. The *Cincinnati Enquirer*. Some reporter from WGUC, the NPR affiliate in Cincinnati. Colleagues from her department and from Jack's. The Dean of Arts and Sciences. The provost. Norris White, faculty advisor to the African American Students Association. The heads of the Cincinnati and Hamilton, Ohio, chapters of the NAACP. The article hadn't explicitly stated that the Barishes weren't black; most strangers had therefore made a logical, if incorrect assumption about race. When the family met over dinner—Genna had baked boneless chicken and vegetables in marinara, served it over egg noodles—Simon said, "Guess what?"

"What?" asked Jack, as much as he'd said to her in three days.

"It's not bad enough that in Tipton, Ohio, I'm gay, fat, and Jewish." Simon heaped his plate, passed the pot to Lizzie and topped his mound of noodles with two plump breasts, a pool of sauce, but as few cooked vegetables as he could manage. "Oh, no. Now everyone thinks I'm African American."

She glanced at Jack, then at Lizzie, who had passed the noodles after taking a single spoonful. Simon cut his meat into larger-than-anyone-else's bite-size pieces and distributed them through his noodles.

"I was walking in the hall, and a couple of the moonfaces pushed into me. 'Hey faggot,' they said. 'You're really light for a—' And then they used the N-word."

Simon swallowed his first wad of chicken-pasta.

Jack asked, "Did you report them to the principal's office?"

Just like him to make this about something Simon failed to do.

Mouth full, Simon shook his head. "I told Mrs. Lindstrom."

"Good for you," Genna said. "What did she say?"

"'It's amazing how stupid some people can be.' Then she got them in trouble. She got Nick Fleming in trouble, too."

"Good for Mrs. Lindstrom," Jack said, perhaps to needle her. "What about you, Lizzie, anybody say anything to you today?"

"No more than usual."

"What does that mean?"

Lizzie shrugged, sullenly, Genna thought.

"Tell me," Jack said.

"Kids are always teasing me about Simon."

Genna recalled her very different experience as Billy's sister. No wonder she and Lizzie felt so estranged sometimes.

"What do you do about it?" Jack asked.

Lizzie's eyes laughed. "I tell them to kiss my skinny Jewish bottom."

"Go, girl," Simon said, and for a moment the Barish clan ate in silence marveling, at least Genna was, at her unknowable daughter, at the challenges that brought them together.

Simon broke in, brightly, "I had a good day at rehearsal." He crammed his mouth with more pasta and chicken. "I know all my lines."

"That's good," Jack said, then apparently couldn't resist. "About time."

Simon grinned, too relieved, she thought, to be offended.

"Fourteen days to opening night. Have you bought tickets?"

"Every performance," Genna said. "I told you."

Later, while Jack undressed, she feigned total involvement with yet another rerun of *Golden Girls*. He didn't bother, as she did, to disrobe in the bathroom when they were quarreling. Jack was still so vain, even now that he didn't have any particular reason to be, although she noted from the corner of her eye—as Blanche swished across the small screen wearing yet another outrageous outfit—that Jack seemed to have lost some weight.

"Can we talk?" He crossed in front of the television wearing absolutely nothing. That brown mole on the cheek of his ass. He stepped into a pair of pajama bottoms then snatched the remote from her nightstand. The screen went silent, green-gray.

"I can't compete with the television."

"Very little can." She allowed him to see her looking at him. His chest hair was graying. "So talk."

"There are things," he began, "you haven't been telling me."

Now you know how I feel. "Like what?"

He gazed at her over his majestic nose, so broad, so honest, so Jack. "Why don't we start with whatever Simon told you Monday."

"Ask him yourself. He's your son, too."

"Why won't you tell me?"

"When you said we should talk, you meant I should."

She was goading him. Later, she'd concede it. For now all she could do was watch the color rise in his cheeks, the vein throbbing in his neck, and think, No way I'll tell you anything.

"You said it yourself, 'He's my son, too.' You should tell me what he said."

"'You said, he said.' You sound like a goddamn idiot. Isn't there anything, or anyone, you want to tell me about?"

"As a matter of fact, there was. But you make me so goddamn mad"—his eyes flashed—"I'd be fucked before I say a word. If anything happens we could have prevented if you weren't being so goddamn offended, or whatever it is you're being, it's on your head, not mine."

Jack lunged at her. Fearing he meant to hit her, Genna flinched, but Jack was only grabbing his pillow. "I'll sleep on the couch."

She heard him pause at the closet to rummage for a quilt, then his footsteps evaporated down the hall. In the morning, with first light washing the gray trunks outside their window, she felt more than heard him slip into the room then under the bedclothes. Last spring, when she was the Woman Who Drove, that's what she'd do, guilty as a teenager, sneaking into their bed so the kids would think she'd spent the night at home. She sighed and heard Jack sigh, the Morse code of tired love. She slept so miserably without his big body beside her. The next time Genna woke sunlight sparkled, penny-bright, in the room, and she knew without reaching behind her that Jack was gone.

Then she realized what had awakened her. A car in their driveway! There was never a car this time of day, but she heard it a second time, tires compacting gravel, Sam barking, defending the realm. A car door opened, slammed. Genna heaved out of bed, nine-forty-seven, tied on her robe and peered through the shutters, remembering the petrochemical stench of the cross. A blue Windstar, what the hell? She hurried towards the front hall, pinching hair behind her ears. Should she call the police? She pulled the front door ajar just as Marge, the soccer mom from Roscoe, reached to touch the bell. Genna hadn't seen her in months. Without practice, which was just starting up, their paths hadn't crossed.

Marge wore jeans under a red and white windbreaker, Tipton colors. Apparently, she'd just had her hair done. Blond to the roots. She balanced a covered dish in one hand, struggling to steady it, while discouraging Sam's snuffling adoration with the other.

"Sam!" Genna grabbed the oaf's collar and dragged him inside. Slammed the door harder than she meant and rejoined Marge on the porch. "Sorry."

A determined smile, which nothing, apparently, could dislodge, was pinned to Marge's lips. Genna was about to ask her business when Marge held out the white and blue corn flower casserole dish.

"I read about what happened. I'm sorry." Marge chewed her lips as Genna remembered her doing the first they met. "It's nothing fancy, but with all the strain you've been under, I figured you might a been too busy to cook."

"Oh." Genna accepted the covered dish. "This is so kind. Please come in."

Marge shook her head. "Can't, I'm on my coffee-break. Looks like a nice house, though."

Genna felt a twinge of shame for how much nicer it was than Marge's. "Thank you."

"Anyway." The woman's eyes narrowed. "I hate them bastards. Maybe you think we're all the same. But you came and talked to me and my neighbors, so maybe you don't. When the Klan marched at the high school ten, twelve years ago, you heard about that?"

Genna nodded.

"Me and my friends, I wouldn't want you to think we agreed with them bastards, hon. Most folks here, we're not like that."

Genna found herself blinking back tears. "I know."

Marge hugged Genna briefly and awkwardly, then stepped back.

Genna asked, "Do you know who did this?"

"I have no idea."

Genna couldn't help herself. "Would you tell me if you did?"

Marge got a funny look on her face, then grinned. "You bet I would. Well, I got to get back. Just so you know, I was making turkey tetrazini last night, and my Megan who plays with your Lizzie, said, 'It's as easy to make two as one, isn't it, Mom?' I kissed her I was so proud. By the way, how's your son holding up?"

"Better than I am." Genna wondered how much Marge knew about Simon and possible motives for the attack. "Honestly, I don't know how he makes himself enter that building every day."

"I want you to know, I voted for the levy and so did my father. Told him it was time."

Genna smiled and raised the casserole, as if doffing her cap. "Thank you so much. This is really thoughtful."

"Forty-five minutes, a three-fifty oven."

Genna thanked her again. She'd always hated turkey casseroles but she'd be sure to try this one, or perhaps she'd keep it in the freezer to be taken out when she needed a bite of human kindness.

"Marge." The heavy blonde paused before climbing into her mini-van. "I'll see you at soccer practice."

"You bet."

✦ ✦ ✦

Friday after lunch, Simon was headed towards his locker, just keeping his nose clean, as Dad said, when Fleming and several of his Smokers dragged up behind him.

"Hey, faggot." Nick preened for his buddies. "You got me in shit with Lindstrom."

"No, I didn't."

"Then why'd she call me to her office and tell my parents?"

"How should I know?"

Nick's hottie face twisted. "People like you," he paused, and Simon felt he was repeating what someone else had said, who knows, maybe his parents, "you live in Tipton, but you don't know shit about it, what it stands for."

Crackerville, thought Simon.

"Next time, it won't be a cross."

Simon was in no mood. Fourth bell, he'd learned he was failing French. At lunch, Rachel said it was his fault Rich's father beat him so badly he had to miss school.

"Next time," Fleming grinned, "maybe someone will torch your whole freaking house."

Suddenly, Simon had Fleming by the shoulders and was slamming him into the lockers. "What's wrong with you?" he shouted into Nick's handsome face. Simon outweighed him by fifty pounds and he slammed him into the lockers a second time. "Leave me alone, asshole!"

Hands grappled, and he swatted them like bugs, like no-see-ums, never taking his eyes off Nick, who struggled to come back to himself.

"Ooh, I'm scared of you, faggot. Ooh, ooh, I'm scared."

But Simon had seen the hot, embarrassed light in Fleming's eyes. "Grow up," he said and walked away.

✦ ✦ ✦

By the time rehearsal started, everyone knew.

"No, no, no," he said to Tina, "there wasn't any fight."

They huddled in a dark corner of the auditeria. On stage, Will Travers, who played the king, and Tom Jennings, the prince, rehearsed a second act number, in which the mute king, using winks and gestures, explained the facts of life to his clueless son. Will was a natural clown, but Tom, a good-looking doofus—typecasting!—still hadn't learned his lines. He'd been having particular trouble with this scene in which he had to keep guessing what his father was trying to tell him.

"Boy flower? Girl flower? Oh, father, I think I understand."

Tina whispered, "Be careful. Nick doesn't like to be shown up."

"He calls me names all the time. He's such an asshole." Sadness pinched Tina's narrow features. "Of course," Simon admitted, "he is totally hot."

Tina covered his hand with hers. "I'm thinking about breaking up with him." She moistened her lips, her tongue a small pink rose. "Should I?"

"I wouldn't throw him out of bed." He waited to see if Tina appeared shocked. No. "But he's definitely an asshole. So drop him like a hot penny, hon."

Tina squeezed his hand. "Have you always liked boys?"

"I had a girlfriend at my old school."

"Really?"

He remembered Janet's living room, all the hours watching television with her family, how the last few months she kept wanting to have sex, but he wouldn't do more than fondle her big floppy breasts, how queasy that had made him feel. "But she wanted to wear the dress in the couple."

Simon grinned to let her know he was kidding. Tina's hand still grasped his. "Last I heard, she was pregnant and marrying her cousin." Tina looked as if she didn't believe him. Simon said, "Her family's from Kentucky."

Tina laughed. Actually, she snorted. You wouldn't think a thin, pretty girl would make such a sound, and loud enough for Ms. Cherry, who was on stage working with the nitwit prince, to turn around and shush them.

Moving her lips to his ear, Tina whispered low and breathy, "Did you and your girlfriend, you know, mess around?"

Simon gazed at Tina in the near-dark. Narrow nose, cheeks, eyes so blue and washed-out they were almost without color, the light stringy hair. She's flirting with me. "Of course."

"Did you feel anything?"

What it had mostly felt was wrong. Janet's soft breasts and moist hands, her urgent needs. Tina was flat-chested. Simon had bigger ones than she did. "Of course I felt something."

"I was wondering, about our kiss." Her lips so close he felt her feathery breath. "If we could make it feel real."

"Definitely," Simon whispered. "We have to."

"Then we should definitely rehearse. In case you're out of practice kissing girls."

She moved her lips near his. For a moment, panicky and confused, Simon thought she was going to kiss him. Then she did, brushing her mouth against his.

"What do you think?"

Simon shrugged.

She said, "We can do better."

She kissed him again, harder. Her lips were thin, like the rest of her. There was a fruity taste, strawberry, that must be her lipstick.

She grinned. "Definitely better. But on stage, you have to kiss me."

She positioned his left hand on her right shoulder, as if she were a dance instructor.

"With your right," she whispered, "brush my cheek, as if you're amazed how soft and wonderful it feels."

He obeyed, wondering what kind of game she was playing, if she were secretly making fun of him, so she could tell her asshole boyfriend she'd kissed the faggot. Then Fleming and his Smokers would have even more reason to kick his ass. Tina smiled, lips slightly parted, and Simon moved towards her, thinking of Danny and the night of sex in Sweets's house. He felt a tingle, down there, and leaned forward stroking Tina's cheek, pressed his large lips against her thin ones and closed his eyes as if he were Justin kissing Britney Spears. That was when the house lights must have come on, and everyone started hooting their names. The first voice he recognized was Ms. Cherry.

"Simon, Tina, may I see you?"

He followed Tina, as if she were the snake head and he were the rattle, weaving through the large room of empty tables and chairs, past the other cast members, every eye on them. They mounted the stage, and with Tom and Will close enough to hear, Ms. Cherry brought her small face near theirs.

"What the hell is going on?"

He was too embarrassed to answer. Tina said, "Honest, Ms. C., we were rehearsing."

Ms. Cherry's eyes nearly spun out of her head. "That's the lamest ever."

"Think about it." Simon grinned, first at Ms. Cherry, then at Tina. "What else could it be?"

"Okay," Ms. Cherry said slowly, and Simon could tell she didn't know exactly what to think. "We'll do your scene next." Then she leaned close and whispered fiercely, "But no more rehearsing in school." Ms. Cherry stepped back and barked, "Five minute break, and I do mean five!"

Thirteen days to opening night.

✦ ✦ ✦

Jack sat in his office Sunday afternoon thinking about Rajiv Menard. That's what he'd wanted to tell Genna. That in San Francisco Rajiv had kissed him flush on the mouth, and though he hadn't kissed him back, he often found himself wondering, what if he had? He could feel the man's lips, the bristle of his moustache. Or was he imagining the moustache? Yes, Rajiv was clean-shaven. Jack had stumbled backwards against a piece of stainless steel equipment, a glistening liquid nitrogen specimen tank.

Rajiv said, "Oh, don't look so shocked."

Jack muttered he wasn't.

"You shouldn't be. You've been leading me on."

That had shocked him. Now Jack wasn't sure, and sitting in his office, he remembered something long forgotten or, he supposed, repressed. The September he was twenty-two, driving to California to start Stanford, he'd picked up a hitchhiker outside Salt Lake City. The boy was his age, perhaps a year or two older. Jack hadn't thought about him in twenty years or more, the memory slumbering like a princess until awakened by Rajiv's kiss. Phillip? Mark? Willowy, a tumble of light hair falling into his eyes and past the collar of his short sleeve work shirt. When this boy, this Mark, climbed into Jack's rusty Bonneville, he emitted a faint stink of sweat. Too many hours under the Utah sun. Jack announced he was Palo Alto-bound, and the boy replied, Cool, I'm hitching to my sister in Berkeley.

Mark carried almost nothing, a sleeping bag, a small pack, while Jack's material possessions overflowed the trunk into the back seat. Even more than sweat, a whiff of street smarts hung on this Mark, the way he said, Sorry he didn't have any bread to chip in for gas. Sorry too, if he smelled funky. By the way, could he bum a smoke?

No, no, Jack didn't, and if Mark was worried about smelling ripe, why didn't he crack the window? Jack paid for the gas, and later, when it was time for lunch, he purchased Mark's meal.

"I can't pay you back, I'm kinda broke."

But Jack had money and a new life waiting at the end of I-80.

They stopped in Elko, Nevada. Jack bought a room in the Starlight Casino Motel. Fifteen rooms. Slots, one craps, one blackjack table. Their own room was pretty rough. Twin beds with dirty spreads, a large stain on the rug in front of the door that looked like dried blood. The bathroom reeked. Disinfectant or bug spray, he wasn't sure, but after ten hours on the road, Jack craved a shower, and he wanted Mark, whose smell had ripened during the afternoon, to have one, too. It was Jack's first time in a casino and he aimed to show he knew a thing or two about blackjack.

When Jack came out of the bathroom in a towel Mark eyed him, but Jack didn't think much about it. When this Mark emerged, a cheap motel towel (white, a blue stripe) wrapped around his waist, dirty blonde hair, water-darkened, swept back from his face, the layer of dirt and stink scrubbed away, Jack saw he was pretty good-looking, but thin as a nail, without a single hair on his chest. A line from his one Shakespeare class floated in Jack's mind. A lean and hungry look.

"I'll wait in the hall while you dress."

"You don't have to."

"I'm in a hurry to gamble," Jack answered, wondering if he were getting a sex vibe or imagining it.

At the table, Jack caught fire. He won fifty, eighty, then a hundred, a lot of money then. This Mark stood beside him and when he was ahead one hundred-twenty, Jack handed him four five-dollar chips. "Hold it, okay, so I don't lose it all back." Then he passed Mark one more. "Play the slots, whatever."

How great to be young and lucky. When Mark edged away, Jack wondered if he'd see him again. Before Jack stopped playing, he'd lost some back, but he still had sixty, not counting the chips he'd given to Mark, who soon returned and stood behind him. Jack took them both to dinner, great big steaks, which cost almost nothing, a gambling town, and a bottle of red wine. How thrilling to be traveling to a new life (where he'd meet Genna), cash in his pocket, red wine in his head.

In their room, Mark said, "I've never been gambling before."

"Me, either."

"You were so good at it." Mark's eyes glowed, half a bottle of wine in him, too.

Jack draped his pants on a chair, conscious of his bare legs, his tight BVD's. He climbed into bed and closed his eyes, the wine and the night's winnings swimming inside him. When he opened them, Mark knelt beside him.

"You've been so nice, paid for everything," his words tumbling fast, dirty blond hair flopping in his eyes. "You can have sex with me, if you want."

Jack remembered being scared and flustered, maybe a little excited, but mostly flustered. No, no, he didn't want to.

This Mark said, "You've been so kind, it's the only way I can pay you back. Are you sure?"

Yes, he was sure.

This Mark said, "You're not mad?"

He wasn't mad.

"My body is all I've got, and I just thought…"

Jack slept uneasily and drove straight through the next day, dropped Mark in front of his sister's house, said, No, no, he didn't want to come in, he had to get going. Then he motored off thinking, and thought for the next few months, he remembered now, until after he met Genna, If I want to, I can. I was just scared. If I want to, I can.

Then he forgot all about it, forgot that naughty Mark, as if he'd closed and locked that door, and had regarded himself always as the most heterosexual of men, like his father, which perhaps he was. Most likely, he would never have thought of it again, if Rajiv Menard hadn't smooched him, and said, Don't look so shocked, you've been leading me on.

Perhaps he had been. Perhaps he was implicated in his new project in more ways than he cared to admit. Not that he had discovered his essential sexual nature, as if he'd bitten into the core of a nut meat hidden inside a shell, and thought, Gadzooks! Or found a pair of socks, Jack thought, gazing out his office window at the wall across the courtyard, a pair of pink socks hidden in a dark closet.

What he had discovered was that for some men, certainly for him, homosexuality, or homosexual acts, were indeed a choice and not destiny: a door, okay, make it a closet door, stepped through, or pulled tightly shut, unopened. And if that weren't an original or rare insight in the larger world, it was a liberating one in his own life, as well as his work.

Think about how different the choice, or lack of choice seemed to be for Simon, and what that implied about the genetic underpinnings of sexuality. What if the gay gene were only controlling if there were input from both gametes, and sexuality remained a choice if there were only input from one? That might explain the 65 percent concordance rate in Whitam's identical twin studies.

Suppose that one half of the twin pairs got the genetic gay *it*, whatever *it* was, and on whatever gene it was located, from both sides, and that for them, homosexuality was volition-less. That meant that one-third of the remaining twins, who'd gotten their gay *it* from only one parent, had to choose to be gay, which would explain the less than 100 percent concordance between identical twins.

Come to think of it, that would also lend credence to the claim of conservative psychologists that they could train some individuals not be homosexuals, or at least not to perform homosexual acts. If homosexuality were indeed sometimes genetic destiny and sometimes nurture, then the worst homophobic assertions—that a more gay-friendly society would encourage more people to choose to be homosexuals—might actually be true. Not a politically correct assertion to make, but what if it were so?

Jack wished he could tell Genna about this. He wished he had told Rajiv, but that would have meant fingering those socks, and explaining right there and then that homosexuality was a choice he'd decided against. He hadn't been prepared to do that. Too insulting for Rajiv, and anyway, he hadn't thought it through yet.

But Jack could no longer feel sure he wasn't the source of some of what made Simon who he was sexually. Consider the implications: what if volition-less homosexuality was essentially a recessive trait requiring genetic input from both sides? In the genetic testing study he wanted to conduct, Jack now saw the need to subdivide questions about homosexual experience into homosexual acts and homosexual desires as a motivator for genetic testing. Jack felt an urgent almost painful need to tell someone about all of this, someone he could talk to about hidden things. He paused barely a moment, then called Marla.

chapter 21

Thursday morning—seven days to opening night!—Simon was hauled out of second bell and informed by a rat-faced senior named Rebecca Boose to report to Badger's office. Boose had the nastiest hair in the school; it looked and smelled as if she styled it with oil from the BK fryer. Either she didn't know what Badger wanted or wouldn't say. Simon tried to weasel it out of her, then gave up, and they drifted down the empty hallway. Near the Media Center, they passed a couple, lips locked, crazy. Further on, outside the office, Boose handed him the pass and snickered. Inside, Mrs. Lindstrom and Dr. Burroughs waited with the two police officers. What were their names? The younger one was superhuman, everything one and a half times normal.

"Good to see you, Simon." Old Cop stuck out his hand. "Sergeant Heinsohn."

"Officer Trent," said the young one. He looked oddly familiar last time, too. Then Simon had it. He-Man with dark hair. "We have good news."

"There's been an arrest. Rich— "

Simon glanced at Mrs. Lindstrom. Rich?

"— O'Brien. Seems this Rich and his father— "

"Maybe the grandmother," added Trent.

"—did the terrible deed. Idea why?"

Simon said nothing.

"The boy was attempting to come forward," Heinsohn continued. "He some kinda friend of yours?"

He wouldn't meet the cop's eyes.

"The dad beat him up pretty bad."

Oh, Rich.

"Two days ago, this Rich ran off to his mother's in Indiana, who convinced him to come forward. We've got the dad in custody. Child abuse and, of course, the cross burning."

The letters! "What about Rich?"

Officer Trent said, "Staying with his mom."

Mrs. Lindstrom said, kindly, "Because he's testifying against his father."

Simon didn't think you could do that, some sort of law.

Sergeant Heinsohn said, "Because we feel he was coerced, Rich isn't being charged. We haven't decided about the grandmother."

"So you see," Mrs. Lindstrom said, bright blue-eyed. "Rich is the hero in all this."

"I'd like to ask again." Heinsohn creased his bald head with his meaty palm. "Any reason Rich or his father would do this to your family?"

Simon glanced at Mrs. Lindstrom, who shook her head so only he could see. He really loved her! "Not really."

Burroughs the Badger cleared his throat. "If you know, it's wrong not to tell us. We're all friends here."

Hell-oooo! Simon said, "May I go back to class now? I need to keep up, you know, for the play."

Dr. Burroughs's eyes narrowed. Heinsohn said, "Tell your parents we'll be calling."

"Thank you," Simon said. "I will."

Mrs. Lindstrom patted his arm. Simon stepped out of Badger's office, full of fear, and headed towards his class. Outside the Media Center, the same couple was making out. Nobody bothered the straight kids. Imagine if that were me and Rich. Then he realized

Rich was never coming back. Simon began to cry, quietly, then great sloppy sobs broke from his chest, and he ducked into the bathroom to wash his face. Who was that? Blond spikes, red, swollen eyes? Oh yeah, that's me.

✦ ✦ ✦

Saturday, Simon slept in. Every other week he had to drive to Cincinnati for Yevgeny, but there was rehearsal all afternoon today and tomorrow, complete run-throughs, no scripts, so Mom and Dad agreed he needed sleep more than a lesson. But Simon could never sleep in, not like Lizzie, who would burrow into her blankets until just the top of her brown head peeked out, and stay there until the afternoon if Mom let her. Simon was awake by nine—five days to opening night—and though he wrestled his comforter as if it were a python, he couldn't fall back to sleep. At ten, he heard noise from Mom and Dad's room, not the dreaded thumping, which was nasty, but distressed voices, maybe Mom crying. When he'd arrived home Thursday, the cops were already there. He didn't know who had said what, but Dad's twitching neck showed how pissed off he was. Simon? The cops looked at him funny. Oh, you, their eyes said. You piece of dirt. But no questions, they had to get going. The whole time there was this thing, like a gob of food caught in everyone's throat. When the cops left, Dad turned on Mom. "How could you not tell me?"

Mom looked at Simon, then back at Dad, forlorn. What hadn't Mom told? Omigod. Simon assumed what he had told Mom, Dad knew, too.

"You think he's not going to show those letters?" Dad shouted. "Of course, he is. Why wouldn't you tell me before you told the cops?"

"Not now, Jack." She glanced at Simon as if they shouldn't be discussing this in front of him, when he knew all about it, when he was the cause.

Now they were shouting again. Simon pillowed his head and thrashed, not hearing. Later, with Lizzie still sleeping, of course, and Mom and Dad's door shut tight (when he was learning to read Dad would tape up block-printed signs: Simon, please don't wake us until eight o'clock, Love, Dad), Simon sat in the kitchen, reading yesterday's comics. Then Dad swept down the hall in running shorts, carrying his workout bag.

"How you doing, Kiddo?"

Simon hated Kiddo. That was a problem with Simon, no nickname, and Dad liked nicknames. Jack or Jackie, though his real name was Jacob. Uncle Russ, or Rusty, short for Russell. Even Lizzie or Liz, not Elizabeth.

"I'm going to the gym. Don't suppose you want to come?"

"Rehearsal."

"You guys ready for opening night?"

Simon nodded.

"I'm really looking forward to it." Dad set his bag down and walked to the dish cupboard. "Any Cheerios left?"

Simon shook the box, which rattled robustly. At least Dad couldn't say he'd finished it.

"Okay if I join you?"

Uh-oh, Simon thought, man-to-man alert.

Dad poured coffee, fished raisins from the fridge, fixed himself a bowl every bit as big as Simon's. Through his first mouthful, "I remember you have a love scene—"

"Not really."

"—kiss a girl?" A milky drop oozed from Dad's lips. "How's it going?"

Weird. Wednesday, he and Tina rehearsed at her house. First the song and blocking, then kissing just like at school, one hand caressing her cheek, the other on her shoulder. She kissed him longer than seemed right, even moved her tongue on his lips. Her eyes shone, and her pale skin? The slightest hint of blood and she was flushed. Oh, hon, he wanted to say, Don't get the wrong idea. I'm not straight!

"Fine, Dad."

"Need any pointers?"

What a doofus, Simon thought, as Dad took another huge swallow.

"I need to ask something, and I expect the truth. That night Rich slept over, anything happen?"

"What do you mean?"

"You know exactly what I mean."

He'd given Rich a blow job. Afterwards, Rich unzipped his pants the one and only time, to jerk him off. But there was no way he'd tell Dad.

"Sergeant Heinsohn called yesterday. I'm pretty sure Rich's grandmother showed him those letters."

"It's my word against his."

"So something did happen?"

Simon wouldn't answer, he couldn't answer. Outside, birds sang and sunlight blasted the new leaves overhanging the deck. Simon nodded. After a moment, Dad said, "I'm glad you told me."

Simon wished there was something decent to eat, not just crappy cereal. He bit his lip till it hurt. "Will they put me in jail?"

Dad reached across to pat his shoulder, and Simon couldn't help it, he drew back. "I don't think so." A moment later, Dad asked, "Is Rich sixteen yet?"

Simon shook his head. Dad looked worried, or sad; oh, who knew what he looked.

"I still don't think so. So don't worry."

Then Dad finished his Cheerios, and left without saying good-bye to Mom.

✦ ✦ ✦

When Jack finished working out, he drove towards Marla's. He'd been twice since calling last Sunday in the wake of his excitement after theorizing about the gay gene. But when he arrived, and she handed him a cappuccino stiff with froth, it was all he could do to tell her, and he only managed because he'd promised himself he would; it came out sounding as if he were more worried about Rajiv than excited about his insight. They'd sat in her sky-lit living room on a designer leather and tubular steel couch. She stroked his cheek, entered his troubled eyes with her merry blue ones.

"Oh, Jack. I can't believe you're worried."

She brought him to her bedroom and stepped out of her dress, her body almost pubescent in its slimness. Breast buds, a thatch of blond hair. She proceeded to fuck his ears off. He wanted to say he wasn't worried; it was more the professional insight he wanted to share. But when they lay spent on her queen-size, staring up at the peaked white ceiling of her A-frame, she murmured, "You want more proof?"

"I think you're missing the point."

"Any time." She rolled onto him, half his weight or less, and lay above him looking down. "You want more of whatever." She nibbled his lower lip. "Just stop by."

He'd stopped Tuesday after class, and they'd planned on Thursday until Marla phoned from her office with news of the arrests and said how surprised she was. She'd been certain it was kids, which was why she'd called in Nick Fleming and some of the other known troublemakers. Jack said nothing. He'd suspected all along it was Rich's father.

Now, on this warm afternoon, Jack was on her road again, which was lined with maples and oaks bursting with life. Everything was whirring out of control. He was here to tell Marla he couldn't see her again. He and Genna hadn't uttered a civil word, they hadn't uttered very many words at all, since the cross burning, how long ago was that? He was sleeping so regularly on the couch the cushions bore the imprint of his body. Yet if he didn't stop this, whatever this was, life as he knew it would be over. It might already be over. Carrying on with Marla was making him less tolerant of Genna's craziness, whatever that was. How could she not tell him before she told the cops? And there was something else she was holding back, he was sure of it; she wasn't skilled at deception. Not like you, bub.

Jack looked across an open field, greening with what he thought was winter wheat. Earlier, running then lifting, he had the unsettling thought that he was buffing up for Marla, as if he needed to lose some gut to be naked in front of her. He thought about Simon and how, if Lamarck had been right, which of course he wasn't, about the inheritability of acquired traits, then Jack's high school regimen of sit-ups, push-ups, and weight training should have made Simon's high school years less pudgy.

Jogging around the elevated track, an odd thought had come to him. While Lamarck was clearly wrong about the inheritability of physical traits (the Lysenko-led demise in Russian agriculture had proved what didn't need proving), in something as complex as the genetics of homosexuality it might be fair to represent societal or familial attitudes as acquired traits, and theorize that acquired traits were passed from generation to generation. Seen this way, the phenotypical expression of homosexuality was, in the instance of chosen homosexuality, determined not only by a genetic predisposition, but by the "acquired traits" or attitudes of the society or family the child had been born into. Which might mean that homosexuality not only "ran" in families because of genetics in the instance of what he'd been calling volition-less homosexuality, but because of familial gay-accepting attitudes.

The Town and Country crested the rise before Marla's driveway. Jack braked and turned in. Sunlight sparked on the trunk of her silver Beetle. Jack parked, then Marla appeared on her porch, looking like a blond flower. When they were inside she said, "Let's have a shower."

"I showered at the gym."

She shot him a look.

Marla's bathroom occupied the rear corner of the house and eyed the woods through two round windows. The shower had clear walls. Jack joined her under the spray.

"That feels great."

Marla was soaping his balls and cock. "I can tell."

Water ran down her hair, face and chest. She looked half drowned.

"Marla." The moment didn't feel apt to say he couldn't see her again. "How'd you afford this fabulous house?"

"What a funny question." She rubbed the bar soap between her hands and lathered his stiffening cock. "To ask now."

"I've been meaning to ask."

Water coursed through Marla's bangs. "Want to wash my mouth out with soap?" She knelt and took him into her mouth, then looked up with her clear blue eyes. "Soapy," she murmured and opened her mouth to the spray.

"What did you expect?"

"This."

Water rivered the top of her hair and the bend of her neck. Then Jack raised her and because he was big and she was small, he impaled her and held her above the shower floor. Legs cinching his waist, she rode him, spray rushing down his back, her face, Jack's hands braced against the glass walls until he thought his legs would give or the shower would explode.

When he was sipping cappuccino stiff with foam—that seemed to be their thing—she said, "My uncle died and left me money. A lot of money."

"He didn't have kids?"

"Forrest never married."

"Enough to move away?"

"Where would I move to?"

"There's lots of places better than here." He thought of San Francisco, Hawaii. "Almost anywhere."

"Trying to get rid of me, Jack?"

This was the opening to tell her. "Does it feel like I am?"

"Or do you want to come with?"

He couldn't tell if she were joking.

"Don't look so worried. I had one husband, who cured me of ever wanting another."

Jack felt totally confused, and stalled, sipping hot espresso through cool froth. "If I didn't have to stay in Tipton for a job, I'd leave."

"You would or I would?"

Again, a thrill. "Both."

"If you think that now, wait till you see what I've got to show you." She opened her purse and handed him a Xerox copy of what looked like a half sheet torn from a spiral, the left edge outlined like baby teeth against the black border.

Faggots are even worse than niggers. A nigger can't help he's a nigger, he's born that way. But a faggot picks being a faggot. So we should get them.

"Where'd this come from?"

"A custodian found it, where else? In the boys' bathroom, Friday after school."

"Is Burroughs going to do anything?"

"He hasn't decided." She squeezed Jack's large hand between her small ones. "We're meeting Monday morning. And you can't call and demand action. No one's supposed to know. Certainly not you."

"I suppose you'd get in trouble."

"You're already getting me in trouble." She raised her eyebrows. "I'm not sure what Burroughs can do, anyway."

Jack could feel himself getting furious. "Handwriting analysis? Fingerprints?"

"Too many people have touched it."

"What about a public forum, some sort of consciousness-raising?"

"Herb Burroughs," Marla said, "retires next December. He's a tired little man without much consciousness of his own to raise. So he's certainly not thinking about anyone else's."

Jack stood and set his cup on the island. Marla stood, too, her large eyes on him. Her hair was still wet, and he blushed, thinking about their shower. He stepped forward and kissed her hard on the lips. She held on then laid her face on his chest.

"You know," she began, not looking at him, and then she was. "I'm the woman who sleeps with married men because I don't want to feel too much."

"So this isn't working out for you?"

"Don't mock me, Jack." She gave him a sad little smile. "I already care so much about Simon, and I'm starting to care about you."

"I better go. I'll call you."

"You better."

Then he was out the door barreling into a perfect spring day. Lambent, he remembered that word from somewhere. And what a great job he did telling Marla he couldn't see her again.

✦ ✦ ✦

Genna had absolutely had it. Nobody worked out at the gym for three hours, certainly not Jack. She'd already dialed his office after promising herself she wasn't going to do that, ever, but banged the receiver into its cradle after two rings, so maybe he was there. Now she lay like a solar panel on the deck soaking up the spring sunlight, trying not to think about Jack, realizing that in an hour or so she could collect Lizzie at soccer practice, maybe exchange a friendly word with Marge, but what to do until then? She'd already run with Sam and didn't dare start driving just to be driving. Drivers Anonymous. But really, how fine that would be. The wheel between her palms, the pedal play, gas and brake, the hum of tires chewing asphalt like so many chocolate bon-bons. Oh, Sweets! How could you! So much empty time she wouldn't have to suffer through, wondering where Jack was and knowing, knowing. All this worrying about Simon, a sense of dread which weighted her like a down comforter in summer. She wanted to rush to Simon's room to check his crib as she used to when he was six months, and they were untested, all of them, to make sure he was breathing.

The phone shrieked.

She'd remembered to bring the kitchen cordless outside and stared at its demanding whiteness. There was no one she wanted to talk to, no phone call that could make all this right. But what if it were Simon or Lizzie, needing her help?

"Genna?"

Jack. "What?"

"I was wondering if you wanted me to get Lizzie at practice."

Where have you been? she wanted to ask, but wouldn't. "I will."

"I'm in my office if you need me."

I don't.

"I was wondering, it's such a nice day, we could go for a hike."

She loved to hike. "I'm busy."

"Genna," Jack said, "we need to talk."

That burned her up! She thought of all the times she'd needed to talk, and all the times he wouldn't. All the times they had talked or not talked, and what difference had it made? He was gone for three hours on Saturday morning, and she couldn't ask where. They lived surrounded by such evil someone could not only burn a cross on their lawn, but Simon might be getting in trouble because of a love note. All along, she'd known who burned the cross, or at least had a good idea, but couldn't tell the man she loved because things were so terrible between them, and now he wanted to talk?

The sun hammered her forehead. "If we talk now, some things might…"

"Sooner or later, we have to." Then he added, gently, "If we're going to have any chance at all."

For a moment, she felt less angry. "Then later, okay? After Simon's show."

She set out early in the Camry, which she almost never drove. What she hadn't told Jack—I'm in my office if you need me—Barish, was that Simon, about to leave for rehearsal, had banged into their room at ten-thirty, an hour she'd never still be in bed, especially not on such a light-bending morning, if she weren't paralyzed with fear. He'd crawled in beside her, nuzzled her shoulder like a cub.

"…rehearsal, see you tonight."

She'd lurched into befuddled wakefulness. One moment she'd lain wrapped in green dreams, the next she rose stammering like Jackie Gleason, hummana, hummana, humanna, trying to match words to thoughts. "LizziepracticeDad?"

"Dad left."

"Where?"

Simon's soft eyes, Sweets's eyes, darkened with anger. "Don't you and Dad talk anymore?"

"Why, Simon!" she exclaimed, "What do you mean?"

"You didn't tell Dad about Rich's father. He didn't tell you he was going to the gym." His eyes accused her. "He didn't even say goodbye."

She prevaricated her head off, with energy but not much skill. Everything's fine, dear, never better! Simon had believed not one word and they argued bitterly when she insisted on driving him to rehearsal to hold onto the Camry. Now she headed west out of town, forty-five minutes before Lizzie's arranged pick up. She'd found Marla Lindstrom in the pint-sized Tipton directory. (Not the directory of pint-sized Tiptonites, though Little Miss Marla would be on the cover if such a book existed.) There were no other Lindstroms; the putative husband had moved away or wasn't listed. Maybe Lindstrom was Marla's maiden name, but there it lay under Genna's finger, big as life, totally shameless. Genna had located the road on a Tipton map; now she drove, the wheel crushed between her palms, the thrumming of rubber working on her like valium. Genna, oh Genna, be calm.

What had she intended? See where the little bitch lived. Pin her neck with a forked stick. No, a soothing spin on an April afternoon. Genna rode with the windows down. The sun warmed her forearm and the fine blond hairs unfurled. From somewhere, the light scent of lilacs reached her. The road dipped and rose. Crop land sloped gently away on her left, while Genna checked mailbox numbers on her right. Only one or two more, she thought, and slowed for a better look as the Camry crested a small rise.

Just in front of her a silver hood edged out of a driveway. Genna mashed the brakes, preparing to stop in case the car pulled out, and she rolled past, barely moving, ten or fifteen miles an hour, still checking for numbers, and looked straight into the astonished gaze of Marla Lindstrom. Oh no, oh no, oh no! Genna thought, raising her hand chin-high. Think I'm spying, and she'd be right, Genna thought, her face fixed in a faux smile, regretting her pathetic little wave. She continued slowly for another hundred yards or so then punished the accelerator. The Camry leapt ahead, tires screeching. Genna exhaled, remembering Marla's startled eyes, and allowed herself a wolfish grin. At least she knows I know.

Genna shot westward, towards Indiana and the great beyond.

chapter 22

Wednesday, Simon couldn't sleep. Twenty-one hours to opening night! And when he did sleep, what dreams! He stepped on stage, and his pants fell down. Again and again, pants big as one of the little pig's houses blew down, and his penis blossomed in the sudden light.

He dreamt of standing ovations. Of having to kiss Tina Murphy in a blood red spot as his pants blew off like cosmic dust. He dreamt of a talent scout in the audience, one-eyed Del Ray Beech, who waved a recording contract like a white flag. Oh please, oh please. Simon Sings Britney. What about those pants? Thursday, he woke with a throbbing erection before the sun had pierced the canopy of new leaves. Opening night, and he had to piss like a racehorse. No wonder his pants kept tumbling, and Simon hurried to the bathroom, fished his little man, ha-ha, through the flap in his boxers and roiled the toilet. When he returned to his room, it was five-fifteen, but he was too excited to sleep. His dick rose like a rocket, and cream in hand, smiling Justin Timberlake on the wall, a medley of *Mattress* songs in his head, —I'm in love with a girl named Fred! Tonight I love you less, than I will tomorrow morning! Hurry, Harry, Hurry, Harry, Harry, Marry Me!—Simon greeted dawn with a thunderous ejaculation that left him wet-bellied, worried he'd shot his whiz into orbit. Opening night!

In Animal Chorus, he shared sheet music for the first time in a long time with Peter, who played Sir Studley in the show. No speaking lines, but Peter sang with the other knights, and paired off for dance numbers with a freshman, Mary LeBlanc. What an excellent dancer, Peter. All the self-consciousness that made him Peter—right hand shielding his teeth, the girlish squeals—melted like a candle when he danced. Watching Peter whirl in rehearsal, and he had been watching, he'd seen a new Peter emerge. Tall, still growing, with fluid movements like a ballerina. Maybe someday, Peter would let out what lurked inside and become a drag queen, dressing in sheath dresses like Uncle Billy's wife, Aunt Carolyn. Peter had such long shapely legs. Standing beside him now in Animal Chorus, feeling Peter's light weight against him, Simon knew a wave of affection. How different life will be for Peter and for me, too, when we're away from Tipton High and the moonfaces.

Glancing at Peter in a corner of the eye sort of way, noting the dusting of freckles, the slightly turned-up nose, he thought, Peter and I could really be friends, you know? He isn't hot like Rich. (Simon still couldn't think of Rich without anger. What a bastard his father was.) But Peter was less messed up. Belting out the final chorus of "(They Call The Wind) Mariah" Mariah, Mariah, they call the wind, what a stupid song, but fun to sing. Wait, could that be where Mariah Carey's parents got her name? He smiled at Peter, and Peter smiled at him. Eight beats later, with Donut's creamy hands vibrating just below his chins, thumbs and first two fingers pinched together, eyes bulging to signal the end of the final ah of Mariah, Simon nudged Peter then whispered, "Let's hang out Saturday at the party."

"What party?"

"Kelly Martin's."

Peter looked like he was going to cry. "I'm not invited."

"Everyone's invited. It's the cast party."

Simon checked to see if Donut was watching them, but he was flipping pages on his stand.

"Oh, drat," Donut muttered, knocking sheet music to the floor.

Simon said, "There's going to be a bonfire."

"I'd love that." Peter covered his mouth. "If Mom will let me."

"I'll drive, I've got my license."

"Cool."

Donut bent, fumbling for the fallen music. When he raised up, his bosomy bottom bumped the stand, and the whole mess crashed to the floor. The kids started to snicker.

"All right, all right." Donut stood and smoothed his shirt "'When You Walk Through A Storm.' And you can stop laughing now." He raised his pudgy hands. "One-and, two-and, three— "

Simon opened his mouth and music flew out like golden birds. "When you walk…"

He glanced at Peter.

✦ ✦ ✦

With Rich gone, and Rachel blaming him (Look, hon, he'd finally said, I didn't burn a cross on his fucking lawn), Simon didn't have anyone to sit with at lunch. Peter ate during a different bell. The popular drama kids—Millie Miles, who played Princess Winifred, Will, who was King Sextimus, and doofus Tom the Prince—nodded, but that was as far as he'd progressed. He still anchored one pole of the misfit divide, while they dwelled in glory on the other. So Simon was alone with his pepperoni slices, salad and twenty-ounce Sprite, going over lines—Eight hours to opening night! Six to make-up!—when Tina slipped down beside him.

"Hey, Sir Harry."

"M'lady, I was just thinking about you."

She colored. "You were?"

He nodded, feeling kind of crazy—opening night!—and took her hands in his, then whispered-sang in his best Sir Harry, "Yesterday I loved you as never before."

On the last note, his voice rounded with vibrato. Heads turned.

"Oh, Harry, you're embarrassing me."

He released her and looked around the noisy auditeria to see if anyone was watching. On stage, the castle flats were already in place. "I'm so nervous I could hardly sleep."

"Me, either." Tina's pale eyes glowed. "I broke up with Nick last night. Told him what a jerk he was."

Oh, hon, you didn't do this because of me? He heard the next line in his head, Or else I was out of my mind.

"Cool," he said.

"I've been thinking about our kiss," she said. "Saturday night, let's hold it a really long time."

I don't know. "Saturday?"

"In case Ms. Cherry gets mad. It's the last night."

"There's Sunday."

"Afternoon. Besides, Nick's coming Saturday." She touched his hand. "You don't care?"

Or else I was out of my mind.

"About kissing me. I mean, you're gay."

"No, it's cool."

"I want Nick to see what he's missing because he's such a jerk."

"And a homophobic asshole."

"Love you, Sir Harry." She smiled, added softly, "I tremble at your touch/Not nearly half so much/As I will tomorrow morn–ing."

Then the bell rang. He bussed his tray and journeyed to Loser Study Hall, arriving without encountering any of the moonfaces. Mrs. Lindstrom sat up wearing a purple pantsuit over a ruffled blouse, very stylish. He sometimes wished Mom dressed more like her. While the other kids were settling in, Mrs. Lindstrom asked, with her sneaky-sly smile, "Are you ready for opening night?"

He nodded. "Are you coming?"

"I don't think I can."

Simon tried not to show how hurt he was. A few minutes later, Mrs. Lindstrom called him up to her desk. "Simon," she began. "Will your parents be there tonight?"

He nodded.

"Of course." She reached for his assignment book.

Oh, shit.

"Are they attending every performance?"

"Mom is, I don't know about Dad."

Mrs. Lindstrom flipped to today's blank page.

"Oh, Simon," she said. "What am I going to do with you?" She suddenly looked so sad. "Don't worry about anything else, but you must get the French." She looked up at him, eyes wide, like another mother. "If you promise to do your French homework, I'll find some way to be there tonight. Deal?"

She offered her hand, which was warm and larger than he would have thought (she was so little), and they shook. A moment later, Simon set out for French, at the other end of the building. What was up with Mrs. Lindstrom? She must really like him. He couldn't make sense any other way. No one cared that much about his French homework, he sure as hell didn't.

He started down the gym corridor. The weight room opened, and two, then four moonfaces appeared in red, long sleeve t-shirts and gym shorts, thick necks and long arms, bowl-cut hair. They looked at each other and then at him, bolts of hate shooting from their eyes. They stepped forward, and Simon didn't know whether to keep walking or run. The moonfaces filled the corridor, shoulder to shoulder.

"Faggot."

"Nigger-boy."

"Hey," said the short one Simon recognized from other times, the thickest neck, crazy eyes. "It's two freaks in one."

The others held his arms, while the small one pummeled his stomach. He brought his mouth close enough to kiss. "Say a word, we'll fucking kill you."

Then the moonface kneed him in the balls and Simon lurched into spinning blackness. It felt like being stabbed and burned. He couldn't breathe! The others ran off, and he slid like vomit down the wall and lay still. No one came, but he refused to cry. When his nausea crept back down his throat, Simon stood and wondered if he should continue to French or return to Mrs. Lindstrom. It hurt to walk, but not too bad. If he saw Mrs. Lindstrom, he knew he couldn't keep himself from telling, and he didn't want to. So he hobbled towards French, holding his stomach, catching his breath, and he did not cry.

✦ ✦ ✦

Genna sat in the sun waiting for Simon. On Thursdays, Lizzie went straight to soccer practice. Jack's class ended at three-fifteen, but she rarely saw him until five or six and had imagined she'd have a few hours with Simon on this most special day for her boy. He said he'd be home right after school, but at three-thirty he still hadn't arrived. She had to fetch Lizzie at five—she'd been certain one of the boys would be home with a car—and couldn't for the life of her imagine where Simon could be. He had to be at the school by six, and he'd said he'd be home right after school. She sat on the deck trying to read an article on the challenges of translating cultures, while Sam slept at her feet. The air on the deck seemed somehow to have missed spring and moved straight into the heat of summer. The weatherman was predicting thunderstorms for the next few days, and a cardinal perched on a nearby branch serenading his lumpish mate, "Bir-die, bir-die."

Damn, the phone. She hurried in, interrupted the third ring. "Simon?"

"No, my dear, it's Sweets."

She hadn't spoken to him in weeks—how long had it been?

"I was calling—"

Through all the miles, he must feel the tension.

"—if I remember correctly, tonight is Simon's opening night?"

"It's kind of you to remember. Is there a message?"

The distance was vast as the Plains, as the Continental Divide. "Genna, what's wrong?"

She saw the burning cross, Jack asleep on the couch. "Nothing."

"How about"—She could see his blue-gray eyes, the small nose like Simon's—"we don't play games. After the week here, I think you owe me…"

"I owe you?" Was that a car in the driveway? "I brought my family. I opened my heart to you."

"I'm so grateful."

"And that's why you bought Simon a prostitute, to repay me?"

"He told you?"

"He's my son!" Genna thought she might start sobbing, she felt that overwrought. Then she discovered what she was really feeling, rage, and it burst out of her. "I'm so tired of the men in my family thinking with their cocks! Young, old, gay, straight, can't one of you think about something besides your own, or someone else's, goddamn penis!"

There was a car. She heard the engine die, the absence of sound.

"I don't know what to say." An awkward silence, then Sweets added, "Marty said I shouldn't."

"You should have listened."

"Danny wasn't a prostitute, just a young friend."

"I don't want to hear it." Just then Simon burst through the garage door. "Here's Simon, he just got in." She passed the receiver. "It's Sweets." Simon's face lit as she knew it would. "Don't talk long."

She returned to the deck to catch her breath. How did this happen? The only male in her family she could count on was this smelly old dog. She stared into the trees, wondering where the cardinal and his mate had gotten off to, and felt the moist air settle like a sheet. Simon joined her, still talking, his face split by a monstrous smile.

"That would be so cool." He palmed the mouthpiece. "Sweets wants to see the show!"

She looked at the phone, aghast. There was no way she could say no, not with Simon listening. Sweets's voice melted against her ear.

"I'm so sorry about the other thing, Genna. Please, let me come. I'll make it up to you."

Simon stood beside her at his most puppy-like. Wide-eyed, begging.

"Sweets, wait." She motioned with her head. "A little privacy?"

Simon didn't move.

"Go!"

He slunk inside, followed by Sam.

"It showed terrible judgement."

"I can see"—there was background noise at Sweets's end—"how you might think that. I wanted to give him. I wanted… "

"Why should I care what you want?"

"…his first sexual experience to be beautiful. So often for gay teenagers, it's not."

"With a total stranger?"

"Welcome to my world. A handsome, skilled stranger. We could all do worse."

She remembered her quick fumble freshman year.

"I apologize from the depths of my being, Genna. On my hands and knees, if you like. I adore you. I adore Simon. So please, please, my dear, let me make this up to you. It would mean a lot to Simon."

"I know."

"I can be on the red-eye Saturday, which gets into Cincinnati at five-thirty Sunday morning. I'll take a cab from the airport."

She thought for a moment and realized she wanted to forgive him. She wanted to forgive someone. "We'll pick you up."

"I'd prefer that, if it's not too much trouble."

"Will Marty be with you?"

"I'm not sure Ohio's ready for Marty." He cleared his throat. "Would you put Simon on? I need to tell him to break a leg."

"Simon!" she shouted, then came back on. "I've been so angry, Sweets, I felt so betrayed, you have no idea." She hesitated, considered she shouldn't say it, then did, it was such a relief to open up to someone. "I thought I'd lost you a second time."

"That's the kindest thing anyone's ever said to me."

Simon bounded onto the deck. If he had a tail, it would have been wagging.

✦ ✦ ✦

Jack sat between Genna and Lizzie in the near-dark, second row center. Simon's first big scene was coming up. Marla was somewhere in the back of the auditeria. She'd arrived ten minutes before the curtain, and he'd gotten up to go to the men's room, passing close by her and smiling—she smiled back, nervously—but not stopping to talk. He was surprised, and a little terrified, to see her. After the drive-by on Sunday, Marla had phoned his office.

"My God, she must have been lurking, waiting for me to pull out of my driveway. She looked right at me!"

Jack disliked talking to Marla about Genna; it felt so disloyal. He tried to explain Genna liked to take long drives, it was how she relaxed.

"If you'd seen her eyes, you'd know she wasn't relaxed."

A sudden absence at Marla's end. She was on her cell, driving, and service was so spotty around Tipton, he thought the call had been dropped. Then she came back, breathless.

"She's behind me! No, it's not her. I'm pulling over."

"Are you okay?"

"Freaked out." Marla's voice pinged, as if she were calling from inside a cave. "Think she was outside when you were over?"

No, no, he'd spoken to Genna—he didn't like mentioning this—as soon as he got back to his office.

"Then what the hell?"

Sitting in the hushed auditeria, he still didn't know. Coincidence? More likely, Genna suspected he was seeing Marla and wanted, what? Marla had said, They'd better be really careful, and she wasn't coming to the show. She couldn't face Genna. Then she'd called this afternoon to announce Simon had begged her and she'd promised. She wanted to see the show, and it would seem too strange if she didn't. Didn't he agree?

Simon entered stage right, in the red velvet tunic and dark tights he'd worn for the opening scenes. He'd always loved velvet, and had somehow convinced Ms. Cherry to let him wear red. A silver scabbard glistened below the wide belt that cinched the tunic, and he looked very knight-like, if maybe a little swishy, as he crossed the stage, right hand grasping the hilt of his sword. Jack replaced grown-up Simon with Simon at three, dressed as He-Man, his hair still blond and curly, brandishing a plastic sword, piping, "Bad Skeletor! I slay you!"

Jack glanced at Genna, her expression in three-quarter profile so rapt and glowing it was an indictment, as Simon joined his leading lady, a skinny blonde with alabaster skin.

> A lark was singing in the trees and you said you'd remember that moment forever.
>
> Yes, Larken, yes!
>
> And then we watched the sun go down? Well, I'm going to have a baby. So you see, a princess for Dauntless must be found…or I shall have to go away somewhere.

How bizarre, Jack thought, the one gay kid, and he plays the stud. Gazing into her eyes, Sir Harry sang, "It won't be long, it won't be long, it won't because it can't be long, before our dreams come true."

Larken answered, her voice indifferent and thin, nothing like Simon's, "In a little while, just a little while, you and I will be one, two three, four. In a little while..."

What a sweet illusion, Simon loving a girl, her swain, her knight. Then he answered, in that God-given, hard-wired, oh who knew what, glorious instrument, "In a little while, I will see your smile, on the face of my son, to be for, ever hand in glove..."

Just playing a part, but wouldn't it be wonderful, Simon having a son, Simon who'd always loved children. Who didn't play a part? Jack squeezed Genna's hand, the proud parents, and she squeezed back without glancing towards him, her eyes fixed on stage until the duet ended, the lights went down, and the auditeria rocked with applause for Sir Harry and his lady fair.

chapter 23

In the halls, strangers chorused, "Way to go, Sir Harry!"

Popular kids, losers, jocks—not the moonfaces, of course—patted his shoulders. Ms. Cherry hugged him, curls corkscrewing away from her face as if her toe were stuck in an electric socket. By fifth bell—lunch!—Simon rode the cresting wave of his life's best day. Hang ten! He'd turned in his French. In Animal Chorus, everyone who wasn't in the show applauded for everyone who was. Then, shyly, eyes glowing as if he wanted to kiss Simon right then, Peter whispered his mom said he could attend the party, and thanks so much!

By the time Simon reached the auditeria, which was cloaked in its daytime drab, Simon and the other cast members were walking with a bop, a bounce, a wiggle. Word had spread like the enticing scent of buttered popcorn that every performance was sold out, and Ms. Cherry was trying to add one for Sunday night. Simon emerged from the food line like Keanu Reeves in *The Matrix* (now that boy was hot), able to dance up walls and pluck bullets, like raindrops, from the air. He craned for an empty table. But King Sextimus and Princess Winifred (Millie Miles, who looked like Julia Roberts, and had the second-best voice after his), both waved him over. For the first, and who knew, maybe the last time, Simon lunched with the cool kids. No one said much, and he felt too intimidated to talk, but at least he was at their table. Just before the bell, Tina Murphy bustled up.

"Hey, Harry."

"Larken, my love."

She dropped her hand on his arm as if she owned it.

Will, who sat across from Simon, was thin, dark and always clowning, just like Sextimus. "Some kiss, you guys." He hugged his own face with both arms, wrapped tight his nose and mouth, then moistly smooched his forearm.

Millie tossed her dark hair, more like a mane than human tresses. "It looked like you'd been practicing."

Tina blushed, that pale skin. "We have."

This was so weird.

"Watch us tomorrow." Standing above him, Tina set her hands on his shoulders. "Right, Sir Harry?"

She gazed into his eyes like they'd practiced—windows of the soul!—and sweat oozed from his armpits. Then the bell clanged, and he escaped to Loser Study Hall. Mrs. Lindstrom took him aside as soon as he entered. Proud of himself, but not wanting to appear too nerdy, Simon said, "I did my French."

Her bright eyes brightened. "And I saw the play. You are so talented."

He longed to tell Mrs. Lindstrom everything. "My grandfather's coming."

"From California?"

How did she know that?

Mrs. Lindstrom's blue eyes held him. "Now, Simon." She led him towards the small blackboard, as far from the others as possible, her nails biting his biceps. "There's something." Her voice whispery. "Someone left a note in the guidance office saying three or four boys beat you up."

He felt tears at the back of his throat, and wanted to flee. He didn't want to tell, but he didn't want to lie. Her nails dug deeper into his muscle.

"Why didn't you tell me?"

"That hurts."

She looked, at first, as if she didn't know what he was talking about, then released him. The whole time Simon was frantically searching as if his mind were a desk drawer, tossing away ideas like balled-up papers. "I can handle it myself."

"Was it Nick Fleming?"

He shook his head.

"Did they hurt you?"

The other kids were watching. Then the first bell sounded, time to get to work. Mrs. Lindstrom faced the Losers. "Take out your assignment books." To Simon, she whispered, "Do you know their names?"

He shook his head. "I can handle it myself."

For a moment, Mrs. Lindstrom looked so, so sad. Then she was just a teacher again. "Sit down, I'll be around to check."

Simon found his seat, feeling he'd gotten away with something.

✦ ✦ ✦

Everyone agreed: Friday night sucked. Right in the middle of "Man to Man," doofus Tom froze so solid you could have skated on him. Will did his bulging eyes, miming best—busy hands, suggestive smiles—like they'd practiced. Tom was meant to interpret, "Woman...like girl flower, Man like bee and boy flower...Man, that's me!"

But nothing buzzed from Tom's mouth, and his eyes swelled until he and Will looked like costumed toads. The audience thought it was part of the dumb act and howled. Will kept swirling his hands. Flower. Bee. After thirty seconds that felt like thirty days, the stage manager croaked, loud enough for the first few rows to hear, "Girl flower, boy flower," and Tom lurched into motion as if he'd been lubricated. Add to that screw-up, the unfortunate incident during "I'm in Love with a Girl Named Fred," (a flat toppled on a dancing knight and lady, and everyone had to stop and pull it off them), and Friday's performance was better off forgotten, which Simon was attempting to do by sleeping in. He couldn't remember ever being so tired; except for getting up once to whiz, he slept like a dead one and didn't stumble upstairs Saturday until almost noon.

"Hey, Sleeping Beauty," Dad called from the kitchen.

Simon scratched his stomach. It felt hairy, even through his T-shirt, and Simon wondered if he should shave it. "Wrong play."

Dad grinned over the sports section. "Some girl called, Tina something."

"Lady Larken."

"Said you'd call back. And Peter's mother, wanting to know if you were a safe driver." Dad paused for an explanation.

"I'm driving Peter to the cast party." Dad wanted more explanation. "She's really overprotective."

Mom entered wearing her jogging gear, blue T-shirt and shorts.

"Hi, Mommy."

"Do you have homework?"

Who could remember? "Maybe a little."

"Do it today." Something passed between her and Dad. "Remember, Sweets arrives tomorrow."

"Of course, I remember."

"What time?" Dad asked. "I'll get him."

"Don't bother," Mom said loudly. "I will."

Simon hated when they fought.

"I was just trying to be nice."

Mom's face looked like a balloon about to burst. "We all know how nice you are."

Simon said, "This is supposed to be a happy day, you guys."

"Mind your business," Dad said, looking more embarrassed than angry.

"You and Mom are always telling me and Lizzie not to fight."

"That is our business." Dad's neck vein was starting to throb.

"He's right!" Mom shouted. "It is a happy day." She looked as if she might start sobbing. "His play, and Sweets coming."

"Even Mrs. Lindstrom thought it was wonderful about Sweets."

It's weird, Simon would think later, how sometimes you know things a moment too late, like he knew just after he'd said it that he shouldn't have.

"How did she know?"

Simon's eyes swung, pulled like a tractor beam by Mom's, towards Dad.

"She called, let me think," Dad looked only at Simon, "yesterday, that's right. There was some sort of problem at school."

Mom looked horrified. "Don't you dare talk to her about my personal business."

"I was talking to her about Simon."

There was a split-second pause like when you're about to sneeze but trying not to. Simon sent Dad brainwaves, Don't tell about being beaten up. Don't tell! Mom looked as if she might start screaming. Time stretched and pulled between them until the silence formed a sheet of ice with a brick falling towards it, and the only thing keeping it from shattering was the power of Simon's mind. Then he thought, Mom's jealous of Mrs. Lindstrom, and the brick crashed through. Dad said, "There's a rumor about Simon getting beat up."

"When?" Mom shouted.

"Thursday."

"And you didn't tell me?"

She turned on him, Dad too, as if they were a team again. The whole time Simon was deciding what to say, to lie or not, his brain was pumping, Dad and Mrs. Lindstrom, Dad and Mrs. …and he took off for his room, hurling over his shoulder, "I don't want to talk about it!"

Dad and Mom shouted, "Get back here, if you think you're going to that play tonight!"

And blah-blah-blah. He was starring in the fucking show, what could they do? He pounded down the steps and slammed his door so hard the house trembled.

✦ ✦ ✦

Later that afternoon, Jack drove towards Marla's, going over what he needed to say. This is no good, it's making me insane. He inspected the hands on the steering wheel. He'd always been proud of his hands, which could palm a basketball. They were larger than Russ's, one of the few ways in which he outdid his brother physically. His father had had large hands, too. But he eyed them as if they abutted someone else's wrists. Dark hair grew between the first and second knuckles on every finger, and Jack recalled his grandfather's hands, the same springy hair, remembering, too, how that had bothered him when he was little Now even his hairy knuckles were someone else's.

He turned onto Marla's road. The southern vista over greening fields, the way the land fell away as if it were part of a river valley was not only aesthetically, but somehow morally soothing. He understood why she liked it, but the view wouldn't be enough to keep him in Tipton if he had the money to leave as Marla seemed to. Using the control pad on his door, Jack opened both front windows, and warm, moist air gusted through the Camry.

After Simon had locked himself in his room, he and Genna had raged at each other. Hours later, he was still upset and needed to squeeze the wheel to keep his hands from shaking. Maybe that's why he didn't recognize them, so white and bloodless. There was a good chance Genna would kick him out. She might have done it today if not for Simon's play and Sweets's arrival. A bitter, bloody fight, conducted in whispers, with Simon barricaded in the basement. And Lizzie? She always seemed to be out when they fought. For a moment he wondered why, then it came to him. Simon was so attuned to his own feelings and everyone else's, there didn't seem to be any point in trying to shield him, while neither he nor Genna would let themselves fight with Lizzie around. And maybe there was revenge in it, too. They were often fighting about Simon.

Jack turned into Marla's drive, parked beside the silver Beetle and started up her steps.

"Jack," Marla said, kissing his cheek after she'd let him in. "I don't think you should be here."

He tried to read her expression, but she turned and headed for the living room. They sat on her leather couch, and skylight-filtered sunlight sparkled in her hair.

"Do you want me to leave now?"

"What I don't want is you sitting here if Genna drives up."

He wanted to say, We've been fighting because of what you said to Simon about Sweets, but that would sound as if he were blaming her. He said, "If I move out…"

"Have you been discussing that?"

Jack nodded.

"I wouldn't want it to be about me."

"It's a little late."

"Oh, Jack." She scooted closer. "It's too much responsibility. What if I don't like you if you're not married? I don't think it will happen, but it could. And what about your kids? They'd hate me. Simon would hate me. You'd be the bad guy, and I'd be the home-wrecking bitch from hell. Have you considered that?"

"Of course."

Her bright eyes searched his face. "Frankly, Jack, I think you love your kids and your wife a good deal more than you love me." She put her hand on his cheek and caressed it; the pads of her fingertips thrummed his stubble. "I think you're a family man down the tips of your toes and I've just turned your head," she smiled, "because I'm so little and cute, because no one's ever made love to you like that in the shower, and because you think you have to save me."

He looked at Marla, who without a doubt was what passed for beautiful in middle age, and couldn't remember what he'd come to tell her.

"I don't hear you telling me I'm wrong, Jack."

He didn't answer.

"Then maybe you better leave before I get insulted." She edged away and folded her arms across her chest. "I'm sure Simon needs a car to drive to the show."

Jack walked towards the kitchen, feeling more relieved and confused than he'd felt in a long time. Had she just broken up with him? Had he come to break up with her? When he turned back, Marla was reclining on the couch, eyes half-closed, gazing up at the skylight.

✦ ✦ ✦

There was a special excitement Saturday night in the auditeria. Genna had felt it grow as the room filled. Last night was also sold out, but tonight even the back wall was lined with bodies, and there were more students, fewer parents. It was also the last nighttime performance; Dr. Burroughs had turned down Ms. Cherry's request for Sunday night. The man had impeccably bad judgement. No doubt the kids wanted to make up tonight for Friday's flop; Genna had nearly died *not* laughing when the scenery toppled onto that poor knight and lady. Afterwards, there was the cast party, to be held at some large house in the country. Simon had told her at least three times not to wait up. If the rain held off, there was going to be a bonfire, and whoever's parents it was (she'd spoken to them, some sophomore girl with a small part), said anyone who brought a sleeping bag was welcome to sleep over. Simon had left for the play, wildly excited, although he said he'd probably come home to sleep because he'd promised Peter a ride. That was adding to his excitement. I'm driving him, Mom.

Genna sat between Jack and Lizzie, who'd tried to weasel out of coming, but Jack wouldn't hear of it. Genna wasn't sure she agreed. Simon rarely if ever attended Lizzie's soccer games, and she was sick to death of being her brother's audience. Genna had grown pretty damn weary of cheering her own brother in high school. But Jack had returned from his office (that's where he said he was), to give Simon the Camry and demand Lizzie come, too. Then he'd taken her aside, and though the last thing in the world Genna was interested in, really, was a heart-to-heart with Jack, he insisted on telling her, with that open Barish face and big nose peering right at her, that she was the one he loved, the only one he loved, and if he'd done anything to make her think otherwise—Like having an affair? Give me a break, Jack—she should put it out of her head.

Genna sat in the second row, her usual seat, in a waking dream. It was already the second act, and Simon's big number was next. The first act had gone without a hitch. The kids, all of them, were performing better than she had imagined they could. The girl who played the Swamp Princess, with that beautiful dark hair, the King, the Prince, even the bitchy queen, perfect. She was holding her breath for all of them, yet felt a certain sadness because it would never be this good again, and Sweets wouldn't see it. That Peter, what a dancer he turned out to be. Simon and Lady Larken had looked so lovey-dovey during their first act duet. Watching them in the soft pink spot, she could almost forget everything she knew about her son and believe he was Sir Harry and he loved this girl, who carried his son, One, two, three, four.

They were entering the empty stage, Harry from the left, Larken the right. Her hair was up, and she wore a pale blue lady-in-waiting satin sheath that outlined her flat belly (hard to believe she was pregnant) and button breasts. Harry, of course, was in his red velvet tunic and tights, and marched forward with his hand on his sword. In the spotlight—Genna sat no more than ten feet away—she could see his eyeliner, and the foundation applied lightly on his cheeks and forehead. Eyelids fluttering to convey modesty and devotion, Larken declared that if Harry didn't love her anymore, why, she'd just go away.

Sir Harry smiled. Even as a cherry-cheeked baby, his smile could melt polar icecaps. He grasped Larken's hand and gazed at her with the adoring eyes of a romantic lead:

Yesterday I loved you as never before
But please don't think me strange
I've undergone a change
and today I love you even MORE!

Genna was swept away, overcome. Her heart turned circles. Of course, as the star's mother, she might be prejudiced. But Simon looked so handsome, he really seemed to adore Larken, and he sang so well it sounded as if Robert Goulet or some other adult actor had landed on stage surrounded by children. Such a robust sound, and for a moment she imagined Simon sang to her, and where was the harm, there would never be another woman he loved so well. Then Lady Larken answered, and though the girl tried, with her pretty, pinched features, and lovely white arms, Simon's voice buffeted hers like a gale moves a leaf, and yet: they held hands and sweetly sang to each other, heads thrown back in the glowing spot, so that they seemed, really and truly innocent (well, not that innocent, she was pregnant), young and in love.

She glanced at Jack, remembering how just this evening he told her he loved her and her only, as never before, and she wondered if that was an act, too. Had he been to see Marla and fucked her that very afternoon? Or had he broken it off? How would she ever know? Simon sang, the girl answered, and they sang together, holding each other at arm's length, so in love, and all an illusion. Then Jack fumbled for her hand and she let him take it. Monkey see, monkey do, and the music swelled to a crescendo. The stage lovers held their last notes, then moved into each other's arms. Sir Harry caressed Lady Larken's cheek. Larken rested her cheek on his palm, then seemed to throw herself forward, pressing her lips and her squirming body against his, her arms wrapped around his neck like death. Their lips met. All Genna could see was the back of the girl's head, her wheat blond hair, and Simon's forearms holding her. The audience began to hoot and whistle.

The kiss went on and on and on, with this little girl grinding her son, until at last they broke apart with the crowd shouting and clapping, and this one voice in the back of the room screaming something she couldn't make out. On stage, Simon looked stunned, a large buck caught in headlights; beside him, his doe appeared exultant and flushed. Then the spotlight dimmed, the stage went black, the kids ran off, and she turned to Jack, who said, "What the hell was that?"

chapter 24

Afterwards, it was all anyone could talk about: The Kiss. When they ran backstage, still breathless, doofus Tom declared, "You guys rock!" He flashed his googly pretty-boy grin, high-fived Simon and raced on stage. Will and Millie, all the dancing ladies and knights, acted as if they'd never seen anyone kiss before. For the rest of the show Larken was a candle, no, a rocket. Her face flushed red and stayed hot until they came out for their final bow, third from last. They bent from the waist, and the house went bananas and nuts, topped by a rousing cheer. "Kiss her!"

From the corner of his eye, Simon caught Mom and Dad. Then, through all the commotion, wasn't that Nick Fleming: *Don't, you faggot!* And in that moment Simon remembered *Bye Bye Birdie*, the boyfriend rushing on stage to prevent Ann-Margaret from kissing Birdie. Pow, right in the kisser! Simon and Tina exchanged a chaste little peck, then joined the principals in a human chain across the front. The full cast bowed. Ms. Cherry bounced on stage to accept roses from the Drama Boosters, and it was all a dream come true. Not gay, not fat, for a day, not failing French.

Afterwards, Ms. Cherry took Simon and Tina aside. "Never, ever do that again!"

They'd be lucky not to be suspended, and blah-blah-blah. If they kissed like that tomorrow, they certainly would be. Then she glanced around, Ms. Cherry, under her whirling curls. She didn't look twenty-two. She looked as if she could still be in high school or anyway in college. She looped arms around their shoulders, whispered, "Don't tell anyone, but I thought Dr. Burroughs was going to piss himself!"

Then she hurried out to schmooze the parents, to help stack tables and chairs. Simon turned awkwardly to Tina. He could still feel her lips and body thrashing against him like a snake. It was all so nasty.

She said, "We really showed them."

Showed them what? "Too bad Badger didn't piss himself."

"We rocked."

Hoping she'd say no, Simon asked, "You need a ride to Kelly's?"

"I'm good." She hugged him, whispered, "You're so cool, Simon, don't ever change."

Then she ran towards the girls' dressing room, and Simon headed for the boys', looking for Peter. At the end of The Kiss, with Tina writhing against him, Simon was fretting, What will Peter think? But Peter waited in the dressing room, stars in his eyes, hand shielding his mouth. They walked out together and found his mother, who was tall, thin, and nervous, just like Peter; no, he was just like her. Then Mom and Dad hugged him, which was so embarrassing he had to get out of Dad's arms right away and hoped no one in the crowded auditeria saw, though of course, everyone did. The gay boy hugging his father.

"You were just so great tonight," Mom said. "I'm so proud."

Mom always knew what to say.

"You didn't need pointers on that kissing." Dad grinned and Simon grinned back. "Maybe," Dad put his arm around Mom, and she let him, "I should get some from you."

Simon wondered, just for a minute, if Mrs. Lindstrom was there. He hadn't seen her and hoped she wasn't. He had a sense lots of people were watching, and not all the eyes were friendly. He whispered, "I love you, guys."

Mom and Dad answered, "We love you, too."

Then Simon asked for twenty dollars, which he knew they'd give him. Maybe he should have asked for forty; meal money on the way to the party. Dad grimaced but forked it over. Mom said, "Drive safe, what time are you coming home?"

"Don't wait up."

Dad said, "No drinking."

"I don't drink," Simon answered, which wasn't one hundred percent true, but close enough.

They stopped at Burger King. Simon wanted to see Mary, and remind her the Fry Guy was coming back. Anyway, he was so hungry he could eat a snake and a horse, all the animals walking two by two, and Peter didn't want to arrive first at the party; he was too nervous. Mary wasn't working, which was disappointing; instead, there was another manager he barely knew. But Simon got his employee discount and ordered two chicken sandwiches, an extra-large fries, large chocolate shake. Peter only wanted a cheeseburger, no wonder he was so skinny, and Simon paid for it all, just like a real date.

They were edging away from the counter with their food on trays, when Fleming and the Smokers blew in. Simon saw them see him, and wished he'd ordered to go. Maybe he could turn back and ask for a bag; they could run out the door and drive to the party. But Fleming and his Smokers blocked the way. They stepped up close before Simon could ask for anything, before he could even reach the condiment table to set his tray down.

"Look," said Nick, in his white muscle tee, dark forelock twisting on his forehead. "It's the faggot with his little girlfriend."

Most nights, Simon would have let it go. But not with the crowd's applause still inside him. "Suck my dick, Nick, you know you want to."

It was suddenly so quiet, Simon could hear the ping-ping of the registers. Fleming glanced at the Smokers surrounding him. Three guys, one girl, and one of the guys, Simon realized, was the smallest moonface.

"You're gonna wish you hadn't said that, faggot."

Simon wondered if he should pitch the tray into Nick's handsome mug. He glanced at Peter, whose lips trembled. Then the door opened, and Sgt. Heinsohn sauntered in, Simon realized, for his nightly meal. "Hey, Sergeant Heinsohn."

"Simon, how are you?"

"Fine, thanks." Simon turned to Nick. "And I wouldn't talk about girlfriends. Yours just dumped you."

He led Peter through the Smokers, who parted around them. They found a table near the front window. Simon's hands shook. Inside he felt like a giant Jell-O.

"Wow," Peter whispered, "you were so brave."

Simon didn't feel brave. "Let's eat, and get out of here."

They wolfed, they scarfed, they lion-ed their food. Simon stood up, clutching his shake, looking for Nick and the Smokers. He didn't see them, but Sergeant Heinsohn waved, his mouth full of fries, his cop's hat still capping his dome. Simon led Peter into the humid Tipton night. The streets were wild with college girls in short skirts and tank tops, boisterous with guys in J. Crew tees. They hurried towards his Camry, parked two blocks away behind Dad's bank. Simon watched for Fleming and his assholes. If Peter was scared he didn't say so. They came up on the car. Simon unclicked the doors, and they climbed in.

"You know when Nick said I was your girlfriend?"

"Don't mind him," Simon said. "He's such an ass."

"I wish I was." The street lamps shone in Peter's eyes. "Your boyfriend."

Simon leaned closed and kissed Peter's mouth. Peter's dancer arms circled his neck. They kissed for a long time.

"When you were kissing Tina?" Peter glanced out the window. "I was really jealous."

"When I was kissing Tina, actually, when she was kissing me?" Simon put his ham hands on Peter's neck and turned him to see his eyes, his crooked front tooth. "I was thinking of you."

"Really?"

"Really."

They kissed again, then Simon put the car in gear. He turned left out of the lot, then right onto Main Street. That's where, Peter would tell me later, Fleming and the Smokers picked them up. And like every other kid in Tipton, they had cell phones, to tell each other they'd found him. By the time Simon cleared the uptown bar strip heading east, a black SUV trailed him. He didn't think about it until he turned right at the stop sign at the edge of campus, and the SUV turned behind him, without stopping. Then another car, a low, white, piece-of-shit Chevy, swung out from the main college lot, cut in front, and the Camry was sandwiched, the Chevy ahead, the SUV behind.

At the next light, Peter said, where they waited to turn left behind the Chevy, Simon realized they were in trouble. The SUV had followed him into the turn lane, then switched on its high beams.

"Asshole," Simon muttered, and glanced in the rear-view.

The SUV's driver, the front passenger, too, stuck their hands out and flipped him off. Simon shoved his out and returned the bird. The SUV shot forward into his bumper, and Simon's head whipped forward and back. The SUV rammed them again. Peter's forehead cracked against the glass, and the Camry lurched into the Chevy's bumper.

"Asshole!" Simon shouted out the window, his heart beating faster than a hummingbird's. And if he weren't scared yet, he was terrified when voices from both cars chorused, "Faggot, you're dead!"

The light greened. The Chevy turned, Simon just behind it, the black SUV nudging his back end. They started downhill towards the university stables. And though the speed limit was thirty-five, and Simon had never in his life exceeded it—he was such a careful driver—he was soon doing forty then fifty, past the slumbering horses, under the clouded sky, then fifty-five past the university police and the Tipton sewerage plant.

"Simon, I'm scared," Peter said.

Simon slowed, and the SUV bumped him from behind. The Camry veered into the westbound lane, but Simon was such a fine driver, he brought it under control. The SUV edged closer, he could hear it behind them. Peter squealed. Simon gunned the engine up the next hill. He caught up to the white piece of shit as they passed the turn into Forest Glen, then roared past, the nose of the Camry almost against the white car's tail, the SUV against his. Peter was whimpering. The best thing, Simon thought, was to pass the white car. He could outrun that piece of crap, no problem. But headlights were sweeping up the hill. Simon pulled back into his lane, and the SUV crept closer. Tears glistened on Peter's cheeks, and Simon swore if he got out of this, he'd kill that fucking Nick Fleming.

The brace of cars, the Chevy, the Camry, and the midnight SUV, started down the long hill east of Forest Glen. The headlights of a pick-up whipped past, then Simon pulled out behind the Chevy and crossed the solid yellow line. And here I can no longer pretend to be the objective eye, the experimenter uninvolved in the experiment. I've tried, but I can't do it! Simon floored the accelerator, racing downhill. He was such a careful driver, my son. We rode together many times; I taught him on this very road. And now he was doing sixty, sixty-five. A half mile ahead, a third, then a quarter, a stale green light glowed, then yellowed at 127. He could make it through, leave his tormentors behind. He was such a safe driver! The SUV pulled out behind him, and they both roared past the white piece of shit. Simon floored the Camry, pedal to the floor, and they shot towards the bloody intersection.

What kind of father would write this? Am I implicated yet in this project?

The light went red and Simon raced through, eluding his pursuers, never seeing the minivan headed north on 127 until the last moment when all he could do, he was such a careful driver, was brake and spin the wheel, which spared the driver of the van, but sent the Camry cartwheeling towards the guardrail, collapsing the bumper and radiator, activating the driver side air bag which shot out at 150 miles per hour, as the Camry rolled once then again, landing driver side down, wheels spinning, engine smoking, as the white piece of shit and the black SUV roared through the intersection without stopping.

Now here we all sit, outside Simon's room in Cincinnati's Children's Hospital Medical Center, Building A, Fourth Floor, Intensive Care. We've been here every day for the past seven, keeping a vigil. Genna, Lizzie, whom we cannot protect from this sorrow, and Sweets, who was already on the plane when we heard the news. Peter comes sometimes, with his mother; Peter walked away from the accident with a concussion, a broken arm. Our neighbors from Forest Glen visit, as do our colleagues. That woman Marge, from Lizzie's soccer team, arrived yesterday with a tin of homemade cookies. There's been a community of voices to encourage us and say they just know it will be all right while Simon lies suspended between death and who knows what. There's no permanent damage, the doctors assure us, but we don't know what to believe. He's healing, the body is a miraculous thing, they say, but he lies there still, so very still, and he does not make a sound. His brain swelled, and they opened the top of his skull the first night to relieve the pressure. Now, the swelling's down, and color's returning to his cheeks beneath the turban of gauze, but he does not make a sound, and perhaps that's the hardest thing of all. Simon without that voice.

The doctors say he could come out of it at any time. He could be fine. Too early to say, they say. When there's news, we'll know.

Until then, Simon's sleeping. *Il dort.* And we wait in this private waiting room outside intensive care, worried, exhausted, waiting.

Genna hasn't said anything about Marla, or what comes next. She's had Sweets here—I did pick him up at the airport—and Sweets's presence has been a comfort to everyone. What's there to say? We wait. There's been a lot of time to think, to hold hands. To push on his chest and shout, Simon, we're here and we love you. Simon, we know you're in there. Simon, can you hear us?

Sitting in the waiting room, I wonder, What kind of people are these anyway? What kind of father-researcher would conceive such a project and call it a novel? What kind of guidance counselor would have an affair with her student's father? What kind of wife, twice burned, would take her cheating husband back? For that's what I want. I want it all back, my wife whom I probably do not deserve, and above all, I want my son.

The day after the accident, they found a black SUV with fresh scrapes on the front bumper registered to Fleming Construction. From what we were told, at first the family denied Nick was involved. But there were too many witnesses to the confrontation in Burger King, including Sergeant Heinsohn, to claim nothing happened. Now we hear, on the advice of their lawyers, that Nick is prepared to say it was all an accident, youthful hijinks, no harm intended.

Of course, none of it, nothing, is an accident or unconnected. Not the American race laws of the 1920s, and the Nazi eugenics of the 1930s. Not those very same race laws, and the cross burned on our lawn. My affair with Marla and her calling in Nick Fleming, fueling his rage, and the girl, Tina, kissing Simon that way. It is all connected. And I find myself wishing, if Simon is never going to be better than this, if he is always going to lie there silently, then let him die, and let that boy Nick Fleming be blamed. Let him pay the price. Let them try to call that an accident.

After a moment, when I realize what I've been wishing for, I hurry from the room and head for the bathroom, leaving Genna,

Sweets, and Lizzie in the waiting room. The doctors have promised to call if there's any change. Go home, they say. Go home.

I relieve myself, wash my hands, and examine my face in the glass. Did I mention they canceled the Sunday matinee, and that on Monday, there was a school assembly with grief counselors? Ms. Cherry delivered a card the whole cast signed, and the guidance office sent one with hundreds of signatures. We assume it was organized by Marla, who left a message on my office machine, but has not called or stopped by the hospital. Flowers arrive every day, and someone from the Drama Boosters took a picture of Sir Harry and Lady Larken on stage, and blew it up to the size of a poster. We've taped it up over Simon's bed. According to Peter's mother, there's been only one discordant note, spray-painted in the boys' bathroom: Ding-dong, the fag is dead.

Assholes.

I've always hated blowers, so I dry my palms on my pants, then start back towards the waiting room. It's not far, but I am so tired, it feels as if I am trapped inside someone else's sleeping body. When I enter, the small room is empty, and it takes me a moment to realize what this means. Genna and Sweets would never leave together unless there were news. I move towards the door to Simon's room, suddenly finding myself in Schrödinger's box. Until and unless I open that door, nothing has happened. Simon is neither alive nor dead.

Genna's voice calls from the other side. "Jack, Jack. Come here!"

I extend my complicitous right hand and push the door open. Inside, I do not find Schrödinger's Rex, either mewing or on his back, legs stiff, but my extraordinary son, reaching for Genna and Lizzie, and past them, towards his grandfather, Sweets.

"Simon!" I cry, sorry to have missed even a moment. "Simon!"

He turns. He looks different. His face is so pale.

"Dad."

His voice is a whisper, a croak, barely a voice at all inside the hospital gown, under all that gauze, but it is enough, it is a symphony, my son's voice.

I catch Genna's eye. She's smiling and crying at the same time. In a moment, I will be, too, complicitous in joy as in sorrow. And then he says it again.

photo by Lynda Koolish

about the author

Eric Goodman was raised in Brooklyn and holds degrees from both Yale and Stanford University. He is the author of three previous novels: *High on the Energy Bridge*, *The First Time I Saw Jenny Hall*, and *In Days of Awe*. Goodman has held residencies at the MacDowell Colony, the Ragdale Foundation, and the Headlands Center for the Arts, and has won several fellowships from the Ohio Arts Council. He resides in upstate New York and Oxford, Ohio, where he directs the creative writing program at Miami University.